# INDIA GATE

# INDIA GATE

## Lacey Fosburgh

CROWN PUBLISHERS, INC.

NEW YORK

Published by Crown Publishers, Inc., 201 East 50th Street, New
York, New York 10022. Member of the Crown Publishing Group.

CROWN is a trademark of Crown Publishers, Inc.
Manufactured in the United States of America

Library of Congress Cataloging-in-Publication Data
Fosburgh, Lacey, 1942–
      India gate : a novel / by Lacey Fosburgh.
         p.  cm.
      I. Title.
   Ps3556.O7545I5  1991
   813'.54—dc20                                        90-28427
                                                           CIP

ISBN 0-517-58493-x
10 9 8 7 6 5 4 3 2 1
First Edition

*To Luz and little Billy, on the one hand,*
*To Sophie and David and Gabe on the other.*

*"The Lord Shiva . . . a mystic dance performs, a cycle of destruction and rebirth."*

*The Upanishads*

# PART ONE

## ❧ 1 ❧

NEW DELHI, INDIA

THE SKY WAS LOW AND WHITE
and windless and by the time the body was found the jackals and
the vultures had already found it too, so there was far less of a
body than there had been once before, but one thing about it was
clear and that was that it was white.

The whiteness might not be very unusual someplace else.
Here on the far shores of the Jumna River where the Taj Mahal
lies one hundred miles to the south, the Himalayas are some
hundreds to the north, and but a few miles to the east is India
Gate, the center of the city, and the boulevard made of deep red
sand called the Road of Kings, it was.

On the Road real kings and queens of the English sort and less
real kings of the Indian sort have traveled in their day, horses
and elephants, low-backed cars and probably even on foot, staff
in hand, but the far shores of the Jumna River was not a place
for kings or, really, anyone.

I went there just to see it. The squalor stretched for miles.
Even the fields were dirty, full of refuse and hard dry earth, this
all Delhi too, same as the Road of Kings. But out here, nothing
seemed alive, not in summertime, and it was hard to believe any
of this would ever regenerate.

The taxi wouldn't take me in, so I had to stop, get out. The
driver agreed to wait. I set off walking. The expanse was large

3

and still, brown along the ground, brownish white above. It was barren, no place for human life. I felt laid out, exposed, and it made me wonder about the man who ended here. What had brought him to this spot? whoever he was.

I walked and walked. The police had told me where to go. I saw people from the shanty towns that started up ahead. They were coming toward me, their bodies standing up in dusty shrouds against a dusty sky, the kind of people who live in huts along a river that has already in the heat of summer trickled down to but a foot or two of something that could be called water but is really only sludge that moves.

They circled round me, all excited, and asked, did I know about the body? I said yes, and then they asked, did I know about the woman who had come? and I said yes, I knew her, she was my friend and I wanted to see the place, too. They led me on, impatient, talking all at once, because although any body that turned up on the outskirts of a capital city would have merited some attention, a white body merited a whole lot more.

A brown body would not have been unusual at all, truth be told, just one more soul who has lain down to die after not enough food has passed his lips for a long enough time and finally the legs bend at the knees and slowly he drops down altogether, to the ground. The jackals and the vultures begin to circle round, sensing the coming of death, for the coming of death has its smell too, and then they all come together, man and the earth, the jackals and the birds.

I kept going. My mind was full of Phoebe, Cully, all of them. It was for them that I was here, and despite the uncleanliness underfoot, I thought of this land and sky out here as beautiful. If one ignored the huts that spread into the distance and looked instead at the pale silhouette of the fort on the other side of the river and the gray of the Moghul mosque, took it as a whole, this vast plain, with its sticks for trees and million shades of brown. I thought of the rains and when they'd come this year, soon or late or not at all, and felt that wish spring up in me for life renewed. Even here in this desperate place where living was at a minimum, hope was perpetual.

The site itself when we came to it was nothing much to see. One of the men, the leader, his face so dark there was no

4

distinction between his eyebrows and his skin, suddenly swooped up his arm and brought it down, a wild gesticulation he must have felt worthy of the event, and announced that it was here.

He himself had found it.

We all looked down, myself and some ten or twenty others, but all I could see were tracks in the dust where the policemen's trucks had come and the butt of a filter cigarette, an old snake skin, torn and wrinkled where it was left, and tail feathers chewed from some hapless bird that must have retained the means to fly because it was nowhere thereabouts, lucky thing.

The man was pointing out the way the body lay, the legs here, the top, or what was left of it, there, arms underneath the rest. It looked like the man had fallen, he said, but from what, death, dehydration, or even a bullet, he couldn't tell.

Nor had he any idea what the man had seen or heard or even when he ceased to be alive. No one knew about the body then, certainly not who it was, just one day, the people said, they began to smell the smell and see the vultures and the dogs, but no one knew when he came or if he came of his own accord or was dumped from the back end of a car.

The man said dust was everywhere. It had blown up about the corpse, the eye sockets and the legs, and obscured whatever tracks or signs of human life there might once have been.

I asked if there was any sign of violence, and he said no, but the other woman had asked the same thing, too.

"What else did she want to know?"

"Everything," he said in his singsong Hindi voice. "About whether he had any yellow hair, but there was none. I am telling her, the jackals are taking it. She asked about what I heard, but I am not hearing anything. I am telling her no one was hearing anything. She asked was there a gun, a truck, a car? and I am saying no, there was not one thing. She asked who else was coming here, so many questions, on and on, and finally I am saying, 'No one. No one is coming here but us. Who else would be coming here?' "

"Was that all?"

"She is asking about the heat and the weather, wanting to know every little thing about this man and his circumstances, and I am saying it is the same as now. 'The smell is barely gone,'

I am telling her, because it is only one, two days past, three at most. 'Nothing is changed,' I am telling her. 'It was just like this only.' I am feeling irritated at her, but then she said this man was her brother, maybe, she doesn't know, and so I am feeling sorry for her for this sadness for her brother and I tell to her, 'No matter. What dies, comes back. What goes, returns. The god Shiva knows it, too.' She is looking with such sadness, I tell to her it is so simple even one child can be understanding it, this matter of rebirth."

"And did she understand?"

The man shrugged elaborately. "But this is all that matters," he said, and with that, he circled his arms up in the air to show the full shape of life, something going round and round. Finally, he said, he told her about the sunset.

"What about it?" I asked.

A sunset that spread purple and gold three hundred and eighty degrees around the spot, a blessing, he said, for the man and his new life. He told the woman this and she promptly sat down on the ground and looked off in the direction of where the departing sun had gone, Cully there among the rays, perhaps. She asked him please would he go away, she wanted to be alone to think about her brother, but they didn't go away, the man said, because no one in India really wants to be alone.

I imagined the sunset and the light. How it would have spread up around and even beneath the wretched corpse, enveloping him in a beauty that was compelling and aloof, inspiring, but, as always in India, scary. If his soul was still there to scare, that is. The sky was so vast and he was so small, this body six feet long, and before he died, whenever he died, he must have felt vulnerable knowing he had nothing left to shed because there was nothing left between him and the heat and the whim of fate, except the last few articles of clothing that protected whatever modesty he had left.

But, finally, fate did come and take the last thing he had left to give and he became part of the jackals, the vultures and the earth, little by little, grinding down, a bit here, a morsel there, for there was a lot less of him when he was found than there had been once before, and certainly not enough to know if he was Cullen Llewellyn Guthrie.

Police came and more people, untouchables most of them.

6

They stood and watched, hands held up against the sky to shield them from the sun. The stench was everywhere, flies and creepy, crawling bugs that eat on human flesh.

It was Sunday, the ninth of May, not very long ago. The body was carted off on a stretcher, put in the back end of a truck and taken across the river to a Delhi police station, where it was parked in the sun while some telephone calls were made, and it was not unapparent to the surrounding landscape what lay cooking in the back end of the truck. Finally, a good bit later than it would have been someplace else where things take a lot less longer than they do here, the body, still unidentified, was taken to the morgue.

Many bodies end up in Delhi's Safdarjang Morgue and many are unidentified, but very few are white and unidentified and not a one in recent years has come in like a piece of trash, torn, thrown out, far less a thing than it used to be.

Had this body had a face or even hair, things might have been entirely different, but since it had no identity whatsoever, it was measured up in a few days' time against a list the policemen had. The list had a title that took up one whole line, but what it meant was "Foreign—Missing," and it lay as a single sheet of paper in a file in a drawer on the second floor of police headquarters. They let me see it. "Cully Guthrie, American," was the first name on the list.

Police headquarters is a large gray building that looked modern when I first saw it years ago as a child, big square boxes set on other boxes, and I used to think it was blue. Maybe it was. When I went there this time it simply looked dirty and besieged, surrounded by hundreds of bicycles and not so many cars.

On Monday, May 10th, one such bicycle carried the "Foreign—Missing" file across town to the American embassy. Inside the building the ambassador made a copy and passed it around. Alongside the name of Cullen Guthrie were some specifications as to size and weight and then the words *art scholar* and two names. They were Jiggie Deeg and Kady Suraj. The first was his employer, the second his friend, and since they were famous, a maharaja and a high government official, they were the reason Cully found himself at the top end of the list.

At some point someone with a sense of history—or, maybe,

7

only irony—thought to send a clerk-chaprassi over to the National Museum of Art on Raj Path, the Road of Kings, to pick up a certain card. "Donated from the collection of Louis Antonine Guthrie," it said, and when he came back it was stapled to the sheet of paper so that now the father's name lay on top of the report that his son was missing.

The card itself was twenty years old, one of the two-by-three-inch labels the museum affixed long ago to the walls beside the 442 pieces of Indian art that once belonged to Louis Guthrie and made him briefly one of the leading collectors of Indian art.

The collection is beautiful. Some pieces are small, others large. The most famous of all, the dancing Shiva Nataraj that lorded over the house at Number Nine Jumna Road, isn't there, sold long ago, but when I go to the museum I just wander through and relish the gathering that remains.

I realized one time, to my surprise, that they were all, all 442 pieces, gods and goddesses of the highest realm, all in various positions of dance and prayer and copulation, lovers, their lips poised in anticipation of a kiss. Shiva, Krishna, Buddha, and Ganesha, countless incarnations as well, for the gods have their incarnations just like us. At least that's what Indians believe. That the house on Jumna Road was populated with these gods and goddesses eventually gave a deeper, even spiritual, dimension to everything for me. But Phoebe, when I told her that, said she'd felt that all along. Their presence had apprised her from the first that matters worthy of their consideration happened in that house of hers.

She knew all these pieces, black or bronze or made of stone. They had grown up with her, things that were Gandharan, Cola and Pallava, Hindu, Buddhist. Once when we went to the museum together, we were contemplating them all together in room after room and the silence and sense of awe inspired us, gave us that vast and searing notion of a universe that is so truly Indian, an all-consuming nothingness and timelessness.

The two-by-three-inch card with Louis' name had one more thing, a date, twenty years past. It was the date of Louis' bequest and the year of Louis' death.

Thalia's death, too. She was his wife.

On Tuesday, May 11th, two days after the body was found, Phoebe Guthrie was notified at home in New York City. An embassy official called to tell her an unidentified male Caucasian body had been found on the far side of the Jumna River.

Cully, her younger brother, was missing. He had not been seen in weeks. Phoebe knew all that. She had just talked to the airlines and was pondering a trip back to India for the first time in twenty years, back into the world where she was born, but who knows if she would have gone had the call not come. The body gave her just the nudge she needed.

Cully had been seen last on Friday, April 2nd, heading out across a field near the city of Deeg in western Rajasthan, some five hundred miles from Delhi.

Deeg was the birthplace of both Jiggie Deeg and Kady Suraj, two names that had come together in many people's minds long before they appeared on the list with Cully's name. Deeg lies far to the west of Delhi out where the high plains of northern India give way to desert and the hills. The land was once the cross-ways for caravans from Europe and the West passing into Asia and the East. Later it became the Kingdom of the Deegs. Today it is still identified with them but has turned into a thriving place in its own right, largely due to Kady Suraj, with factories and movie theaters, a regional government, hospital, university and an ice-cream parlor called American Ice.

Most foreigners know it only as a tourist center. Four stars or five they give it in all the books and the Deeg Palace Hotel, where Jiggie and his ancestors were born, is said to be among the best hotels there are, complete with a vast indoor swimming pool that has garlands along the sides and overhanging swings where girls in saris used to fly aloft, then tumble down to swim.

Tourists bear down on this city in droves and Cully himself joined them in September of the year before he died. He was not a tourist, this is true. It was the past that drew him there.

Specifically, it was the art. He had taken a job at the palace.

Seven months later, on April 2nd, he was last seen walking diagonally across the large alfalfa field that abuts on palace land, midway between where the city of Deeg ends and the lands of the maharaja, popularly known as Jiggie Deeg, begin. He was heading west toward the open desert. He wore khaki pants and

9

a blue shirt, items the male Caucasian body didn't have. His sleeves were rolled up past the elbow and because of his hair, he was recognizable anywhere.

His hair was the color of something that has lain in the sun so long, all pigmentation has been cooked out of it but for a yellow glow. It fell down over his left eye and rolled in curls along his neck almost to his collar. It was a lovely thing and a servant from the palace watched him go, watched him, she later said, because she marveled at the sight of the sun shining on his hair.

But afterward it was not known if Cully headed farther out into the desert, for whatever reason, or caught a train or a plane and went to Delhi or in some other direction altogether. No one was known to have seen him after that, not in Delhi or in Deeg, although it did develop that someone might have seen him, or maybe just heard him, in an antique shop in Delhi that specialized in art and sculpture.

A man was found murdered there that day, an Indian, small and slight of frame, skin so dark it was nearly navy blue, hair still laced with the scent of almond oil.

He had been beaten about the face, then strangled.

Cully's whereabouts then and later were unknown. The two real friends he had besides me were Kady Suraj (Indians pronounce it *Kay-dee Sur-ahje*), who lived in Delhi, and Jiggie Deeg's granddaughter, Mirabai, who lived in the palace in Deeg, and they professed as much confusion about him as anyone else.

It was dusk when Cully disappeared from sight. The servant said he was not carrying anything in his arms or on his back. She specifically said his arms were swinging at his side, "like a march," but those who knew Cully well understood that when he was angry, that is the way he walked.


Call it a story. Call it history. To me it's just what happened, a thread that wove its way through people's lives, binding them together in ways they didn't know and didn't suspect, making them responsible for things they didn't even see or begin to understand.

I didn't know it, either. I was never part of it. I just knew the players, but it was not my life or history. I just encountered it along the way, the way one does storms and sunny afternoons, things that come, then go, then come again, bringing with them each time round greater care and familiarity.

By the time the male Caucasian body was found, this entanglement of things had already come down through three decades of Indian time. It had twisted its way through three families and three generations, Guthrie, Suraj and Deeg, caught them up and spit them out, half of them innocent and undeserving of what they got.

Without Phoebe and Cully Guthrie, the whole thing might have been different. Had first Cully, then Phoebe, stayed in New York and not returned twenty years later to India where they were born, the story would have played itself out until everyone was dead and gone.

Jiggie Deeg was the one who chose Cully's name from all the other job applicants, setting in motion his return. His staff at the palace was looking at the names of people who'd applied for a new job—someone had to catalog the vast collection of art down there—and when they spotted the Guthrie name, it brought up memories of the past and they knew the matter had to be referred to Jiggie and Jiggie alone. He himself was no longer in Deeg at that time then. He had retired to live as a religious hermit in the watery parts of Benares City, so an aide went down to see him and Jiggie was the one who said, "I'll take that one there, Cully Guthrie." I can control him, is what he must have thought.

Had Cully not headed East to pursue his work, the secrets would have stayed where they were, bits of brain within a few men's skulls. One woman's, too, lodged back behind her orange eyes. Without Cully, then Phoebe, people would just have died and fallen away, taken their lives and history off into silence and oblivion, the memories of not one, not two, but three families, sinking into the funeral flames and drifting with their ashes into the waves and swirls of one Indian river or another, there where their ashes were scattered to mingle with the gods, their souls free to come again, or so the Indians say.

Instead it happened that in one long Indian summer, the whole thing that had been lying unmoved for so many years became unraveled.

The gods would say that was why Cully and later Phoebe

went back, not to do the things they thought they were going to do, but to do what they had to do and resolve what had been left undone.

Maybe it happened because it was supposed to happen. Or maybe obsessions pulled it along from beginning to end, obsessions and love.

## ❧ 2 ❧

I DON'T REMEMBER MEETING
Cully in India when he was a child, but they say he was quiet,
seldom said a word, and that when you went to the house on
Jumna Road, he hung back, his feet on one side of a door, like
as not, his head peering in across the frame. That if he came any
closer you could see how he stood, with his head slightly bent
over toward the left, like it was heavy or something drew it
down, his hair falling in his eyes, drapery covering half a window pane.

He told me once he'd always worn his hair long. He said it
with surprise, like it was a mystery why. I thought it was obvious, a device to hide behind, but it was awfully attractive. It
made you like him. He was always a handsome boy, athletic and
increasingly gifted in his field, which was Indian art, but the
hair gave him an air of neediness. Later, when I knew him
better, I understood that for all his good looks, he could dazzle
you with his charm, quick as a flash he'd be gone, hidden inside
his head, as if another person entirely had taken up residence in
there.

If I can't remember Cully in the early days, I remember
Phoebe vividly. Unlike her brother, she has such a strong presence that I sometimes think I can recall every single thing about
her from the moment I first saw her as a teenager in the elegant

Gymkhana Club in Delhi with her father and Kady Suraj, to the last time, a few days or weeks ago. For this reason Phoebe's always had meaning for me, first as someone I was jealous of, although I was eight years her senior. Later I just loved her as my closest friend. More recently she's come to represent the spirit of life itself.

She is tall, dresses well, even elegantly, with a flair for long skirts and a casual look, but she doesn't pay much attention to the whole thing. Dresses quickly, can look good in jeans or a floppy T-shirt, rarely shops, never peeks in mirrors or judges her friends by their appearance.

Aside from her looks per se, though, what's most conspicuous about Phoebe is the confidence she projects. No matter that she doesn't always have it; one assumes just from looking at her she's the sort of person who can do anything, and it's almost true. Even when she's as insecure or intimidated as the next person, she never lets it stop her. One of our friends in New York says she's like a Mack truck that just keeps on going. The going part is right. The truck isn't. She isn't pushy or aggressive. She's just tenacious, as well as soft and dedicated and deeply kind.

Her face is just like Cully's, with high cheekbones and a warm, enveloping smile and, of course, the blue eyes, long thick yellow-white hair, and skin that looks perennially tanned, but isn't. Her eyes are different from his, though. If his can be dull and opaque, hers have startling shifts of expression and sometimes you can watch them like a movie screen and know exactly what she's feeling.

Her life in New York, before she went back to India, was not all that different from anyone else's we knew at the time. It revolved around her friends and her work. She started a foundation years ago that became a kind of adoption agency for talented adults in need of money and these people, as well as myself, her ex-husband, Stephen, a college roommate named Alice who helps run the foundation, and an assortment of friends, were the focus of her life.

And Cully.

Cully was everything. He always came first. Divorced, she had no apparent interest anymore in commitment, serious relationships or children. The future didn't seem to exist for her.

She had an avowed attitude toward India, too. That it didn't interest her either. She never saw Indian films or went to Indian restaurants or followed the country in the news. Lots of people had no idea she'd even lived there, been born there, for God's sake.

But I always thought it was closer to her than she knew.

Without even thinking about it, she kept piles of money in her pockets and handed it out to beggars and the homeless. When taxi drivers gave her loose change or even bills, she put it in her pocket. At checkout counters, movies, it was the same.

"Be sure to spend it on food," she always said when she handed it over to people, quarters, singles, even a ten or twenty, an expression of sadness on her face.

"Did you do that in India, too?" I asked her once.

"No," she said. "I wish I had."


Phoebe and I have lived curiously parallel lives. We both were born and raised in India, both settled in New York City and lived there as single, working women, both eventually returned to India, all at the same approximate times. My father was in the diplomatic corps there, hers in business. They didn't particularly like each other, her father too eccentric, mine too establishment. I rarely saw her there. I went to the embassy school, she an Indian one. My memories of her there all date to our teenage years but they were so striking that when I ran into her again some eight years later in New York, when we were both in our twenties, my first impression of her was that something was missing, gone.

We were waiting for cabs downtown and after confirming that we did indeed recognize each other, I asked had she ever returned to India, and she said, "Oh, no," as if it was clearly out of the question.

If I hadn't run into her again, that one encounter would have turned me off. Her rejection of India was so complete, I was tempted to take it as a rejection of myself.

Our next encounter was also on the street, but this time we hugged and apologized for not getting each other's numbers, talked about the pressures of life, etcetera, and then she took me home and I stayed for dinner. We had a very good time, and she ended up telling me something revealing about herself. So from this point on, you might say, our real friendship was launched and I knew what Phoebe Llewellyn Guthrie was really like underneath all that poise and sophistication. Because of that, my true devotion to her began.

She told me she used to sleep alone in the streets of Delhi. I couldn't believe it. I was horrified. But it was the truth.

Curled up against the walls of a building or the back end of a hedge. Did it for years, in fact, from about age ten to thirteen.

Sometimes she even walked far into Old Delhi, never afraid, she said, in and out of shadows and congested areas, past people sleeping or walking, sharing glances, them dark, her light, and the sharing of night seemed to mean they were all alike in some plight. They none of them had a place to go, she said. They were on their own.

But why did you do it? I asked, and later asked again and again. She answered in various ways, to be on her own, to be independent, because she was curious and it gave her an odd and wonderful feeling to be so intimate and involved with India.

But that first night all she told me was that she just felt like it. She wanted to get away from the house. I didn't press her then, partly because I didn't really know her yet, but mostly because I sensed she had reached the edge of what she could see and understand.

She just loved to walk. That's what she said.

"I wanted to be out of the house," she said later, during the long Indian summer after she returned to see the body and we were both living in New Delhi. "I didn't think much about it then. It wasn't like I was lying in back of a hedge thinking about my mother or father. I wasn't feeling anything in particular, except that I loved being by myself. It was dark. It was quiet. You could hear cars and dogs and bicycles. Sometimes I thought about my mother and what she was doing. She was home, in her room, and my father was out, he was always out, even then, and Cully was asleep, and sometimes it seemed strange that they were there and I was here, but mostly it was just wonderful. One place in particular was cozy, and safe. Under the hedge where no one could see me, even if I slept till dawn. There was a stream nearby, except it wasn't a real stream because it was filled with sewage and yuck, but I could hear the water flowing and it made me fall asleep."

❧

If Phoebe and Cully had the same hair, eyes and body structure, except that she stood straight and he did not, neither one resembled Louis or Thalia at all, except that Phoebe had the same extraordinary presence as her father. That's what I noticed the first time I saw her. At the Gymkhana Club in Delhi.

I know exactly when it was, twenty-three years ago, early one summer. I was taken by her right away. She seemed so confident I couldn't take my eyes off her. I immediately wanted to know who she was, everything about her.

She was standing across the room near the potted palms, their branches hanging over her like outstretched arms. She was clearly younger than me, only thirteen, it turned out, with no makeup or allure as such, flat shoes, no breasts at all, but I felt an overwhelming stab of envy. At the same time, I was drawn to her.

She stood there under the palms looking at everything. She even saw me watching her. She was entirely her own person. That was the thing. Self-contained. Flat shoulders, no hips, androgynous, and calm. It unnerved me.

She was standing with her father and his friend, Kady Suraj. I'd seen the two men before, always together, of course. Phoebe stood slightly to the side and back.

Everyone at my table stopped and stared. That's how gorgeous they looked. Louis Guthrie was lighting a cigarette, his head bent over toward a match. Suraj was in a dark suit, tie. He was so handsome, my breath got caught in my throat. No one ever dreamed in those days then he'd go so far, but he was certainly someone who was going somewhere. As I watched a bearer came up, asked Phoebe what they wanted to drink. He didn't ask the men, just her, and she said something, smiled, then ordered for the other two, and the mere way she cast out her arm to include them made me feel she had some inner superiority I'd never match.

Then a man at my table said he was always there, and I wondered who he meant, Guthrie or Suraj. "And now her, too," he added. He bet from now on it was going to be the three of them, and I thought, What was he talking about? And then suddenly I knew. Louis was the kingpin and the other two, the younger ones, were his entourage, because right then Louis stood up tall, pulled away from the bearer who was holding the match, and looked out into the room with the same command as Phoebe, and I got a vivid sense of this unusual and seductive threesome, with him at the vortex, three people held together by some mysterious and unseen bond.

I told my father when we got home and he said, "Oh, I wouldn't be envious if I were you. She's got a hard life."

"How," I asked, firmly disbelieving.

"Just think about it," he said. "You'll see."

He was right. Next time I saw her, she was at a lunch party sitting alone up against a door. She was reading *Jane Eyre*, her father and Suraj somewhere about—her mother wasn't there, of course—and she looked lonely and a trifle sad. I thought I'd go talk to her, but when I got up close I didn't know what to say. She seemed so different. So I just stuttered out something about, "Where's your mother?" and she said her mother was sick and couldn't come. I said, "Oh," knowing that wasn't true at all, and promptly drifted away, knowing something awful must have led her to lie about her mother. I was never envious of her again.

Now let two decades pass and I see Phoebe Guthrie someplace else. She's in India now. She arrived in New Delhi in May on account of the male Caucasian body, but by now summer has come and gone, taking with it everything that happened then. The body by now is long burned and returned to dust and ash. It's wintertime, heading into spring. The skies of Delhi are bright and blue and Phoebe and I see each other nearly every day in a big old house not far from the one on Jumna Road.

Spreading out for miles around us is the sprawling plain of grass and trees cut by boulevards and gates and old colonial houses that is called New Delhi. It's where we live, those of us who can, because these environs are as protected as India gets from the poverty and population that threatens to devour it. But, in truth, it's not really protected at all.

Whole villages of wretched huts, complete with campfires, naked babies and water buffalo, proliferate outside our gates and the roads themselves, at the edges of our lawns, are as clogged with life as the rivers get with death. There's no escaping tumult and depression here. It's why tourists don't want to come to India and Indians want to get away.

The house I'm talking about where I see Phoebe now is two stories high and it has pillars and palms just like the one at Number Nine Jumna Road, but if that one had no veranda, this one has no art, no lovers' embrace to hint at the finer things in life. Instead it has wood paneling and chintz and the kind of expensive porcelain things that belong to people who model themselves upon the British and know they are safely upper class. This is where Phoebe came to stay with Indian friends when the long, long summer was finally over and fall, or winter, as they call it here, set in.

I had already returned to India before first Cully, then Phoebe, came. My husband, an economist who specializes in the Asian subcontinent, was on loan again to the World Bank down on Lodi Road, my son in boarding school near Boston, and one day—I'm talking about the fall now, late October, long after the body had come and gone and I had made my trek over to the other side of the river—I went over to see Phoebe.

When I was leaving, she asked if I liked to play cards.

I didn't and I couldn't imagine that she did, either, but the cultural ethic was just right, that's what Indian women did, and so I said yes, why not.

I showed up the next day and the bearer brought the cards out, but he must have understood as much as us because he just put them down and didn't even ask if he should bring the table. Phoebe and I talked and talked. Or, rather, she talked and I listened and after that we met every day. There we were, two American women some years apart in age, one tall and blond, the other short and dark and physically somewhat round. One, myself, was often knitting and busy with her hands. The other was invariably still, her hands hanging at the end of a chair, head back against a cushion, her eyes often closed.

I remember one day late in November. Phoebe was positioned on the veranda, facing the back lawn, on the chaise. She had a stack of books beside her, but not one was open. Someone had brought her a nimbhu pani but she hadn't touched that either, and the liquid looked flat in the fresh, still air. There were newspapers on the floor, the *Express*, the *Times*, *Herald Tribune*, and I saw a Sunday *New York Times* I had brought round a few days earlier still tied up in string. Her sunglasses had fallen down on the papers. A note pad was lying there, too, but it also looked untouched, so I knew she hadn't been doing anything at all. She was staring out across the lawns, and when she heard me she looked up and brushed the hair out of her eyes—something she always did—and asked if I liked peacocks.

I said yes, and she said they'd cried all night and I knew what that was like, didn't I, their sad and mournful cry penetrating the darkness? and then she added, "But I can't think about that, can I?" I said, "No, you better not."

I sat down. The bearer brought more nimbhu panis but she said no thanks. I took one and he left.

She hadn't washed her hair in days. It looked dirty and stringy. She had pulled it back off her face, only it had fallen again, strands around her face, just like Cully, inevitably. "I look a mess," she said suddenly. "But I just can't . . . . I don't know."

I said never mind, I'd just come around to drop something off. I didn't tell her I'd gone to the museum again or that I'd had dinner with Kady Suraj the night before. It was better, I thought. Let her rest. She'd talked enough. These days one story produced another, one memory gave three more. I felt like she was drinking in the sun and all its energy, soaking it up and quietly replenishing herself, like some amoeba reproducing itself a millionfold.

She said wouldn't I like something to eat? I said yes, and she called out, not too loud and not too soft, her voice raised just the right amount, and the bearer appeared instantly, his voice solicitous and obviously caring.

She ordered pickles and chapatis, samosas, too, just put them on a little tray, would he? and bring some napkins, please. I knew the composure was not all true, no matter how much at home she felt in India.

Still, I loved this feel of her nowadays, alone, outside in the shade, so preoccupied she couldn't read or drink, just talk day after day about the inner worlds of people I'd known for years and years, people named Kady Suraj and Jiggie Deeg, and Louis and Thalia Guthrie. And Cully, too, of course, always Cully at the back of everything, and the woman with the orange eyes named Durr.

Today Phoebe was quiet for a long time. She leaned her head back against the wicker lounge and stared out at the lawn where a crow was pecking at the ground. I shifted over to another chair beside her and stretched out, too.

"I thought I might go to Bombay," she said finally, letting out a long sigh. "But then again, I might go to the south of France. Or I could always go back to New York. . . ." She closed her eyes and breathed for a while. I watched the rise and fall of her chest. "Or I could just stay here."

By the time the tray came, she was fast asleep.

# ❧ 3 ❧

IN NEW YORK PHOEBE AND
Cully lived with Granny, Thalia's mother. They shared a Fifth
Avenue apartment that had nothing Indian in it. It had long
burgundy curtains tied with velvet rope, statues of Airedale
dogs, nineteenth-century prints of people in long dresses skat-
ing on country ponds, and one of a collie dog with a hat on
barking at a kitten.

When Phoebe and Cully left India, they brought clothes and
a photograph and things the servants packed, but that was all.
They only had two suitcases each. Louis and Thalia never even
had a funeral, things happened so quickly. The children were
on the plane the same time they might otherwise have been
singing hymns and looking at coffins in a nave.

Granny left Phoebe the apartment when she died, and
Phoebe, who had just divorced Stephen, moved right back in.
Went right back into the same bedroom down at the end of the
hall where she'd slept since she arrived from India, aged sixteen.

The apartment was big, with twelve rooms, long corridors
and windows six feet tall overlooking Central Park. All Phoebe
eventually contributed—she didn't have much from her years
with Stephen—was the books, hundreds of them, and stacks of
magazines and newspapers that seemed to grow until someone,
either herself or the cleaning woman, threw them out. The

books were piled everywhere, in corners, on shelves, in the hall, up and down the walls. She loved to read, history, philosophy, biographies, occasional thrillers and best-sellers, anything she could get about America. She rarely watched television, and unless friends were there, she never used any of the rooms except the kitchen, although she barely cooked, and the bedroom.

That's where she lived, down at the end of the hall, right next to Cully's old room, propped up in a pretty bed, with the same pillows and ruffles it had always had. Whenever I went over, Saturday mornings or at night after work, sometimes Cully was there, sometimes not, she was invariably all packed in with books and work, pads of paper, extra pens, magazines, a box of cookies, all in a slightly oversize single bed with the now faded picture of some artist's idea of a little girl in the middle of the headboard.

But if the bed was small, Phoebe would occasionally pat it affectionately and announce with a wicked grin that men loved it, referring, presumably, to the intimacy such a narrow space required.

As far as men were concerned, however, post-Stephen, most of them didn't last long and if they did, they had very nice apartments and big beds of their own.

For Phoebe and Cully, uprooted and alone, without a home, a family or an accessible past, Granny's twelve-room apartment above Fifth Avenue became a land and a territory in itself.

I understood that, of course, but, gradually, the older we got (she was thirty-six when the male Caucasian body turned up), the more the apartment seemed too big. There were four guest rooms, for example, and walls of china that were never touched. At some point after she left Stephen I began to be concerned about her. I had left *Newsweek* to work at the *Post* in Washington, and we still saw each other on weekends, talked constantly on the phone. I eventually got married and came back to New York, went on working as a stringer, but in New York, with a husband now, things between Phoebe and me shifted imperceptibly. My life began to center more and more around a stable relationship and eventually the yearning for a child. I began to notice that Phoebe didn't want the same thing.

When my son was born, we talked about how life evolved and you went through phases, were one thing one time, became another another, but she didn't relate it to herself. "I'm still young," she said. "I'm not in any hurry."

But, as life will have it, that's exactly what Phoebe was thinking about that day in May—thinking about what was happening to her life—when the phone call from New Delhi came, telling her about the body six feet long on the distant side of the Jumna River (Indians pronounce it Jamuna or Yamuna, either way).

Cully being missing for six weeks before the body was found was the first real crisis in Phoebe's life since her parents died. I was already back in India and she wrote me wild letters. She said everyone was trying to reassure her he was just wandering around. You know Cully, he'd lose his head if it wasn't screwed on, but it was easy to tell she was locked on to some awful dread and foreboding. It was the terror of losing all she had.

The call came Tuesday, May 11th. She'd just come back from buying a present for Alice who worked at Guthrie and Guthrie, the foundation. That had turned into a very successful enterprise. Other investors, taken with the one on one of it, had joined in. Phoebe had made a name for herself, sitting on boards, being quoted in the paper from time to time, but what it all came to on an emotional level was that she provided her beneficiaries with intense interest, money, encouragement and devotion, and they gave her much the same in return. What she didn't get—or give—in relationships with men, she got here.

On May 11th she bought a pitcher with leaves around the handle for Alice's birthday, and as she handed her money over to the clerk, it suddenly struck her that the only things she ever bought for a house were for other people, never herself, and just as suddenly she knew the reason why. It was one of those breakthroughs life can provide.

"I wish I could get one for myself," she heard herself saying to the saleswoman, "but I live in New Delhi, India, and the house's so full of art and things, there's no room for me."

On the way home she knew she'd had a warning that she had to do something about herself. Maybe it was because she was worried about Cully and already had India on her mind, or maybe it was just time, time to face the past, but she suddenly realized her childhood and her past were as shut off from her as India itself.

Back in the apartment she opened every drawer, cupboard,

closet. Sure enough, everything was Granny's, nothing was hers.

She called Pan American Airlines and when the woman asked where did she want to go? she said, "India."

"No. I mean where?" the woman said. "Where in India?"

Phoebe said, "New Delhi," and felt herself reeling. Standing by the sink, she saw her life as a block of ice, frozen, and after she hung up the phone, she actually started to yell. She raised her voice to its highest pitch and yelled and yelled and thought of Cully dying.

Then the phone rang.

But for that one second before it rang, she remembered the night they arrived in New York twenty years before and how, when Cully was in bed, she'd been so afraid he was going to die, alone in his own room for the first time in his life, she peeked in on him over and over again just to hear his breathing, life itself still alive in there, just because their parents had died didn't mean he was going to die.

She picked up the phone, her throat sore from yelling. The woman from the embassy, Harriet MacDonald, said, "I have to tell you we've got an unidentified male Caucasian body here. I wonder if it's your brother. You've been calling me enough about him, I thought I ought to tell you right away."

"Tell me what?"

"About the body."

"Oh my God, it's not Cully," Phoebe said.

"It might be him. There's no way to tell."

"But it can't be."

"I hate to say it, but there's a chance. We just can't tell from the condition of the body."

"What does it look like? Tell me. I'd know him anywhere."

"There's nothing to tell," Harriet said. "There's nothing left. No hair, clothes, head . . . well, parts of a head, that's all. But it's the right size, same body type and skin color as your brother. There's not much left. The back side of the head is gone, and the—"

"Does he have a scar on the left shoulder?" Phoebe persisted. "A big long ugly scar that looks like it should have had stitches, but didn't?"

"I called down to Deeg," Harriet said, unable to answer the

question. "Someone's coming right up to look at it. They're getting here as fast as they can, even chartering a plane, though frankly I don't think there's much chance they can identify him. I told them there was no need to hurry, but they seem to think there was. You're the only one who can really help. Do you think you can Air Express some dental X-rays as soon as possible?"

Phoebe bought a ticket to Delhi; she was leaving the next night. Now in bed she kept thinking of the past. Fear was rumbling in her chest like a swarm of ants or bees, something small and on the move, fear about where she was going and what she might find when she was there.

She sat up in bed and turned on the light, but all she could see were various versions of half a head—"the back side of the head is gone"—and Cully's one big toe. Is that what she was going to see in India? His toe? She could never forget the toe, so oversize it looked like two. They used to tie a string around it, make it a pet for the day.

She turned out the light again and stared at the ceiling, wondering how she'd get through this and whether this was the worst or only a taste of what was ahead.

India was so close, she could hear it. She'd forgotten till now how tall and thin her parents were, that Thalia spoke with a nasal twang and Louis had smelled of alcohol. She remembered the heat of India for the first time in years and how her breath used to stop in her throat and crack the walls of her mouth. She heard lizards on the walls and buzzards in the trees and remembered how the air felt full of people breathing. Even if she couldn't see them, they were there, breathing everywhere, and, remembering now, she understood why she had avoided India and pushed it from her mind. The suffocation and the fear were too real. The minute she thought about it, her chest went tight and everything narrowed down inside.

Gradually even the smells came back, the smell of dirt and underbrush, smoke and kerosene. India was all around her, India on and on, endless and still. It echoed in her ears and hallucinated in her mind. Remember me? it seemed to say, like a half-remembered dream thumping inside her skull. She could hear hyenas howling in the woods of Delhi and bicycles whining as they zoomed past in the street outside. Her heart was pounding and powerful. She felt it with her hand, thump, thump, Cull-lee, Cull-lee. In her mind it was night and the guard outside Number Nine Jumna Road was clicking his heels as he walked up and down the road. She could even tell which guard it was because one had limped and one had not and this one didn't.

He'd be dead by now. All her relatives were dead, Louis, Thalia, Granny. Maybe even Cully.

In the darkness, Phoebe saw herself and Cully on their knees in the Indian garden and Kamala, the ayah, pointing at a vulture in the blue-white sky—she called it a "kite"—and saying to watch out, vultures swooped down and carried babies off. It was her first memory, but it was also, oddly enough, one she had remembered almost every day ever since. It floated back into her mind like a piece of music, something printed indelibly on her life, and registered itself fleetingly, always with the same feeling.

The ayah with her arm pointed up, and Phoebe with her first sudden terrifying intuition that Cully was then and always would be in danger.

Phoebe, three, Cully in diapers, and Kamala's red-brown sari level with her eyes, Phoebe had looked up at the sky and seen the circling dark shape of the bird descending slowly low. It was hot and the garden was silent with the noise of India away, off in the background, leaving them and stillness inside here in the garden, and Kamala's arm was up and pointing, and the girl saw the bird and knew that Cully didn't.

The danger was circling now. It could strike at any time, unless she warned him, and swoop down unnoticed on nine feet of feathered wings and stab its beak into Cully's neck and lift him up off the ground and disappear, the two of them, bird and boy, off into protected, horrible oblivion, a place where she could never go.

But the bird had sailed up, danger averted for a spell.

## ❧ 4 ❧

PHOEBE PUT ON AN OLD T-SHIRT
of Cully's and went to his former room.

Switching on the light, she looked at his bed. She imagined his
hair flopped on the pillow and that she heard him breathing.
Somewhere there was a photograph of Louis and Thalia. He left
it when he moved out on his own after college. "You keep it,"
he said to Phoebe. "I have plenty."

"I don't want it."

"You should at least have one. One can't hurt you."

She found it in the top drawer of the bureau, still wrapped in
the tissue paper she herself had put it in. She had thought the
paper would protect it. Protect it? she thought now with the
wisdom of some distance. Or protect me?

She unwrapped the tissue. In her hand was a three-by-five
black-and-white picture of Thalia and Louis, taken outside
Number Nine, but she didn't look at it.

She left it facedown in her palm.

She remembered holding Cully's hand as the picture was
taken. She was all dressed up, a long way from anyone who wore
heels or even a bra. They were standing together outside the
bounds of the picture, looking in. Cully's hand in hers was
moist. Her parents were lined up like strangers who hadn't been

introduced and she had felt like waving at them to draw their attention to her so they, in turn, would draw her in to them.

Instead she tugged at Cully's hand and led him farther out across the lawn, as if they, the children, lived best out there, but what she wanted was to protect Cully from the feeling she herself already had.

Now Phoebe turned out the light in Cully's room and went down the hall to the kitchen. There she laid the picture on the counter, filled the teakettle with water and put it on the stove. She kept staring at the back of the picture.

Finally she turned it over and looked at it. She was surprised. These people were handsome. She'd put them so far out of her mind, she barely remembered what they looked like. Now suddenly they seemed tall and unalike, one dark, the other fair, and they stood not touching, Thalia in a patterned dress with shoulder pads, Louis in white pants and white shirt, and they hadn't smiled for the photograph.

Louis' hair was sleek and dark. He had a high forehead and good bones. Phoebe reached up to her cheeks to touch her own, big hard things that felt like lumps and looked like his.

Thalia wasn't as pretty as she had been when she was younger, but she still looked lovely and Phoebe remembered the one clear memory of her mother that she had: Thalia bending down over a baby and a crib. Maybe it was a photograph, maybe it was reality itself. She didn't even know.

The baby could have been Cully or it could have been her, she had no idea, but it was on its back with its two legs and two arms up in the air as if reaching for Thalia, and Thalia was reaching in to it.

Her memory showed the fine, rounded line of Thalia's back curved in over something, someone, that deep down she didn't want and didn't like. A baby. Her face was turned toward the camera—or maybe toward Phoebe, who would have been no more than three if Cully was the baby—with a dazzling smile.

It was the smile Phoebe remembered. It stretched inches, maybe feet, across her face, lips full and soft, opened slightly. They looked so soft and pliant, a kiss would push them in. The teeth inside the smile were white and even. The eyes, a grayish green, were crinkled, and the beauty seemed absolutely overpowering to Phoebe as she remembered it, so much so that she leaned her head back, away from the kitchen counter, as if the memory was so overwhelming, the only relief was distance.

She put the photograph next to the faucet and ran the water, daring it to splatter, and found herself looking at Louis' eyes. She hadn't thought of them in years. Her most persistent memory of him was one night when he was weaving and falling, drunk, climbing stairs on his hands and knees. He smelled of alcohol. It was the last time they went to the secret house in Golf Links, just before he died, the house where he and Kady kept the whiskey, perfume and German bikes, contraband for India.

Phoebe wiped her wet hands on her T-shirt and lifted the picture with the sides of her fingers, bringing it close to her face. She felt Louis' eyes looking at her in ways he'd never looked at her in life. For all the time they spent together, she was the one who watched him, Phoebe the observer. Watching him at this, that, in his fancy office where he lorded over the largest soft drink company in Asia, or later, watching him head across a room to join Kady Suraj, seeing his eyes light up with pleasure as nothing else could do, because, in that odd way life does things, Louis was as fond of the young Kady Suraj as anyone he ever knew.

Phoebe jumped down off the stool. "You're full of nonsense, both of you," she said aloud to her parents. "India wasn't good for either of you and twenty years without it has been just fine for me."

"Don't you want to go back?" Stephen had asked years earlier.

She said no, she never had, not since she arrived in New York, aged sixteen. "I was too intent on fitting in," she told him then, and nothing had changed since. "Can you imagine? Having yellow-white hair there? And being Indian here? I don't belong anywhere. Knowing gods are alive and the dead live and flies ground into paste can cure infections? You have to hide that kind of knowledge here. I want to be American."

She'd been attracted to Stephen then. He reminded her of Vikrim Ali Seth of Number Five Jumna Road and the time they'd had rolling around one night in the prayer room of Nizamuddin's Tomb.

Her skirt up around her neck, shoes off, there in the dust and probably four hundred years of pee, although it didn't smell of pee but it was so dark and private that surely four hundred years of people had gone in there to Nizamuddin's Tomb to do lots of things they should only do in private.

Including sixteen-year-old Phoebe Guthrie who was about to be an orphan and had just had her first and last sexual experience with anyone but herself for a good five years.

# ❧ 5 ❧

LOUIS AND THALIA WERE MARRIED
six weeks after they met. Louis said Thalia reminded him of
Jean Arthur, with her little hips and full breasts. She wore
stylish clothes and had her nails painted red and liked to lunch
with her friends every day. She was, all in all, the sort of woman
who might have done quite nicely with another man, another
life, New York a better parameter than India.

But she and Louis fell in love. He took her swimming at night
and ordered champagne when they met for breakfast, things
she'd never even heard of before. She told Granny he was
"wildly interesting and romantic," which he was, of course, but
his ambitions turned out to have little to do with her or their
children.

He was offered a job in India and she read up on all the history
and didn't pay attention to how his mother died when he was
six. Granny warned her he was difficult and needed someone to
take his mother's place, but Thalia didn't listen. Granny warned
her about India, too, but Thalia argued it wasn't that far away
and besides, it was just the place for Louis. His talents would
stand out there.

She was right. They did. But everything went wrong from the
start after they arrived in Delhi. Louis wanted constant attention and she refused to give it. Further, there was India itself.

32

She told people she thought it'd "be like Italy." But it wasn't. It was bugs and heat and food that made her sick and poverty that made her cry and crowds that made her nearly hysterical, and, finally, it was the Indians themselves. Their eyes were too big, their lips too full, their hair too black and they looked at her too much and picked their teeth in public.

But Louis loved it. He couldn't become a Hindu or join a caste, but he made Indians his closest friends, and if other Americans balked at taking off their shoes when they went in a house or at eating with their fingers, he perfected such customs as an art.

"I took to India like a duck to water," he used to tell people, but Kady Suraj claims that wasn't true at all. He says underneath, India scared Louis, and that no matter how much he tried to belong, eventually his exclusion, simply on the grounds he remained foreign and white, perpetuated the very thing he struggled with, namely anger and depression.

From the beginning Thalia retreated to the safety of her room, leaving everything, including her children, outside. But one day, when Phoebe was six and Cully three, she came across an article in the *International Herald Tribune* about a local orphanage on the other side of Delhi. For some inexplicable reason, she had the driver take her there, and in a sense, she never came back. These babies became her life. She spent hours there every day, taking care of these little brown motherless, fatherless creatures.

I myself saw Thalia only once. I went to a party on Jumna Road with my parents. They said I had to see the art, but because everyone important was always at a Guthrie party, I had to wash my hair, have it set and wear a brand-new dress the tailor made just for this occasion.

Thalia was sitting on the couch in the living room, not far from the statue of the Shiva Nataraj, and didn't move at all. She looked perfectly nice, I suppose, but even at my age I felt there was something strange about her. She was dressed in an unattractive brown skirt and blouse that matched her hair. She wore no makeup. Her hair was poorly cut. Her hands were crossed in her lap, and she reminded me of a missionary.

Her husband was across the room, laughing and loud, full of life and vigor. Phoebe and Cully were upstairs, never allowed to come down for parties.

33

Phoebe says having Thalia as a mother was terribly confusing. Eventually people talked about her as if she were a kind of saint, but Phoebe barely knew her. Kamala the ayah took care of her and her brother, got their clothes, made them do their homework and sat at the table while they ate.

Louis, for his part, not only disliked his wife, he disliked his son. The boy's timidity enraged him and eventually, when he adopted first Kady and then Phoebe as his nightly companions, he expressly saw his wife and son as little as possible. Ironically that made him all the madder and toward the end he yelled at Thalia whenever he saw her. Cully, too. His face would turn red, he'd near burst with rage, and Thalia would only ignore him all the more.

"Why d'you always blame me for the fact it's hot?" Louis screamed at her one day when Phoebe was standing in the bedroom door.

"What's that?" Thalia asked airily from her couch in the alcove. "Were you talking to me?"

"Of course I'm talking to you. Who else blames me for the heat and the flies? Are you trying to drive me crazy?"

"I thought you might be interested in me for once," Thalia said calmly, knitting something for the babies. "You're always talking to Phoebe or Kady. Anybody but me and Cully."

"I'd love to talk to you," Louis yelled, beating his hands up and down like there was something there to strangle or destroy. "But you don't talk to me."

Phoebe slipped away and found Cully outside in the hall sitting on Kamala's lap, his head nestled up against her breast.

"Did he hear?" Phoebe asked.

The boy shook his head.

Louis had an executive's position with a new but promising American company that eventually sold packaged food and soda drinks throughout Asia. He knew at a glance that everything in India was who you know, and from the start he had the perfect knack for deference and condescension. In no time at all he became quite the pukka sahib. His business thrived, and he became one of the preeminent Western businessmen in Delhi, a position he enjoyed enormously but was unable to maintain.

The papers called him "fun-loving" and "unpredictable."

34

That wasn't the half of it.

It was, however, as a top man in Delhi business circles that he met K. T. Keshri Suraj and discovered art.

All Phoebe knew about this was that when Kady and her father met for the first time, Kady was standing in the middle of his own living room and Louis was at the front door. She had no idea how her father got there but she knew what happened next. The room was full of attractive, worldly things that contrasted sharply with the young and unsophisticated Kady, but Louis, at a glance, understood the younger man whose name he didn't even know.

Kady was just nineteen and twelve years Louis' junior. He was tall and impressive but he wore a jacket that hugged him tight around the chest, pants that were too short, and his hair had been cut in some bazaar. He was clearly not long out of the backwaters, but Louis instinctively saw he was full of promise, talent, and aggression. For all their external differences, they were a perfect match. Louis had everything to give, and Kady wanted it. Louis spotted him for exactly what he was, a comer who needed what he could provide, and so they stepped out together into Delhi society, mentor and protégé, undisguised best friends.

Two years later Phoebe joined them, a bizarre, if crucial, turning point.

"I don't want you to hurt yourself by thinking you mean anything to your father, darling," Thalia said to Phoebe, sitting her down for tea one day then. "He's using you for himself. He can't be alone. He wants to hurt me. It has nothing to do with you. You must admit, it's awfully strange for a girl to go out at night with her father and a black man—"

"He's not black."

"—who has a wife he never lets anyone see. But are you having a good time?"

"Yes."

"Then I suppose it's all right. This is India, after all, no one will know. Just don't think it means anything to him. That's all I care about, darling. What happens to you."

"I know."

"Just remember he was really very clear about it."

"About what?"

"Not having children. He was very matter-of-fact." She

35

handed Phoebe a cup of tea. Phoebe put it down untouched. "He always said there'd be no children. I ignored it. I thought he meant we wouldn't have one *yet* or for a while. I didn't tell him for months."

"Tell him what?"

Behind Thalia the sun was shining on the Shiva Nataraj, four arms and two legs, dancing on the dwarf of the world. Phoebe looked at the statue, her father's prized possession.

"That I was having a baby, silly darling. You."

The Shiva was dancing inside a circle of flames, the flames of life and the universe, Shiva on one foot, the dance of life itself.

"Finally I had to tell him I wasn't just fat or having a strange reaction to the heat, although that was true. I did get hives. I told him over breakfast. It was our only time together. At least we still had that. Now I wouldn't recognize him if I met him on a bus, would I, darling? I tried to tell him you were a mistake."

"Why didn't you just say you really wanted a baby and you knew he'd love it when he got used to it?"

"I was afraid. I hated India and I wanted to go home. I didn't know what to do. I told him I hadn't thought it could happen so fast. I told him I was sorry. I was in tears and all he said was . . . Phoebe, I can't tell you how much it hurt." She looked out the window, and now her daughter, too, looked away. "All he said was, 'How long do you think it takes? a month?' You know, dear, the act itself. 'Can't you get rid of it?' and I said, 'No, of course not,' it was too late, and I wouldn't want to anyway, now would I, darling? and he said, 'But I'm not ready. I have to deal with this first. . . .' "

" 'This' what?"

"India. Everything was India to him. And I said, 'But you're more settled here than you've ever been in your life,' and he said I didn't understand a thing. I thought everything was easy for him and it wasn't. He said I didn't pay any attention to him now, how could I if I had a baby, too? He was very angry, and I said, 'Well, maybe I don't understand, but I want children and I'll have them,' and he said, 'Well, then, you'll have them on your own,' and I kept expecting him to turn around. . . ."

"What do you mean, 'turn around'?"

"Because he was buttering toast in the other direction. I wanted him to look at me but he didn't."

"Didn't what?"

"Aren't you listening? He just kept hitting at the toast with his knife and I stretched out my hand to beg him and he flung it at me, and I realized he wasn't buttering toast at all. He didn't even have any toast. There wasn't any left. It was all hacked up and he'd just been hitting at these little crumbs."

## ❧ 6 ❧

IT WAS NOVEMBER NOW AND I
left Phoebe sleeping on the lounge chair out on the veranda.
This was Kitty Chandradas' house; she'd been Louis' friend, and
now Phoebe was staying there. Kitty always left Phoebe and me
alone to sit and talk. That day I told the bearer, never mind, I'd
come back later, better let her sleep, and he said yes, because she
didn't sleep at night, which I didn't know, and he said yes, her
light was always on and sometimes she came outside and sat
here and they found her asleep in the morning.

The driver was taking me home when I remembered Kady
was at his office. I had him take me over to Raj Path, the Road
of Kings, to the Secretariat Building overlooking India Gate and
all of Delhi. I went up to the top floor—"Deputy Minister,
Public Works," read the sign—and Kady himself came out. He
ushered me in through the maze of rooms that were his domain.

I told him I was just passing by, thought I'd drop in, that's the
way things were done here, even with people of his position. He
was pleased—our bond was Phoebe—and in his inner office he
shut the door and I looked around. He acted like he had nothing
else in the world to do but entertain me, although people were
lined up outside waiting for him and the phones were ringing
madly.

The office was tasteful. I knew it would be. I complimented

38

him and he seemed very pleased. He pointed out an antique desk from Burma Louis'd given him and I commented on how handsome it was, then asked didn't he have any pictures of his children? There were none around. He said he kept those at home, and besides, they weren't exactly children anymore. I was going to ask him more about them, I wonder what he'd have said, but my eyes caught sight of a beautiful piece of cloth that had been framed and positioned along one wall. I thought it was one of the most unusual things I'd ever seen.

"What's that?" I exclaimed.

He told me it was a rare Kashmiri piece, an antique, and then said Durr—she was his wife, the woman with the orange eyes—had given it to him. That surprised me. It suggested an intimacy and a caring I didn't think they had.

Kady was relaxed, asked how I was, what I was doing today. I said I'd been to the museum, didn't mention Phoebe, although he probably knew I'd been with her.

It was odd seeing him there for the first time. The allure of the place made him even more imposing. I was struck by how he did personify the new India, even to an outsider like me. He towered over me, so unlike an Indian, and his dynamism was inescapable. He wandered around the room picking up things to show me, his physical stature alone commensurate with his terrain, roads, dams, power plants, forging rivers and deserts alike.

"Do you really think you represent the future of India?" I asked somewhat breathlessly all of a sudden.

He flashed me an amused smile. "Oh, don't get into that," he said.

"But that's what the newspapers say."

He shrugged, obviously irritated with the subject. "I'm just impatient," he said. "That's all it is. More people should be impatient around here. I just want to do what I want to do." He sounded awkward all of a sudden, terribly human. "I don't care about any of the hoopla anymore. I hate it, actually."

He asked if I wanted tea. I nodded and we sat down, and with his long legs stretched out in front of him and his face so beautifully shaped, yet always enigmatic, he looked even more like the new India, but now it was his clothes. They were expensive and aristocratic, but for all that, he acted like he'd just picked them up blind and thrown them on, his tie askew, jacket wrinkled.

39

Kady was unusual looking for an Indian. With his long nose and high cheekbones, he didn't have the round look Indians usually have. He was more Semitic. His eyes weren't Indian, either. Not soft or languid, they were direct, even aggressive, and, in fact, the only truly Indian thing about him was his skin, the color of mahogany or coffee with just a speck of milk.

I didn't mention Phoebe, neither did he. The clerk-chaprassi brought us tea and eventually we did get around to the things that tied us together. I asked about May 11th, the day he saw the male Caucasian body in the morgue.

It was 95 degrees fahrenheit and the air-conditioning unit that serviced the entire building had gone off. Phone service had been erratic since morning, telephone lines in Delhi more like a mass of vines than anything meant to work. Electricity had ceased for over an hour around noon and in the afternoon there was no water anywhere because all the water around Connaught Circle, the heart of town, had trickled to a drop, then stopped, not that anyone knew why except that maybe water wasn't meant to move through pipes hundreds of feet above the ground.

That was the time of year when most men, even in Kady's position, wore short-sleeved white shirts hanging loose over their trousers, but not Kady. On the day before Phoebe Guthrie returned to India, he was wearing a beige cotton Nehru jacket, custom-made several years earlier in London and especially fitted so that even without lining it looked exactly the way it was supposed to look. He had undone the top two buttons, however, it was so hot. His undershirt was showing and there were perspiration stains underneath his arms.

Papers were spread out on his desk. The list of messages was high, appointment book full, and he was working just as he always did, blinders on, his only focus, his job.

A beautiful English tea set Jiggie Deeg had given him sat on the desk, an ashtray unused nearby, and if there was the scent of something vaguely cinnamon in the air, it was left over from the day before. Because he had not smoked as yet before the telephone call came in. He had already drunk five to ten cups of tea. He didn't drink anything else except water and nimbhu

40

panis, a drink of lemon juice and soda water, which he spiced with salt, not sugar. He didn't know the Taj Hotel had an open-ended reservation for Phoebe Guthrie starting for tomorrow. Or that across town the smell of an unidentified male Caucasian body had hung over the far shores of the Jumna River for days and had now ceased to be.

But Cully Guthrie was still at the back of his mind.

He always was these days and right now there were lots of reasons, but one was that Vishnu Bhave, the little navy blue man who had been Louis Guthrie's art dealer and a friend to Cully in recent months, was sitting outside his office.

He'd been there since eight o'clock that morning when the doors opened. His son had been murdered April 2nd, six weeks past, in the antique store and residence where they lived in Old Delhi.

Vishnu Bhave didn't have an appointment, but he told the receptionist he was waiting to see Suraj and he had even brought his lunch, pakoras wrapped in a newspaper, telling the woman no thank you, he wasn't in a hurry, he could wait all day. In fact, he could come back tomorrow and the next day and the next and wait as long as was necessary.

"It was most extremely peculiar to see him without his son," Suraj's driver, Samiji Jabu Mal, said later. "I am never seeing Vishnu Bhave anywhere, not even anywhere, not here, not there, for twenty, thirty years, have I seen him without this one son."

Kady Suraj knew why Vishnu Bhave was outside his office but he didn't want to see him. In fact, he had no intention of seeing him, so much so that when he went to the bathroom he used the sweepers' door, where only untouchables go, just so he could avoid him.

At about three in the afternoon he turned to the newspapers to give them a second read. There was the impending famine in Bihar, the inevitable speculation about whether the monsoons would be early, late, or not at all, more Hindu-Muslim unrest in Kashmir, more Hindus killed by Sikhs in the Punjab, soldiers now positioned heavily around the city.

Outside in the reception room, the American ambassador called.

He was put through to the Deputy Minister's First Deputy

Assistant, who was not to be confused with either the First Secretary, who was far lower in rank and caste than he, or the First Deputy, who was far higher.

The First Deputy Assistant told the ambassador that Deputy Minister for Public Works Kady Suraj was not in.

The ambassador had probably expected as much, only intending to leave a message. That's the way things were done here: be as indirect as possible. "Please tell him I have a delicate and fairly urgent personal matter to discuss with him," he said, which, translated, meant he didn't want to be put off to talk to the First Deputy and that he regarded the matter as not "fairly urgent," but very urgent.

As Suraj remembers it, he was looking up when the knock on his door came and Mr. Kuldip Ramchandran, his Deputy Assistant, was standing there saying the first assistant had just taken an important message from the American ambassador.

Kady told Ramchandran to ring him back right away. "I have a feeling he's calling about the Guthrie boy," he said. "Tell me immediately what he wants."

# ❧ 7 ❧

K. T. KESHRI SURAJ'S OFFICE
above Raj Path was both palatial and attractive, but there were
few people who knew much about his first office.

In fact, it is inaccurate to describe it as an office at all because
it was more correctly a chair, and not a real chair at that, just
a straight-backed job that had no indentation for a seat and was,
worse still, physically attached to a desk. It was someone else's
desk at that, one of four like desk and chair arrangements, all of
them in the onetime very small dining room of a onetime very
low-ranking British officer's bungalow, now converted to a
transport office far out in the beautiful regions of Rajasthan.

That it was a Central Transport Office, not a branch, and was
located in the city of Deeg itself, was its one redeeming feature
and Keshri Suraj, a tall, skinny boy about the age of twelve, was
affixed to his one chair as a part-time clerk. That was putting it
politely. He was really an inner-office note carrier, which is
several castes above what was next below it on the rung, but a
very long way from whatever it took by way of birth and caste
to occupy the desk itself.

By all rights he shouldn't even have had that chair. He should
have been out in the Rajasthani Desert in the family village
where there was a view across the plains to Umaid Mahal Palace, home of Maharaja Juggernathan Bisamillah Rajender Baha-

dur Singh, otherwise known as Jiggie Deeg, and he should have been plowing with a hoe, watching a bride, some ten years old with a sari across her face, pull water from a well.

But his father, taking Kady with him, had left the village long ago to follow a divinely inspired career as a healer and a psychic. His inspiration was his son, he said. He knew he had a future and he saw it as his duty to help him find it. Their travels led them to a back street in Deeg where he established a considerable reputation for himself and a life for the boy that was even more out of the ordinary than his own.

He got Kady into first one school, then another, finally the best in town. Meanwhile, his divine calling exposed him to so-called and actual dignitaries, as well as the general riffraff of life. When the boy was twelve, one of the lesser elite, an administrator in the Department of Transport, had a tooth inhabited by a bala or demon. After three sessions he was freed of the demon and as a gesture of his appreciation, he gave Kady a part-time job in the local transport office.

Media profiles say Kady was already a member of the local Congress party by this time. Other articles pinpoint the start of his political activities to a few years later when a local school burned down, killing twenty-one children, and he led the effort to rebuild it by protesting the lack of schools in general. He focused his attack on the legacy of Maharaja Juggernathan Singh. "He can't keep us backwards anymore," he was quoted as saying at a political rally. "Everyone deserves an education."

The school was finally rebuilt and public pressure was such that the maharaja not only donated the funds, but set in motion construction of more. Kady, precocious as he was, was quoted as saying the school was symbolic of India. It had to rise from the ashes of feudal control.

Today the local newspapers have thick files on Kady Suraj. His name comes up after the fire in a steady stream of articles. He was certainly older than his years. One wonders if he was ever a child at all. He got involved in building a health clinic; he spoke at a rally calling for government-sponsored birth control; he was at a meeting that declared dowries should be illegal because they undermined the whole economic system from the village on up by forcing everyone into debt. He spoke at a conference on the need for electricity and said the sun should be used to provide energy.

These clips are so yellow now, they look like cornbread. I had to handle them gingerly lest they crumble, but they certainly show, among other things, that one of Kady's ongoing themes was criticism of Jiggie Deeg.

At one political meeting he said the root cause of India's problems was people's tendency to cede responsibility to others. "Whether it's Jiggie Deeg or the British, it's all the same," he said. "What good was independence if Maharaj-sahib still dictates what happens to us?"

I was interested to discover how completely the later articles ignored this early criticism. They focused instead on how the maharaja eventually became Suraj's patron and never wondered what caused the boy's turnaround or led him to give up a local political career in Deeg, to go to Delhi to work for Deeg Enterprises.

The press was endlessly fascinated, understandably, by the partnership that developed between the two, the young man with the older powerhouse as his backer and his guru, the older man changed and informed by the spirit of the young. But in all the millions of words there was never a hint of the single most important thing of all, namely what bound the two together.

The journalists are to be forgiven. Only six people knew of it, and they never told. They were Kady and Jiggie Deeg, Durr, Jiggie's two aides, Shyam Singh, a barefoot peasant, and Attar Singh, landed gentleman, and, finally, Vishnu Bhave, the art dealer.

Later Louis Guthrie learned and, eventually, Phoebe and myself. But that was all.


Of the change in Kady Suraj's status, the newspapers simply say that Jiggie Deeg decided to sponsor the boy's advancement and within a few years he was married to a Kashmiri woman named Durr and living in a tiny flat in New Delhi. He started as a clerk at Deeg House, home of Deeg Enterprises. He went to college at night and spent every penny he had being tutored in economics and elementary engineering.

They say Jiggie Deeg befriended him and everything else came naturally.

They were not all wrong.

45

I heard the basic stories about Kady Suraj long ago from my parents. He always interested me, in part because of the way he looked, but also because he was so different. His rise in life gave him tremendous distinction. It stood out in people's minds as emblematic of the change and turbulence that characterized postcolonial India.

Despite the rigidity of the underlying structure of just about everything in India, from Hinduism to the caste system to the regularity of trains and mail delivery, the country, nonetheless, has an almost pioneering mentality that soars from time to time. It shows the explosive energy that's contained just beneath the repression and the rules, whether in the spectacular marital affairs that rock the press from time to time, the mammoth wealth onetime street cleaners accrue or even the mind-boggling violence that cuts its swath.

India is a place of change and no change. Some things are positively medieval, others the opposite. Take women. A woman is legally described as property and chattel. She is owned by her husband, same as a house or a car and, if divorced, becomes something of a waste product. In some cases her family won't even take her back, she is so disgraced. People won't invite her to their home and her children can't be married, on the assumption they'll turn out as bad as she.

But, for all that, even at the time Kady first showed up on the Delhi scene, some few marriages were being arranged across caste-class lines, and the notion of democracy had certainly taken hold. Election turnout was regularly some seventy-five percent. The economy itself was wide open, if corrupt, accessible to thieves and opportunists. Anything and everything, from traffic tickets to passports, could be bought and sold on any street corner. Nowadays there are computers and fax machines and even high-rise buildings, but telephones still don't work and privies in the classiest home or office can be two holes in the floor. For all these reasons, the phenomenon of Kady Suraj, while astounding, was more acceptable than you might think.

People didn't care about his origins. The time was right. He had money—although no one ever suspected it came from the black market—and no one minded where, or what, he was born.

Kady, for his part, was open about the whole thing: his caste, his background, family, work, mission, and, most especially, his benefactor, Jiggie Deeg.

"I am what I am," he often said. "I have no secrets."

## ❊ 8 ❊

ON MAY 11TH, KULDIP RAMCHAN-
dran left Kady's office and placed the call to the embassy. The
American ambassador came right on the line.

Mr. Ramchandran apologized, but not too profusely, and said
the Deputy Minister was unfortunately detained "out of station" longer than expected, and could he please take a message
in his stead.

The ambassador told him a male Caucasian body had been
found and was now lying in a Delhi morgue. He had to wonder,
he said, if it was Cully Guthrie. "It's the right size and all, and
I wanted to notify the minister right away."

"Yes."

"I also wanted to ask if, do you think he could visit the morgue
and take a look? I know it's a lot to ask, but we just had Jasdan
Singh up from Deeg, the maharaja's son. He came on his own
plane, and, to be perfectly honest, he couldn't tell a damn thing.
He's all in a snither, says he's got to know who it is right away.
I have my own problems with this body, and I wouldn't bother
you except . . ."

"Yes?"

"Well, it's hard to identify. In fact, I gather it's downright
disgusting. But do you think the Minister could take a look?"

Mr. Ramchandran made no reply except to say that he would relay the message the next day when the minister's return was "anticipated," but that his schedule, as always, was very tight.

I'd been in his office a good half hour that November when Kady suddenly said we should go out.

"Go out? Where?"

"Anywhere. Let's just get out of here. Take a drive, eat, I don't care. I'm sick to death of this place."

He took me by the arm and led me out. Elbowed his way through the crowds in the hall and didn't stop for anybody, although they pushed up around him like flies on jam. It would have driven me crazy, but he was obviously used to it, just pushed them away. He seemed on edge now, restless. He pulled out one of those cinnamon cigarettes and lit it. Outside he gave it to a beggar, patted him on the head, and treated him with warmth. Someone else might have just kicked the fellow aside.

Inside the car he leaned forward to talk to the driver. "Samiji," he said, "go to the Wyndham." I realized we weren't going for a drive at all.

The Wyndham is a dreary old hotel in Connaught Place. I hadn't been inside in ages. It was all the thing in English days and later when I was growing up, but no one goes there anymore. The dining room was almost empty. It was dark, too. There were no windows and the only lighting was a chandelier hanging from the ceiling. We sat down in a corner booth that gave a look back across the floor toward the door and I could barely make out Kady's face at first. He seemed that dark, but his eyes looked white and I was reminded of a child's book my son used to have with all the animals' eyes gleaming white in a jungle darkness.

We didn't talk at first, watched a group of German tourists who were wearing short shorts and socks with sandals and then a couple from south India who had newspapers. He said they were studying marriage ads in the classifieds, looking for people of the right caste to fix up with their child.

The atmosphere was private. Even the bearers didn't recognize him. His allure of wealth stood out, however, and they hovered around until he shooed them away.

"So how is she today?" he finally asked.

"Same," I said, feeling a huge sense of relief that at last Phoebe'd been mentioned.

Then he started drawing on his napkin with a pen, an intricate mandala of circles and things. "Why'd she wait so long to come back to India?" he asked. He glanced at me briefly, then returned to his drawing, as if to say he was only halfway interested in my reply. His face looked handsome, but blank now. Phoebe had said the thing she liked about it was that it showed everything. But it didn't to me. I wondered what was back behind it, sadness, anger, hurt. I couldn't see a thing, just that smooth dark skin and those wonderful eyes.

"I don't know," I said. "I don't think she ever wanted to."

"Then why did she? Just for Cully?"

I didn't know how to answer. I knew what he wanted to hear, but I didn't think it was my place to say it. That was between them. So I just told him what she'd said about being "frozen" and how she knew she had to break out.

Then he asked about her ex-husband, Stephen. He wanted to know what he was like and again I couldn't tell if he was really listening or not, because he tried to look as if he wasn't. By this point I liked him tremendously, so I knew what he was going through. Besides, the vibrations were flowing out of him, like an engine under the table. I said Stephen was terribly nice, one of the most decent people I'd ever met.

"Then why did she leave him?"

I said he was too perfect, his life, family, manners. He was safe. There was something staid about him. He even opposed her return.

Kady nodded, but I began to feel he was getting impatient. I didn't know why.

He kept asking me questions, about Phoebe and the past, her American past, not the Indian one they had shared, and I gradually began to understand what he was feeling. That as far as he was concerned I had access to the missing twenty years, the gap between the times he and Phoebe had known each other. And he wanted it. America and those missing years had become inextricably mixed with his own missing pieces and he was trying to pick them up and sort them out.

The bearers brought us three rounds of tea and some Indian sweets. He asked about her friends, her work, this and that, a steady stream of questions that accompanied his drawing on the napkins and allowed for lots of chitchat, too, about American art and the banking system, the problem of drugs and how he'd tried a skateboard once outside his hotel in Washington.

I tried to picture it, laughed. So did he. "Didn't you fall down, at least?" I asked.

"No. I was rather good. Even though I must have looked silly." He shrugged, indifferent at the thought.

"Did you bring one back for your son? A skateboard?"

"No," he said, and I thought of asking him more about his son but didn't.

See, I didn't know anything about his children yet. Except that he had them, two daughters and a son.

"Tell me more about Stephen," he said.

"What can I say? Living apart made them closer." I told him their common understanding was that her devotion to her brother had effectively ruined the marriage. "Cully always came first. He'd call, she'd say did he want to have dinner and cancel any plans she had with Stephen."

Again, Kady nodded. "What else?" he asked, his arms and elbows on the table as he bent over and fiddled absentmindedly with the bowl of sugar.

"What do you want?"

"Anything."

She and Stephen always argued about movies, Cully, her work . . .

"What about her work?"

She'd never leave work to take trips with him, and he said she was more married to it than to him.

"Did she ever think about her parents' death?" he asked.

"No," I said. "Never."

"She didn't wonder about it?"

"She never said so. Why would she?"

"No reason."

"She didn't even think about them," I said. "Not until the day she left for India. Then she couldn't get the accident out of her mind. She even called Stephen and asked him what, hypothetically, could have happened to the car."

A burned and charred car, would it have been taken away, you know, removed? Or would it have burned up in the fire?

Kady nodded. "Perfectly good question."

## ❧ 9 ❧

In New York Phoebe still had
to get Cully's X-rays and pick up something at her office, but she
lay in bed in the morning, unable to get started. She couldn't get
the body out of her mind.

The phone rang. It was her friend Alice. "Are you all
packed?"

"I keep thinking about what I'm going to do at the morgue."

"Why don't you just send the X-rays, Feeb? You don't have
to do it in person. It's too gruesome."

"Death is so commonplace over there, you wouldn't believe
it. I mean, there's death everywhere. One year Samiji, he was
our driver, he had seven children up in his village. The next year
he had five. Just like that, he lost two. I'm not crazy to be
worried about Cully, am I?"

"It's been six weeks."

"I mean, even if there wasn't this body, it'd still make sense
to worry?"

"Given you and Cully, absolutely."

"I mean, he wrote every week. At least he did in the beginning
when he first got there. Here, we talked every day. You'd understand, you really would, if you had a younger brother."

"What's going on?"

"I've been up all night looking at old pictures. I found one of Cully that just makes me cry."

Phoebe held it in her hands and stared at it as Alice talked. It caught Cully looking over his left shoulder, eyes slightly glazed. His yellow-white hair looked like hay burned by the sun, the eyes were as blue as blue, and if you didn't know him, you'd see nothing dissolute in the face, just someone handsome, even dazzling, only the faintest suggestion of anything else.

You bum, she thought to herself, making half a smile.

She had another picture, too, showing her brother standing in front of the Secretariat Building on Raj Path with Kady Suraj.

Phoebe always looked at Cully, handsome and happy, his hair flowing out in some rare wind, his head bent ever so slightly toward the left. But now, as she listened to Alice, she looked at Suraj.

He had one arm around Cully's shoulder. Something about the way they were standing made her think he had just given Cully an embrace. She looked at his face. She barely remembered it. She hadn't thought much about him in years. "I wonder what's happened to him," she said aloud.

"Who?" asked Alice.

"Just someone I used to like in India."

The dentist came right out of his office and gave her a hug, then led her back inside and sat her down on a stool. "I wouldn't worry about Cully," he said. "He can take care of himself." He patted her on the back, then pointed to charts that were lined up against a fluorescent lamp behind him. "Ready?" He flicked a switch. Suddenly Cully's teeth stood out naked and pointed like an anthropological display.

Phoebe gasped.

"I'm sure they have dentists over there who can do this, but . . ."

"I want to be able to do it."

She watched as the doctor began going over Cully's charts with his tiny pointed instrument, noting marks of distinction. She remembered a room covered with moss and bugs and bottles where Cully had taken her years ago.

They had gone to visit Brinj, Samiji's village, so poor there wasn't one car in the whole place, and there was moss growing on the doctor's walls. The doctor had looked at an infection in her leg and said not to worry, it would heal, and she thought it was amazing he could even see it, the room was so dark and wet. The infection was a big round hole above the thigh and he poked around, the light so dim she couldn't even see the pores on his face. He gave her some medicine and she was sure he said something about ground-up flies, but whatever it was, the infection disappeared by morning.

"He has thirty-two teeth in all," the dentist was saying.

"What works for them works for us, Feeb," Cully had said in the doctor's office. "But you have to believe. Do you?"

"Yes," she'd said.

"And don't worry," he'd added. "Because it's going to work. You're nearly Indian anyway."

And he was right, or, at least, he was then. She had been nearly Indian once.

"He's had his wisdom teeth out so you won't see . . ." the doctor was saying.

Phoebe stared at the fluorescent lights and the naked teeth that looked like fangs. She didn't want someone else to look at the body, she was thinking, and say, Oh yes, this is your brother, or, oh no, this is not your brother. She wanted to do it herself.

"Look at this filling in the back left molar," the dentist said. "It's very distinctive. You have to think about how you'll recognize these teeth if you see them again."

"What do I do?" she asked. "Put a mirror in the mouth?"

"That might work, but it isn't always as simple as that. If rigor mortis has set in, sometimes it's impossible to get anything in the mouth and the jaw has to be broken."

"How do I do that?"

"Get someone to do it for you."

"But what?" she pressed. "Do you break the jaw in back at the hinges?" She touched the side of her cheek at the right place. "Crack the two sides apart?"

The doctor grimaced disapprovingly. "Don't expect him to look familiar," he said, "because unless the body's fresh, brand new or something, the gums will be rotten. Eaten away by maggots."

54

"Oh, good," she said. "Just what I need. Maggots." She flashed him a smile. "And why would his head be halfway gone?"

"Your guess is as good as mine," he said.


At her office in a small building on lower Madison Avenue, big photographs of the beneficiaries covered the walls. One showed a California fisherman standing against a boat Guthrie and Guthrie had bought, another, a woman in the window of a kite store that had become a national enterprise. In yet another a woman was leaning over a microscope with her head turned out toward the camera. Phoebe had drawn a cartoonist's circle and written the words, "I'm going to discover the cure for AIDS" coming out of her mouth.

She took Alice into the storage room, to a big cabinet, and pulled out a file entitled "Louis Antonine Guthrie." Inside was a manila envelope and inside that a smaller, white envelope.

She handed that to Alice. "Open it."

"What is it?"

"My parents' death certificates."

Alice pulled out two sheets of paper and looked at them. "It says they died on the road to Agra. Where's Agra?"

"Where the Taj Mahal is."

"It's signed by a doctor." Alice put the paper down. "What are you going to do with these?"

"Look at them," Phoebe said. "I've never even opened this, if you can believe it. Maybe I'll do it there. Maybe I'll even go to Agra."

"But why?"

Phoebe shrugged. "Find the place. I don't know. They never even had a funeral, you know. They weren't even buried any-where."

# ❧ 10 ❧

IT WAS THE SIXTH OF JANUARY twenty years before. The winds were blowing, the cold had come down from the north, and Phoebe and Cully stood at the gate, bundled up in sweaters and woolen socks, looking out at Jumna Road. It was a thing they did at dusk, watch and listen, bullock carts and wagons going by, taxicabs and men on bicycles, everyone headed home, dogs howling in the distance, hyenas, too, and somewhere far away on this particular night they heard a procession starting up, a wedding or a death, the singing told its course.

Peacocks swung from the trees, their feathers hanging like blankets meant to dry, and the sky stretched purple from front to back. It was a fantastic shade that gradually tinged everything with its glow and Phoebe stared in awe as first the trees, then everything, assumed a veneer of the elegant light. She should have gone inside, but she couldn't leave. The procession winding its way through the distance held her to her spot. She knew it was a funeral now and, in retrospect, the only hint she had that something was going to happen came not from the house, or from Thalia and Louis inside, who would die before the night was over, but from the procession itself, because she gradually perceived it was coming this way and the closer it got, the more she felt it was being played out for her benefit.

56

The noise was getting louder, the cries distinct, and then the servants, one by one, as if summoned by a call, were coming out of the house too and standing beside them along the fence, death something to behold, even in India where lives never die but go on and on in perpetuity, from bird to ant, man or saint. They had all seen bodies before, but never here on Jumna Road.

"A burning, miss-sa'ab," said Kamala, the ayah.

Phoebe stood riveted to her spot. It was incredible to her that of all the places this procession could go, of all the streets and houses it could pass, it was going to wend its way down this very street, past her house and her lawns. Death was commonplace, that was true, but she'd never known anyone up close to die and that a death should come her way did not seem a random event. She had lived too long in India to disregard the coincidence of fate and she whispered in Hindi, "But why is it coming here? What does it mean?"

Kamala shrugged and the way she did it meant who was she to speculate on the interactions between man and the gods that led death directly past their door. "Maybe it's not for us," she said.

"For who, then?"

Now the drums were beating loudly, coming ever closer, the sound of tympanum filling the air, and Phoebe and Cully leaned far out over the gate, waiting to catch a glimpse. Phoebe listened hard to the chanting and shrieking that heralded the great lament of death. The men's voices yodeling in pain fascinated her, and for all her efforts to suppress it, she heard the relentless beating of the drums with an apprehension she couldn't ignore. She knew there was meaning here. "They're headed for the river," she whispered in Hindi to Cully on her left.

Even before they saw the procession, they saw its lights coming closer through the trees, its fire right outside the house, when a few hours later, this very same night, there would be another fire down in Agra in the white Ford car. Finally the procession turned a corner and came in view. Flares were burning, rags were soaked in kerosene and strung high on sticks. The people filled the street, scores, hundreds of men, all dressed in white, with woolen scarves and shawls around their heads and necks, torches aloft, their faces streaked with red and white and yellow paste, religious marks meant to make connections with the gods.

The drummers were drumming hard, announcing that this, a newest arrival, was on his way to the gods on high, but it seemed to Phoebe they were unburdening a fury, not helping the journey of a soul, so tense was the beat, and then she saw the newest arrival himself.

He was stretched out on a board carried by a dozen, twenty men, and any glance would take him to be dead, surely not asleep. He was all but invisible for the mounds of flowers lying on top of him, orange, white, pink, and red, a profusion of color to mark the absence of life, and he, poor man, was just a face at one end and a foot dangling off the end of the platform at the other, looking like he wasn't wedged on well enough, but was still too secure to topple off.

That was all that was left to see. Phoebe stared at the face just a few feet away. It was a truly ghostly white, especially for a man who surely not so long ago was closer to a shade of brown, and the whole thing, flowers, the man and a board, was held aloft like a platter kept from leaping dogs.

The man's eyes were shut, his face settled, but what struck Phoebe was that he had, not a restful air, but an absent one, as if something was there, but not him at all. He was gone.

Death, then, for Phoebe, became a thing of remnants—the person gone, relocated, a shell in his place.

She drew back in awe and stared at the body passing. The drummers never paused. They led the procession on down Jumna Road toward the place where the banks along the river were lined with woodfires meant for burning and the voyaging of souls, waiting for flames and the wind to carry them aloft.

Finally the flares were all that was left, flames still visible through the trees, and the servants receded, pulling back into the shadows toward the house.

Soon Phoebe and Cully were alone again, and as the noise ebbed away, Phoebe realized it was much darker than it had been moments ago, the purple gone, but even before they turned from the fence, Moosselman, the cook, suddenly yelled at the door of the house and came running out to them, his white clothes flying wide.

"Be coming now for dinner," the cook said urgently, grabbing hold of Phoebe's wrist and pulling it. "Hurry, miss," he said. "Before he does something."

But when she found him, Louis Antonine Guthrie was doing nothing at all. He was sitting.

Louis Guthrie could make polo ponies dance to his slightest touch—or, at least, once he could—speak with the charm of harpsichords and rustle cards until the highest pairs came out, but now he was sitting in a corner of the living room, his long fingers wrapped around a cigarette that had burned down almost to his hand. His back was bent, his head was leaning over toward his knees.

But if he was not doing anything right now, he had been moments before. Right beside him, not inches from the lighted cigarette, was a series of small, round, black holes burned along the top of a table. The scent of burning wood was still in the air and what Louis was doing when Phoebe and Cully arrived was eyeing the marks closely, pathmarks to a getaway, one leading after the other right up to the brink of the table.

When the children came in, his eyes shifted away from his handiwork and landed first on the children together as a pair, then on Phoebe. There they stayed.

Cully tugged on Phoebe's sleeve, pulling her away, but she stared back at her father. His dark eyes kept looking at her. "What's going on?" she asked.

He didn't answer. He was staring at her as if she, or he, was a long way away, cloaked in far more than the lighting of a room, and Phoebe felt the anxiety she had felt outside come right back in.

"Go upstairs," she said to Cully.

The boy gave her a worried glance and left. She took a step closer to her father.

"Get back," he commanded.

"What are you doing?" she asked. "What's going on?" She sounded more angry than worried. "You have to get yourself together."

Louis didn't say a thing. The ash fell off his cigarette. He didn't notice.

"Have you been arrested?"

He frowned, confused, and then, understanding, said, "No, no," impatiently, but her question had broken the spell and he looked away from her, reached out and stubbed the cigarette down in an ashtray. The moment was gone, the intensity over. "Can't you get out of here?" he said, his voice almost breaking.

"Has something happened, Louis?"

"Yes."

"What?"

"I moved to India."

"No. I mean now. Tonight. Where's Mother? What's happening?"

"I married your mother."

"No. I mean now. What's going on?"

He didn't answer.

"You can't just burn tables. You've got to do something." Her sudden pleading made her sound like a child.

He looked at her again and then his eyes traveled away to a spot across the room where the Shiva Nataraj was dancing, arms aloft, framed against a window. The statue was caked, even now, with old food he had angrily thrown at it two days ago when Jiggie Deeg was there for the first and only time, and even as Phoebe watched, she saw the muscles along her father's face and jaw, down his neck and along his arm, grow taut and thick. She could see them throbbing, up down, up down, independently alive with some preoccupation that was pounding through him.

She cast a quick glance around the room, looking for help, but there was no one there, of course. The room was empty but for the constellation of gods and goddesses he had brought into the house in such profusion that they had taken over first the public rooms, then the whole downstairs, and in time made their way up to the bedrooms, encroaching the same way jungle creepers took over outside when the rains came.

"Louis?"

He didn't answer.

There were gods dancing and gods sleeping, black sculptures from the Deccan and Buddha heads from Sanchi, and Louis Guthrie, despite all, was still as handsome as they.

"Shall I get Samiji to help you?" She could smell whiskey, but she saw no glass.

He didn't answer, maybe he didn't even hear.

Phoebe knew that something was wrong but when Thalia suddenly stormed into the room, arms everywhere, her voice raging with a rare shrillness, Phoebe knew that whatever it was was spiraling out of control.

"Get up and come for dinner," Thalia yelled at her husband. "Hours, I've waited for you. Hours. And here you are, closeted with her. Don't you care about anything? Anything at all?"

Phoebe saw Cully in the hall outside, his head down near his shoulders, and she rushed to him. "Go back to your room," she said.

"He will not," Thalia countermanded, flowing through the hall on her way to the dining room she rarely used. "We are a family."

In there everything happened fast and suddenly the focus came round to Cully, and then, just as suddenly, it was over, the children gone, all before the meat had even come. But first they had to go through salad, then prawns, and from the very beginning the servants were nervous, circling around, platters in their hands. They were Thalia's targets now—why was the food so hot, so cold, would they never learn, how often did she have to say it, and all the while her remarks pierced the air like a pick and could surely be heard across the street, across town. Was there any place, Phoebe wondered, safe from the hideous tones of anger?

The servants just bent their heads ever lower and made their way slowly around the table. Louis stared at his plate, food untouched, and Phoebe watched the muscles in his neck and jaw, the veins along his arm.

Thalia didn't seem to notice and only when Louis started to talk did she calm down. She sighed then, picked up a fork and started to eat, and when Louis began to unravel, she just turned her head this way and that, strikingly unperturbed, caught up in a world or scene of her own imagining.

"You've got enough rope around your neck in that tie of yours to hang yourself," Louis began, Cully his target, not his wife at all. "Is that what you want? For God's sake, can't you even hold your head up, Cully? It's not such a hard thing to do."

Louis' voice was scathing. He didn't even look at Cully, Cully with his head bent over toward the shoulder.

Phoebe was scared. "Mother, don't you hear it?" she wanted to say.

"Is that what you want?" Louis continued. He started to eat

61

now. "Hang by your neck? I'd be glad to help you." He looked at Cully for the first time and suddenly he turned his fork around like a slingshot and pitched a prawn at Cully's face. "Is that what you want? Hang you by your neck. I'd love it. Who needs a head? Why not cut it off. This is India, after all."

"Yes, sir," the boy mumbled.

"Or strangle it, tie it in a noose."

"Yes, sir."

But Cully's head was odd, Phoebe thought, bent so far over toward the left a magnetic force must have been at work, pulling the two protuberances, head and shoulder, together.

"Is that all you can say?"

"Yes, sir." The boy reached for his glass, going through the motions of eating a meal, and bringing his arm up and over the table, he overturned the glass.

Phoebe threw him a napkin and using it to blot out the water, the boy accidentally brushed a prawn off his plate on the floor.

"Oh, good," Louis cried.

Phoebe's heart was pounding.

"I was waiting for that." He smoothed his hands along the line of his head. "I knew you'd spill your water or drop your food. I never dreamed of both."

Phoebe pushed back her chair to get up.

"But why be so conventional, why keep food on a plate, when you can be different," Louis went on, his voice rising. "And why be different in an interesting fashion, when you can do it in a plodding, miserable way."

"Yes, sir."

"Choose the most mundane way to make your mark on the world," his voice loud now.

What had Cully done? Anything?

"And maybe, knowing you, you can actually find a way to leave no mark at all. With any luck we'll never know if you're present or not because you'll say nothing, do nothing, be nothing, and we can despise you in your absence."

Thalia was eating placidly. For God's sake, Phoebe thought, what's she doing?

"Yes, sir," Cully said.

Then, reaching for his glass, he overturned it a second time, and this time the glass rolled slowly, steadily, toward the edge of the table, Cully staring at it, and it seemed to Phoebe that

Louis was waiting for it to fall. Then it crashed on the floor, glass on wood, glass on glass, and then as Cully stepped off his chair to get the glass, was halfway down to the floor where maybe he thought he belonged, Louis was halfway up, then fully up, and he had his own glass in his hand and finally he was yelling, "Here, you need a glass? Here," his voice ecstatic in its noise. "Here, let me give it to you."

With that, he swung the glass hard against the table edge to break it, and holding the jagged piece by the stem, he reached his arm back, ten feet tall by now, and threw the glass, hard as any knife, straight at the half-bent body of the boy.

The glass penetrated the boy's shirt and wedged itself, broken pieces sticking out, in the fleshy part of the back of the shoulder, the very shoulder the head itself preferred.

Louis' hand was still uplifted, the boy bleeding, the blood showing the glass now ever starker against the growing red. It had probably taken no more than a second or two to happen, and then the two of them, Cully and Phoebe, rushed from the living room and up the stairs, hand in hand, Phoebe pulling him, with not even a last look at their parents, not even a backward glance, Thalia turned, never actually seeing them go, Louis' arm still uplifted, locked in its awful trajectory.

Up to their room, slam the door, and all in all, it took close to one minute, certainly no more, to leave their parents forever, but however long, it was the last minute of the first half of their life, because later the car drove off, one or two people inside, they never did find out.


But Louis had left. That was for sure, Louis in his white shirt, glass broken on the floor, and either Thalia had left then or else she had joined him later, because somehow, by the next day, Wednesday it was, Louis and Thalia both ended up in a car crashed on the road to Agra.

Kady said—and for some unexplained reason Maharaja Jiggie Deeg was there, too, in the living room, when he barely knew Louis himself at all—that the car crash was so terrible, the car burst into flames and the fire spread to a village and burned some huts and cows and people, too. "Five people," he said once, "six," the other.

But that night, Tuesday night, when they were still two chil-

dren with two parents, still a family in name, at least, they saw
the car leave the driveway and Phoebe, fixing Cully's cut, shirt
gone, glass pulled out and bandages ready in her hand, felt relief.

Cully had looked at the car and then at her, responsibility all
over his face, as if he had thrown the glass, made the wound, and
started the fight, he a nice boy with not too many faults besides
gangly legs and a vagueness that echoed inside his head and
made him forget meals, plans, everything.

Phoebe was kneeling beside him at the windowsill, bandage
ready in her hand, up in their big room above the lawn that was
a fortress within a fortress within the protected environs of
New Delhi.

So that night they had stared out the window and the chowkidar, the guard at the gate, had opened the gate for Louis and the
white Ford car, and they heard him say, "Sahib," one long
Indian syllable without a consonant or a break in the middle,
just a string of vowels, "Saaaaaaa'ab," and then Louis was gone
forever.


Samiji drove them to school in the morning in the other car,
and when they asked about the white Ford car with the sky blue
curtains, he said Louis wasn't back, and they didn't think to ask
about Thalia.

That afternoon Mooselman picked them up at their school,
and when they got home Granny was on the phone calling from
New York to tell them the news, but Kady was already there.
And so was Jiggie Deeg and Mr. Smith, the CEO from Louis'
office, and Samiji, too—right there in his cotton dhoti with his
bare legs showing in the middle of the living room, not in the
hall where he was supposed to be—and so Phoebe and Cully, if
not the last to find out, were certainly not the first.

## ❧ II ❧

IT WAS A HOT SEPTEMBER TWENTY years later when Cully Guthrie arrived in India. He took the train from Delhi to Deeg.

He wanted to see India for himself, the land going from city to country, finally villages and the desert. He envisioned himself sitting on the train all night long watching his future arrive, Deeg and his new job coming up ahead, but instead he slept the whole way, his head propped up against the wooden slats, bobbing back and forth like a melon on a stick. Soot flew in through the window, settling on his yellow hair, India peppering him with herself, an idea he would have liked, but he slept so soundly he didn't notice, the heat, the dirt, the land passing by, one day back into the place where he was born.

He didn't even wake up during the night when the train stopped at places like Agra and Jaipur as it made its way across the plains.

Then morning came. He looked out and saw nothing but desert and the hills and the kind of grass that grows when nothing else will, a gray-green scrub with prickles on the ends.

This was not an India that he knew, and turning to the man beside him, someone who said he was an apothecary, he pointed toward the great expanse outside and said, "Kya hai?"

"Deeg hai," the man replied.

He disappeared eight months later in April of the following year.

Leaving behind a few friends, like me and Kady Suraj, an apartment in Old Delhi, a room at the palace in Deeg, one important piece of sculpture and not much else.

Those eight months I saw more of him than I ever had before. In the beginning it was whenever he came to Delhi but that became increasingly often and, finally, he moved here full-time. He reminded me very much of Louis, in one regard, at least, because he liked to be the Indian expert. He delighted in showing me things I never dreamed existed. Like the bird bazaar and the slaughterhouses, odd people he'd come across, a dancer-prostitute, bless her, who supported her mother and two sisters, and a band of eunuchs who insisted he come for tea, bringing me. Another was a man he said imported Afghan hash into Delhi, not that Cully ever smoked it much himself, but he would actually sit with the man while he made his deals. There were other things like that, all part of Cully establishing that he knew Delhi "better than anyone" and that, like his father, he was comfortable on the edge.

When I first heard about Cully's disappearance, I didn't take it seriously. He was always a hard man to locate, vague about his comings and goings, and I assumed he'd be back.

With me he was incredibly sweet. I knew he could rail about his landlord in New York, or Granny, that he had the capacity to obsess about people, but I only saw his gentleness. He appreciated that I never pushed him one way or the other, trying to get him to do things, the way Phoebe did, he said. "That's just because she loves you," I explained.

And that I "believed" in his art collection when she didn't.

The truth was, I didn't believe in it, but I chose not to press the fact. There was no doubt, however, that in Delhi Cully's life often revolved around Vishnu Bhave, the art dealer. Baa-vey, as Indians pronounce it, would send his son, Anant, over to tell him his father wanted to see him and Cully went.

I saw Bhave's place twice. For someone whose patron was the great Jiggie Deeg, it was as innocuous-looking as you could imagine. It fronted on the street, big steel shutters pulled down at night so that after hours or when the place was closed, you had to creep in underneath, like a fence. The shutters were the only lock.

Which was why, in regard to the murder of his son, Anant, it was important that the steel shutters were up all day.

Anyone could have gotten in.


The one time Cully took me inside Vishnu Bhave's house and we sat down with him and Anant to look at things, Bhave seemed indifferent whether Cully bought anything or not. He was polite to him, but it seemed clear he had no particular interest in him, except out of obligation to Louis and his patron, Jiggie Deeg, who was Cully's employer. Indians are like that; they find duty in everything.

Cully obviously liked Bhave enormously, but he ignored his son, Anant. He acted like he wasn't there and afterward referred to the day as the time when "the three of us," Bhave, himself, and I, had tea.


The job announcement was signed by a Mr. Jasdan Singh and addressed to no one in particular. It was a flier that had been sent to schools of fine arts all over the country, and it showed up one day on the employment board at the New York University School of Fine Arts in New York City. That a friend of his noticed it at all struck Cully as a sign of providence.

The friend tore the sheet down—"Come to India," it said across the top—and handed it to Cully over lunch. Cully worked as an assistant in the Asian Arts Department at a Park Avenue auction house, a position far beneath his academic credentials. He took one look at the paper and knew the job was meant for him.

"A position has been established in cooperation with the Government of India to study and chronicle one of the great private art collections still extant in India today. . . . Come to Deeg. . . . Residence provided in Umaid Mahal Palace. . . . Job requires ability to identify and catalog Indian art objects dating from the 8th to 19th centuries."

At home later in Soho in his two-room apartment full of books that were stacked in islands all around the living room, Cully emptied a drawer at the bottom of his desk and put the notice inside as if it were meant to soak up all the air in there and assume a stronger life. For a couple of weeks he thought about it. He never mentioned it to Phoebe, though he saw her several times a week and could count on her showing up with things like groceries, razor blades, and new sneakers.

Then one day he opened the drawer and laid the paper out on the desk top. He spent the day working on a response, but by nightfall he still couldn't get it right. He called Phoebe and asked her to come down.

"Why?" she asked.

"I'll tell you when you get here."

He was waiting for her. The few pieces of furniture in the room, couch they'd bought at the Salvation Army, chairs, a table and an icebox he'd painted green, stood out in the middle of the room, away from the walls.

He started explaining as soon as she walked in.

"Why didn't you tell me about this before?" she asked.

"I wanted to wait until I was sure."

"Sure of what?"

"I didn't want you to get excited until I knew what I was going to do. This is my big step. I've fooled around enough. No, don't argue, Feeb. I have. I know I have. I've wasted a lot of time but now I'm ready to make a change. I can't get the letter right, though."

Cully's eyes sparkled. He couldn't stand still. He walked around the circumference of the room, making Phoebe turn in order to follow him with her eyes. Jasdan Singh's announcement was in his hands and as he moved he read it aloud, line by line.

"Just say: 'Dear Mr. Singh . . .'" she suggested when he finished. "That's what you'd call a maharaja's son."

Cully kept going in and around the stacks of books.

"Can't you stop walking like that?" she said. "I'm getting dizzy."

He sat down at the desk.

She pulled up a chair next to him.

He started writing. " 'Dear Mr. Singh,' " he said aloud. "What should I say next? I've rewritten this so many times I can't—"

"Just be straightforward." Phoebe watched him, thinking he looked good, his skin healthy, she surmised that he'd been eating better recently. "Tell him you were an art student and that you specialized in Indian art. Mention all your degrees, grades. Tell him you grew up in India, speak Hindi, etcetera."

"But what do I say about the collection?"

"What collection?"

"Mine."

"You mean Louis'?"

"No, mine."

Phoebe's heart stopped a millimeter of a second. "What collection do you mean?" She looked out across his room, listening for his answer. When it came, she heard excitement in his voice, conviction.

"That's what I'm going to do there," Cully was saying. He held her with his eyes. "Let me explain. Come on. Give me that." He sounded firm.

"I'm listening."

"It's what I've decided to do. I'm going to collect art. I'll never be as good as Louis, of course. I have no illusions about that. But one or two pieces. Just one. A great piece. Can't you see it? You'd have a collector for a brother. Do you know what that would do to me?"

Phoebe didn't answer.

"Feeb? I have to know what you think."

"You know what I think. You know more about Indian art than Louis ever did."

"That's just not true," Cully exclaimed, getting up and starting to circle the room again. "He had a masterful understanding of the subject."

"So do you."

"I'll never be as good as him."

"He may have loved it," Phoebe said quietly, following him with her eyes, "but he didn't know very much about it. You do."

"Don't you want to hear me out?"

"I do," she said. "I was just trying to put your knowledge in perspective. You already know far more than he did."

"Don't tell me that," he said impatiently. "I don't want you to flatter me."

"I'm not flattering you."

"Are you going to listen, or what?" he said angrily.

"Yes."

He walked at a slower pace now, still circling the room, touching the couch, the icebox, the walls, as he went. "My only real

69

question is whether to tell Jasdan about the collection now or wait. What do you think?"

"I'd wait. It should get a little more concrete before you tell him."

"But it is concrete."

"Then tell me more about it."

"It's what I'm going to do," he said. "That's all. What use is my knowledge if I don't own anything?"

"It's got every use."

"That's not what Louis'd say. He'd say you have to own—"

"Who cares what he'd say? He's dead. He died because he was too drunk to drive."

"That's your opinion."

"Opinion!" Phoebe exclaimed. "He was drunk. He drove straight into a village. He killed five or six people."

"Maybe he had a lot on his mind." Cully kept walking. "Remember how upset he was? Don't you think that fight affected his driving?"

"That doesn't get away from the fact he was drunk."

"Don't you even remember our fight?"

"Of course I do."

"We disagree about him, that's all," Cully said with finality.

"You have this fantasy about him."

"It's not a fantasy," he argued. "I feel part of that accident." He sat at the desk.

"But what about money?" Phoebe was beginning to feel helpless. "Louis had money."

"I have plenty of money. Besides, it's cheaper in India and with my connections . . ."

"What connections?"

"Louis'," he said. "Remember Vishnu Bhave?"

"Who?" Phoebe asked, brushing her hair out of her eyes. "The art dealer?"

"Oh, yes," she said. "Him."

"Besides," he added, "I could always stay there."

"Stay in India? What a silly idea. Listen, Cully, let's get back to the letter. I think the job sounds great. You're perfect for it and it'd be a great deal of fun. In the letter, mention Louis' collection. Tell him you're his son. Remind him that his collection is in the National Museum in Delhi."

Cully sat down and started writing. "And tell him how close

70

I was to Louis," he said without looking up.

Phoebe was quiet. She brushed her hair out of her eyes again.

"Why do you do that?" he asked, looking at her.

"Do what?"

"Touch your hair so much."

"It's in my eyes. You could even tell him you met his father," Phoebe went on. "Remember January sixth? He came to the house with Kady Suraj? And say your father knew his father."

"Did he?"

"They met at the house. Two days before he died."

"But did they meet often?" he persisted.

"Not really," she admitted.

"Then why's it important?"

"It's a part of your life," Phoebe said. "That's all I'm suggesting."

"It's not my life. It's yours. I hate it when you say that, pretending we're the same. You had one life and I had another. I never went to the Gymkhana Club. I never heard stories about 'Jiggie Deeg.' I never went out in the car at night. I never did any of those goddamn things."

# ❧ 12 ❧

A 1936 SILVER-BLUE ROLLS-ROYCE
with a metal statue of two upright lions and a unicorn on the
front fender met Cully at the Deeg train station. The driver was
wearing a uniform that was way too big and he had rings on all
his toes. Cully was standing on the platform. "Coming, sa'ab?"

"What?" Cully was thirsty.

"Coming?"

Cully got in the car. He couldn't drink the water, he was
thinking, too many germs. He'd have to get some tea.

It seemed like a long ride to him, first through the city of
Deeg, then out along a road where there were fewer houses, huts
they were, really, fields all about and wells with wooden pulleys
that camels and bullocks moved. The Rolls traveled about ten
miles to the hour, never got above fifteen that he could see. The
driver pointed out Pushtu Fort, far away, on a hill above the
city.

Cully barely looked, wondering if he should start carrying a
canteen of boiled water. He'd never needed one before, but he
was only a child then, so he was calculating what a canteen
would weigh and whether . . .

He noticed the gate at the entrance to palace lands only because the car slowed to an absolute halt. He saw a high iron
archway looming overhead, then the car moved on, past a large

72

stone carving. He turned to look back at it. It was near human size, showing two upright lions and a unicorn. They were a threesome, one the same size as all, dancing, their paws touching but not linked, all their eyes facing in, the lions seeming masculine, the unicorn delicate and feminine. While some might have seen it as an emblem of the might of these three equal creatures, two men and a woman, this ancient emblem of a feudal Deeg, Cully took it as a triangle.

Two against the one, was what he thought.

Turning face front again, he saw a flagpole with no flag. He wondered briefly why, since flags flew for maharajas, this one was empty. He speculated on where the maharaja was, outside, inside, working, reading. He assumed he'd come out to greet him at the palace, art an important thing.

As the car slowly moved forward, he spotted three roads branching out ahead. The driver took the narrowest of all, unpaved and barely as wide as the car itself. It circled in through a garden, past fountains and what used to be a zoo. Cully made out the high-wire cages of an aviary and an animal pen big enough for elephants, both empty now and overgrown with weeds, and then he had a view of a lake coming up on the right. As they approached, the lake became all blue and gray and he saw laundry spread out flat on the shores, drying in the sun like patches of a giant quilt. There were palaces all around the lake, their walls coming down in sheer rock cliffs to the water's edge.

It looked like a tourist poster for a special spot and Cully's reaction was excitement. But he wasn't used to groups of people, he reflected, so they'd have to take him for what he was, scholar and collector, and suddenly for no reason at all, he wondered if Louis smoked or not.

He didn't remember, shocking as that seemed, since he remembered so much else about his father, and he determined to ask Kady Suraj as soon as he could. Suraj would tell him how to find Vishnu Bhave, too, and then he'd start his collection.

"Lake Pichiti," the driver said.

The road ended abruptly right in front of the main portico of one of the palaces. The palace stretched along the water, its walls coming down in cliffs on one side, the desert off to its left on the other. There was lawn everywhere in between, acres of it.

"Umaid Mahal Palace, sa'ab," the driver announced, turning

73

off the motor. He pronounced it Um-eye-id Mail.

Cully peered out the window at the palace. Made of sand-stone, it was a bright pink that lent the place a sleepy air. It looked like it had two long wings, but this was really just the front side of a 310-room building designed in the shape of a giant E. It had balconies and cupolas, walls of filigree as finely carved as any temple frieze, and it had as an appendage, square and squat, another building off its flank to the far left. This was where the women lived, the zenana.

But what Cully was noticing was that he saw no one at all. He wondered if he was being ignored.

The driver got out, came around, opened his door and waited for Cully to move. When he didn't, he poked his head in. "Coming, sa'ab?" he asked in English.

"Where is everyone?" Cully asked. "Go get someone." Louis would never put up with this.

The driver shrugged. "Someone coming maybe sometime soon." He pulled his head back out of the car and stood waiting. Green parakeets swooped in and out of the portico of the palace.

Cully felt nervous. As a rule he didn't visit people much. Then, despite himself, he began to notice that edges of the palace steps were crumbling and discoloration had set in. He wondered if that was due to heat or a structural defect of the design, and then he dated the palace almost to the year and noted Moghul antecedents to the filigree. The professional observations made him feel more secure.

"Better getting out, sa'ab," the driver interrupted. "Hot soon."

"Are you sure they know I'm coming?"

"Mostly very busy people here."

"But there must be enough servants to—"

"Many people waiting here, sa'ab. Waiting in car, waiting in hall, waiting in salon, waiting, waiting, all time waiting."

"But that's rude."

"No, no, it's just being done, always done, always, always."

"What? Being kept waiting in a car? That's outrageous."

"No, no, sa'ab." The driver sounded confused now. "Everything," he said.

"Everything what?"

"Everything now always the same as always." The driver was

almost pleading now, his voice had taken on a whine, and finished, he stepped away from the car and pulled out a cigarette.

Cully wanted to slam the door on him but he leaned back farther in the seat and crossed his legs, looking for a position that seemed most casual. "So," he began conversationally, "where do you think the maharaja is right now?"

There was no answer.

"Where do you think the maharaja is?" he said louder, irritated he had to raise his voice.

The driver came in closer to the car. "Maharaj, sa'ab?"

"Yes." Cully calmed his voice down some. "Where is he?"

"Benares, sa'ab."

"Benares," Cully exclaimed.

"Always living Benares. Maybe five years, maybe ten, maybe twenty. Having old-time palace there. Washing all times in the river."

"But why?"

"For living with the gods. For showing sorry."

"Sorry for what?"

"I am not for knowing, sa'ab."

"Then who's in charge here?" Cully asked. "Who takes care of everything? The art and all?"

"Same," the driver said, wagging his head. "All time same as always."

"But—"

"Not for worry, sa'ab."

"I'm not worried. Why should I be worried?" Cully cast his eyes back along through the gardens and the driveway. "What's over there?" he asked, anything to keep on talking. "What about those roads? Where do they go?"

"One goes to palace hotel. Five-star deluxe, sa'ab. One time palace, now for paying guests."

"What about the other?"

"Very, very short and unimportant road coming here to this one and only palace, sa'ab. Only for peoples walking or on bicycle."

"For servants."

"Exactly right. For peoples not good enough for front side here."

"Where does it go?"

"You not interested in servants, sa'ab."

"No, I want to know. I want to know everything."

"Going straight to kitchens and the back side. Far and distant back side. No good peoples' going there."


The road to the kitchen and the back side did not end there.

It kept on going, past the palace and the grounds and headed on toward the fields beyond. It narrowed down after a while and went in through what was sometimes barley, sometimes wheat, twisting this way and that, as if it had some direction in its mind, landmarks that used to exist that now did not, until finally it came to the spot where a river used to be.

The river had dried up and turned to dust. But hundreds, maybe thousands, of times before, the river had dried up and turned to dust, so now it remained a place where sometimes there was a river and sometimes there was not. From time to time enough rain came and then floods and then the river once again regained its life, but then, after a few years, it dried up all over again and all that was left were the lines that told where a river and its waters used to be.

It was there, in among the dust and water marks, that Jiggie Deeg and Kady Suraj met for the first time some twenty-five years before. Jiggie came by car, Kady on a bicycle that was too small.

## ❧ 13 ❧

Jiggie was not the oldest of the Deegs, not by far, but he was something else, the firstborn of the firstborn of the firstborn, on back into the days when the name of Deeg first came up out of the desert, and as a consequence, the whole thing, every last bit of it, the zoo, the elephants, the Rolls-Royces, the palaces and the people, from the servants to his son, all belonged to him.

But that he was still a maharaja was just because he was the last. The title was honorary now, Deeg just a district, 120,000 square miles in all, in a western state of India. Democracy was in place and Juggernathan Bisamillah Rajender Bahadur Singh, who was crowned sovereign when he was six and had an army and a council at his command before he knew how to read, lost it all when he was twenty-five.

By rights, he was only one more Mr. Singh.

He was a short man, overweight, with a pockmarked face, big dark eyes, and a panoply of power that only India would allow. There was no mistaking that he, and just about everyone else, still thought of him as a minor king. In the days before Jiggie removed himself to isolation in Benares City, he never went anywhere without an entourage of aides. He was always addressed as "Your Highness"; only a few people ever used his name. Indians bowed low before him and even touched his feet. The deference was total, in Delhi and Deeg. He lived in both, had influence in both and people everywhere were said to be beholden to him for favors, money and protection.

Because Jiggie was dangerous.

He was the kind of person who made it his business to know secrets and to use them, and there was an aura of fear about him. No one would choose to offend, ignore, or disturb the man, and the sycophants were legion.

Kady stood out strikingly by contrast. His relationship with Jiggie was known to be largely private, but he had gone from the great man's clerk to his near equal, and while they were rarely seen together in public Kady was frequently heard arguing with Jiggie and was even known to contradict him outright in front of people.

But Jiggie accepted it without a budge. More surprising, he didn't even seem to mind. Whatever the complexity of his feelings for Kady Suraj, he treated him with more respect and deference than Suraj treated him.

The truth was, as everyone knew, that if Kady Suraj was beholden to him for his start in life and a whole lot else, Kady, in turn, was one of the very few people Jiggie himself was indebted to. The younger man had had a profound influence on him, exactly why, no one really knew or understood, but there was no getting around the fact that a good measure of Jiggie's continuing credibility came from the fact that some of Kady's progressive, even radical, politics had rubbed off on him. And so while everyone might wonder why Jiggie allowed himself to be so influenced by this younger, even arrogant, man, there was no getting around the fact that he himself wasn't an anachronism to be written off, as most of his peers were, and a good part of the credit was due to Suraj. Jiggie Deeg maintained substantial political influence for decades and that he managed that was in large part because he was able to change and grow with the times.

Further, no small item in itself, Kady was the one who upgraded Deeg itself. The palace hotel was his idea and so, too, the ways of investing Jiggie's money that ended up giving Deeg a relatively high standard of living.

Umaid Mahal Palace in Deeg could sleep hundreds and my parents were regularly among the group that was invited down for tiger shoots and cultural events. Prime ministers would be there, visiting heads of state, artists, diplomats, socialites, the very ones Louis himself preferred. My father admired Jiggie and found him entertaining, even interesting, but he had all kinds of stories about how he fired people at will, made and broke careers over lunch, and earned lifetimes of favors by handing out things like houses and dowries. He was like a Mafia don, but legal, he said.

He had one story. One night at Deeg a man got drunk at dinner and Jiggie asked him to leave. No one thought much of it, but later my father saw the guest outside.

He was walking down the road carrying his suitcase, his wife following along behind.

Jiggie'd denied him even the use of a telephone or a taxi.

How Louis Guthrie met Jiggie Deeg was one of Delhi's famous stories. That the two did not like each other ever after was not a secret.

It was at the Gymkhana Club, several years before Louis met Kady Suraj, who then would have been just a boy in Deeg. Jiggie was conspicuous as always, standing in the bar, now inviting people to his Delhi house for an evening of sitar music and orissan dancers. This house covered an entire city block, part mansion, part palace, and any invitation there was highly coveted.

Louis, listening in the crowd but not invited, was said to have pushed himself forward until he got to the great man's presence, and then, standing tall and far more handsome, sleekly dark and noble beside the fat little pockmarked king, he looked down and fashioned his eyes conspicuously on the man's skin itself.

Then he turned and walked away.

The two men may have encountered each other socially after that, but they were never known to have talked again. Louis never got an invitation, and why Jiggie Deeg appeared not once, but twice, at Number Nine Jumna Road on the very last days of Louis' life was one of the unsolved mysteries of Phoebe Guthrie's childhood.

At issue for Jiggie Deeg was his face.

One did not look at it.

For all his power and wealth, it was the most important thing about him.

He wore jewels constantly, earrings, finger rings, necklaces, so that, on an ordinary night at the Gymkhana Club, he might have a million dollars around his neck in emeralds the size of walnuts, strands of pearls as big as jelly beans, or uncarved rubies that looked like rocks; but, for all that, the most striking thing about his appearance was his face.

The pockmarks scarred it hideously and he looked decidedly strange. Small round pits an eighth of an inch in diameter covered his entire face, scalp, and neck and God knew where else as well, presumably his whole body.

As a child he nearly died from smallpox. An epidemic spread to Deeg and struck near as many people as it left alone, so since the age of six he'd had a polka-dot face.

And thus he remained: someone with exquisite attire and a rough, scarred face.

But it is with the face and the marks that the story of the woman with orange eyes begins.

She fell in love with him without even knowing who he was. The love affair took hold months before she knew and from the very beginning she gently touched his face, smoothed her palms over his uneven cheeks and told him she loved him just the way he was and she even loved his face most particularly of all.

She said the marks meant he was lucky. He was marked by the gods and he hadn't died. There must have been a reason they let him live, she said. He just had to find it.

She also said the pits themselves looked like art. They weren't dirty or the least bit like acne. Instead they were round and roughly symmetrical, and she viewed them as a beautiful design and said that they served to remind her just how poor India was and how virulent its diseases were, but that its beauty and its art could be found anywhere.

Even on a face like his.

Jiggie loved her devotedly and profoundly, and that's at the heart of everything.


The last time I saw Jiggie it was up in Kashmir. It was just before he renounced and went to Benares to live as a religious recluse. I didn't know, of course, that even as we spoke, he was on his way to see this woman and tell her he'd never see her again.

I just knew he looked different.

He was wearing old sandals and a cotton dhoti. The dhoti is the sheer white gauzy cloth Gandhi wore. It's wrapped around a man's waist in such a way that the leg from the knee or thigh down is exposed, and the upper leg shows bare through the cloth. It leaves a man almost naked by Western standards and yet there was Jiggie Deeg wearing peasant clothes on the streets of Srinagar, Kashmir. And no jewelry.

He wasn't very old, eight years ago now, so he'd have been about fifty-five, Louis' age, but he looked a hundred, and he seemed depressed. There was nothing whatsoever to suggest he was the famous Jiggie Deeg.

It was the fall season, long before the Hindu-Muslim fighting started, and my husband and I were walking along one of the beautiful streets lined with chinar trees, when suddenly Jiggie was there. I recognized him right away but did nothing about it.

He was walking along with Shyam Singh, although I didn't know who he was then. They were going fast, single file, Shyam behind, their heads down, very intense, but I recognized Jiggie and let him go by.

Only to regret it instantly and run back to catch him, tap him on the shoulder and introduce myself. He said he knew exactly who I was and gave me a buff on the cheek, English style, but I saw in a flash fatigue and sadness all about his face. I was tempted to turn away, not bother him anymore, but instead I introduced my husband, then the men were shaking hands and Jiggie, to my surprise, was inviting us to have a drink.

My immediate assumption was that we were providence to him. For some reason he wanted delay and procrastination,

and we were it. He called out, "Shaaaaaaa-am," to his servant and with him in tow went into a cafe nearby, leaving
Shyam to sit on the ground outside. Drinks came, snacks and
fruit, and Jiggie played the host, obviously distracted but
going through the motions. He asked us questions, my husband's work, my parents' whereabouts. I wondered why he
was bothering with us. We didn't merit this attention. He
asked what had become of my father, recalled various exploits
they'd had, on and on.

Then he asked where he was now and I said he'd died, and
then I said where was his wife? Back in the hotel? I should have
known Yosant too had died, but I didn't. He told me she'd had
malaria, "God knows, must have been ten, fifteen years ago,"
and died, and I said, "Oh, how sad," and then he said, very
clearly and distinctly, "Yes, but a place like this reminds me how
much sadness there is in life, don't you think? There's no getting
around the fact life's sad and Kashmir tells me just precisely
that."

"Kashmir?" I said, aghast. "Remind you of sadness? A place
as beautiful as this?"

And I instantly regretted it, because he looked right through
me and I knew it was over, the drinks, the moment. "Yes," he
said vaguely, and stood up to go.

We shook hands, none of this kissing anymore. Shyam Singh
darted up to leave some rupees on the table, and they left, gone
from us as quickly as they'd arrived.

Then, odd how fortune smiles on us, my husband said he was
tired. I said I wasn't. He headed off and I stayed. I thought to
do some shopping, but just as I stood there outside the cafe, I
saw the disappearing back of Jiggie Deeg, with Shyam Singh
trotting along behind.

Two dhotis headed single file toward the lake, and I followed.
Why? Just because I did. Because he was the famous Jiggie Deeg
and he wasn't at the golf course or the club, he was right here,
right in front of me, and I wanted to know what he was doing.

The two men were going quickly. Shyam stopped him once
and was obviously asking about a taxi or a rickshaw, but there
were none in sight, so they took off again at an even faster clip.

Eventually they came out on Dal Lake. I was sweating and I
hoped they'd stop, but they didn't. They kept on going, almost
at a jog, right along the edge of the water where the mountains

start. The boatmen ignored them because they looked ordinary and made hysterical motions at me instead, "Shikara, memsa'ab? shikara?" Then suddenly, up ahead, I saw Jiggie go down a staircase to the water's edge and climb into a boat of his own.

It was tied up, far from the others, and a woman was leaning back in it, resting against the multitude of cushions piled on the banquette that filled the stern. The boatman was standing up in the front, his single pole positioned vertically in the mud, waiting for the latecomer to arrive.

I kept going to get as close as possible.

Jiggie stepped onto the cushions alongside the woman and told the man to push off.

I couldn't see the woman's face, just the way she turned her head to him and was half leaning, half lying, on the banquette. As I watched, her arms reached up to draw him down.

He sat beside her, his face to her, and then he slipped his arm in around her neck and moved in closer, but not too close, that was the thing, and I knew from the way he looked and sat with her, and she with him, they'd done this a million times before, he with his arm back around her neck, she along his side, but that they still enjoyed it, a sense of love exquisite and longstanding, and then the boat took off.

Then Jiggie must have remembered Shyam Singh.

He withdrew his arm and turned around to look back at shore where Shyam was standing. He waved, a big wave that must have meant something to the two of them because Shyam gave a signal back, and then Jiggie turned around again, Shyam forgotten, and I thought that would be the end of it. But the woman turned back too and so I saw her face.

She waved a great big wave at Shyam and smiled.

That was it. She smiled, an extraordinary smile that spread all across her Kashmiri face. She had olive-white skin and Aryan features, high cheekbones and eyes that seemed enormous even from my distance away, and even from there I could see a kind of light in her skin as if a torch inside her was imbuing it with a beautiful, warm and calming glow. She had full lips, thick black hair pulled high above her head and eyes that even from a distance seemed to burn with flames, their color so vivid, almost neon or fluorescent, something only an artist could produce.

I was overwhelmed by the sight of her. Lying on her side,

surrounded by the arm of Jiggie Deeg, she seemed Elizabeth Taylor, Helen of Troy, I don't know, but I was struck for all the world by the sight of the most exquisite woman I had ever seen.

It was only afterward that I realized something else about her.

Her eyes were orange, the color of pumpkins and southwestern sand.

# ❧ 14 ❧

YEARS AND YEARS BEFORE, WHEN
Kady was only seventeen and Jiggie in his prime, the two men
met for the first time on the shores of the dusty river in Deeg.

By the time the meeting occurred, however, letters had gone
back and forth for weeks. They were sent by post, unmarked,
no name or return address on any, that's how secret it was, and
virtually no one had an idea a correspondence was under way.

It was only by luck that Jiggie saw the first letter at all. It was
not the custom for him to read the mail, but occasionally he
picked out one in the office pile and this was such a time.

The letter had nothing to distinguish it from the outside. It
was like hundreds of others he received. The paper was bought
from any bazaar and it was written with an old-fashioned pen
that made the words look like two thin parallel lines running up
and down the page, but the penmanship was good, the look of
it strong and male, and, as Jiggie later traced it in his mind, if
he had picked up this one for any reason, it was because he
surmised the writer had a mind.

So, pick it up he did, tore it open, but then, never very good
at Hindi, he had to read it slowly, pondering occasionally over
the verbs.

Someone else might have thrown it out, said it was oblique,
rubbish, not worth the effort to decipher. It was not clear, for

example, what the writer had actually seen or heard or what, precisely, he was proposing.

But Jiggie went out into the garden to read it in private and to him it made perfect sense. He also knew the writer, fearing another eye might see it first, had taken precautions to protect his message and assumed, correctly, the woman in question was a secret.

Of the other woman, Jiggie's wife, Yosant, the writer spoke with the greatest respect and said, among other things, he shared "maharaj-sahib's every wish for her continued well-being and serenity of mind." Translated, that she should never know anything of what was being discussed and said.

What Jiggie discovered as he walked around his lovely garden, green now even at the height of the Indian summer, was that he got no sense of a threat from the man at all, this K. T. Keshri Suraj who described himself as a functionary in the Department of Transport, Central Branch, Deeg.

He had written that he was "not without some skills." Jiggie had recognized his name immediately from the newspapers, so he had a clear sense of these "skills." For all of the man's obvious youth and social inferiority, Jiggie Deeg had absolutely no doubt he was dealing with a personal equal, so he, far more than Kady, knew exactly what was getting under way.


He answered the letter immediately. Every day counted as far as the woman was concerned, her future in the sway. His strategy, however, was to leave the particulars to the other man. He wanted to see just how clever he was and he told his aides henceforth to save all such epistles for himself.

After that the letters came steadily and the terms got clearer. Suraj assumed ever-larger dimensions in Jiggie's mind. He graciously indicated he understood why Jiggie could never marry the woman. Caste could not be defied, he said. He eventually thought of everything, even Jiggie's need to make the woman financially independent. As to the child, he spelled out what it would or, more specifically, would not be told, what contact there would be—none, of course—and on the matter of inheritance he was just as clear and to the point.

The child would have none, even if it was a son. None, except that which its legal parents would provide, and if it were male, no claims would ever be made on Deeg. Which, of course, was not legally binding and Jiggie knew it.

As to "the appropriate sum and recompense" that was to be part of the bargain, Suraj admitted to uncertainty. He made it clear his interests were entirely professional and that he wanted "advanced training and opportunities," not wealth per se, a notion that gave Jiggie some peace of mind because he saw it as admirable, if pathetically naive.

It was also perfectly stated in the bargain that all future contact between the maharaja and the woman would cease as soon as the marriage began.

The plan was so risky and unorthodox, Jiggie couldn't believe he would go through with it, but he did. He agreed to the most generous terms possible, saw that as the best way to control the man, and understood that from now on he'd know more about K. T. Keshri Suraj than anyone else in the world and there could, eventually, be some gain in that. He knew his man well; an investigation by Shyam Singh had helped in that.

He just thought he could handle him.

Mostly, though, he considered everything from Durr's point of view. He believed he was building a life for her, giving her a future she couldn't have with him, life with honor and normality and, specifically, a husband. He knew he was protecting her from the isolation and shame an unmarried mother must accept and the ignominy and shame that would pursue her into her future lives.

He loved her so much, he was willing to give her up. That he'd never see her again, or the man, either, for that matter, seemed a small price to pay for her well-being.


Jiggie chose the site.

It was the emptiest place he knew but in truth he'd been there once before, with her one night when she said upstairs in his suite of rooms, "Oh, Jiggie, can't we go for a walk? Do I have to hide inside all the while?"

That's where Jiggie took her, to the riverbed, and where, later, he told Suraj to meet him.

He hadn't said anything to her about what was happening. It

hadn't even occurred to him, so assured was he that he was right, he no longer the lover, but a father, in effect, planning an arranged and suitable marriage.

"Out where the road that goes past the palace turns off into the fields," Jiggie wrote to Kady Suraj. "It goes straight for a mile. Then veers off to the left where the river used to be. There," he wrote. "I'll meet you there."

Jiggie thought nothing of telling the man to come out through the palace grounds, but Suraj balked.

It was the very first thing that hinted to him at what was getting under way. Even though every last bit of it was his idea—had burst full blown into his mind as he stood outside his father's door and listened to the maharaja talk inside about the possibility of an abortion—he hadn't considered the psychology of it all. The thought of riding past the huge palace that sprawled in the dark like a monument itself was almost more than he could bear.

He considered writing back to say, Let's meet someplace else.

What changed his mind was simple: knowing that Jiggie would then know more about him than he wanted him to know, know, at the very least, his fear. So he agreed.

# ❧ 15 ❧

Jiggie arrived first, alone in a jeep, early on purpose, to wait and watch, remember her. There was nothing to see in all directions. Not even the mountains and high terrain that rimmed the city, forts on all the hills, were visible in the heat of the night. There was only flatness all around.

Jiggie leaned against the jeep, his legs crossed in front. After a while he walked up and down, feeling the air, relishing the sadness. He appreciated the fact that the meeting that would arrange for them to part forever would take place here at the very spot he associated so intimately with her.

He told himself driving out that he still had a decision to make, he could still see her again and again, year after year, but standing there, wiping the sweat as it dripped slowly down his face, he knew he'd accepted the man's proposal even before he finished reading his first letter.

He watched the darkness ahead, waiting for a sign of life approaching. He remembered her hand in his as they had walked along the dry riverbed, how she'd delighted in hearing some animal there, a ferret or a mouse, how they'd found comfort lying one on top of the other in the fields where only scrub could grow.

He kept eyeing the road, looking at a watch, tension rising, knowing the sooner the man came, the sooner he'd tell her and lose her forever.

Then he heard the squeak of a bicycle in the distance. He looked at his watch again. The man was on time. The bicycle squeaked when the front wheel turned and it didn't have a lamp, so Jiggie only knew it was coming at all because he heard the squeak of the wheels turning and finally he saw the shape of a tall man hunched over a bicycle that was too small getting closer in the darkness.

That was the first thing Jiggie noticed, how tall he was. Kady, for his part, saw a man up ahead leaning against a jeep.

He got off his bicycle, touched the bar with his foot to hold it upright in the dirt and came over to stand beside the jeep. He had one hand in a pocket, the other hung straight down.

Neither said a word.

Jiggie reached onto the front seat of the jeep and took out a pack of cigarettes. He passed one to Kady, took another for himself. He had the match, too. He found it in his pocket and struck it against the jeep, held it out near the other's chin and studied the hairs standing out upon his skin. Not much of a growth for a man so big, he thought, but he was clean and if his clothes were appalling for their fit and style, at least they too were clean.

He looked at his shirt, saw it was new. Saw he'd trimmed his nails. "No rain as yet," he said aloud. He spoke in Hindi. It didn't occur to him there was an option.

Kady looked up at the heavy sky and said nothing. "I prefer a cinnamon taste in mine," he said in Hindi and Jiggie understood him to be talking of the cigarette.

"Do you?" he replied. "I shall try to remember that next time."

And heard himself say "next time," sensing already that his plans were changing.

He puffed on his cigarette and watched the tall slender form of this man he'd never met. He was surprised by how young he was, young, he thought, to conceive so audacious a plan. Then he realized the man never looked at him and he felt relieved, so intent was he on watching him, fixing every inch of him in his mind's eye, thick hair, narrow structure, good looks, yes, he was good-looking. It was the only thing that unnerved him. Not that she would prefer this boy to him, that wasn't his worry, but that the boy himself should look this good, how could it be?

It was the second sign that something was different from what he'd thought and it made him feel uneasy.

"When is the baby due?" Kady asked as he puffed on a cigarette. He could smell the man, something sweet, a powder maybe, and he imagined him coated in perfume and that to touch him would leave the scent on him.

He backed away, put his two legs together, knees almost touching, and stood up taller. That was when he noticed that Jiggie was short and it gave him a slight measure of confidence, even as he knew that confidence overall was the last thing he had right now.

"It's coming in five months," Jiggie said. "That's why we had to hurry. She's healthy," he went on. "You should know that. There shouldn't be any trouble."

"And there's enough time."

"Yes."

"Get squared away beforehand."

"She'd rather die than go back home by herself with a baby."

"She's right."

"Or go anywhere, for that matter. It's why I'm doing this."

"Where is she from?"

"Kashmir."

Kady made a noise of surprise and almost looked at Jiggie, but he checked himself.

"Her mother approached me there," Jiggie said, surprised at himself again, now for talking so much. He'd had no plans to say anything at all. Just meet the man and dismiss him. "I saw her in the marketplace," he went on. Maybe it was because the boy wasn't obsequious, wasn't obsequious at all, and he wasn't used to that. "She was showing men some pictures. Stopping them, trying to get them to look at her photographs. Then she came to me. I tried to push her away. She wasn't a beggar, but she was . . . well, you know . . . not the sort one . . . Anyway, she said she needed money. She sounded desperate. Ordinarily," he said, "I wouldn't . . . but . . ." Jiggie stopped, at a loss suddenly.

Kady heard it. In spite of himself, he was intrigued.

"You'll see," Jiggie said in a second. "Her face. Her eyes . . ."

"So you looked at the pictures?"

"They weren't very good. But I'd had a dream about her. Before I even met her. Her eyes."

91

"Her eyes."

"Yes, you see, she has these . . ." He paused.

"Yes."

"But in the photographs they came out white, and I asked her mother, 'What about the eyes?' and she said, 'See for yourself.' I did. I didn't want to. It seemed not quite the thing. One doesn't . . . you know . . . But you see, it was this dream, and I couldn't forget it, and it turned out she'd had a dream, too. And when I saw her, it was the same as the dream. The orange eyes. . . ."

Kady looked at him for the first time. "Orange?"

"Yes."

The two men stared at each other and Kady felt like reeling, the man's presence, his scent, even his skin. His face seemed cavernous and repulsive.

The older man lowered his gaze first and looked away.

"Is she illegitimate, too, then?" Kady said.

Jiggie himself nearly reeled, hurt by the man's coldness. Maybe the man wouldn't do after all, he thought. She couldn't survive around anyone as cold as he. He took a few breaths to give himself time to recover. "I don't think so," he said carefully. "She says she remembers her father." Then he had an idea. "Your father," he began. "He's a healer. He takes care of people. Is this something that interests you? Or is politics all that matters? Politics and your ambition?" He waited, watching the man's profile as it was outlined vaguely against the night.

The younger man didn't answer. He heard the subtle slur. He kicked at some dust and then patted it down with the flat soles of his sandals.

Jiggie sensed his uncertainty about how to answer and felt relieved. The man wasn't as cold as he pretended to be. "Were you tempted to follow in his path? Help people?"

There was no answer.

"I don't remember my father, of course," Jiggie went on, pleasantly now, feeling the other's reluctant interest. "He died even before I was born, so I can't say I know a blessed thing about fathers."

Kady stood up straight, careful to put his knees together and show his height. "I see politics as the only way to help people," he answered in a firm tone.

Jiggie was surprised by the strength of his reply. "So you don't think the soul important?"

"It doesn't buy flour or build a dam."

"So are those your interests?"

"You can see the answer for yourself. Why do you think I've got you to help me? I want the same things I wanted before. Only more. I want the education and money to do them."

"Well, all you'll get is—"

"I'll get what I can, won't I," Kady retorted with arrogance.

"You'll get what I give you, nothing more or less."

"We'll see, won't we."

"Don't 'we'll see' me, boy. Without me you're back where you started."

"And what about me?" Kady answered in a tone that was quiet and nearly sinister.

"What about you?" Jiggie said with disgust.

"Don't I have you by the balls, too? Or doesn't she mean anything to you anymore?"

The air was still. Nothing moved, not a breeze, not a sound. Kady feared he'd said too much, but a thrill was pulsing through him, and he felt more stimulated than he'd ever felt in his life. He held his breath, afraid the man would hear the tension in his throat.

Nobody said anything. The silence lasted. Kady barely risked a breath. Eventually he began to calm down. Wished he had a cigarette, but didn't move. Jiggie wiped his face, hands across the little pits. Finally he talked. "She's had some school."

Kady held in a sigh of relief.

"Four or five years."

Silence.

"She speaks some English."

"I've had nine."

"Oh, have you, very good." Jiggie was surprised, and his voice showed it. It made Suraj feel good.

"You must get to know my aide," Jiggie said. "His name's Attar Singh. He'll set you up with everything."

"Yes."

"I was thinking of Delhi."

"I've never been there."

"Maybe now's the time. Tell him everything. He'll deal

93

with it. If you want anything, you or her . . ."

"Yes." He realized how fully the man had capitulated.

"Just . . ."

"Yes. . . ."

They were silent again, no sounds at all except, far away, the jingle of some bells on a bullock cart as it rumbled through the night. "She likes music," Jiggie said quietly.

Kady didn't answer. The notion of music hadn't occurred to him.

"I'd like her to continue with her singing."

"She takes lessons, does she?" Kady asked, seeing suddenly for the very first time the vague outline and shape of a woman he didn't know.

"Well, no, not as yet, but I think she'd like to."

It sounded like a request, even a plea.

Kady didn't answer. He replayed the words in his mind. He was torn. He had nothing against music and he had nothing against the woman, but he didn't like standing next to this man. He'd watched him before, seen him in crowds, giving speeches, seen him most recently inside his father's house when he came asking about the abortion, but if he'd criticized the man before for all he represented, now he didn't like him.

Mostly because he didn't like how he made him feel. He'd never stood one on one with a man like this, and for all his success right now and his public protestations earlier, that one was as good as the other, he knew he didn't know what he really believed.

Over and over inside his head he heard the tone in the rich man's voice. He rolled it around in his mind. It sounded like a plea. It sounded something like anguish, it had a throb, but since he himself knew precious little about love, it didn't occur to him that this man beside him, one of the most powerful men in India, was actually in love and in pain.

He only thought instead that he, Kady, was about to get something the other man wanted. It was a novel idea and one whose full implications he knew he hadn't yet considered.

"Shall we say you come for lunch at the palace tomorrow?" Shocked, Jiggie heard himself say the words. That had never been his plan. His intention had been never to see him again. Now he had already invited him to lunch at his family table no less. "Come around noon. Get set up. You'll do," he added, almost talking to himself.

Kady felt his heart thump in anger at the condescension of the phrase and wanted to yell, "Look at me, I'm smarter than you," but instead he was too nervous to move at all.

She'd be asleep by now, Jiggie was thinking. He pictured her curled up like a monkey on the floor of his room, in a corner where he'd laid some rugs, more like home for her, beds and kings nothing she'd known before, any floor a home to her, and her orange eyes would be locked tight inside her wedded lids.

A peacock called, its haunting noise never sounding like a human cry to Jiggie or Kady. They'd heard the birds too often to take them for anything but what they were, but still, its sound pealed out over the night with a sad and painful feel, and Jiggie imagined it was the girl herself, reaching out to him. He felt her reaching and pulling, doing things to him no one had ever done, loving him for all his ugliness and this kept him rooted there, a father more than he'd ever been before. If I ever have a daughter, he vowed, I'll teach her how to ride and shoot and be damned if it isn't the thing for girls to do. Let her be as powerful as she can be so she'll never be as vulnerable as this girl here, wrapped in shawls, lying on a floor, her power over him that she had no other power at all.

"Do you have a name for the baby?" Kady asked after a while, his nerve come back.

"I don't want to know anything about the baby. I want nothing to do with it. I want nothing more to do with you, either. You'll work for me, maybe I'll see you sometimes but that's it. Lots of people work for me. They always have and they always will and you're just one more."

Anger burst in Kady Suraj.

Jiggie turned and headed toward the jeep. He got inside and prepared to go.

Kady dropped a dead cigarette in the dust and squashed it. He swung his leg up over the back of his bicycle, then put it down and turned to face Jiggie. "Oh, one thing," he said, looking in the jeep and not knowing where he got this last bit of nerve, not even knowing if the man could hear him now.

Jiggie saw his handsome face through the window and hated it.

"What's her name?" Kady asked.

Jiggie couldn't answer. Giving her name seemed the most precious thing of all. He pretended not to hear. He started up the motor.

"I say," Kady repeated, because now he knew the man heard every word. "Will you tell me her name?"

"What's that?" The motor hadn't caught yet.

"Her name?"

"Durr," Jiggie said, knowing the boy had bettered him from beginning to end. "Her name is Durr."

# PART TWO

## ❧ I ❦

PHOEBE POSITIONED HER SEAT UP-
right. The plane was descending. India and a continent were up
ahead, and she pressed her nose against the window and stared
out. Her hair, piled up on top and tucked in by combs, was
falling out in all directions, a blond spray around a face that
looked tight and intense, lines around the eyes, mouth serious
and not at all relaxed.

Outside everything shimmered a shade of brown and the land
below seemed no more a destination than the sky. India was
virtually invisible and peering down, Phoebe waited for India
to show itself. Dust seemed to be rushing headlong into her eyes
and the dull brightness of the sun obscured made her squint.
Somewhere in the brown bilge of the air below was an airport,
a city, a brother and a past, but whatever she'd expected of the
moment when she finally returned to India, it wasn't that she
wouldn't be able to see anything at all.

Then suddenly the tarmac reached up and slapped the plane
on its stomach. India was present: a seared, brown flatness that
stretched as far as she could see. She stared out the window.
Peasants with sheets of cloth wrapped around their bodies gazed
dumbstruck at the plane as if a god were landing and she was
taken aback by how small they were, their thinness appalling
even from a distance.

Low flat buildings with a clock and a tower were straight ahead. Lined up along the runway were rows of men, police or army, who's to know, in khaki uniforms, bullets in bands across their chests and semiautomatic rifles in their hands.

Her face was right up against the window, and as the plane slowed down, she saw that the soldiers were half-asleep, eyes almost closed, these not men on guard, just men at work, and if their uniforms fit, their shoes did not. They were big old heavy leather boots, one size for all, with no laces in the place where laces were meant to be, just a yawning tongue of leather, opened wide in the heat. There were dozens of men, dark, light, turbans, no turbans, short, tall, Dravidians, Aryans, a hodgepodge, no more role, in fact, than a fence.

This was India once again and Phoebe's stomach was knotted up with an anxiety that was nearly nauseating. What had it done to Cully? She reached for a brown paper bag she didn't need, held it, then dropped it on the floor and kept on staring, head against the glass, blue eyes looking out at the brown flat land.

"Don't you want to get off?"

It was the stewardess.

Phoebe looked up. The plane was empty.

"You'd better get off," the stewardess said. "You're not sick, are you?"

"Sorry. I wasn't paying attention."

The stewardess led her down the aisle. "Hardly a place for a vacation. . . ."

"That's for sure."

"Either you love it or you hate it."

"Yes."

"But if you're not staying very long . . ."

"Well, thank you," Phoebe said, and with that she stepped out onto the staircase that headed down to the tarmac and felt the heat, like a block of cement, hit her in the face.

My God, she thought. Her eyes evaporated to pinpoints and her face didn't sweat because the sweat disappeared instantaneously in the air. Her skin cracked like chalk in the dryness. She took a step down the stairs. Soldiers half-eyed stared at her. Her stockings felt like sleeping bags. She glanced down at her clothes—hanging wet already?—and took another few steps.

Her last thought before she touched the ground, other than that Cully wouldn't be there to meet her, didn't even know she was coming, might even be dead in India, like all her relatives were dead in India, gobbled up by gods and goddesses to mingle with the stars before being reborn, her last thought was to wish she had brought her sunglasses.

Not to protect her from the sun, but to shield her from the stares.


The great gray room had a high vaulted ceiling and a few stray fans, leggy upright things, to keep the air moving, but for all its size, it was mostly bare, a line of three-hundred-odd people down the middle and one counter, one official, way up in front to check their visas. That was all, but for a handful of soldiers who stood around looking no more purposeful in here than they had outside.

After a while a sweeper, an untouchable, made his appearance. He was dark brown, with blue shorts that were really underpants and brass studs in both his nostrils. Without looking at anyone, he bent his knees almost to the floor and, balancing low on his haunches, reached his arm out in front to sweep up, back and around in broad circular motions with a thing in his hand that resembled a broom.

Long and feathery it was, with three or four naked branches, but because he didn't have a dustpan or even try to sweep toward any one place of deposit, all he did with his slow rhythmic moves was endlessly relocate the dirt, from here to there to there.

It was hot. All the doors in the room were closed. There were no windows to open and a fan on the ceiling swirled steadily but did little to affect the temperature. Phoebe was sweating profusely. Her body felt as if it had a massive attack of poison oak. Everything, limbs, torso, neck, and arms, didn't exactly itch or throb but was dynamically alive in some special relationship to the substance that was coating it.

A thermometer against a wall registered the temperature inside at 101 degrees.

The sweeper continued his broad circular path around the room. Phoebe kept following him with her eyes: reach, pull, and sweep, reach, pull, sweep, on and on. He continued this slow, scything motion as the line of people he never looked at gradually became shorter, and if perchance he ended up in the path between the immigration counter and the door, some people walked around him. Others simply stepped over him.

Given his size, it was not a very hard thing to do.


Two hours later Phoebe finally pushed open the door of the airport and stepped out with her one suitcase and a shoulder sack. The immigration officer had looked at her place of birth and stamped her passport with a flourish meant to welcome her back home, but now outside, in the hot sun, she felt desolate and alone. She looked up and down the arrival area, cars and taxis that were not for her, and when she set out to find a taxi, red-turbaned coolies chased her in packs across the parking lot. She brushed them away with swings of her arm. "Go away," she cried, remembering again, for no reason, that her parents had never had a funeral.

"Taxi, jaio," she called. A cab came and she got inside, escaping the coolies, only to remember something she had forgotten to do inside.

She told the driver to wait. He nodded and she went back in to the cashier where five hundred dollars' worth of traveler's checks got her a stack of bills six inches high. Then she found a telephone booth.

She knew the number. She had called it from New York enough, but when she dialed this time, nothing happened. There was no ring, no click, nothing. She tried the number again and this time it finally rang. A man answered and said, "Dr. Kumar here, sexologist speaking. How may I be helping you?"

Phoebe hung up.

She dialed the number again, same one as before, and this time an operator answered and said, "American Embassy yes," but before Phoebe could say anything, the line was disconnected.

She tried again. Four coolies had their faces pressed up against the glass, inches away, staring at her.

She turned her back on them to face the wall, but there was less air that way, so she turned back. They were still there, mouths open, and she could see their tongues resting on their lips, as though they were dogs and mere contact with air provided some hydration.

The phone was ringing now, but it rang so many times, she

was about to hang up. Finally a man came on the line and said, "American Embassy, please."

She asked for Harriet MacDonald.

When she got put through to the consular office, she identified herself by name and asked for the woman again.

"Holding, please," a man said, and when he came back on the line, he announced Mrs. MacDonald was in a meeting, "not being interrupted."

Phoebe pleaded with him to get her anyway.

"May I be knowing the nature of your business?"

"She knows all about it," Phoebe said. "I've talked to her many times. She wants to talk to me. It's about my brother."

"She is having no brother."

"No, my brother."

"You are wanting to talk to your brother?"

"Well, yes, but—"

"He is not here. There is no Guthrie here. He may be having another department."

"No, no," Phoebe said. "You've got it all confused."

"But there is no Mr. Guthrie here."

Four sets of eyes stared at her. They were open wide, brown and ringed with white. She looked at the ground, breathed in deeply, looking for some peace, but all she got was dust off the floor and traces of her own sweat.

She started again. Speaking very slowly, she said, "Will you please tell Mrs. MacDonald that Phoebe Guthrie is here in New Delhi. I am staying at the Taj Hotel and I'd like to see my brother as soon as possible." She paused. "Do you have that?"

"Of course," the man said, offended.

"I'm at the airport now and I'll be at the hotel in one hour. Will you be sure she gets the message as soon as possible?"

"My greatest service to Mrs. MacDonald is to be giving her each and every message."

"Yes. No doubt."

Phoebe pushed open the door and stepped out, shiny as a piece of fruit. The coolies scattered, back now impassive along a wall, indistinguishable among the rest. Not one moved in her direction. They'd sized her up for exactly what she was—not a chance of work—and didn't waste effort in her behalf.

With her suitcase and sack, Phoebe Guthrie set out across the parking lot for the second time. She could picture herself and the image made her feel even more forlorn than before, because she knew she stood out as someone who did not belong. A tall white woman with an expensive purse hanging from her shoulder, flat shoes, skirt that reached midcalf, shirt, belt, jewelry. She saw lazy eyes following her path across the dust and she wished she could hide.

The taxi drove out of the airport, blowing up clouds of dust, and reached a four-lane highway headed toward town. The road was full of potholes and if twenty years before, desolate villages stood along the way, now there were cement warehouses on the side and piles of handmade bricks, encampments of squalid huts, and naked babies.

The air was thick with dust and smoke. She could smell it, too. She leaned back and inhaled deeply, sending India down to her guts, the scent of diesel and heat and something unpleasant, garbage or sewage, she couldn't tell. She looked steadily outside and tried to adjust to the fact that this was India, not New York or some odd dream. Finally she realized she found everything beautiful, if poor, and it calmed her a bit. She felt less alien, more familiar with it all. Her face relaxed and she thought about how fear had brought her back to a place she'd never thought to see again, but, despite herself, she felt herself smiling because she had the glimmer of a sense of coming home.

Trees and the little stick figures of Indians were lined up along the road. They quivered, as in a mirage, and were gone, only to be replaced by more. There were already multitudes, even here, outside of town, and she watched them go by, India and its people, proof of its reality mounting up. The road reached the city from the south, past huge housing projects, miles and miles of low-slung buildings that stretched in parallel lines, block after block, without a break, past people, cows, boys on bikes, and men squatting on the side of the road to do you know what.

Soon the taxi reached the lush, inner parts of the city where wide boulevards stretched out beneath high spreading trees. Just off the sidewalks were walled estates. Some extended for acres, nothing visible from the road except hints of mansions, lawns as big as golf courses, peacocks roaming full bloom across the greenery, and that it was green at all spoke volumes, for May was considered summer here, no rain in almost a year, and water for grass was near as precious as gold.

Phoebe realized she knew where she was going. She started following the street signs and anticipated exactly what they would be. Then she turned in her seat to look off to the left.

Because, over there, beyond the huge green trees that spread their branches above the land so far they must have had generations, even centuries, to grow so big, over there was Number Nine Jumna Road.

## ❧ 2 ❧

THE MORNING PHOEBE ARRIVED,
our water filter broke in the kitchen and then the electricity
went out, taking the stove with it, and since all the bearers had
been gone since the night before, off for a wedding, and weren't
due back until tomorrow, I was busy with the cook carting
buckets of water out to the woodfire in back by his hut so he
could boil it there, then carting them back into the kitchen so
we could use it. The farthest thing from my mind on Tuesday,
May 11th, was Phoebe Guthrie or Cully or anything except my
own monumental inconvenience.

Kitty Chandradas was the one who told me she was back.

It was only a few days later. We were at dinner with the R. T.
Ramsinghs who had just returned from their house in the hills
in Mussoorie, and they had a few people round, including one
banker, head of the local Lloyds, who wanted to meet my husband. The rest were mostly import-export types, one, I remember, who said he dealt in "arms." Everybody knew it was really
interballistic missiles he got from the Israelis and sold wherever.
Delhi's like that. Behind the scenes a lot's going on. It was
almost midnight, dinner was just being brought out, and when
I saw Kitty coming in from a stroll outside, I went over to help
her up the steps, take her arm.

I asked her if it was any cooler in here with the air-conditioning and she said a little, but she couldn't get used to the idea of staying inside. She still thought summer nights were meant to be spent outdoors, and she told me how when she was a child they all slept on the roof, men on one side, women and children on the other, and I said, "Oh, how wonderful," and then, lighting up a cigarette, she said she'd seen Phoebe Guthrie the other day, did I know she was back? I exclaimed in surprise, and she said Phoebe said something about how she was looking for Cully. "Had I seen him," Kitty said, "and I couldn't tell her I didn't care if I ever see her brother again, so I just said, no, I hadn't. I didn't keep up with him. Let it go at that."

I asked Kitty where Phoebe was staying and she said she saw her at the Taj picking out newspapers in the bookshop, so maybe she was there. "How'd she look?" I asked, wondering why Phoebe hadn't called me yet.

"Well, I don't know, actually," Kitty said, "I recognized her hair and so I just said, Excuse me, but you remind me so much of someone I used to know and all that, and she was terribly nice, asked about Jyoti, and how was he, did he still play poker, and I was amazed she remembered his name and everything. She was just a child then . . . well, no, not a child, I suppose. But still, as soon as I said I didn't know anything about Cully, she just sort of . . . Oh, well, I don't know, but she didn't have Louis' charm. She was lovely looking, in that sort of breezy American way, you know what I mean, her hair everywhere. But then, you never really knew Louis, did you? So how can I expect you to remember his charm?"

I said, "Well, thanks for telling me, I'll have to track her down," and Kitty said, "Do you still see Cully, by the way?" and I said, not in a while, had she? and she said Jyoti ran across him somewhere, not long ago, and I said, here? in town? and she said, "Oh, very," and then she gave a fake shiver and said, "Uhhhh, what an odd boy." I said, "Oh, he's not so odd, he's just . . ." and she said, "Well, you must be accustomed to them since you're American, too."

The next morning I called the Taj, but she wasn't registered there. I called back later and asked to speak to the manager, remembering that he was a friend of mine's second cousin and had gone to Yale and spent the weekend in Greenwich once with my husband's college roommate, so he came directly on the line, India's like that, and said she'd left for the palace in Deeg.

I asked if she was coming back and he said she asked the clerk would there be any trouble getting a room again? When he himself heard that, he called her right up and told her none, none at all, not for her, she could come any time, nothing too much for a relative of Louis Guthrie's, and she said, Do you remember my father, then? and he said, Of course, who could forget Louis Guthrie, even if twenty years had passed? not telling her he'd never actually met him, just heard the stories.

I asked him if he ever saw her and how was she, and he said he didn't know what to make of her, she did the most remarkable things and had everybody so worried, he literally assigned her one full-time bearer and one taxi driver in order to keep track of her. He had no choice, really, did he, it was his duty to her father to look after her and let the staff know she was favored because of her family and all.

That was awfully nice, I said, but what did she do? wondering if he meant men in the room, that sort of thing, and he said, Well, she went to the morgue and she went to the untouchables' slums out on the other side of the river and to Safdarjang Hospital, he didn't know what to think, and she never did do a single thing tourists do, except make inquiries about taking a trip to Agra, and I said, Well, she wasn't exactly a normal tourist, after all, but I was surprised myself, to say the least. He said the taxi driver was so concerned, he didn't let her out of his sight, but for all that she could be very charming and so he had asked her the second night if she'd like to join his family for dinner, but she'd said no, thank you, she was sleepy, she wanted an early night. Instead she went right back out and had the driver take her to her brother's apartment in Old Delhi, where she spent the night; the taxi driver slept in the car.


I put in a call to the American ambassador, but he was out. I decided to call the palace in Deeg, give it a try, at least, but the lines didn't work, so I gave up for the time being. I was worried myself. Had something actually happened to Cully? It seemed extraordinarily odd, hospitals, the morgue, so I went round to the hotel, saw the manager in person, and made up some story

108

about why I was so worried, and he put me on to Tulsidas, the taxi driver, so I talked to him.

Aside from the fact that I was worried and I loved Phoebe, all this interested me from the start. This was Phoebe on the move. Furthermore, something was obviously happening with Cully and I wanted to know what it was. I'm not a prying kind of person, but if there's something I want to know, I want to know it. I was also thinking, who else was there to look after Phoebe and Cully anymore?

When I got home I looked up Kady Suraj's office number in the phone book and rang over there, thought he might know something about her, but I got switched from one desk to another, going steadily up the ranks, from assistant to first assistant. Then I hung up abruptly without even leaving my name. I didn't have the nerve to talk to him, was what it came down to. What was I supposed to say? "Oh, excuse me, Mr. Suraj, but we met at so-and-so's house one night and I'm the woman with dark hair who sat across the table from you and asked you about the Sikh problem, but you weren't in the mood to answer because you were having an affair with some woman there, so you ignored me"?

I called the ambassador back, left another message, and wrote a brief letter to Phoebe care of Maharaja Juggernathan Singh, Deeg, Rajasthan. Even though I knew he didn't live there anymore, it was the quickest way to reach her. "Personal, Urgent," I wrote on the envelope, and figured I'd done all I could.

## ❧ 3 ❧

HARRIET MacDONALD NEVER
called Phoebe back. Phoebe finally tried her again and when she
came on the phone, she said she'd never gotten her message.
Then she tried to persuade Phoebe not to do the very thing she'd
come to do. Said Jasdan Singh of Deeg and Kady Suraj had both
gone to the morgue to see the body but neither one could identify it. Why didn't she save herself a lot of grief and hand over
the dental X-rays, let someone else do it, it was pretty awful, but
Phoebe insisted. So Harriet said she'd try to arrange to get her
into the morgue as soon as possible.

It might be difficult, she cautioned, because the director of the
morgue was away until tomorrow conducting marriage negotiations on his daughter's behalf and she wouldn't be able to see the
body until at least six P.M. when he was due back.

Why? Phoebe asked, upset at the delay.

Because he left no instructions authorizing anyone to be let
in.

But that made no sense, Phoebe argued. Someone had to be
in charge, capable of making a decision. Harriet said she agreed,
but that was the way things were done over here, and what
could she do?

Phoebe was so persistent, Harriet said she'd call Deputy Minister Suraj to see if he would use his influence.

But that proved of no avail, either, because Suraj was "out of station," which could mean anything, Harriet explained when she called Phoebe back. "Either it's true or it's false, but I left a message about you anyway."

"Where's the body now?" Phoebe asked.

"Safdarjang Morgue."


Phoebe asked for Suraj's phone number and the location where the body'd been found, then called Suraj's office herself. The receptionist over on Raj Path, Road of Kings, took her name and number, transferred her to someone else, who also took her name and number, and then on to someone else who again took her name and number, and finally to Mr. Kuldip Ramchandran, who wrote down her message, then told her Suraj wasn't there.

"Where is he?" Phoebe asked, exasperated. "I've been on the phone half an hour."

"I am not his appointment secretary and so I don't know his whereabouts."

"But he is due back?"

"I suppose." The man's voice was vaguely familiar.

"So you'll tell him I called? And that I'm in India?"

"Yes, it is my complete and utter understanding that the Taj Hotel is in—"

"No need to go through all that," Phoebe said irritably and hung up.


Downstairs she told the hotel taxi driver, named Tulsidas after the poet, he announced, to take her to Safdarjang Morgue.

But at Safdarjang Morgue the deputy director refused to let her in. "I am not letting Indira Gandhi in," he said, barring the door with his foot.

"But she's dead!" Phoebe screamed.

"I am not for letting down my job. My job is being all specified and I will not change it for you and I will not change it for my cousin and I will not change it for the director of the bus company and I will not . . ."

❧

She got to the other side of the Jumna River about five in the afternoon, the sun was still high in the sky, and after an argument with Tulsidas who tried to convince her in a mixture of Hindi, Urdu, and English that only untouchables lived out here and that for all her talk about bhais and how she hadn't seen hers in a year and he may have died out there, it still wasn't right for her to go there alone.

She said, Well then you come with me, and he said, no, he wasn't going out there with untouchables, and so she set off by herself.

But he kept her in sight.

A man who was so dark you couldn't tell where his skin left off and his eyebrows began showed her where the body was found and where the police trucks had driven in and he answered all her questions, told her about the maggots and the flies and eventually drew a picture on a piece of paper of the sun going down with giant rays stretching all across the page. Phoebe sat down on the ground to study it, with some twenty or thirty people spread out around her like the rays of the sun itself.

Afterward Tulsidas took her back to the hotel and upstairs Phoebe, who hadn't slept much in three days, sank into a fitful sleep that was full of dreams and memories that were trying to reach the surface but couldn't.

# ❧ 4 ❧

T<small>HAT</small> <small>EVENING</small> <small>WHEN</small> K<small>ADY</small>
Suraj returned home to the spacious colonial bungalow set out
on acres of grass on Viceroy Circle, he did not seek out the
company of his wife. That was not unusual. He seldom saw her,
although invariably in the natural course of events their paths
did cross in one hallway or another. Instead he sat downstairs
in the library, which he used as an office. He had never adopted
the British custom of having a whiskey at night, so he asked for
tea. He did not turn on the fancy lighting system or play music
on his elaborate and foreign stereo system. He rarely did because he liked his music live and he associated the lighting racks
with entertaining, something he never did. Instead he turned on
a small pin light on his desk, as was his custom, and worked,
surrounded by the dark of the rest of the room.

There were a couple of bronze and terra-cotta gods for decoration, but otherwise the library was sparse. Kady did not appear
to notice the deities, but he may have sensed their presence and
taken their radiance for granted. They were all gifts from Louis
Guthrie. As he read, he tried to still his breathing and his mind,
to focus ever more sharply on work and problems that were at
hand.

Night was coming late these days of mid-May. The skies were

white, not even heavy yet with rain, and in the paleness of evening, he eventually reached out and pressed a button positioned by his chair.

When the bearer came, Kady asked where Kumari-sahib was. She had gone out, he was told, something he already knew, and would not be back until after dinner, something he also already knew.

Then he asked to have dinner by himself in a corner of the library, just as he did almost every night. With only one of the lights turned on, he was in near darkness as he ate, his eyes at peace with the shadows and the quiet, and afterward he went to an office adjacent to the room, where he worked until after eleven. It was what he did every night when he did not go out to someone else's house.

Among other things, he studied his telephone messages from the day and handled some papers to do with a small house outside of Delhi that he owned. A flower garden had been planted there, the blossoms were in bloom, and he was studying arrangements he had made for guests who were due there in a week or so. He called it the Garden House.

At some point he heard a car pull up, a door open and close, voices that were indistinct, footsteps within the house. Then it was quiet again, but he traced the sounds, every one, picking up even the nuances that indicated the person was tired, more tired than usual.

Kumari-sahib, Durr Suraj, had returned home and gone to bed, and sometime later Suraj-sahib himself went up the stairs to bed but at the top of the landing he took a different direction from the one his wife had taken, and he went to sleep without seeing her.

If he had been asked, he probably would not have been able to say exactly when he had seen her last, but it was not recently, not within the last few weeks, at least.

If asked, however, he would have been able to describe almost everything about her. There were certain spots he had not seen very often, some he had not seen in a very long time, one might even say years, and some he had never seen at all, but of those he had seen, he had a memory that was perfect.

Upstairs in his bedroom, which was empty but for a bed, a table, and an armoire, he reached into a pocket of his jacket and pulled out the sheets of paper Mr. Ramchandran had given him.

There were four of them, all with the woman's name, saying she had called.

He barely remembered her, he had so completely put her out of his mind, and now he inadvertently gave her the face her brother Cully had. He felt indifferent to her.

He put the notes on the table by his bed and just about then became aware that he was nervous. This was unusual. He blinked and did not move. He picked up the slips and put them farther away in an ashtray, as if their proximity had caused the disturbance in his chest. But the feeling did not abate. Deep inside his stomach he traced the perceptible movements of anxiety as they came in contact with his stomach, his throat, and various muscles in between.

He tracked them with precision and sensed their origin in the woman's name. He began to breathe a bit in a yogic way. He found himself staring across the room at the tip of one piece of paper just visible on top of the furniture and he stood up, picked up the slips, and threw them in the trash, saying to himself she'd be gone soon enough and he wasn't going to see her, even if he did have to acknowledge he was curious about what she had become.

His intention, specifically, was to subdue his curiosity about the woman he'd known so long ago and he found it was not difficult at all. Before long he forgot her altogether.

## ❦ 5 ❦

EARLY THE NEXT MORNING, IT
was May 12th, Tulsidas took Phoebe to India Gate. She got out
of the taxi and went over to stand underneath its mammoth high
red arch as it loomed over the small park in the center of the
great wide boulevard. But for its color, it reminded her of the
Arc de Triomphe in Paris. Pigeons flew in and out of the intricate carvings overhead.

Waving good-bye to the driver, Phoebe took one last look up
at India Gate and was conscious as she set off that she was
headed into the old and the past, Old Delhi ahead.


She walked and walked, never noticing that Tulsidas followed
along behind, in the maze of streets of Old Delhi, she kept
steadily apace, knowing exactly, without maps or directions,
where she was going.

Walking itself was hard to do and required her full attention.
The streets, two lanes wide, were dense with bicycles, rickshaws, bullocks, cows, and cars, all moving in both directions on
both sides of the road as fast as each could go.

There was no "your side–my side" here, just get wherever you
want to go as fast as possible and pay no attention to whatever's

in your way because God has made it your duty to accomplish whatever it is you are doing. So Phoebe plowed ahead with something that looked like confidence; to fall back and cede the way ran the risk of leaving her at the side, unable to get back into the flow again. She felt exhilarated.

Her head was high, she was almost smiling, her hair was thrown back long over her shoulder, her face ran with sweat, and every few yards she stopped to buy something, oranges and packets of spice, bits of colored thread and little amulets. She stuffed them in her pockets, along with rupee notes and change, and forged ahead, stopping all the time to dole out coins to beggars whenever they came along. At a stall where there was a vat of boiling oil, she bought some orange sweets shaped like pretzels, ate them fast before the flies could settle. She stopped at a faucet dribbling in the street and washed her face, careful not to let any water pass her lips, and walked on, smiling. She felt happy. To her it all just looked and felt and sounded great and she couldn't understand why she'd stayed away so long.

Noise hammered in her ears. Wired to most of the storefronts, rooftops, and even posts at intersections were loudspeakers with different radio programs blaring from each. No two sounds or songs were alike, all of them declaring, It is my God-given right to give the world my sounds and make it listen whether it wants to or not. To Phoebe this was India reintroducing itself to her. That she hadn't, as recently as yesterday, ever wanted to come back again was completely forgotten.

When she finally reached Cully's building, she stood across the street from it and looked up, hands on her hips, pockets bulging with trinkets and cash, head running with sweat. Her heart beat hard, Cully's presence suddenly overwhelming.

She barely had time to notice because, abruptly, she was besieged by urchins, beggars, lepers, everyone pressing in around her to sniff her smell and touch her clothes. She started waving her hands and pushing them away, and quickly they all moved back, afraid of this living thing that flayed her arms: maybe she was a lunatic. One woman, more brave, peered at Phoebe from a spot not two feet away.

"Jow," Phoebe barked in her face, "jow," waving her arms as though she was shooing at a fly. The woman backed off a couple of feet, no more, then Phoebe slipped into a tea stall, sat at the back, and the woman stared in, but came no farther.

"Chai, please," Phoebe called out to the shopkeeper, relieved to be alone.

The man, standing in undershorts at the open fire, ignored her. Phoebe called again, an order for tea with a cardamom seed in it. He still ignored her, so the next time she added a line Samiji, the driver, always used. "And hurry up because I don't have all day to wait for you to figure out that it's your karma to serve me tea." With that the tea man hopped to and brought her something white in a glass with a seed floating on top.

Phoebe thanked him graciously.

"Hanh, jee," he said, wagging his head, but the way he moved showed he felt ashamed and was asking her forgiveness.

She bowed her head in a way that said, of course, she forgave him, and he immediately set off to bring her another cup, gratis.

Drinking now in solitude, Phoebe looked across the street at Cully's building. It had shops at the street level, nothing except windows at the second, a wooden balcony along the third, and at the very top, the roof itself, where Cully lived, a balcony with double glass doors and a screenlike railing made of the same stucco as the walls.

The building had once been white, but now it was streaked and gray, with daggers of dirt extending vertically up and down the walls like icicles. It was not unlike the hundreds, thousands, of other buildings pressed in here in Chandni Chowk because year after year rain pounded on the roof two or three months at a time, overflowing daily, flooding the sides, and removed in the process all the filth that had accumulated on the roof the other nine months of the year. The dirt then lodged in the crevices, as if the ground below were not big enough to receive it, and ended up making dirt and waste as much a part of the building's design as the walls themselves.

So it was in a striped gray-and-white building that Cully lived. Had lived, did live, might live.

A staircase stood in the middle of the building sandwiched between two open-air shops, and with it in mind, Phoebe gave the tea man an enormous tip and crossed the street, made it to the wide stone steps, and headed up.

At the second level there were two doors, one on either side of the landing. Both were closed. Two doors stood at the third floor, open with cloth hanging down, and at the top, Cully's, there were two doors again, both closed.

Steel locks four inches square and one inch wide were stuck through the loops in the doors. The keyholes were big enough to take a thumb.

Phoebe knocked on one door, then the other. There was no answer. She hadn't expected any, but she still felt defeated. She tried to decide what to do next. The walls were gray and dirty, marked with hands, grease, and apparent streams of liquid that seemed to have been directed from just below the waist. Phoebe had no doubt what that was, but she didn't think the place dirty, only dark. The air didn't smell and she understood why Cully lived here.

She walked down a flight of stairs and rapped at one of the open doors. The cloth flapped against her legs, a fan was whirring inside, and in a minute a woman appeared. She wore a sari, but the end had been pulled tight between her legs and stuck in the waist in front, so she looked like she was wearing pedal pushers. Her legs were revealed to her knees and, perspiring heavily, she was drying her hands on a cloth.

When she saw Phoebe she brushed her hands over her hair and face, primping quickly, threw the towel to the side, and wagged her head from left to right in a way that said, What can I do for you?

"My brother lives upstairs," Phoebe began, speaking English. She pointed up the stairs.

The woman's face was blank, as if Phoebe hadn't spoken.

Phoebe tried again. "My brother is living upstairs since one year," she said slowly, taking on the singsong rhythm that distinguishes Indian English. "He is scholar loving Indian art, and I am coming from America"—only she pronounced it "Am-ri-ka"—"to see him. May I be asking if you are knowing where he is?"

The woman broke into a big smile, pulled back the cloth, and gestured Phoebe inside. "Coming in." She pulled Phoebe's arm. "Coming my house." Then she yelled off to the side and Phoebe saw another sari dart through an open door ahead. "I am just telling servant bring for tea," the woman explained. "You must be having tea, for we are just now greeting you to India."

Still holding Phoebe by the arm, she directed her to a single bed lined up lengthwise against the wall in what was apparently the living room and pushed her down on it to sit. "I will just now be getting tea," she said, and with that she disappeared through the door into what was apparently, by the nature of the sounds, the kitchen.

The woman returned with one cup and one saucer and put them on a little table near Phoebe. Then she disappeared again. When she came back she had a teapot, a bowl of sugar, and a little pitcher of milk. "So you are being Cully's sister." She sat beside Phoebe on the bed. "But of course I am knowing that just from looking at your . . ." She would have blushed, but for the color of her skin, and didn't finish the sentence. She had drifted perilously close to the personal. She started pouring the tea.

"Are you knowing him, then?" Phoebe asked, deferring sugar—it looked awfully speckled—but taking milk when she saw the scum on top that meant it had just boiled.

"My children are playing with him every night."

"Now?" Phoebe exclaimed.

"They are loving him," the woman went on, "and he is having such fine ways taking them to ice cream."

"When did he get back?"

"Not that I am having to teach him Hindi, but he is enjoying this practicing with me. . . ."

Cully was fluent.

"And I am doing my best to instruct him in our Indian ways."

"When did you see him last?"

"Oh . . . ," The woman's arm waved elaborately in the air. "It is being not quite so very recent, I am suspecting now," and with that her hand plummeted to her lap and she looked at Phoebe as if admitting that silence was far more accurate than words.

With effort Phoebe raised her cup and drank some tea. "So he's not here?"

No answer.

"So he is not being here right now?"

"Yes, that's right," the woman said energetically, as if that's what she'd been saying all along, only Phoebe hadn't understood.

"His door is being locked."

The woman nodded.

"I'd like to look inside."

"Yes," the woman said sympathetically.

"But I am not having the key."

"So many peoples coming to look for him," the woman said. "Police and this one inspector sa'ab, and just now this morning, not yesterday morning, but this morning, these two mens. Asking where is Am-ri-kan sa'ab?"

"What two men?"

"Coming from Deeg just to ask for him, just to look for Am-ri-kan sa'ab only. Where is Cully-sa'ab? they are asking, but I am saying, I am not knowing, and they are saying, I must be knowing, they have this one letter from him, they wave it in front of my eyes, but I am not knowing." She laid her hands out in hopelessness.

"I am wanting to get into his room," Phoebe said, "but I am not having key."

"Embassy woman getting in."

"How is she getting key?"

The woman looked blank.

"Is she having key?"

"Of course."

"Where is she getting it?"

"From me," the woman said, throwing Phoebe a sideways glance that intimated Phoebe was strange or stupid or both.

"From you," Phoebe exclaimed. "Why you?"

"Because I am being landlady," the woman said. "I am very first one calling embassy because Cully-sa'ab is not paying rental and I am needing rental, so sorry"—only she pronounced it "sod-die"—"because my brother's wife is having baby and I am needing to give her some very things—"

"That's all right," Phoebe interrupted. "Are you getting rent now?"

"These things are being taken care of, I am sure."

"Who is paying?"

"Indian go-wer-ment," the woman said proudly.

"The government?" Phoebe repeated doubtfully. "Paying his rent? Are you knowing when you are last seeing my brother?"

"I am not knowing. Time. Time." The woman waved her hand to indicate the irrelevance of time.

"I am most loving to talk to you, but do you think you could let me in his room?"

They walked upstairs. The woman unlocked the door on the left and held it open as Phoebe went inside. "This is all you are wanting, then?"

"Yes, that's very nice. Thank you. You can go now and I'll give you the key when I leave."

"So you are not wanting any more?"

"I can't think of anything."

"So it is that you are not wanting key to other room as well?"

"What other room?"

The woman gestured across the landing. "It is also Cully-sa'ab's."

"Why didn't you tell me?"

"You are not saying and so I am not knowing."

Phoebe silently counted to five. "Yes, I am very much appreciating if you will get me key."

"I am not having it."

Phoebe inhaled deeply. "I am very much appreciating it if you will go downstairs now and be getting me this one key I am needing. Please be leaving it outside on the floor."

The woman nodded and reached out to pat Phoebe on the arm. "We will be doing everything we can to find your brother. I am sure he is only somewhere thinking in his mind, but all of India will be helping you, I am being sure."

She left to get the key. Phoebe went inside, shut the door, and slid down against it to sit on the floor of her brother's room.


Sunlight streamed through the double glass doors, casting columns of dust across the room. It glared in Phoebe's face but she could still make out the shape of Jama Masjid Mosque outside, its high rounded dome a gray, almost shadowy thing that loomed over the horizon. All she could see, just as Cully had written, was the shape of the Moghul dome framed in double glass doors. It was the same dome she'd seen yesterday from the other side of the river.

She looked slowly around the room, slowly because the room was so overwhelmingly Cully's and the effect of his presence so strong that she felt stunned.

It was mostly the furniture, none of it pushed against the walls, out in the room instead, like islands. The books were decidedly his, too, stacks of them, ten, twelve high, piled all over the floor, just as they were at home. She would have recognized it anywhere, Cully reproducing himself one place to the next; the contrast between his presence here and his absence everywhere else was so intense, Phoebe, briefly, had no doubt at all that he was alive.

She heard the landlady come up the stairs outside and the telltale sound of a key being placed on the floor.

The room was hot and stale. She stood up. It'd had no air in days, maybe months, hard to tell. Sweating from her tea, she had a sudden image of him, half a head, maggots, and a corpse.

She pushed her hair back behind her ears and, negotiating her way around the books and furniture, crossed the room and pushed open the doors to the roof to let in the hot but comforting breeze and noise of Old Delhi.

The room was the same size as the landlady's but it seemed larger, airier. She liked it. She looked around for a place to sit, double bed, chair, or the desk itself. Chose the bed, partly because she knew Cully would have taken the desk, and she leaned back against the pillows and imagined him sitting across from her, pen in hand, hair hanging over his forehead, color in his cheeks, and the ability to look up and smile at her that threw her into a turmoil of love and warmth and even desire.

There was something elusive about her brother. She wanted him forever but one could never hold him. He slid away, an eel, out of touch and gone.

Phoebe paused in her train of thought.

No, she corrected herself, pushing aside the sexual nuance. It wasn't that she wanted him. She needed him.

And it was her weakness, not his. "You bum," she said aloud with a half smile and stood up.

An antique bronze horse three feet high with long ears was pushed up in one corner of the room. Phoebe studied it with interest. It was a good piece, from what little she knew.

So he had started his collection after all, she thought. His letters were right. "Louis would be proud if he knew what I am getting now," he had written in his last letter, the end of March.

The horse had lost its tail and the bottom half of the back left leg, but it gleamed with the rich color of antique metal, and more than that, the animal had a bearing that was not so much proud as imposing, and yet serene.

But if Cully planned to be a collector, by the looks of his one-room apartment, he hadn't progressed very far. The horse was the only piece of art. There were gods, though, everywhere, dozens of them, enough to remind someone of Jumna Road and Louis Guthrie. They covered the walls, just like home. But if Louis' were beautiful works of art, Cully's gods were found on cheap posters and calendar pictures, bright and garish, a few rupees at best. The colors blazed red, green, purple, yellow, all around Cully's room, like a carnival, an outlandish mix, nothing subtle or subdued about the way Indians preferred their gods.

Only one picture was different. It was a black-and-white art photograph, a good three feet high, that had the grainy, porous look of Indian sculpture, and its gray-pitted quality stood out dramatically in this cheap room.

Phoebe recognized it as a picture from the Elephanta caves near Bombay, a close-up of the huge, placid, transcendent face of Buddha with the closed eyes and sensuous lips. The lips were thick and round, as soft as any breast or buttock. She looked at the picture, felt reassurance from its beautiful calmness, and wondered if Cully's absence could be attributed to love or an extended sexual encounter. But even if it was true love, that still didn't explain why he hadn't contacted her.

She got off the bed and walked through a door on the side of the room. Inside she found a tiny alcove, shelves up and down the walls, a water faucet, and a stone platform deeply gutted in the middle. This was the kitchen. She glanced around quickly: a tin for tea, but that was all, no razor, hairbrush, toothbrush, no food at all, and no clothes.

A foot or two away was the bathroom. Phoebe opened the door and looked inside. It was barely big enough to turn around in, a pit on the floor, a mount on each side for the feet, and, high above, a water container and a shower head, toilet and shower in one.

She gave the cord a pull and watched the water swirl down into the pit, circulate around the sides, and then disappear downward, headed God knew where, into some ditch or gutter in the street below.

She went back out to the living room. Wherever Cully was, he had left the apartment on purpose, taking everything with him.

There were two pictures of Kady Suraj on the walls. Phoebe looked at them, curious. His face seemed to come from a place even farther away than the photos of Louis and Thalia the other night.

Cut from magazines, the first picture showed Suraj walking away from the Parliament Building wearing a three-piece suit, looking very patrician, head erect, nose certainly not a minor one, firm shoulders, all giving him a wellborn look as he stared out into the camera.

In the other he was wearing a Nehru jacket and was surrounded by hundreds of people pushing to get close to him. He was namasteing them, hands up, head slightly bent, looking genuinely devout. He had garlands of flowers around his neck and was obviously the focus of considerable acclaim. The photographer had apparently climbed on top of something, a bullock cart, maybe, or gone to a second-story window to get the shot, because the angle was looking down, and it caught masses of bodies, heads, men on bicycles and bullock carts, no cars at all.

But there was someone on the side of the photograph who was not Indian, his hair not dark enough, probably even blond. He was taller than the rest, the face obscured by someone waving, and he was pressed in among the crowd. There was something about the way he held his head out over his left shoulder that made Phoebe certain it was Cully.

She went through the desk. There wasn't much. One drawer had manila files with headings like "Suite #1," "Suite #2," with lists of objects from the palace down in Deeg. The next had paper, pens, an envelope with strips of negatives, and the last, workbooks, full of notations about the art in Deeg. She looked at these and found the most current was four months old.

Maybe the more recent were in Deeg, too, she thought.

She unlocked the door across the landing. Inside it was mostly books, stacked up everywhere, English, Hindi, Sanskrit.

She went back to Cully's room and packed everything from

the desk, files, notebooks, negatives, all into an empty pillow-case, and then shut the double glass doors to the balcony. Out-side, she locked the doors to both rooms and, going down the wide stone steps, stuck the keys in her purse and left.

She went straight back to the hotel and fell asleep with her clothes on.

## ❦ 6 ❦

WHEN SHE WOKE UP IT WAS AL-
most dark. She went to the window and looked down, saw
someone the size of a pea riding a bicycle toward the condensa-
tion of buildings that was Old Delhi. She stared at the pea and
saw herself as minuscule as well. How can I find another pea,
she thought, even if it does have yellow hair? She turned on the
light and looked in the mirror. Mascara had spread in a great
dark blot across her cheeks, and her hair was falling around her
face. She turned off the light and went in the bathroom, where
she washed her face and hair. She remembered Kamala, the
ayah, who had painted her arms with red designs so the gods
would see her.

Let me paint my arms in red, too, Phoebe thought, and go on
a hill so the gods can see me. Tell me my brother is alive. On
the ceiling the fan circled slowly round, and she watched each
blade as it moved north, south, east, west. What am I? she
thought. If she was one thing in New York, what was she here,
where gods live, the dead are reborn, and all contradictions are
the same?

Still wet, she went over to the window and looked down
again. She remembered Louis and Thalia, both of them ten feet
tall. She shivered despite the heat and went in the bedroom; no
sign of them, only a picture of Cully stuck in the mirror. She

blew it a kiss and went to another window that looked straight across into Raj Path and the great red sandstone buildings, and there they were, floating above the gum trees in the darkness, Thalia trailing photographs and Louis with the Shiva Nataraj dancing on his back.

They looked comfortable flying that way, an undulating easy mix to the way they rose and fell, and she imagined if she opened the window she'd hear their voices, so she turned off the air conditioner and opened the window but all she heard was herself, thinking, Is Cully in the morgue, waiting for me like he always used to do, waiting for me to come home?

It was a strange night.

Phoebe remembered being caught in a mixture of hunger, jet lag, and fatigue, eating from room service one minute, dozing the next, deluged with memories that seemed to last for hours, the past unleashed, as if all she had to do was touch the Indian soil, return for but a day, and the connection was made.

She told me about the past one weekend the following November when we ended up eventually falling asleep on Kitty Chandradas' veranda, then woke up later to find the moon shining on us and blankets the bearer had brought protecting us from the cold. We moved the lounges closer together and talked on through the night until it was almost morning and we could see the frost on our breath.

We had breakfast inside, then moved back out to the veranda, the lawn all green and freshly cut. Had lunch there, then walked—she said she had to exercise—then back to the veranda, where she had the bearer bring her sandwiches. She had ice cream, too, and a tart, later tea and cookies in the afternoon and at night a big dinner, served on the veranda.

She laughed afterward, saying she was eating too much.

I didn't bother to tell her it was her body coming alive again, the summer, thank God, ever farther away.

All that weekend Phoebe told me about the night in May when she was waiting to see the male Caucasian body, lying some miles away inside a morgue. She said she kept remembering the past and a dream she'd had in New York. In it she and

Louis and Kady Suraj were in Delhi in the backseat of the white Ford car. Samiji was driving and he turned around to her and said, "Shall I tell you now?"

She had said, "Tell me what?" and woken up.

Telling it to me that day at Kitty's, she saw the dream as prescient, some inner part of her knowing or sensing what the rest of her ignored.

"Tell me what, Samiji?"


It started when she was twelve and wore thin white cotton ankle socks folded over so the lace just touched the edge of her shoes, white in summer, black in the winter. The first day they went to a horse race and a luncheon party. Louis was wearing white pants and a pale pink shirt and Phoebe had a sky blue dress that covered her knees and matched her eyes.

Thalia was in her room in the alcove before they left, and he was in there, too, Phoebe heard him from the hall, pleading, "Please, just this once come, see if you can have a good time at a party. Just give it a try."

But Thalia, clear and slow, said, "What can I possibly say to them I haven't already said a million times before?"

Phoebe shut the door of her own room, never doubting for a second the "them" refered to a national population of somewhere around eight hundred million people colored various shades of brown and white.

"What's happening?" Cully asked when she came in, but then Louis was in there, too, momentarily confused, because he looked at Cully, as Cully stared at him worshipfully, then found her and said, "You want to come with me?"

"Where?"

But he was gone.

She ran after him, her heart thundering with excitement, heard him on the stairs going down and then her mother calling, "Is that you, Phoebe?"

She dashed in.

"Want to see what I looked like?" Thalia offered her daughter a snapshot.

Phoebe looked with glazed eyes at something that had an air of prewar war, girls with bobs and expressions of surprise, all of them so much alike it took her a second to find her mother, and for a flash she felt the fear her father must have felt at being stuck with this woman.

She handed the picture back, and her mother looked up, something she didn't always do, and said, "And do be careful with your skin, dear. Her skin's so fair, Louis," she added, except that Louis wasn't there.


The racetrack was crowded and Louis took her to the lunch party afterward. People there were the usual mix of Europeans, a few Americans, and rich Indians, both those who were Westernized and the traditional. The only other girl was American, too, but she already wore makeup and had breasts, so to Phoebe she seemed years away. It never occurred to her to look for Indian girls because they were rarely allowed out except for teas and weddings and rounds of shopping with their chaperones.

She followed Louis around. He didn't pay much attention to her, seemed to assume she could take care of herself. Once he took her aside. "Want me to fix you up?"

"Clothes, you mean?"

He nodded. "Everything."

"Sure," she said, excited. "Yes."

"Think you know how to behave if you come out with me?"

"I can learn. Please, can I?"

"You won't embarrass me?"

"No."

"Because you're bored at home?"

Phoebe nodded, a bit of guilt.

"Then it's a deal. I like having people about, an entourage, you know, like Jiggie Deeg. You'll like Kady when you get to know him."

"What will people say? I'm only twelve."

"Do you care?"

"No."

"Fine," he said, and abruptly turned away.

From then on he took her almost everywhere, told Kamala what kinds of dresses the tailor had to make, how the barber was to cut her hair, and she followed happily as his shadow.

At that very first party she noticed a tall dark young man watching her.

The next time she went out with Louis, a few days later, this time for drinks at the house of a man who, people said, "invented plastics," he was there, too, a different suit this time, raw silk, standing by himself looking out a window. He was tall, dark, almost Muslim looking, and when she turned away she saw him following her with his eyes. When she moved to face him better, he had disappeared altogether. She had no idea who he was.

A week later they went to the horse races and then a dinner in honor of one of the owners. Everyone was very fashionable in their cotton saris and astrakhans, and Phoebe listened while several talked about needing a new plane, what did they think? The Lear? She moved away. She sat at one end of a couch, and he came over and sat at the other end. He didn't look at her at all.

Phoebe was eating with her fingertips. She used chapati tortillas like everyone else to hold her food and watched him with his fork and knife, the fork overturned, knife a pusher, strictly English. Finally she said, "You don't own a horse, then, do you."

He looked across at her. "Are you quite possibly talking to me?" His accent was stilted, and she had already noticed his fingers. They were big and long, meant for use inside the ground.

"I don't own a horse at the moment," he said, "but why do you ask?"

"I wasn't asking."

That's how she met K. T. Keshri Suraj.

## ❧ 7 ❧

He had fingernails that were surprisingly pink for a man so dark, and his hair was long, like Louis', only it was fashionably oiled so it lay flat along the side of his head, swept down from a part in the middle that was as clearly demarcated as a road through the woods. This lent a basic severity and seriousness to his appearance that went a long way toward offsetting its somewhat overwhelming natural beauty and elegance. His clothes were tailored with great style, although occasionally he seemed uncomfortable in them, and once, when he complained they were just too much, Louis said no, they made him look older and more sophisticated. He was only twenty-one, after all, "and if you're going to be important, you have to look important," Louis said. "Besides," he added, "you have to play by Jiggie's standards."

Kady said he felt he was just an actor or a poseur. Louis told him he was, but not to worry. He'd get used to it soon enough.

Phoebe was taken aback by what was going on. She didn't know what to make of Kady. They hadn't told her about the black market yet, or about Durr or the children—that they never would—but she wanted to know everything. When Kady told her Louis took him to his tailor two weeks after they met and showed him what to buy, she wanted to know who paid.

"He paid, but I'm going to pay him back."

132

"How?"

"I'll figure it out."

When she asked about the English lessons, he said Louis'd told him he could have an American or English accent. He'd picked American, and Louis arranged for elocution lessons and sat him through round after round of foreign movies.

She said didn't it seem strange not to be in his village anymore? He said no, he hadn't been in his village since he was little anyway. "Well, in Deeg," she said then, and he said no, he'd never felt right in Deeg. In fact, he'd never felt he belonged anywhere, and so this, being a protégé of Jiggie Deeg, his employer, and now a protégé of Louis', too, was nothing new in that regard, he was no more displaced than ever. Besides, it was helping him get where he wanted. "You can't do anything in a village," he said, "except be a better farmer. I didn't want to be a better farmer or a better bureaucrat. I wanted to be more and do more and—"

"More what?"

"Anything. I'm not sure."

"More clothes and things?"

"No," he said, surprised. "These are a waste of time. I get impatient. I want to work. I want to accomplish things. If I could be great," he added, shy all of a sudden, "I would be."

"Then you have to study," Phoebe advised.

"I know."

Louis had tutors for him for business, international affairs, everything. Kady wanted Jiggie to send him to the elite Indian Institute of Technology so he could be an engineer. Louis said that was too ambitious for now. "You'll have to persuade them to accept someone who never went to school after the age of fourteen," he said. "They'll never do that unless Jiggie Deeg tells them to, and he'll never do it unless you show him what you can do first. You have to take him on," he continued, talking one night when they were driving around Delhi in the backseat of the white Ford car. "You have to compete at what he knows best. You have to show him what your mind can do. You have to give him ideas for Deeg. For everything. If you aren't sophisticated and don't give him things he isn't getting someplace else, you'll get nowhere with him. Besides," he added ominously, "if you ever want to break away from him one day, you've got to be bloody daring."

The black market operation started on a very small basis a few months after Louis and Kady met. That they eventually let Phoebe know about it never struck her as surprising. It seemed natural; she did everything else with them, why not that? She went out as much as four or five nights a week and did whatever they did, so why not share the carton boxes and the smuggled whiskey? Why not count money and wait for shipments? They operated like there was barely any danger anyway, although she knew there was, but in their minds there was no risk to them, so why should there be risk to her?

For Phoebe it started one night when they unexpectedly drove to a place she'd never seen. There was no preamble or explanation; Louis just gave Samiji the address. They parked in the shadows and Samiji shut off the engine. A moment's lull before they left the car gave Phoebe a hint something was afoot. Outside, she looked up at the building with rather more care than usual. It was five stories high, tall for this part of Delhi, and had stairs front and back, the back for servants, she knew, and as they walked in through the hall and up to the second floor, she wondered where they were going because it wasn't a place where friends lived. It was too ordinary, too middle class, just cement blocks piled one on top of the other.

Kady, ahead, called out to Louis that this was just like the apartment where he used to live. "Remember?"

"Only yours was bigger and had all those bloody rooms and magazines," Louis said

"What do you mean?" Phoebe asked.

"Jesus, Kady," her father went on, "I knew the truth about you the minute I saw you in the middle of that goddamn room. Just like I knew this country like the back of my hand the minute I got off that goddamn plane. Came here for the night and knew I'd be back."

Ahead, Kady had opened the door to the apartment and was holding it for Phoebe. His eyes were on her, and she knew something big was happening. She looked at him questioningly.

He gave her a reassuring expression and urged her inside.

There she saw cartons and cartons of whiskey. They were piled all over the room, in some places as high as the ceiling.

There was no furniture, just an overhead light, a fan, and boxes.

"Don't worry," Kady said, "I'll explain later. There's nothing to be afraid of. I'll look out for you."

He told Phoebe it was Louis' idea. It had grown out of a series of conversations in which Louis pushed him to figure out how he could get enough money to pay him back for all his clothes and tutoring and also establish his independence from Jiggie Deeg. For that, especially, he needed money, at least if he wanted to meet his own ambitions. Everybody knew you couldn't do anything in India unless you had enough money to live in a certain style and could bribe your way to what you wanted.

At Louis' prodding, Kady came up with the idea of the black market, using Louis' high-level diplomatic connections to bring things in in the diplomatic pouch and his own low-level Indian ones to do the work and front the operation.

"Aren't you scared by the idea?" Kady asked Louis once.

"No," Louis said, "and neither are you. You live on the edge anyway."

I knew Kady Suraj socially long before Phoebe or Cully came back to India. I saw him at receptions and once at a wedding when the family was rumored to have spent over a million dollars and we talked about the extravagance. Then, a couple of months before Phoebe returned, we were at a dinner party together. He was wearing a black dinner jacket, cummerbund, and tie, and even though we only exchanged pleasantries, he was by far and away the most interesting person there. I found myself acutely aware of him and realized he stood out in my mind like a bachelor on the loose.

Not because Durr wasn't there; she never was. Plenty of women here don't socialize, even at the highest levels. They rarely go out except to shop. That night there was at once a restlessness and a calm to Kady that made him stand apart from the stereotype of other men whose wives were at home. I felt he was available sexually.

He seemed distracted. He picked up hors d'oeuvres, put them

down uneaten. He didn't look like he was listening to the conversations or participating more than necessary. He excused himself to make phone calls, which is understandable in a man of his position, but, somehow, he seemed all nerves. Like he'd rather be free to pace up and down unobstructed. I asked the hostess, was he always like this? and she said, "All he thinks about is work. He's much too serious for his own good."

But that wasn't what I meant.

Eventually some late arrivals showed up and as one couple came in the room, I saw him look, obviously surprised, at the woman. He clearly knew her, and she him, but hadn't been expecting her. From then on, however, he was more relaxed. It made perfect sense, given the two of them, because she was beautiful. But she was also more: she was conspicuously available.

She had a maroon-colored tikka right between her eyebrows and a choli under her sari that was as low cut as anything I'd seen in so-called polite company. Most telling of all, she made eye contact. Women here don't. They're not meant to look at a man but instead to look away first, bat the eyes a bit, establish their good character, and then proceed, carefully, to build a relationship. After that, they can establish eye contact, but holding it too long is taken as proof of bad intentions and is even the hallmark of a prostitute.

I noticed this about the woman right away when she looked at my husband, full in the eyes, the kind of thing that's all very second nature to Americans. My husband gave me a knowing wink.

Then she did it with Suraj. I was fascinated. It was a frank invitation. Plenty of married women have affairs in India, but you never never never, heaven help you, see signs of it. Any misstep and a woman's scandal accrues to the entire family, daughters sullied, marriage negotiations out. Only an astronomical dowry can change the fate, if that.

At dinner Kady was seated directly across the table from me. The woman was beside him.

The subject of corruption came up, it invariably does when any two people talk about government, and here the man on one side of me was talking to the man on the other side, laughing, all very in the know, about how everyone had two sets of records, one white, the other black. I wondered if Kady would inject himself because if he was known for anything, it was reform, technology and anticorruption, but he paid no attention. He was talking to the woman.

I tried to overhear what they were saying. I was convinced they were having an affair. There was a sense of privacy between them, the way their shoulders touched and that they ignored the people around them. His hand was even out of sight below the table for long periods of time, and I could only imagine what it was doing there.

Then when everyone was saying good-bye she stood with her husband, a short chubby millionaire she'd married for virtually no dowry, her beauty for his wealth, and she barely paid Suraj any mind at all. That was confirmation enough for me. Otherwise she'd have been more cordial.

The episode made me believe Kady did have affairs, and plenty of them. Because while the woman was beautiful, she was clearly beneath him, not worthy of a prolonged relationship, she was just not interesting enough. I asumed she had to be one of many.

The evening gave me a real feeling of the loneliness of Kady Suraj.

A few days later I went to the embassy library to see what I could learn about him. There were lots of articles about how he'd done this and that, flood relief and programs for immigrants coming in from rural regions, persistent efforts to introduce solar energy and new types of technology. In one he complained that during a drought he finally had to turn to UNICEF in Paris to find out how many well drilling rigs India had because here tradition, local politics, and caste got in the way of information sharing and he couldn't find out any other way.

Mostly I learned about his relationship with Jiggie Deeg—that Jiggie had sponsored him at the Institute of Technology, sent him to England for a couple of years to study, and brokered him into politics at the national level.

According to a piece in a local political magazine, their relationship had turned uncertain in recent years and less was known about it than before. "The two are believed to have had no contact since the former maharaja renounced eight years ago," the article said. "But Deeg still wields immense influence in capital circles, and his support from far-off Benares will still affect, even determine, what happens to Suraj. Suraj got into politics knowing he had the maharaja's backing, and the common wisdom is that he won't—maybe even can't—go on forever without it. Deeg's position on this is unclear. The matter has not been raised, but when Hari Narayan, Chief of Public Works, retires next year, the matter of Suraj's future will be front and center. Oddly, both his strength and his liability is Jiggie Deeg."

# ❧ 8 ❧

For Louis, Phoebe, and Kady Suraj, that was a time, over twenty years ago, of drink parties and weddings, receptions and dinners. Phoebe had her place at the table, same as everyone else, India receptive to any eccentric as long as he was as rich and entertaining and foreign as Louis Guthrie. Kady kept up with his lessons and his work, but at night he became part of this stream of events that tied him together with Louis and his daughter, always with the same set of people Delhi had thrust up to the top. Some hadn't worried about money in centuries, others had newfound riches and heli-copters to prove it.

"This is India," Louis declared one night as they headed along a darkened road. "Don't forget it, Kady. It tolerates anything and everything in others it doesn't tolerate in itself."

"What's that mean?" Phoebe asked.

"He's warning me," Kady said. "It means I have to be careful about everything I do because I'm too bizarre to begin with to be out of step about anything else. He also means," he added, "that he's free and I'm not."

"But we're working on that," Louis went on gaily. "One way or the other, your declaration of independence is coming."

Samiji sped along through the streets, paper and garbage blowing up against the windshield. "Look at that," Louis cried

139

as they passed a colony of people, none bigger than a good-size child. "Have you ever seen anything like it?

"Feel that cold?" he asked, opening the window and sticking out his arm. "People are bought and sold here. Money will buy you anything, Kady."


They drove down to Agra one night, just to see the Taj Mahal, a narrow road that went through town after town and was clogged with bullock carts and trucks even at that late hour. Another time Louis bribed a guard to open the National Museum and they went through and looked at the art, inspired by its calm and serenity.

"Learn from that," he said to Kady, pointing to a deity with its magnificent pose and peacefulness.

Kady and Phoebe exchanged knowing glances, an open secret among the three that Louis'd had nothing to do with art until Kady led him to it.

Other times they drove to the airport and watched planes coming in from Tokyo and New York, one, they knew, with their contraband aboard. And often Louis took them to the veranda of the Imperial Hotel, where he sat them out on the very same steps where he'd sat his first nights in India long ago.

"It was the mosquitoes," he said one time. "It was the sky," he said another. "The heat. God, was it hot."

"But you loved it, right, Louis?" Phoebe asked.

He laughed. "No one but an imbecile would love this place. At least that's what my damned wife says."

But if he complained and railed against Thalia, he rarely mentioned Cully.

Phoebe knew he was ashamed of his son, her brother, how meek and awkward he was, thoroughly nondescript but for his looks. Cully seemed almost repulsive to him, as if he was the thing Louis feared the most, a pitiful creature who couldn't lift his head above the road. It got so bad between them that Cully never talked in his presence, just stared at him, and Louis curled his mouth whenever his name came up.

Phoebe didn't mention Cully, either. But she took great comfort in the fact that she thought her brother's life on Jumna Road had in fact improved since she started going out with Louis. She told herself it took the pressure off him and noticed that he didn't cry as much. He was eating more, two meals a day sometimes, and at night when Phoebe left, he always said he was going to miss her, but he seemed generally happier than before.

Often he was asleep at the window when she came home, waiting there to see her car pull in, his arm curled up on the shelf, his head down, hair fallen in his face.

In the room she changed for bed, then nudged him awake. "Cully," she whispered. Sometimes she knelt first and kissed him on the cheek or brushed his hair up out of his eyes, and when he woke up he always looked at her with something like pain at first, then, relieved, crawled into bed.

In the morning when he woke up, she sat on his bed and told him everything. How they'd driven around looking for hippies strung out on the sidewalks or bands of eunuchs wearing lipstick and skirts, singing in the streets. She told him stories, names, places. He soaked it in. Sat up in bed wide-eyed and stared at her, India coming alive for him, too. If he felt left out, it never showed.

Louis' first piece of art was the Shiva Nataraj. After that he accrued art with intensity and they sat with Vishnu Bhave in his storefront shop time after time. They drank tea with a cardamom seed while Bhave or his son, Anant, brought out things for Louis to see. A little god an inch or two tall or something so big only a sheet would protect it from the eye.

But Kady didn't like their visits there. "Don't you like art?" Louis asked him once.

"Of course," Kady said. "I just can't stand Vishnu Bhave, and neither should you. He's too close to Jiggie Deeg."

Some nights they didn't do anything at all. A pall came down over the house on Jumna Road. Phoebe and Cully ate in the kitchen. Louis stayed in his room, depression settling over him so even the servants were scared to take him food, Phoebe had to do it. And Thalia stayed away, out with her babies.

All because Kady wouldn't leave wherever it was he lived and he was the force holding them together.

Kady wouldn't go to Deeg or go to work or even make it to the phone. He never left his house. Once Samiji told Phoebe it was because Kumari-sa'ab Durr-sa'ab was away.

Another time he told her Kady-sa'ab was sunk down in a pit where Indians never never never wanted to go. Phoebe got scared. Samiji told her Indians were afraid of solitude.

"But he's not alone," she argued. "He has his wife."

Samiji only shrugged.

Then Louis would get a call and it started up again.


By November, the year before Louis and Thalia died, everything began to unravel. Phoebe turned sixteen. Louis rarely went to work at all, and Mr. Smith, the CEO, stood in for him full-time. Then one night they were at a party not far from the Prime Minister's house. Cars were coming and going up the block, and people were milling on the lawn in coats, it was winter. Suddenly Kady told Louis and Phoebe he'd made a decision. He knew he couldn't go on "with" Jiggie, he said, although he hadn't yet decided how to make the break. But it was coming, he said. It was only a matter of days or weeks until he figured out exactly what to do.

Unexpectedly, Louis proposed that he himself be the one to "make the deal" with Jiggie.

"No," Kady cried explosively. "You can't."

"But I have an advantage. I'm his equal."

"I said absolutely not."

"But I know all the facts, yet I'm not part of it."

"I don't want you talking to him," Kady said with unusual intensity.

"All right, all right," Louis said, throwing up his hands and laughing, in case anyone was watching. "Why would I want to talk to the old Jig himself anyway?"


But Kady didn't make the break, and the last couple of months were terrible, for him and for Louis. It got so a dread settled over Kady whenever Jiggie was in town. He said Deeg House repelled him. Louis told him not to do anything rash. One night Samiji drove them over to the huge white mansion with balconies and gardens and they parked in the shadows, none of them ever invited inside the tout monde there.

"Don't you hate it?" Kady said.

"Yes," Louis answered. "But I'm getting back at him through you. You'll hurt him better than I ever could." Then he told Samiji to drive around. "Anywhere," he slurred. He'd drunk too much.

They drove for what must have been an hour or two. Phoebe was very aware of Kady, how he brooded now. She saw Samiji watching him, too, in the car mirror. She wanted to ask him why Kady didn't just go home. But she knew he'd explain for the umpteenth time that no Indian ever wants to be alone, "because he's afraid he'll be—" and then he'd use the Hindi word for overwhelmed and swamped.

"Overwhelmed by what?" she'd ask.

"By all the peoples. So many peoples. Very greatest fear Indian has. Being lost alone in all these peoples. Only family and caste saves you from this fear."

The night wore on. They drove past India Gate and up and down through the streets of Old Delhi, where near as many people slept outdoors as inside. Phoebe thought about how she used to sleep in places like these herself and how last week Kady'd talked about how he'd gone to Deeg just to take a wedding sari to Jiggie's daughter, who was getting married, but first he'd had to go to Benares to get the sari.

"What does he think I am?" Kady said suddenly, breaking the silence in the car.

Phoebe leaned forward to look at him across her father's lap.

"But what do I think I am?" he went on, talking to no one in particular. "I left my village, my father, my community. I gave up everything. And for what? To be his errand boy? Louis, you tell me," he said. "What's my duty? I'm Sudra caste. I must be farmer, husband to my wife, father to my children."

"Why don't you just leave him?" Phoebe asked.

"Oh, Feeb," he said, looking back at her with sudden softness and attention. "Don't ask me. It's not that simple. You know I can't tell you."

"But—"

" 'Duty,' " Louis interrupted in a drunken but formal tone,

"You ask what duty is, Kady will tell you. It's what you must do. It's obligation to family and to caste. It's the only way you can fulfill your caste obligations and be assured rebirth on a higher plane."

"Do you understand, Feeb?" Kady said. "It's the only way I can belong."

"But, Jesus," Louis cried, "you gave up that bullshit years ago. You knew the price you were paying. You knew what you were doing when you set it up with that two-bit king. Leave him, if you want, but don't regret what you've done."

Kady leaned back in the seat. "It was a bargain I should never have made."

"So just break it and forget it. I did," Louis added abruptly.

"Did what?" Phoebe asked.

"Give up more than he thought," Kady said. "He's talking about your mother."

"Get away from him," Louis mumbled. "Get it over with, any way you can."

Samiji took a puff on a bidi cigarette, then opened the window to drop it out. Phoebe closed her eyes and thought about the girl in Deeg who was about to be a bride. They were the same age.

She leaned forward to look at Kady again. "Aren't you better off without 'duty'? So you can just be what you want?"

Kady smiled at her. "I'm Indian. I want to belong, whatever your father says, but maybe I have given up my chance." He took out one of his little cinnamon cigarettes and lit it. The scent hovered in the car. A cow came up in front, blocking the road. Samiji backed up and drove around it.

Louis started talking, his words slurred. "That woman has chewed me up and spit me out." He paused, nudged Kady. "You still want the answer to your question?"

Kady nodded.

"You'll know what your duty is when you know what it is. It'll come to you. It's as simple as that. Believe me. You'll get a sign. You Indians are like that. You just bloody know." Then Louis slapped his hand on the young man's knee and laughed. "What am I? Can't figure anything out for myself, but I can . . ." He drifted off again.

Kady opened the window and breathed deeply. Phoebe could smell it, too, India and the dust, the odor of refuse, the scent of wood and fire. Kady looked at her from time to time, she looked back, Samiji made a U-turn in the street, and they headed home.

The next night she asked Kady, "What does Durr say when you talk to her about duty?"

"I don't talk to her," he said.

## ❧ 9 ❧

BY EARLY DECEMBER CULLY HAD
a cold and stayed home for days, seldom went to school. Phoebe
believed it was because she'd moved her bed to the other side of
the room, wanting privacy for herself, and now he clung to the
room obsessively, his primary link to her. She had tried lipstick
by now and wished she had a bra, and while Kamala would read
aloud to them in Hindi from her position on the floor, she would
lie back on the bed and think about the ironies in her life. How
the ayah had bought her "the necessary" a few years back, one
month's supply a time, and asked her was she sure she knew
what she must never do, even though she would never do it?
Phoebe had said yes. Then Kamala had reminded her that at
sixteen Indian girls got married and had babies. Phoebe felt
miserable. By sixteen American girls had probably already lost
their virginity, and she hadn't even been kissed. She was still
wearing the low, flat shoes of a child.

Mostly, though, she spent her time worrying about Louis. She
didn't go to school much anymore, either, and everything was
even more strange around the house than usual. Louis spent all
day now downstairs. He drank and brooded, Thalia upstairs
in her room or out with the babies, he below with the Shiva
Nataraj.

146

"Hell, I'd give the whole collection up," he told Phoebe one day when she looked in on him. "Keep the Shiva Nataraj and still be proud."


Mid-December Louis was drinking at the bar in the Gym-khana Club and Phoebe was in a corner, feeling sad. Kady had gone to get them salty lemon drinks. Now, as she faced the wall, she heard him coming back. She smelled the cinnamon, and suddenly he touched her. He took her by the shoulder and was slowly turning her around, when he shouldn't by rights be touching her at all. It didn't seem strange at first, because they were just looking at each other, but then he put his hand on her face and held it and said, "You look so sad."

A piano was playing in the background, and a man with an accordion took over and was holding the notes longer than he should, so they trembled, sending uneasy, sentimental sounds out over the room. Kady moved his hand in soft circles on her cheek, then touched her lips with his finger, when he'd barely ever touched her before at all. "Phoebe," he said.

That was all. But she held her breath, and he traced his finger around her mouth. Her eyes began to fill with tears.

"What is it?" he asked, letting his finger drop.

She shook her head.

"Tell me," he whispered.

"He doesn't have anything to say to me, and she doesn't, either. If it weren't for Kamala I wouldn't even—"

"What happened?"

"Nothing, that's just it. Sometimes I go in there and she's reading and she doesn't even know I'm there."

Kady looked out toward the accordion player, then looked back and put his hand on her cheek again, wiping her eyes with his fingers. "I just want to touch you," he said.

"I'm all right," she said as he removed his hand.

The accordion player stopped, and someone in a booth nearby offered a toast in Hindi to a bride and groom.

"At least you and I are friends," she said.

"Has anyone ever touched you, Feeb?"

She watched his eyes, dark brown rimmed with a darker color, study her face.

"Tell me."

"Who would there be but you?"

"You'll tell me, won't you, Feeb?"

She nodded. "What about Durr?"

"What about her?"

"Does she know we're friends?"

Kady didn't answer, just rubbed his fingertips against hers along a glass.

"Does she?"

"She knows everything," he said at last.


"Look at that face of hers."

It was a few days later and the voice was loud and Indian, and thinking back, Phoebe remembered music. There was always music in India, except at Number Nine Jumna Road. This time it was violins with their whiny sound, and there was a breeze and a great big shamiana tent, and somewhere inside it, a bride whose name she barely knew, a girl who'd been washed in buttermilk and brushed with leaves and twigs, sat with her fiancé. Out here people were talking, lights and flares, and now, right up close, someone was dancing.

"You got trouble on your hands, Louis," the voice was saying. "Next wedding better be hers. Girl's not so cold as she tries to be. You tell him, Suraj."

She remembered a scent of cinnamon and the movement of someone dancing.

"He'll believe it from you," the man said.

"He knows it," Kady said.

In the memory she couldn't see Kady but she could feel him, close and strong, and her father dancing by himself, a glass in one hand. The air carried the scent of food and fire. The bride was even now sitting in front of the fire, her legs crossed, her head and body hidden under pounds of gold and cloth, a virgin who'd walk seven times around the fire before the night was out, purity changing over into impurity, one more life launched, Indians believed, from the bedrock of a childhood.

The night was special. It was the first and only time she'd ever met Durr Suraj. Phoebe and Louis had walked in together from the car. Kady hadn't driven with them. But then, suddenly, there he was at the entrance, turning and saying he wanted to introduce her to someone.

A little thing was all she was, standing beside him. She only came up to his chest, had a veil across her hair. Phoebe couldn't see her face.

"Phoebe," Kady said, "this is Durr."

The woman was only several years older than Phoebe, and Phoebe reeled in a kind of awe. She was beautiful, but it was more than that. She had thick dark hair, red lips, high cheekbones, and skin as sheer as light itself, but the most startling thing of all was that Phoebe felt drawn to her, overwhelmingly, as if she were a beloved aunt or sister, trusted to the depths. The woman's eyes, big and clear and soft, were welcoming too, eager to take Phoebe in as well.

"Say something," Louis barked.

"She has orange eyes," Phoebe stammered.

The woman pulled the sari across her face so she was hidden behind the filmy silk. So traditional was the move that Phoebe was startled by her shyness but she could still see her eyes, back behind the cloth, studying her intensely.


Kady and his wife disappeared in the swarm of people. Phoebe peered through the crowds, looking for another glimpse of Durr. Why had she come, why tonight when she'd never come out before? And why did she seem so interested in her, a girl six years her junior?


A few hours later Phoebe was watching her father dancing on the veranda of the house. His eyes were closed, his back bent as if he was turning in toward someone who wasn't there, and then she spotted Durr sitting with the women inside the house. Men were on one side of the room, women on the other, in a row of chairs, their saris hanging from their knees like rolls of cloth. Durr seemed out of place, dressed in an old-fashioned, if expensive, sari, her hair attractive but not stylish.

Around her neck were what seemed like yards of pearls and emeralds. Phoebe was amazed. Where had those come from? Did Kady have such things to give?

Then the memory of Durr faded and Phoebe found herself someplace else, and the man was saying, "You tell Louis about the girl, Kady. A word to the wise. A stitch in time saves nine," and she had turned to watch her father.

Her father made her sad.

Phoebe could still feel that sadness twenty years later, sitting that day in May in her hotel room high above the street, waves of emotion coming across her as she remembered yet another encounter with Durr that night when Durr appeared for the first and only time.

"He's coming apart, Phoebe," Durr was saying. "I have to talk to you. You have to be careful of them."

And Phoebe had asked, "Who?" but that's as far as the memory went right then. Back on her bed in the hotel room, Phoebe knew she didn't want to think about what Durr had said and who was coming apart. Not yet.

Instead she remembered the man's voice saying, "Tell him, Kady."

And herself looking up, twenty years ago, and seeing Louis.

"Get me another drink, Feeb," he had said.

"I can't. I'm talking to Durr."

Then Louis went away.

"You hear that?" the man said to Suraj, chuckling. "I do love those two Guthries. No one'll ever get the best of that girl."

"Phoebe, I must talk to you."

It was Durr again.

"Oh, shut up," Kady said to the man, "and go away."

"I must talk to you," the older girl said.

But Phoebe didn't want to think about it. She got up off the bed and washed her face.

The night after the wedding they made the rounds again, two men and a girl, a brief stop to check the perfume, scarves, and cigarettes that had just come in on a plane that flew from Colombia to Paris to India. Phoebe kept thinking about last night's bride. She would have come out of the bedroom this morning and stretched her arms for her husband's family to see how many bangles were still there and thus know how many lay broken in the bed inside. Proof they wanted of what had gone on in there. Proof they had even before the servant brought out the sheets, virgin blood for everyone to see.

Samiji drove them through the dark, past bicycles and bullock carts. They were headed for a poker game. Finally they pulled in through a long driveway, crowded with guards and jeeps. Inside, the table was covered with green felt, just as it always was, and four men were there. She knew them all. "Make room, make room," the host was saying, fluttering hands willing chairs to move. A raja at the table was holding up a string of jewels, diamonds and rubies so big they looked like fruits, and Kady, his eyes alight, told him he shouldn't gamble with those, they were too precious, but the man just scoffed. Plenty more where those came from.

Phoebe said, "Can I play too tonight? With sticks, of course?" They agreed and she sat down.

"I trust you're not going to talk about your wife again," someone said to Louis. "For God's sake, you used to be more fun."

Phoebe looked at her father and tried to will him to sit up straight, but he just looked depressed and said, "I can't stand your mother."

"Don't talk to me about it."

"She'll get me one day, Feeb."

"Don't say it."

"She will. She'll have me round the neck so tight I'll . . ."

A bearer opened a window. The game went on. Phoebe could hear the cold wind blowing in through the trees and remembered how the rain had flooded out a colony some time back, hundreds pushed by a wall of water and debris into the people living just behind, and those who weren't drowned were killed in the melee that came afterward. There was a paragraph about it in the paper.

Later she excused herself and went to lie on the couch. She heard others excuse themselves, too, and she watched her father and Kady. Sometimes Kady looked across at her and she knew for the first time that she loved him. The feeling was so strong, she wondered how she'd missed it before.

She also knew he was determined to win those jewels.

She awoke near morning. Kady was shaking her shoulder. "Get up," he said excitedly. "I've won."

And that's how Kady Suraj got the necklace that belonged to a Mysore raja. Proceeds from its sale helped set him free of Jiggie Deeg.


In her hotel room, the telephone rang.

Phoebe went over to the table by the bed and picked up the receiver. It was almost dawn outside. Birds were up, crows cawing in the trees, cars honking in the streets below.

## ❧ 10 ❧

"Miss Guthrie?"

"Yes?"

"I am Kuldip Ramchandran." She recognized his voice; she'd heard it before somewhere.

"I am calling to express to you the most enthusiastic welcome to India from Deputy Minister Suraj."

Phoebe's heart started pounding.

"He is sending you the most gracious good wishes and asking me to convey his apologies for being out of town and unable to see you. He is wanting most strenuously—"

She sat down on the bed.

"—to know how long you will be here."

"When is he coming back? I need to talk to him."

"Business takes him away from—"

"But I need to get in to see the body in the morgue. They won't let me in. Not until six o'clock tonight. I've been waiting for almost two days. Can you get me in?"

"I know Mr. Suraj is eager to know your fullest plans and intentions."

"But I need him to help me right now," Phoebe said. "I can't wait all that time. Besides, I'm not staying very long. When will he be back?"

Mr. Ramchandran didn't answer.

153

"Can you call the morgue for him?"

"I will have to consider this possibility."

"What's there to consider? He went to see the body. I know he'll want you to take charge and make the morgue let me in. Tell him he must do this for me."

As soon as she hung up, the phone rang again.

It was Harriet MacDonald. "Sorry to wake you, but did Suraj call?"

"No."

"I hear he's in town after all, and I'm trying to locate him. As far as I can figure out, he probably got your message yesterday."

"Someone else just called for him."

"What'd he say?"

"Nothing, really. So Kady is here after all?" Phoebe asked, confused.

"Yes."

The day after the poker game Louis didn't go to work and she didn't go to school. Cully stayed home, too. It was colder than the night before. Samiji told her Kady had gone to Deeg for the night, Jiggie's daughter was getting married in a month and there was a lot to do.

That afternoon Phoebe met with Vikrim Ali Seth. He liked to ride his bicycle after school, so that's what they often did, but today it was too cold and they crowded into a pedicab, their knees and legs pressed in together. It was so cold he had to put his arm around her to keep her warm. They had tea at a stall, but there was nothing to talk about, so they broke up sweet orange jelabis and ate them until he said, "Shall we go home?" and she said, "Yes."

The next day Kady was back, so they all went out, Samiji driving. It was the last night.

It was the last night of all for them together. They didn't know it then—although they might have, from the feel of things—and talking about it in November on Kitty Chandradas' veranda, Phoebe remembered looking out at the rounded dome of Nizamuddin's Tomb as they passed it in the dark. She had new shoes on, long, shiny, black, with heels half inch off the ground.

"She's too involved," Kady said irritably as the car drove toward the house in Golf Links. "The black market is no place for her. We've got to stop taking her with us."

"Then she's been too involved for years," Louis argued. "What's the difference now?"

"We have to be careful. It's one thing for us to get caught. It's her whole life."

"Be quiet, both of you," Phoebe said impatiently. "Let's just do what we have to do and get it over with."

The car reached its destination and they got out. Kady looked tired. He was always tired after he came back from Deeg, but this time he had shadows under his eyes and she could tell he hadn't slept at all down there.

Louis insisted on carrying the suitcase full of money. Kady told her to go on ahead and get inside the house, but she hung back, stayed with him.

The lights were on and Kady's man, Kuldip, was waiting at the door. He had sandals with socks on and said he was cold. Kady told him it was all in his mind and went upstairs. Phoebe followed, smelling cinnamon as she went. The rooms were bare, just cases of whiskey piled everywhere. They went from room to room, checking labels. They were alone, but being in the house at all was dangerous, even though it was shielded by trees and a fence.

"Phoebe," Kady finally said, and stopped right in front of her, "we have to talk." They were in a small room with a sloped ceiling, a child's room, boxes stacked under the window and along the wall, and outside she could hear Louis crawling slowly up the stairs on his hands and knees.

"It smells in here," Louis yelled up, his voice echoing in the stairwell.

"Phoebe . . ." Kady wore a suit and sweater, the scarf she'd knitted him around his neck.

"It's your damn cigarettes," came his voice again.

Kady pressed her arm, then let go. "Everything seems strange, doesn't it?"

She nodded.

There were stereos out in the hall left over from last week and the shades hadn't been pulled down; the sky outside was black. The room was small and airless, but intimate. She looked at him. "Was Deeg bad?"

"Jiggie got mad."

"Did you get fired?"

"Fired?" he said, surprised. "No, it wasn't like that. He can't fire me."

"Why not?"

"I'll tell you, soon. I promise. But, Jesus, I never realized you were so old. You used to be just a child."

Phoebe felt unsettled, even scared. "Do you think he'll be all right?"

"Louis? No." He shook his head. There was no sound from the hall. Kady went out to look at him, came back, and they stood close again, boxes piled up behind them. "He's sitting on the stairs."

"Maybe he's sick."

"I wouldn't be surprised if he killed himself, Feeb. I worry about him all the time."

"He doesn't have a gun."

"He does. I was with him when he bought it. A month ago."

"I don't think he'd have the courage to use it on himself."

"I don't want to scare you, but—"

"You never scare me."

"But I think that's why he might do it," Kady said. "Just to prove he has the courage. To do something, at least."

"Why does he have to prove something?"

"He can't leave Thalia. He can't leave India. His job's in trouble. He's lost too much money at poker."

They were quiet. "I think about you all the time now," Kady said, his voice low. "I've never known a woman, or a girl, like I do you."

"What about Durr?"

"That's different."

"Why?"

"Because I see you every night. I eat with you, talk with you. Jiggie's daughter is marrying a man she's never even met, and she's sixteen."

Phoebe shivered.

"Are you cold?"

She shook her head, but her arms were bare, her sweater in the car.

"Want my jacket?"

"No."

"I like your new shoes."

She rubbed her arms.

"Durr says you shouldn't be doing this," he said.

"But you shouldn't, either. What if Jiggie found out?" She gestured toward the whiskey.

"He knows everything anyway."

Phoebe sat on one of the cartons. He sat beside her.

"We should go downstairs," she said. "They'll be coming."

"I wish we could stay here forever. Stop time."

"I never liked this house," she said. "I don't like any of these places. When they're empty . . . I don't know. I wonder who lived in them before, what they were like, where the people went. Don't you ever feel that?"

"Not really."

"And I feel haunted by the missing people, even though I don't know them. Does that make any sense? If there was furniture, it'd be different. And I wonder if there were ever children, maybe a brother and a sister." She could hear Louis. He was humming on the stairs, maybe it was a groan.

"Sometimes when I'm alone I imagine you talking to me," Kady said. "What you'd say."

"No one lives the way I do," Phoebe went on. "They go to school, talk to their mother, and in America they probably go to the beach and have boyfriends, and someone my age would have a bank account. Here—"

"Kady?"

"Coming, Louis. Go on," he said to her urgently.

"If I ever have children, how can I explain all this? It's such a strange life we have. What would I say? That I had no friends but two men?"

"Don't tell them."

"Oh, I couldn't do that."

"If you were Indian, you'd be married."

"I want ten children. Come on." Phoebe stood reluctantly. "We've got to go. This is getting dangerous. They'll be here any minute."

"Finish counting, then."

She left him, counting boxes, her assigned job, and when she came back in the little room, he was still there. "There's only one hundred and twenty-one," she said, starting toward the stairs. "Nine are missing."

"Wait, Feeb. I don't want to leave yet."

"Neither do I."

He came to her and took her hands, started moving his hand up and down her arm. "You feel so wonderful."

Phoebe shivered.

"You feel it?"

She nodded.

"Do you?" he whispered.

She nodded again.

"That's my kiss. Feel it?"

"Yes."

"Promise?"

"Yes," she whispered.

"For as long as . . ."

She nodded.

He gripped her hand. "Then let's get going," he said. "We don't want it all to end right here getting arrested, do we?" He was smiling now, as though something had changed, shifted. He started down the stairs. She heard him step over Louis and reach the bottom.

"Everything okay, sa'ab?" she heard his man Kuldip ask. She didn't want to leave. Maybe she sensed this was the last night.

"Phoebe?" Kady called.

"Coming."

At the stairwell she looked down at her father and felt a lurch in her stomach. He was curled up, head against the wall, groaning. She stared at him. "Ready to go?" she finally asked, her voice almost inaudible from the pain of seeing how bad he was.

He sat up, slid down several steps on his fanny, and stopped, embarrassed. "Jesus, Feeb. Give us a hand."

Kady came to the bottom of the stairs and suddenly Phoebe started to cry. "Kady . . ."

"It's okay," he said softly. "Help him."

She started down. Tears were pouring out of her eyes. "You want to use the bathroom, Daddy?" She stopped beside him and put her hand on his shoulder, then suddenly she sat on the stairs

158

and wrapped her arms tight around his chest. "Oh, Daddy," she said. "Daddy, Daddy."

"There's no water, remember?" he said. "Can't use a john without water."

"You can go outside," she said, clinging tighter to him and staring down at Kady all the while. He was watching them, Phoebe with her face in her father's hair. Then Louis started to get up, pull away from her. He slipped out of her grasp and slid the rest of the way down the stairs. She bent her head and started weeping fully. Louis was in a heap, trying to push himself up with his hands.

Kady went to him. "Come on, Louis," he said. "I've made my decision."

"You have?"

"I'm going to break the whole thing off. Finish it. As soon as I can."

"You are?" Louis hoisted himself up.

"Leave everything. Durr, Deeg, politics. Start over."

Kady was terribly serious, even grim, like the weight wasn't fully off. Phoebe knew his words were meant for her.

Suddenly Louis saluted him, and it all went comic, because he looked a little silly in his drunken pose. Kady started to smile in spite of himself.

"Congratulations, sa'ab," Louis was saying. "So you got your sign? Told you. Didn't I? You're rich now. You can buy anything. That necklace did the trick."

Kady shuddered in distaste.

"Stop," Phoebe said. "We're all nervous, we've got to get out of here. Where did you put the suitcase, Kady? I have to pay the driver. It's time to leave. People will be coming any second. You don't want to be here, do you? Let them see your face?"

He shook his head. "She's right."

"It's in the kitchen," Louis said.

She found the suitcase and started counting out rupees. In the other room Louis was laughing. "It's life," he said. "You take your best shot and in the end you get shot down anyway."

"Not me," Kady said, a sureness to his voice she'd never heard before.

But she was thinking about money and the whiskey now because there were one hundred and twenty-one cases upstairs, which meant nine had been stolen, everyone on the take, even truck drivers. She went out on the lawn. The truck driver was crouched down on his ankles, smoking a little brown bidi. He jumped up when she approached. She handed him the money, smelling the bidi on his breath. She planned to ask him about the missing boxes, instead she just said, "Thank you."

"What are you doing here?" he asked in Hindi. He reached to touch her hair.

She pulled back.

Louis came to the door, leaning against the frame. The man turned away, headed back into the Indian darkness.

"Let's get in the car," Louis said. "See it happen."

"We should leave. It's not safe. We can get the money from Kuldip tomorrow."

Kady came out. "Let's hurry." She could feel his tension. He shut the door of the house, Kuldip still inside, and ushered Phoebe to the car, holding her by the elbow. Then he got in, pulled Louis in after him, and because Louis insisted, Samiji drove over into the shadows, backed the car up against the hedge, and they waited.

"Had enough, Louis?" Kady said in a minute, impatient. "Let's leave before they come. Anything could go wrong."

They were in the backseat. She could hear Kady breathing, feel his arm pressed up against hers.

Louis took a drink from a bottle on the seat. "They won't see us. Who'd think of looking here?"

"You sure he's all right?" Kady asked nervously.

"Samiji? Of course he's all right. Never hear a word, do you, Samiji?"

"Right, sa'ab."

Then Kady came closer so that his arm touched hers, and with his right hand he began a slow-moving caress up along her bare arm, past her breast, and down, slowly, not as if he had any plans, but as though he couldn't keep away. She could barely breathe.

"Got the suitcase, Feeb?" her father asked.

She thought of Vikrim Ali Seth.

"Phoebe . . ." Kady was looking down at her. "This can't go on," he whispered, feeling her breast.

" 'Course it can," Louis answered. "What's the problem?"

A car drew up and parked, a man got out and ran toward the house. The door opened, closed. In a minute the man came out carrying a case of Chivas Regal, drove off. There were more cars, one by one, people running in, out, throwing cases in a car and taking off. The night was dark, the neighborhood quiet, everything at the house hidden behind the fence, the sound of a chowkidar somewhere, click, hitting his post against the street, *click, click*, but it never came any closer, and a dog barked out in the road and in the distance she saw an elephant go by, someone asleep on his neck.

It took less than an hour. No one talked. Samiji started to light a cigarette, then stopped, stubbed it out. Louis went on drinking, the car smelled. Phoebe felt Kady holding his breath, too, just as he was still holding her arm, sliding his hand up and down along the top of her breast so that it was alive and warm beneath his touch, and she could tell from the way he was breathing and leaning against her that he felt exactly the same as she.

The last car was gone, the lights went off in the house. The man with the mustache opened the front door, shut it; they didn't hear a sound.

Louis rolled down his window. "Over here," he yelled. "Over here."

"Shush," Kady muttered, and she felt his body, tense and hard, pull away from her.

"It's all right," she whispered to him.

Kuldip came over, his hands full of money, pockets stuffed with it, more inside his shirt, pulling it out and throwing it in the window. Louis said, "Here, Feeb. Kady."

She handed Kady piles of money, their hands touched, he held her tight, and then he let her go.

## ❧ II ❦

THE NEXT DAY KADY WENT TO Deeg. Days passed. He didn't come back, and she wondered why. Christmas came and went, and still Kady didn't come back or call her. He spoke to Louis on the telephone, but Louis didn't tell her. Samiji did, and Moosselman, the cook, about how they talked and talked. Something was going on. Louis went to work one day but came back right away. Mr. Smith, the CEO, was with him, and she knew things were bad. Thalia was talking about how she wanted to go to New York to live, and Louis had moved into a guest room and didn't come out.

Phoebe dreaded her mother and her father, and she asked Samiji why Jiggie kept Kady in Deeg when Kady had a family in Delhi, and Samiji said he didn't think Jiggie was in Deeg, but he also said he didn't think Kady's family was in Delhi, either. Hindus didn't celebrate Christmas, Phoebe knew, and so maybe Durr had gone to Kashmir to visit her family, now that her husband was away.

Then Kady's calls stopped altogether.

One day Louis had a visitor. She knew who it was because the Rolls-Royce bearing the flag of two lions and a unicorn was outside when she came home from school. In the dining room there was food still untouched, platters of sandwiches and one empty plate. In the hall the Shiva Nataraj was coated with bits of egg and bread.

Someone had thrown them all over his four arms and two legs, food dripping down like moss.

Louis and the visitor were back in the library, the servants said, and she waited in the hall to find out what was happening. Soon Jiggie Deeg appeared.

He wore earrings and rings and a winter achkan jacket. She stared at his skin as he came slowly closer, amazed that he was so ugly, pits all over his face.

At first he didn't notice her, but the closer he got, the bigger he seemed and the more she began to feel the power and the strength of this man who had taken Kady's life and held it in his grip. Barely conscious of what she was doing, she stood up as tall as she could and felt a determination rise up in her that if he could humiliate her friend and humiliate her father—she knew that's what he'd done there in the library out of sight—she was going to show him the Guthries as a whole could stand up to him.

He must have sensed her, too, because he went slower and slower and scrutinized her all the harder, until she knew, before he'd even reached her, that she'd won—won something, at least. She could actually see his mind shift over from whatever it had been thinking about her father to taking account of her.

He observed her closely, his forehead fixed in a frown of concentration. When he was beside her, he stopped and said, "This must be the daughter, then."


There were only two more days until the end. Still Kady didn't call. Twice Louis went upstairs and yelled at Thalia through the door, although it wasn't locked and she wasn't even there, then left and sat downstairs underneath the room like a bomb waiting to explode.

She saw her mother once, downstairs in the living room not far from the Shiva Nataraj, which Louis had forbidden anyone to clean. She was standing with her chin raised, looking at herself in the mirror.

"Oh, there you are," Thalia said when she noticed her, as if Phoebe were someone she'd been looking for. "How do I look?"

"Fine." But it wasn't true. She looked like Louis, gray and dingy, both of them dying before they were dead.

"How can I?" Thalia said, fingering her wrinkles. "I just hate this house," she added suddenly. "A husband who hates me. But if I don't take care of you and Cully, who will?"

Kady still didn't come back and he still didn't call. Phoebe was desperate. The servants were worried, too, this end of all routine spelled no good, disaster even, but she couldn't imagine what the disaster would be.

She saw Vikrim Ali Seth again, and they went to Nizamuddin's Tomb, lay down among the leaves, because, for her, the rough weave of his jacket reminded her so much of Kady Suraj. Her shoe came off in the dark and she left it there and they took a taxi home. He left her at the door with a kiss. Inside, Louis was waiting, the tall dirty Shiva at his back.

Someone was knocking at the hotel door.

It was the bearer bringing newspapers and her breakfast, three eggs so small they fit in a single spoon.

She took the tray and looked at a paper. A motto at the top said, "Duty Is the Path to Liberation."

A Pakistani jet fighter had been sighted over the Beas River project, but officials insisted it was a navigational error. Outside Nagpur in the south, Hindu villagers had attacked a Muslim found near their well and hacked him to death with an ax. The item was in a box.

She also read a story about a man who keeled over and died after he refused three times to feed a cow who came to his door.

Durr Suraj's eyes were orange and gold. When the image of her finally emerged in Phoebe's memory, Durr was talking while Louis was dancing around the floor with a partner who wasn't there, while somewhere else the bride was circling around a fire. Even now, years later, Phoebe had the impression of talking to a woman she'd never seen before or since, but who was linked up with her so tightly, she had from that time on counted her among the most important women in her life.

"I was knowing Louis first," Durr said. They were seated side by side with their knees pointed in against each other as if they had been friends for years. "He wanted me to run away with him. He followed me down the street and wouldn't go away. He was saying, 'Run away with me,' 'Do anything with me. Have a drink, have dinner,' and I was werry much frightened. Finally I had the decision to let him drive me home because there was his driver to help me out and I thought it was the only way for getting away from him, but then he followed me up the stairs."

"Where was this?" Phoebe asked. "Where did you meet my father?"

"I didn't meet him. I was truly busy with someone else and so I didn't 'meet' him or even 'see' him, but he saw me and outside he was right in front of me and I saw he was werry handsome and I wasn't knowing what to do."

"Were you with Kady?"

"No."

"Someone else?"

"Yes."

"Was it a restaurant or something?"

"A restaurant."

"And Louis followed you when you left the restaurant because you were so beautiful?"

"Yes, but—"

"He was inside the restaurant and saw you, but you didn't see him? Is that it?"

"Yes. But this person I am with was seeing him and ignoring him, trying to get him to leave and go away, but your father didn't go away. He wouldn't. He was trying to make himself known to this one person I am with. They are knowing each other and this man is not liking him, but your father was trying to get his attention and have one talk, but this person was not wanting this talk and it made your father mad."

"What happened to the man?"

"He went off to his one car and left me on my own. He should not have left me so alone with him. He knows it now. He regretted it right away when I told him what had happened."

"And Louis saw you with this man and you were attracted to him," Phoebe said. "Is that it? And you had an affair, but you don't want to tell me?"

"No. No, absolutely not, in no way. I would never have an affair." Durr pulled her silks about her.

"Then why are you telling me this?"

"Because all that is most precious in life is before you now waiting to happen, marriage, family. Your life is just up ahead, waiting to begin—"

"My life isn't 'waiting.' Why are you telling me this?"

"And you must be careful. That is what I am wanting to tell you."

"But my life isn't 'about' to do anything. It's been happening for years."

"You don't understand," Durr said urgently. "I am feeling all of a sudden it is my urgent duty to worry for you. Kady has instructed me to help you. They're . . ." But instead of finishing her sentence, she took Phoebe's hand and gripped it.

"But I'm fine. Really. Nothing is happening to me."

Louis came dancing by. He was bent in against a dancer who wasn't there. Durr pressed her hand harder. "They're strange and powerful mans."

"But I'm all right." Even as she said it, though, Phoebe knew it wasn't true.

"Each one for the other one is perfect, but for you they are not perfect."

Phoebe tried to remember the color of her mother's eyes but couldn't. There weren't any eyes in the world now except these orange eyes, and she felt like curling up and putting her head in Durr's lap.

"And you must take care, Phoebe. You can be hurt. Your father is not now the same as he used to be, but he is still a powerful man for so young a daughter. I am not knowing everything and you are not knowing everything, but your father was one time the very most powerful thing that was ever happened to Kady and so he must be powerful for you, too. You are too young to be knowing everything—"

"I'm sixteen. You're not much older."

"But you're too old to be doing what you're doing," Durr said. "You must be careful."

"Are you warning me about sex?"

166

Durr looked away. "Maybe," she said finally. "But it is more than that."

"What is it?"

The woman paused, her orange eyes huge and soft and important. "Ruin," she said finally. "It is about ruin I am warning you."

"Ruin," Phoebe said, disbelieving.

"Then let me tell you how powerful he is. He followed me into the apartment and saw Kady standing there, and he looked him up and down, up and down, oh, my God, and Kady was standing as tall as he can ever stand and I was thinking to myself, This man, he is not surprised to see my husband. I should have known, he was knowing very well that I was not for allowing him to come to an empty apartment. He must have guessed I had a husband."

"What surprised him, then?"

"Without a word, he picked up this stack of magazines and was just there dropping them one by one on the floor. I am never reading them, but Kady is. He is studying them all the time, and Louis was saying, 'You work for Deeg Enterprises, don't you?' and Kady was saying yes, and then Louis said, 'That's what I thought,' and then he was taking off, going through the apartment. He went in all the rooms, each and every single room, the baby's room, the boy's room, the kitchen, the dining room, each and every one, I am telling you, not one, not two, but every single one."

"Why did you let him?"

"Nothing like this had ever happened to me before. You must be knowing that. A man, he just came to my door and walked right in and I am hearing him opening doors and shutting doors and he was in my closet and my bedroom and then Kady's bedroom and then he went up the hall and I was picking up the magazines and then he came back down the hall, and Kady, he was excited. I have never seen him so much alive, and I am thinking, Is he knowing this man? Is this man a famous man? Then he is coming back, your father. He lit a cigarette, watching Kady all the time, and I am proud of Kady because he looks so fine to this gentleman. He was very quiet now, your father. Then he sat down. Kady and I are just only standing there, looking, waiting, and I am thinking, Should I offer tea? But I couldn't think of tea, and he looked at Kady, your father did, and

Kady was looking at him, and he was, oh, so distinguished he was then, not so sad as he is now. Just like a maharaja he was then, only he was thin and tall, not a little bit fat and short, like some maharajas, and he said, 'And she's your wife?' Kady nodded. Of course I am his wife. Would I be standing there, sharing an apartment with him, if I wasn't his wife? Does he think I am having no honor? And then your father said, 'And you know about the man in the restaurant?' And Kady nodded and—"

"Didn't Kady mind you having an affair?"

"And then he said, 'Do you know who I am?' and Kady said he had seen his picture in the newspaper, and your father said, 'I can help you. Do you want that?' and I am thinking, Help with what? But Kady was nodding. 'Any-ting,' he said. 'I want any-ting and every-ting.' 'Good,' your father said, 'that's what I thought. I know exactly what's going on and I can help you deal with him. I can help you fight him.' "

"What are you trying to tell me?" Phoebe interrupted frantically. "I don't understand."

Durr stopped. "Maybe it is about sex and love?" She said it as a question. "I don't know if you are ready or if you are not ready. If you are, it will be bad, but if you are not, it will be bad, too, because to be werry, werry frankly honest, I was one of the ones who was"—she laid out her hands to make a word or shape—"ready . . . and it was a bad thing, yes, but not actually a werry bad thing."

"Why are you telling me this?"

"Because you have no mother and I have never before made the decision to see you, but Kady has talked to me and told me to come and talk to you, and now I am here and you are my friend and my responsibility."

Phoebe didn't know what to say. "I'm right here all the time," she said finally, "anytime anyone wants to see me."

Durr removed her hands. "I don't speak werry good English. I am not having so much experience as Kady. Maybe I don't . . ."

High above them the broad strips of the shamiana tent enfolded their silence. A bride was on her way, journeying over from what Indians thought was nonlife into life. Phoebe didn't know what she felt except that there was this bride here, another in Deeg, and they were all sixteen. Just as if she'd read her mind, Durr said:

"I was sixteen when I got married. It turned my life. I was

being oh so much in love and the world was this, oh, my god, this great big, werry big thing, and it is still for me, this love, even though it is not my duty, and from one minute to the next then I was not knowing what to do, because I was only sixteen and had only monkey mind, child's mind, and didn't know my duty, but then I got married and it changed my life."

Phoebe didn't say a word, but she understood. A band was playing "On the Street Where You Live," and she thought how she'd never even seen the street where Kady lived. "I'm only trying to help Cully," she said. "That's why I go out with them. But it's not working and I can't help my father, either. I thought I could, but I can't." She stopped and looked around.

Her father was coming, still dancing by himself.

"I used to like it because I got to be with him and it was fun and exciting, but now . . ." Phoebe started to cry.

Durr held her. Her hand played with the length of Phoebe's hair. "I am all the time thinking about Kady now and what will happen to him. I just worry, worry, worry, all the time for worry. What did we do wrong? Everything is wrong, but now he is talking to me about you, and when he is talking it is so werry rare, because he never talks to me, and so I must listen. He is worried, too. He says you are not Indian, but you are not American, either, and . . ."

It was then, right then, that Phoebe knew how much she loved Durr. The feeling came up and over her like a wave that could carry her out to sea. Durr's hand on her face and cheek and forehead felt soothing, and she said dreamily, "I love you," and closed her eyes while Durr held her tight, the two of them not many years apart, but one was long a woman, the other not.

# ❧ 12 ❧

after the fight between Cully and her father at the dining room
table, the white Ford car drove away, one or two people inside,
they never did find out, but they heard the chowkidar at the gate
say, "Sa'ab," one long Indian syllable without a consonant in
between, and then the car was gone.

Samiji drove them to school in the morning in the other car,
and when they asked about the white Ford, he said Louis wasn't
back, and they didn't think to ask about Thalia.

That afternoon Moosselman picked them up at school, and by
the time they got home Granny called from New York to tell
them the news herself, and Kady was already there with Jiggie
Deeg. None of it made any sense at all. Jiggie Deeg was standing
right there in the middle of the living room, and Mr. Smith, the
CEO from Louis' office, and Samiji, too—in the living room, not
in the hall where he was supposed to be, but right there with
Jiggie Deeg and Kady Suraj—and so Phoebe and Cully, if not
the last to find out, were certainly not the first.

Kady stood up when they came in. Then Mr. Smith was
saying Granny was on the phone, and Phoebe went to the phone
wondering how she'd tell Cully whatever it was she'd have to

tell him, but she already was sure Louis had shot himself.

So when Granny told her about the accident, she had to tell her twice because she couldn't understand there'd been an accident, not a suicide, and then Granny said they were coming "home" in two days' time, she and Cully, and Phoebe said, "I want to stay with Cully."

"Yes, dear, of course." Granny was so distraught, Phoebe knew she wasn't thinking clearly, either.

Phoebe took Cully in the dining room and sat down while he stood up between her knees, and she held his arms with her hands and told him what had happened.

"What will become of us?" he said.

"We're going to New York," she said, as though it was the most natural thing in the world. "We'll be all right. We have each other."

When they went back to the living room, Kady was gone, summoned to the lawn by Jiggie Deeg, and Mr. Smith was saying how sorry he was. Kady came back and took her hand and held it with the two of his, the three of them standing side by side. "Do you want to know about it now, or do you want to wait?" he asked, talking to them both.

"You say, Feeb," Cully said. "It's up to you."

Cully hadn't started to cry and neither had she, but her legs were wobbly. She wanted to know about the accident right away, everything there was to know, but she didn't know if Cully should hear, and besides, along with everything else, almost the biggest thing of all was the fact that they were leaving.

Kady made the decision. Told them where the accident was, that it happened in the night, in Agra, and when she said, confused, maybe she hadn't heard, "Where?" he said Agra, Agra District, "Agra, the Taj Mahal." He said some huts had burned, a bus and cows as well, even people, and that it was "a terrible fire and everything burned," and she said, "But how did it happen?"

"Wasn't he very drunk?" Kady said, still holding her hand. "Yes."

"Well, that was it," Jiggie Deeg interjected, coming in. "The car went out of control. It spun around and hit everything in its path. It exploded."

Phoebe wondered why he was there. "Was my father driving?"

"Yes," Jiggie said. She noticed even then how closely he observed her. "It was an awful accident, and the authorities down there are stunned."

"Did you see it?" she asked. "How do you know?" She slipped her hand out of Kady's.

"No one saw it," Jiggie said.

"Then why are you here?" she asked. "You and my father hated each other."

"It wasn't hate," Jiggie answered calmly. "Life is too complex for anything as one-dimensional as hate."

"You didn't answer my question."

"I talked to the police," Jiggie said. "That's what I did. They told me everything."

"But how did you know that—"

Kady answered. "Samiji called me in Deeg last night, early this morning, really, and I came right up. Jiggie dealt with the authorities. He has connections."

"Then why didn't you tell us when we went to school?" She looked at Samiji.

"Not for me, miss-sa'ab," the driver said miserably. "Granny's job for telling you this."

"So Samiji called you and you came back from Deeg?"

"Of course I came back from Deeg," Kady said.

"Then why is he here?" She pointed at Jiggie Deeg.

"He flew me up in his plane."

"I came to help," Jiggie said, "to see if there was anything I could do."

"I want to see the accident," Phoebe said.

"There's nothing to see," Kady said.

"The place, then. I want to go there. I have to see it. I want to know how it happened."

"It's too far away, and awful, and besides, Granny wants you home. She wants you all together, and she's right. The sooner you leave, the sooner everything will be normal."

He said they should have something to eat, and Phoebe said she didn't want to eat. Jiggie Deeg went out in the hall to the Shiva Nataraj, and she saw him looking where the eggs had splattered across the dancing figure.

She remembered Durr then and wanted to see her. She was about to tell Kady when suddenly Cully started to sag. His eyes closed, skin went white, and Kady swept him up in his arms, so the boy was stretched out with his legs and head hanging down.

"He's all right, he's just fainted," Kady said, and he headed toward the door, she following. She led the way up the wide stairs with gods and goddesses on ledges on the walls, the man and boy behind her, to her room.

There Kady laid him out on the bed, Cully's eyes still closed, his body limp. Turning, Kady suddenly reached for Phoebe and took her in his arms, lifted her off her feet till her head was next to his, and he held her so tight, and she held him back, she could feel the buttons on his coat and his thighs, and she put her head right up next to his and held it as he moved his hand up and down her back. She began to tremble.

He kissed her cheeks and hair over and over again. "You'll be all right," he whispered. "You will. It's not so far away."

"You said he'd kill himself. I never thought about an accident," she said, winding her arms around him and pressing her lips tight against his neck. "Why were you away so long? Why didn't you come back to me?"

"Don't ask."

"But what happened?"

"I can't tell you."

"But if you don't tell me now, when will you?"

"Oh, Jesus, Feeb." He held her tight, kissing her hair and ears, and she could hear his breath coming in and out. He was nearly crying, too.

Then he pulled his head back so he could look at her, and she suddenly felt afraid, because she knew this was the end, almost the very last second before she left for America. "I'll be all right," he was saying. "Nothing matters except that you're going home."

"Home?"

Cully groaned, and Kady let her down. She crouched beside her brother. The door opened. Kamala rushed in crying, followed by Moosselman, who looked as if the conflagration were right in here, not in Agra, his eyes blazing with terror and alarm. "Good-bye, Feeb," Kady said, and headed for the door.

She saw his face for a second before he disappeared, a smile upon the lips, sadness everywhere else. She leaned over the long shape of her little brother, his eyes open, and she fell down beside him on the bed and burst into tears.

✤

They didn't sleep much that night or the next, and they didn't leave the house, just watched as Kamala and other servants who were allowed upstairs took care of them. Still other servants stayed outside in the hall, never allowed inside a bedroom. Moosselman brought breakfast, lunch. Phoebe knew they were being kept up here on purpose, because the house itself was too large to support such a monumental vacuum. The thought was that smaller spaces for the bibiji would somehow make the hours easier.

Kady came back just once. "I wanted to see how you were." He looked only at Cully.

Phoebe watched him from across the room. The scarf she'd knitted was around his neck. "Isn't there going to be a funeral?" she asked.

"No need for that," he said.

"But in India they bring the bodies home so the dead can be comforted before they're burned. Why aren't they coming home?"

Kady didn't answer. He left the room.

# ❧ 13 ❧

THE LAST NIGHT THEY WERE ON their knees at the window staring out. There were crickets and peepers and hyenas howling and barking, animals moving in and out through the woods and shrubs of the sprawling city. All the noises of India were there, cars, bicycles, and bullock carts, bells tinkling and babies crying.

Kamala came in at midnight, and as they dressed, Samiji rushed around with one more suitcase and went through their desks, tables, drawers, packing everything left behind, feathers from the mynah bird, stones from Simla, baubles from the bazaar. He pressed a photo of himself as a boy, years before they met, into Phoebe's hand and said, "Tell Granny Indian things are good. You need Indian things, not just store-bought." Phoebe and Cully, getting smaller by the minute, were rushed down to the car, Samiji's picture in her pocket.

Scores of servants were there, their families, too, and Phoebe didn't know what to do because you weren't supposed to touch servants and even though she had, she'd never touched an untouchable, but now, suddenly, there were masses of them, seeming more terrified than usual, as if their own plight were magnified in that of Phoebe and Cully, the children now cast out, too.

Samiji and Moosselman tried to kick them away, and they backed off, untouchables know their place, and went almost to the lily ponds, but in the confusion of so much emotion, Phoebe and Cully grabbed them too for hugs, contamination no concern. Then the car was ready to go.

At the very last minute Kamala and Moosselman edged up to it and darted in the backseat and crouched on the floor. "Just don't make any noise," Kady said from his position in the front near Samiji, and they were off, the servants at their feet like suitcases, Mr. Smith, the CEO, following in another car, Jiggie Deeg inexplicably there once again, now in a silver Rolls-Royce with his flag on its fender, the fourth and last car occupied by his chief aide-de-camp, Attar Singh, and a barefoot man in a dhoti and a turban. They were along, Kady said, "just in case."

At the airport hundreds of people were asleep on the floor. More flowed through the crowded halls. Light bulbs hissed and sputtered. People cooked, ate, and talked, excited and noisy. Phoebe and Cully were shepherded through customs, lines and checkpoints. Attar Singh from Deeg saw to everything, special rooms were made available, tea served, then it was time to move.

Phoebe and Cully, Samiji, Kamala, and Moosselman all held hands. Walking to the gate, Jiggie Deeg went in front with Attar Singh, then came Kady and Mr. Smith, then all the servants and the children. Suddenly the end was upon them. The children and the servants hugged, the maharaja left; unexpectedly, Kady interrupted everything.

He took one step backward, put his hands together, palms aligned, fingers pointed up, and he namasted the two Americans, or just the one, herself, she couldn't tell. He bent his head low in a deep respectful bow, fingertips almost reaching his forehead. Everyone was silent.

The children, commanded by a great and superior force, did it back. "Namaste," they said, hands up, palms aligned, head bowed.

Phoebe and Cully headed out alone into the night. Kady remained apart from the little crowd. He stood still, his shoulders perfectly positioned, his dark head bent, two hands together saying farewell.

Phoebe and Cully lifted their faces into the cool fresh air of Indian winter. It blew clear and sweet across the tarmac, and when Phoebe looked back, Suraj had left.

The stewardess strapped them in, first class empty and quiet after India. Immediately the plane was moving, down the runway, then off.

"Cully," Phoebe exclaimed.

Cully leaned over near the window, their two heads, yellow and indistinguishable, boy from girl, pressed against the glass. But India was gone. A few lights blinked along the highway back toward town, but precious few lights there were, because India, after all, wasn't a land of lights. The country behind them was gone. It had disappeared faster than they ever would have dreamed.

## ❧ 14 ❧

PHOEBE WAS IN THE DEPTHS OF
sleep, stretched out on the bed with all her clothes on, when
there was a knock on the door.

She woke up groggily. The knocking came again, more persistent, and she finally got up and made it to the door.

Outside stood a tall man with a thin, neatly clipped mustache,
wearing dark trousers and a white shirt. He looked like an
accountant or a teacher. He was holding something out in the
palm of his hand.

Phoebe looked at it. It was a detective's badge.

He said his name was Nasrut Sardar, from Tees-he-zari, a
district in Old Delhi, and he was investigating a robbery.

Phoebe brought him in, curious, not alarmed, musing, actually, on what India had brought to her door. He said there'd
been a robbery in Tees-he-zari at an art dealer's house and the
art dealer's name was Vishnu Bhave. He wondered if she knew
him.

She said oh yes, she did know him. Or, rather, she used to, and
then she explained about Louis and his collection and only realized at the end that she wasn't telling the man anything he
didn't already know. He seemed intelligent and patient.

He asked if she'd had any connection with Bhave recently.

She said no. She'd just arrived. What'd been stolen?

An antique necklace, made of pearls and diamonds.

She asked how she could help, not very interested yet, except to see why he'd come to her, and he asked if her brother knew him. She said she had no idea. "He never mentioned Vishnu Bhave," she said, although now she remembered that he had. "So I don't know."

"No," the man said patiently.

Phoebe began to feel nervous. She asked, was there anything else? because she had things to do, and the man said, was she planning on going to Deeg? Surprised, she said, maybe, but she had come to look at the body first, and he said, yes, and she wondered how he knew about everything. Then he asked, again, when was she going to see her brother? and she said she didn't know, maybe he was dead, for God's sake, but by now she was really nervous, her stomach in knots.

"Do you remember Anant Bhave?" he asked.

She shook her head.

"Vishnu Bhave's son."

"Oh, his son?"

"Yes."

"Isn't there something wrong with him? Retarded, maybe? That's what my father said."

"Well, there is now."

"What?"

"Something wrong with him. He's dead. He was murdered during the robbery."

"I don't understand."

"Didn't Cully write you about it?"

"No."

"Tell you that it happened?"

"No," she said impatiently. "I told you that. How was he killed? What happened?"

"He was hit on the head. Then strangled."

"What has this got to do with me or Cully?"

"A man with yellow hair was seen at Vishnu Bhave's the day of the murder and was heard fighting with him."

"But that's not proof of anything," Phoebe said hotly.

"Your brother has a temper."

"So what? So do I."

179

"Bhave says he has a bad temper."

"So do lots of people. What's that prove? When was the murder? When was the blond man there? Was it the same time? That's what counts, not all this other mishmash."

"Didn't he tell you what time he was there?"

"He didn't tell me anything at all," Phoebe said angrily. "I told you that. When was the robbery, and when was the man there? What are the exact times? Don't pester me with all these questions when you don't have the answer yourself."

Nasrut Sardar smiled patiently, as though he had all day and all week and all month to hear her out. "The man with yellow hair was there the morning of one day and the body was not found until the morning of the next day."

"See. It could have been anybody."

"Oh yes, that is just my thought exactly."


Phoebe arrived at Safdarjang Morgue an hour early. The building was set off from the road by a thicket of trees that disguised the fact that it was a long flat grimy structure the color of Indian dirt. The two floors that rose above the ground were the hospital, Delhi's depository for the sick and poor. The morgue itself was in the basement.

Phoebe knocked. An official opened the door a few inches wide but stared at her coldly and refused to let her inside until her appointment. She argued, but he closed the door in her face and locked it.

Angry, she stood there a few minutes, then began eyeing the hospital entrance only a few feet away. "I'm going in there," she said hotly to Tulsidas, and marched off.

The driver ran after her. "Is no place for memsa'abs," he cried.

"Maybe he's sick."

"Not in Safdarjang. Only Indians," the driver insisted.

"Maybe he had an accident and they brought him here." She disappeared inside, only to come right back out because an official had told her visitors weren't allowed there, either.

Tulsidas said that was nonsense, "just some werry person," he said with disgust, and taking her by the arm, he walked straight in past the official, and with him as escort, they walked up and down the wards of Safdarjang for an hour.

The place was vast, hallways so long they disappeared in darkness at the end. There were no private rooms, just ward after ward with beds lined like dominoes. There was little light, nothing white, not even much that was clean, mattresses nearly putrid, and the patients seemed as wretched and dirty as when they first came in. Some still had gaping wounds, others green-ish white infections. People clawed Phoebe's clothes and asked for help. She bent to talk to them and handed out silver and rupees. After a while she started crying. Most people said they had never seen a doctor or had any treatment. She ended up giving away so much money, Tulsidas thought she was crazy, until he began to understand what sort of person she was.

They didn't see any male Caucasians. The only doctor they saw was standing by himself at the top of a stairwell, yelling at no one at all.

Harriet was late getting to the morgue. By the time she ar-rived, Phoebe was already in the basement. The room smelled of death and disinfectant. One drawer had been pulled out from a wall of drawers. On the drawer was a sheet and a body, only one hand showed, and Phoebe was standing next to it. When Harriet walked in, she turned, acknowledged her with an ago-nized smile, and then looked back at the drawer, leaving Harriet with the memory of a tortured face above a neat, straight body dressed in something blue. Phoebe had obviously been crying because her face was streaked with mascara.

As Harriet watched, Phoebe and a man who was obviously an untouchable lifted the sheet, and the male Caucasian body lay exposed.

It was naked but for the remnants of a pair of khaki trousers that had been cut off above the knees to make Bermuda shorts. The body was blue in some places, deathly white in others, but the flesh was so ragged and torn, it had obviously been ravaged by animals. For all the devastation, though, it still had two legs and two arms. Worms, apparently still alive in this nonre-frigerated refrigerator, lay around the corpse looking like large kernels of white rice.

"Is it him?"

Phoebe didn't answer. She was looking at the man's feet. Then she took in an enormous gulp of air, and with a rush of energy that came out like a torrent of wind rising from her feet, she cried out with exultation, "There's no big toe." She waved her hands out in the air and brought them together in a loud clap. "He had a toe on his left foot as big as a thumb! It's not Cully."

# PART THREE

## ❧ I ❧

Now roll back the months to fall of the year before, to the time when Cully returned to India and to the palace in Deeg, where the seat at the head of the dining room table remained forever empty and unused, reserved for Maharaja Juggernathan Singh, who was never going to return.

"I met a man," Cully wrote Phoebe in a letter. "He wasn't very old and he looked ordinary to me. He said his aunt came to live with him and that it turned out she was inhabited by a devil. First, he said, his wife died because of her, then his eldest son, then his daughter, and then, before she could kill his youngest and last child, he called in an exorcist and had him put a spell on her. The exorcist told him that in three days the aunt would die, and in three days, she died."

It had been a big reception at the palace. What Cully remembered most was the man's story and the sense he got from it of all that power, the aunt's power, the swami's power, and the realization that he, Cully, didn't have any power at all, didn't even know what it was.

He wrote Phoebe's address on the envelope. Of all the impressions left over from the reception, the strongest was the sense that there was something he lacked. I mean, how, he thought, could one person die, then the other, then the other, all because of an aunt? He'd never made anyone do anything, except Phoebe.

The fan was twirling, the shutters closed. He opened them. It was night. The cool air of Indian autumn moved in through the window and overtook him. He stood gazing out, then abruptly stepped back into the room and looked out instead from a spot closer to the center, as someone might do in a city where privacy was of concern.

The room had views on three sides, toward the lake, the lawns, and the desert at the back, but Cully was careful never to be seen now. That had started when he saw the girl, Mirabai. She was Jiggie's favorite granddaughter.

She had been alone on the lawn looking up at him, and after that he never showed his face in the window if he could help it.

The garden had been empty that day, just a few weeks after he arrived in Deeg, so Mirabai had stood out as something exceptional, all alone when a girl like her wasn't ever supposed to be alone. Even when Mirabai took a bath, a maid was present, so after that Cully stood far back from the window and wondered every single time if she was there.

He thought about her now and why she'd been outside on the lawn.

She had maids all day and all night, old women, called lallis, who took care of the children and the women, their chief responsibility to chaperone. One slept in the hall in front of her door, another on the floor beside her bed. More were beside her mother and her sisters, and during the day they all sat on the floor outside the dining room, like a flock of landed birds colorful in their plumage.

Mirabai wasn't too tall. Cully didn't even know if she was fully grown. She had a long thick braid, nice lips, and a wide face, skin so fair she barely looked Indian at all, although the short fuzzy fringe of hair that circled her forehead could only be Indian. At least he'd never seen it on an American girl before, little short hairs like pubic hair, an inch long, framing her face, sticking up in curls and waves.

Her eyes were dark and so round they were almost circular but for an almond twist at the side and her eyelashes thick as a piece of cloth.

To him the eyes were expressionless. He'd had a good view of them at dinner the first night he arrived when she had looked at him. She wasn't supposed to. It was a long searching gaze across the table, but it held not a trace of anything he could fathom.

A couple of times after that, she glanced at him again.

Maybe an Indian would know what she was thinking, but to him her face was as blank as a wall, and that she even existed had barely occurred to him until he suddenly saw her in the garden when it seemed like a relationship, full blown, had started.

She was near the fountain and she was looking up at his window as if she'd been doing it for hours, although he knew— he'd seen it all in a flash, or so he thought at first, but now he wondered if he'd been conscious of her for longer, far longer— that she had actually been running up and down the garden and had only stopped seconds before he looked at her, as if they had an appointment and both were there on time.

Cully lay down on his bed, a four-poster with mosquito netting wrapped around the top.

The girl had no shape that he could see. She was little and flat, no hips at all, no breasts, probably not even much of a waist. Her arms were thin, little-girl things that came out under a sleeve, wrists so small they could fit in napkin rings. And she was getting married. How could someone that young get married?

In the garden she had been running up and down, or at least that's what she'd been doing until the second he saw her, when she wasn't doing anything at all except looking up at him. He realized she had a dog and was throwing sticks for him, something he'd never heard of.

First of all, Indian girls didn't run. Second, they didn't own dogs as pets.

Her braid had been swinging out behind her head, and he had thought how he didn't like braids and he hated dogs and how could she be running like that if she was Indian and how could she be getting married because she didn't even look old enough to dance.

The dog was big, friendly, and reddish brown with floppy ears and a long nose. The maharaja had gone to Europe to get him years ago, a dog for Mirabai, unheard of, then brought him back to Pakistan and bribed officials to get him in overland to

India, foreign animals illegal without a quarantine.

The silver Rolls-Royce was waiting at the border, and it brought them back, man and beast, across the Rajasthani Desert to Deeg. The Rolls had been sent on such missions only twice before, he'd been told, once to bring the Prince of Wales to Deeg, the other time, twenty-five years ago, to get a blackboard for the school.

"Just to get a blackboard?" Cully had asked Jasdan, the maharaja's one and only son. "All that way?"

No, Jasdan said, it really went to get a trunk full of Jiggie's clothes that had come from Kashmir. The trunk was so heavy, four men had to carry it up the stairs and down the halls to Jiggie's room, no short walk in a palace that size, and the trunk had holes in it so the clothes inside could get the air, not turn stuffy in the heat. There it stayed in Jiggie's room a good ten months until out it came out again and was carried to the train, Jiggie's clothes heading north to Deeg House in Delhi.

Cully thought it was crazy. So, too, did Jasdan, because he was talking about his father's old-fashioned eccentricities, all in connection with the fact that he had renounced and become a religious hermit.

Cully thought about the maharaja a lot. Yearned to know his opinions about Louis and art. Wondered at how much he loved Mirabai. How he'd gone to Europe just to get a dog for her, then to Pakistan, a border town, to collect the dog, and now wrote letters only to her, when there were plenty of other grandchildren, six by Jasdan, two by the daughter, five in all were girls, but Mirabai, the youngest and most modern, alone was singled out.

He decided the girl must be a good deal older than she looked.

## ❧ 2 ❧

His work focused on two floors in one vast wing of the palace. All the rooms were locked, and there were many more than he'd expected—Jasdan never wrote him anything about thirty bedrooms, thirty baths, all of them suites, so it meant thirty sitting rooms and dressing rooms as well, all filled with art—and after Jasdan took him through, he avoided the place for weeks. One hundred and twenty rooms. Of course he avoided it.

Jasdan had unlocked the doors, and Cully had smelled the air inside, so dusty it would have been ruled illegal in New York. There were shrouds, shapes, boxes, backs, hips, heads, and cartons everywhere. There were even bird droppings from pigeons that had flown in through the broken windowpanes. They went through room after room. Sometimes Jasdan just opened up a door briefly, then shut it again, and Cully was relieved every time he heard a closing. Found himself listening for the old servant who accompanied them to fit the keys in the lock and turn it back in place. Separated by lock and door, he felt a brief immunity from what lay on the other side.

Jasdan explained it all standing in one of the bedrooms where everything looked as brown and parched as the desert outside. The art did not belong to his father or his family, he said, but to Deeg itself. Whenever it was bought or acquired, anytime in

189

the last four centuries, it was done in the name of Deeg, but now the House of Deeg didn't exist. Everything Deeg had been had been subsumed in the central government in Delhi at the time of independence in 1947, and the art had to be given over to it, too. Deeg as such was gone. It wasn't a kingdom or an army, just the name of one of India's lesser towns.

The more Cully listened, the more upset he got. Jasdan obviously didn't care. To him this was just history, not his life, but Cully felt it as a kind of plunder that was personal. It reminded him of Jumna Road. Everything gone and given away, a disappearance he hadn't seen or been part of, and now this man was perpetuating that very act, but didn't care, that what had once been his and his family's was now a government's.

"Are you all right?" Jasdan asked.

"I'm just hot." Cully sat down on something that turned out to be a statue of a god. "Maybe thirsty."

Jasdan told the servant, his name was Shyam, to bring some water. "This climate is hard for foreigners."

"Foreigners?" Cully repeated, wiping hair off his face. "Yes."

He's got a nerve, Cully thought, and then and there began his dislike for Jasdan Singh. He didn't hate Jiggie Deeg himself until April 2nd, the next year.

The servant Shyam brought water. Cully drank it. Jasdan was saying, "I have no more right to the art than that man there," pointing to Shyam Singh. But the art had to be counted and chronicled, he went on, so that in the transfer to museums and warehouses the government would know what it was getting and it would be less likely to be stolen.

"That makes sense," Cully managed, "but if all this happened because of independence some forty years ago, why didn't you do it sooner?"

Jasdan shrugged. He was short and fair and heavyset, after his father, it was said. "It takes time," he explained. "Everything takes time. That's the first thing you learn over here. Look at that hotel," he said, pointing across the lake to the Deeg Palace Hotel. "We had this man, Kady Suraj, used to work for us, and he had the idea to make that into a hotel. Took us years to get it going. That's how things work here. What I'm trying to tell you," he went on, "is that you may finish, you may not."

190

It bothered Cully, all that dust and the thought of the irreplaceable objects obscured beneath it. He wanted to rescue the art—he imagined its bronze and terra-cotta substance the way others would dream of gold and wealth—but at the same time he was put off by the dirt and felt that time, malevolent, was choking the art itself.

He walked the halls, elbowed his way past the crates lined up along the corridors, and every time the same old servant, Shyam, appeared to keep him company, unsummoned, keys in hand, fuchsia turban on his head. The old man didn't seem to want anything, just handed him the keys, then took them back again at the end, but never left his side.

Cully told himself he was getting ready, that once Phoebe sent the cartons of art reference books he left behind, he'd be set to go. But when the books came, he had to have shelves made. Old Attar Singh, Jasdan's aide, asked wouldn't the cupboards in his room do? Cully said no, the cupboards had doors and he had to be able to see the titles of the books, so that took some time, getting them made, and meanwhile he did a lot of reading and ordered carton boxes.

Attar Singh asked why he needed carton boxes, and Cully said, "To store things in, of course," but when they arrived he realized everything was too dusty to transfer to carton boxes, so he organized a cleaning effort. Actually, what he did was tell Attar Singh and Attar Singh did it.

Everything was brought out of the first suite on the ground floor and taken outside under the gaze of one whole set of servants who were assigned to watch the other set of servants, and there the things were dusted and taken back inside. But they hadn't gone very far before Attar Singh said they shouldn't go any farther. "It's too much," he said. "Clean it as you go along if you have to and forget about carton boxes."

By then Cully had gotten excited. He had seen a bronze peacock with Radha riding on its neck, terra-cotta bulls, statues of Shiva and Vishnu, Saraswati figured as a bird herself, rakshinis from Rajasthan, and rock sculptures cut from the caves at Ellora, and he felt exhilarated by it all. It was nearly infinite in its beauty and depth, and his hands touching it gave him a joy and satisfaction nothing else in his life had done.

Luckily he seldom saw Jasdan except for meals. The man was invariably closeted in his office. Everyone said he was too preoccupied with the marriage negotiations that were in full sway for Mirabai to handle anything else. Cully questioned his judgment, to have so little time for something as important as the art.

But as time went on, Cully recognized a feeling of relief at Jasdan's preoccupation and the fact that there was no pressure to hurry. He doubted whether anyone even cared about the project except himself. They were just having it done because the government required it.

The plan he eventually put to work was simple: he just began making a list in his notebook. Doing one room at a time, he cataloged first this object, then that, noted that he was off to a good start, and proceeded. Filled up pages. His system was to do all the objects in any one place, everything on top, then whatever was underneath, and sometimes when things were piled on top of each other, like one Nandi cow, Shiva's mount, which was covered with sheets of paper that turned out to be Rajasthani folk art paintings, the paintings he put off in another place to do later.

What he did was trust his luck and think about collections. Louis', Jiggie Deeg's, and his own.


The animals unnerved him. Often he saw hundreds, maybe thousands, of camels, walking as a group. The land, as far as he could see, an undulating thing.

"You'd like them," he wrote Phoebe, "but I keep thinking, what if they go wild or start running away? I mean, how do you control them?"

The camels made a noise that Cully thought was the ugliest sound he ever heard. It had all the hallmarks of something choking to death at the same time as it was making a pathetic attempt at animal communication.

Other times there were goats, hundreds, thousands, to a herd, and he watched as two or three men or boys, walking sticks in hand, barefoot, white cloth wrapped around their heads to shield their precious windpipes in some ineffective way from all the dust that did grave damage down inside, walked beside their herd across the palace land.

He imagined what his sister would think, her wonderment at the bleak course of the boys' lives, moving up and down a desert, keeping track of animals as they looked for leaves and drink in a land that had almost no leaves or drink to give.

"You think about things like that," he wrote her. "You like animals. You like people. You don't mind all this chaos and tumult. You probably don't even notice it, but I get overwhelmed by it. I have to watch myself and be careful. That's the only way I can get anything done. I'm not the kind of person who has time to think about animals. I'm more particular. You can probably do anything you want, but I can't. I have to do what I like to do. Luckily I know myself well. I'm not saying you don't, I'm not trying to be critical, but we're different. You spread yourself around, try to take charge of everything. I only want to do a few things and do them well. Like my collection. I already know what I want to get. See, that's how my mind works. I'm planning it all the time. I've almost finished the first stage. My next move is to go to Delhi and meet Kady Suraj."

## ❧ 3 ❧

"WHAT DO YOU THINK OF MY grandfather?" Mirabai came in the room and plopped down on top of a bronze cow three feet high. The dog was with her.

Cully examined the Ganesha elephant he had in his hand. He put a magnifying glass up to the garlands around its neck and saw, out of the corner of his eye, her maid outside the door with Shyam Singh. They didn't have to worry about him, he thought. The garden had been just fine: she was far enough away. He certainly wouldn't tinker with the maharaja's prize.

"What do you think of my grandfather?" she said again.

"I don't know him."

The girl started swinging her legs under the cow's belly, and Cully caught a glimpse of her feet, little toes and sandals. The servants didn't move, but now at least they were talking to each other.

"Do you think it's a good thing?"

She looked older than before, and this time he got a sense of a waist beneath the sari.

"Do you think it's a good thing?"

"What?"

"What he's doing?"

"I don't know what he's doing." Cully concentrated on the figure in his hands. "I told you that."

"You said you didn't know him."

"I don't."

"But that doesn't mean you don't know what he's doing. Everyone knows what he's doing. I bet fifty people have told you what he's doing."

Cully sat down at the table and went on studying the Ganesha with the magnifying glass.

"That's bad for your eyes."

He continued his work. The Ganesha reminded him of the one Louis had in his bedroom.

"You don't have enough light."

But that Ganesha was bigger. Louis bought him from Vishnu Bhave, the art dealer who—

"Why don't you have Shyam bring you a light? . . . Shyam?" she called. "Can you get Cully-sa'ab a light?"

Shyam nodded and sat down, didn't move at all.

"See?" Cully jeered. "Not everyone does what you tell them to do."

Mirabai tilted her head back. She had a dimple on her cheek.

Another servant appeared outside and bowed to Shyam. Shyam told him to get a lamp.

Mirabai laughed. "See? Even Shyam has a servant."

Cully went back to the Ganesha. Shyam and the maid were seated, talking again.

"You probably don't know who he is, do you?"

"Who?"

"Shyam."

He started writing in the notebook about the Ganesha, the century, derivation and so forth.

"He's my grandfather's closest aide."

"Then why isn't he in Benares?"

"He was. Now he's here to watch you."

"You mean the art, don't you?" Cully said angrily, and jammed his pen down on the table so hard it broke in half.

Mirabai turned her head away.

"Goddamn you," Cully muttered. "It's not me they care about and you know it."

"I don't know why you're so upset," Mirabai said carefully. Cully could tell he'd scared her with his anger.

"What can I do if you're here, bothering me?" he said. "I've got work to finish." His chest was heaving. He turned his back on her, remembering his fight with Louis, when Louis, mad, had raised his voice and thrown the glass at him.

"I didn't mean to be rude," the girl said. She sounded young and hurt. Cully ignored her.

"I know your work is important, and I know you're important, but I think you're being rude to me."

Why couldn't she just leave?

"It makes me feel bad," she said almost in a whisper, talking to his back.

"I'm sorry," Cully said. He turned and smiled at her for the first time. "I guess I don't like it when people criticize me."

"I wasn't criticizing you. You just act so indifferent. I just wanted to know what you think of India. But you don't like me, do you."

"I just don't like you hanging around."

"But you do like India?"

"I guess." He felt sorry for her now.

"It's very different from America, isn't it?" Mirabai was smiling, eager for a talk. He didn't know whether to like her or not.

"There you get to do what you want," she said, "and you go places by yourself. I'm not allowed to. I hate it. I wish I was English or something. Are you married?"

He shook his head.

"But you must have a girlfriend. Everyone does. I've read lots of magazines. Especially someone like you who's an expert, I mean, there must be lots of girls who like you."

"What do you mean, an 'expert'?"

"Well, you actually do something special. I never met anyone like that, except friends of my father's or grandfather's and they're very old." She paused. "Well, anyway, I think it's a terrible thing."

"What's terrible?" He noticed she'd put oil on those short fuzzy strands of hair because they were lying flat against her head. She was leaning against an armoire now, he could see the shape of her breasts. He wished she'd leave.

"I think it's terrible he's away," she said. "I miss him every single day."

He changed the subject. "Where's your dog sleep at night?"

"With me."

"Why not outside? I never heard of a dog in an Indian house."

"I get whatever I want. Everyone's afraid of me."

"Isn't he going to come back?"

"My grandfather? He went to Benares to die, but then he didn't die. He hasn't been here in years. But he writes me letters and I write him. Sometimes I talk to him on the phone."

He knew she had something on her mind. "Was he dying when he left?"

"No, he just said he was ready to die. That he had to get ready to die, really. It's a very important Indian custom. It's called renunciation. He said he had to resolve all his bad karma and cleanse himself for the next lifetime. Try to, at least, or else he would take the karma with him and be just as bad next time. We believe people get older and wiser as they go through different lifetimes, so that I might really be two thousand years old, although I don't think so. I'm more stubborn than wise. That's what my grandfather writes me. I haven't learned enough to be very old, he says. I'm hoping if I get married, he'll come back. Just to see me."

"I thought you were definitely getting married."

"That's what everyone hopes, but negotiations are still going on. We're waiting to hear back from the other side. I've more or less agreed in principle, but I don't know whether to change my mind. What do you think?"

Cully knew instinctively that's what she'd been leading up to all along.

"I already changed my mind once," she said. "That's the problem. Everything was all scheduled, contracts signed. Then I ran away. It was awful, but luckily it wasn't much of a scandal. I only got as far as the train station, then I came back. But now we don't know if the other side still wants me. What do you think I should do this time? That's why I came to talk to you. I wanted to ask your advice."

"I thought you couldn't change your mind." Cully peered at her. "When it was arranged it was arranged." He thought she seemed sad. She should go, he thought irritably. Jasdan should take better care of her.

"They had to call my grandfather after I ran away," Mirabai said. "He talked to me and said not to worry. He said he'd get them to put it off a year and get a better contract for me this time. I said the other side wouldn't even accept me because now I was tainted. He said not to worry, he'd take care of it. Shyam would do something."

"What can Shyam do?"

"I don't know. But do you think I'm ready now? Do you have duties in America? I wish we didn't."

"We can do whatever we want. That's what my sister always says. 'You can do whatever you want.' Except she acts like I'm her duty or something. I mean, she even does my laundry."

"I don't know what I think anymore. The boy's probably all right. My grandfather picked him. My father didn't like it one bit."

"Why not?"

"He's from another caste. But my grandfather insisted. He knows the boy. Knows of him, at least. He went to Oxford; although his family is very conservative. My grandfather likes that a lot and thinks he's modern. With him I'll be more independent than with someone else. But the first contract was too strict. My grandfather agreed with me and said my father should have consulted him about it, but my father didn't and so he was the one who really got in trouble with him."

"I thought you weren't supposed to run away."

"You're not. It's very dangerous. . . ."

"And stupid."

"But my grandfather's not angry. He wants me to be like him."

"Like him?" Cully exclaimed.

"He likes it that they're all scared of me. He told me on the phone to keep it up."

"You shouldn't be telling me this."

"But I want to. I trust you."

"Why?"

"I just do."

Cully had to change the subject. "Tell me about your fiancé."

"He's not my fiancé. It's not settled yet."

"But what's he like?" Cully noticed the way her eyes moved and her lips moved. "If your grandfather went to all this trouble, he must be okay."

"He has a sister. I know that much. She's getting married next summer and my grandfather says she's very nice. I think the parents are difficult, though. In the first contract we were supposed to live with them. I told my grandfather I couldn't do it. He said I wouldn't have to. He'd fix it. Now we're waiting to see if they agree. The family's so conservative. That's why everyone's so nervous. Whether they disapprove of me too much."

Cully didn't know what to do or say. "You should meet my sister," he said abruptly. "She knows everything. She always knows what to do or say."

"You don't like her?"

Cully started writing in order to look like he was busy, but he was writing his own name over and over again. Cullen Llewellyn Guthrie, Cullen Llewellyn Guthrie, Cullen Llewellyn . . . He wished she'd go away. He had other things to do. He had a plan and he was almost ready to move into the next phase, the Delhi phase, Kady Suraj, Vishnu Bhave, and now this girl was confusing things.

"He came for lunch once."

"Who?"

"He came down from Delhi with his father, two uncles, and an aunt, and all his aunt wanted to know about was my dog. Why I had a dog. I was hoping she'd vote against me."

"Did you talk to him?"

Mirabai shook her head. "If they accept the new contract, I get to travel," she said wistfully. "I'd like that."

"Who was at the lunch?" he asked.

"The same," she said, meaning the assorted aunts, uncles, cousins, and other relatives who lived in the palace and never numbered less than thirty at the table. "But Kady came," she added brightly. "My father asked him to bring them down in the plane from Delhi and he did."

"How can you ask a Deputy Minister for Public Works to bring someone down in a plane for you?"

"I don't know. You just can, I guess."

And that was how Cully learned that Kady Suraj was born in Deeg. Mirabai told him about how her grandfather saw him in a field one day, liked him, and "brought him up, really, didn't he?" And how Kady learned so fast and got so rich and smart and eventually became the person he was today, and how her grandfather hated him, or loved him, no one knew which, but that she loved them both and thought that was only fair.

# ❧ 4 ❧

JIGGIE DEEG LIVED IN BENARES IN
an old palace. Room after room was empty, no windows as such,
just panes of broken glass and empty holes to let the hot air in;
no furniture, art, or beds, just whatever had been carved or
painted on the walls all that remained of what must once have
been a lovely furnished place. Jiggie had only bedding now,
frayed cotton blankets stretched along the bare stone floor in the
room that was originally used for religious celebrations. When
he slept he saw the water through the windows and could, of a
night, meditate to the sound of it lapping against the ramparts
of the building.

Some hundred years ago likenesses of Krishna and Shiva,
Vishnu and others, had been painted on the walls and traces of
them remained, streaks of red and blue, black, yellow, and
white, so faint it was hard to tell the walls had once been ablaze
with color and life.

Shyam Singh, Jiggie's servant since about the day he was
born, tried to persuade Jiggie to have the walls repainted, but
Jiggie refused. Said if they were going to eat nothing but rice
and grains, not even have bottled water, and curd only once a
week, then how could artists be brought back in?

Jiggie had nothing of his own anymore, the clothes on his

back, that was all, a few little gods Vishnu Bhave's ancestors had brought the Deegs, a shawl Durr sent from Kashmir and a pile of letters. They were from Mirabai, little missives about her dog and her schooling, how her Hindi was coming along, and, always, that she missed him. Jiggie wrapped them in string and placed them on the wall by his bed, nothing else to accompany him on his journey to the great beyond and whatever Benares promised, but items from these two women, one quite young, the other not so old.

Shyam set up cooking facilities in an adjacent room and bought scraps of food every day. The cupboards were bare but for utensils, a pot, two plates, cups, and a box of tea. They had no sugar, no salt, not even the instant coffee Jiggie had loved so much. Jiggie had given up everything, even privacy and solitude, the greatest luxuries of all. After one month he moved Shyam's bedding from the kitchen and put it in the room with him.

"You must sleep in here," he said when Shyam protested. "I won't have it any other way. There must be no luxuries at all anymore."

The palace was six stories high, erected right up and down the side of the River Ganges like a cliff. The bottom had caved in sometime back and lay under the surface of the river now. Boats slid in and out under the stones when they got close to shore and water was lapping inside the room where Jiggie as a child had slept.

Everything had been allowed to decay and disappear. Nothing from the past was left but the shell of the building itself, the river right outside, lapping, lapping at the old man's prayers.

There were the outlines of an altar set in the wall of the bedroom but it didn't shine anymore. Jiggie expressly forbade Shyam Singh to clean it or Vishnu Bhave to restore it to its former beauty. It was what it was, he said, and he sat before it day after day. Or else he sat outside on the ghats or in the river itself, almost naked, water flowing about his waist.

How'd you get down to the ghats? Phoebe asked old Shyam one time.

That was easy, Shyam said. A path led from the third-floor level down along the side of the palace to the river. It was only used by cows and animals too thirsty to reach the water any other way and sometimes Jiggie even bent down to scoop up hot and steamy cow pies, pack them into balls with his hands and shape them flat and firm.

It was the same as the untouchables did. It was their work to do, noncaste that they were, the lowest of the low. They did it to sell for fuel.

Jiggie did it for penance.

# ❧ 5 ❧

THAT JIGGIE WAS LIVING IN Benares, never to return, Phoebe knew; but on Friday, the fourteenth of May, she went to Deeg. It was not for him she went. She went looking for traces of her brother.

As she packed in the hotel that morning, she was acutely aware of being in India and that what she had seen the last three days was its most appalling, public hospitals and the outer slums, the morgue and the male Caucasian body. She knew that had she been someone with no idea of what to expect, she'd have been overcome by the tragedy of just about everything she'd seen.

She finally stopped packing and took a bath, turned on the fan full blast, and sat underneath it, naked; maybe the wind would clean her. Cully was on her mind constantly, if with less urgency now. She remembered Kamala, the ayah, holding the little boy, the two of them curled in against each other, ayah and the boy, dark and light, and Kamala saying, "See, gods, I'm the one with red henna designs and this little boy. Please don't forget this little boy."

Please, God, Phoebe thought now, remember that little boy, wherever he is.

❧

The phone rang. It was Jasdan, calling from Deeg again. He seemed frantic, his words tumbling over themselves. She couldn't imagine what he was like. Someone on triple speed. This time he wanted to know which plane she was taking, when she'd already told him, but he said he wanted to make sure she was still coming. She said, yes, of course, she was still coming, what was the problem? We're just so excited to see you, he said, but she didn't believe him.

Phoebe placed three calls that morning. One was to Stephen in New York. Another was to Suraj's office, to tell him she was leaving for Deeg, didn't know when she'd be back, and was sorry to miss him.

There was one other, but the clerk wrote down the wrong number in his records and Phoebe's forgotten who it was. I look at those numbers and see the house on Jumna Road. Five of the six numbers are the same as the old number there, so I see her up in her room at the hotel, ringing through to Jumna Road.

Who did she think would answer, Thalia, Samiji?

"What are you going to do about looking for Cully now?"

"There isn't much we can do," Harriet McDonald said, taking up a glass of Coca-Cola. They were downstairs in the hotel cafe, Harriet with her brown hair, friendly face, and open warmth. "This is our biggest problem," she was saying. "Tourists don't write home or they forget their mother's birthday. Everyone calls us but we have no idea where to begin to look."

"He's hardly a tourist," Phoebe replied.

"I have a brother, too," Harriet said. "I think they're really difficult."

"Not for me. We're very close. I'd do anything for him, he for me."

"Then you're lucky. I like my brother's wife, but if it weren't for her, I would have given up on him."

"Why?"

"He's just so unreliable," Harriet said.

"I accept Cully as he is," Phoebe said. "He has problems. We all do. But I don't let them get in the way of our relationship."

"Wish I could do that. I used to fight with him about it all the time, trying to get him to change."

"Did it make any difference?"

"Not a bit." Harriet laughed. "Now I just try to arrange to see him on home leave but he can never work out when his vacation is or where the children will be or whether we should meet on the Cape or . . . I'm from Boston. Anyway, I think brothers are everything that's worst about men. You're not in a position to 'educate' them, if you know what I mean, like you can your husband, but emotionally you still want to rely on them utterly and you can't."

"Our situation is better."

Phoebe paused for a what seemed a long time. "Although I do more for him than he does me," she said thoughtfully. "And he doesn't always like it. Maybe he resents me more than I think."

Harriet watched her, yellow hair, blue eyes, an intense look on her face.

"What about the body?" Phoebe said.

"He'll be cremated, the ashes saved. In case someone shows up to claim him. The Indians aren't very interested in it," Harriet added. "It's just another body to them. Sometimes no one ever claims these bodies. It happens from time to time. A world traveler lost forever."

Phoebe met Tulsidas outside the hotel where he was waiting and told him to drive to Number Nine Jumna Road. There, he parked in the street. She opened her window and looked in past the gate and the trees at the big old house with columns and a lawn.

The gate was closed and there were no cars inside, no one in sight, not even a chowkidar on watch.

Her first impression was that the house was empty. She imagined no one had lived there for twenty years and that all traces and smells from the past were still inside, dirty handprints and echoes of their fights, Louis' intensity and Thalia's denial, bits of food and even mildew, that it had all been locked in there for twenty years and allowed to germinate.

Phoebe felt her stomach tighten. She opened the car door and got out, as much to get away from her own emotions as to get a better view.

Outside, it was no better. Tulsidas got out, too, watching her with curiosity, and as she moved in closer to the house, she felt her tension increase. She leaned against the fence and looked in. She imagined a wind blowing through the halls, Louis dressed in white, Thalia upstairs going through her photo books, and she and Cully not there at all. They were in the banyan tree outside. Phoebe looked for them, two yellow whites climbing over there.

She opened her purse and found a candy bar, took a bite, then handed the rest to Tulsidas. "Want this?" she said, taking pleasure in looking at his face. "It's from Am-ri-ka."

"I am wanting any-ting from Am-ri-ka," he singsonged, and she wondered if Thalia had wanted any-ting from Am-ri-ka, too, and saw a child born here as not really hers at all.

She looked up at her old bedroom, then the alcove on the side and out of sight, and knew Thalia certainly didn't want a child when she had one. "Let's drive on," she said abruptly, getting back in the car. "I've had enough of this for now." In the car she fanned herself with her hand. "It looks like an awful place, don't you think? Too many trees, must be dark inside."

In fact it was very light.

# ❧ 6 ❧

THE DRIVE TO THE AIRPORT WAS different from the trip a few days before. Phoebe looked at everything, not with the sense of returning, as she had, but of staying, and she visualized the road out through the southern end of town as a path headed toward the future. She remembers at one point worrying how long the foundation in New York could run without her, and when she realized it could survive indefinitely, she almost told Tulsidas to follow the road as far as it went.

Instead she stared into the rose-colored light that lifted off the dust and mulled on the peculiarities of life that had brought her here, to Cully's world, and her world, but that she didn't know where he was, nor he, she.

At the airport Tulsidas took her suitcase, checked her ticket and told her where the gate to Deeg was. She could have done it without him, but she liked his protective company and endless fussing. When they stopped at the arrival and departure boards, she affectionately pointed out places where Cully might have gone. "Patna and Bombay, Nagpur and the south," but he shook his head and said, "Maybe brother just right here, missus, not for going anywhere. Just right here in town."

The possibility aroused her worries again, Cully close in worse than Cully traveling, but she dispelled the thoughts and noticed, distinctly, that she did feel different. The anxiety of the last few days had given birth to something new and she looked at the departure board with the sense of time wide open, nothing to do, the future free, introspection and discovery her only clear agenda.

She passed through the metal detector and was about to board the plane when an airport official tapped her on the shoulder. "Please for coming this way only."

"Why?" she asked uneasily. "What do you want? Is it my ticket?"

"One minute only," he said. "Just something for our foreign guests," and with that he led her back across the lobby to an unmarked door, which he opened. She went in. He closed the door and left.

Phoebe found herself alone in an office overlooking the runway. The room had a metal desk, sea green walls, and an upright fan that was whirring toward the ceiling. She glanced at her watch. The door opened and a barefoot clerk-chaprassi in oversize khaki trousers came in carrying a tea tray.

It had two cups and two saucers.

He put the tray down on the edge of the desk and poured some tea. "Sue-gar?"

"No."

"Mil-ik?"

"No. Whose office is . . . ?"

He handed her the cup and left.

She put it down and was facing the window when the door opened again. She turned around and there was Kady Suraj.

He was big and tall and so striking Phoebe was shocked. Everything stopped, sounds, thoughts. The airport and the sea green walls disappeared and she couldn't hear anything except the wind of decades bringing back the past, when she had yearned for Kady for years until she'd dispelled him from her mind completely.

He wore a Savile Row suit and a silk tie. His hands were on his hips, but instead of coming in and closing the door, he stood there, eyes on her, taking in every inch of her, unable to move, and his presence was so overwhelming to her in turn, she realized instantaneously that time had disappeared and he might mean as much to her now as he had twenty years ago.

An airplane engine was revving outside. Kady closed the door and came in, a kind of daze on his face as he looked at her, and she watched his arm move, his head bent ever so slightly to receive the hand, the other still at his hip. He was looking at her, confusion in his eyes, so familiar, yet older, more appealing, and she nearly leaned in toward him, a tree falling in his direction, ready to go to him and welcome him in her life again, when something unmistakably held her back. She felt afraid to respond to him, afraid of what would happen, and even as she knew she was as drawn to him as she'd ever been to anyone in her life, conflicting emotions paralyzed her.

Kady was yanking at his tie, widening it at the neck, rubbing the back of his head, more Indian than anyone she'd met in two whole days, but he was so unexpectedly worldly and sophisticated, she knew she could meet him anywhere. This was no one to take home for a week or two or keep at arm's length for years. This was brand new, and every bit of Phoebe Guthrie felt their years of history, first together, then apart, culminating in this reunion; but if he felt the same thing, too, a crisis for him as well, it didn't occur to Phoebe. She was so catapulted into a netherland of attraction and anxiety, she had not an ounce of attention left.

Kady was frowning. The airplane sounded like it was coming in the room, noise so deafening no one could speak a word. She focused on his skin, shades of brown, the slightest shine, she gulped the air and turned away, she couldn't stand it anymore, and the engine stopped. Silence crashed in on them and rang in her ears.

"I can't get used to it," Kady said suddenly, a voice so English and aristocratic, there was barely a trace of India left.

"Used to what?" Despite herself, she began to smile.

"You. You had bangs."

"I did?" Her smile broadened.

"Or at least your hair was always falling in your face."

"It still is."

"But something's different."

"It's you. You used to have funny suits and—"

"But what are you doing here? Why'd you come back?"

209

"I grew up. That's all. I'm not sixteen anymore."

"Jesus, Feeb, I can see that." He suddenly smiled, a smile so full and dazzling, Phoebe nearly reeled backward. "You're definitely not sixteen, I agree with that."

"Stop," she cried, grinning wide.

He was laughing now.

She was, too, hands up to hide her face. "Stop looking at me like that. I can't think."

"Then don't," he said, mocking. "Didn't it ever occur to you what you look like? Jesus, Feeb, you're beautiful."

"It's just my hair."

"It's not. It's everything."

Suddenly the door opened and they both jumped, startled.

A man started talking to Kady in Hindi. Phoebe turned toward the runway, the plane poking its nose in at them, intruding. "Pilot just for having tea, sa'ab," the man was saying. He left and she heard Kady coming toward her, wondered if he'd shake her hand or embrace her, what would she do? But he stopped, poured a cup of tea, then didn't pick it up.

"This has been a dreadful day," he said. "Meetings, from seven in the morning until . . ."

She turned around, hair curling around her neck, skirt way below her knees, pastel blouse, a soft look, colors that made her glow.

"My life is very different than it used to be," he went on. "I don't even know what I have to do until my staff tells me. I know it's not a good excuse."

"Didn't you get my messages?" The question was the first note of reality, and Phoebe felt it dispel some of the romance and memories from her mind.

"I planned to call you," he said. "Luckily at the last minute I got the time to get here. I realized it might be my last chance to see you."

She listened to his voice; it sounded easy, but something was wrong. She sensed it. She kept on talking, mulling the impression in her mind. "A friend of mine at the embassy said you might be the next minister of—"

"Yes. But that's not until next year sometime."

She listened more. There was a ripple in his voice, a pause; he wasn't telling the truth. That was it.

"It's not definite yet," he was saying.

"Did your flight just get in?" she asked, testing him.

"Flight?"

"Yes. The man said you were away. The man on the phone."

"Oh, yes. I travel a lot."

But there hadn't been any plane and his man Ramchandran had been lying, too; she knew it, and she wondered if her whole life, past or present, was what she thought it was. For a second Phoebe felt so uneasy, she wanted to go back to New York. "How's India?" she asked preposterously.

"I used to think about you all the time," Kady said, "but I haven't now in years. I made an effort to forget you, I guess."

"Me too," she answered.

"Remember how we used to go out every night and Louis'd prop me up and go on and on about pronunciation?"

"I thought you owed everything to Jiggie Deeg."

Kady shook his head. "He doesn't bother me anymore. I haven't seen him in a long time. You knew about him, too, didn't you. You knew everything."

"No, I didn't," Phoebe corrected. "You never told me, whatever it was, between you and Jiggie."

"I do remember," Kady said quickly, obviously trying to dismiss the subject. Then he broke into a smile again. His dark eyes were still tracking every change in her face.

Phoebe felt herself pull back from him all over again, his gaze too strong. "How are your children?"

"Fine."

"And Durr? Does she still take singing lessons?"

"Yes. I'll tell her you remembered. Why did you come back? Was it just because of Cully?"

Only then did Phoebe remember Cully, and worry spread across her face. "Kady," she said urgently, "do you have any idea where he is?"

He took his cup for the first time and started stirring the tea. "I don't."

"He must want to make a break. Be alone. That's what my friends say. He hasn't written much. He's not what you'd call really competent. Maybe he resents me. I've become overprotective in my old age." She grinned, trying to relax and feel comfortable in his presence.

"Oh, he's all right," Kady said lightly. "I wouldn't worry about him. I didn't think the body was him."

"Why not?"

"I just didn't."

She didn't believe that, either. He had a reason. He just wasn't telling her what it was.

He was looking at the desk as if there were things he was trying to see among the memos and the clutter. "I gather you're going to Deeg."

"How'd you know?"

"In my position . . ." He sounded apologetic.

Phoebe laughed again. "Now I remember you," she exclaimed. "You're the one who liked my new shoes and I had such a crush on you, it was awful."

"You did?" He looked both surprised and pleased.

"Don't you remember?"

"Yes. But you shouldn't have been there. That was no place for a girl."

"No place for 'a child.'"

"You weren't exactly a child."

"But was I a 'girl'?" she challenged lightly.

"I don't know," he said, grinning. "You tell me. You certainly weren't a boy, but were you a woman? You tell me."

"I was pretty close, that's for sure." Phoebe started to chuckle.

"What's so funny?"

"I don't know. You. You certainly got out from under Jiggie Deeg. It's incredible what you've done. Let's shake hands and pretend this is all utterly normal and routine." She stepped forward and put out her hand. He put out his, too, but when she felt it, it was so exciting, she dropped it as fast as she could and immediately remembered the lie about the plane. "Where'd you just come from?"

"Calcutta."

She took her tea. It was cold and almost white. He sat down on a vinyl couch and stretched his legs. Had they always been that long? She looked at the line of his chest as he put his arm up along the couch, so that the chest was there, long and lean, but not too lean, plenty of him, and imagined herself there, held in the curve of his arm. She turned and went over to the window to get farther away. "If you want to know the truth," she said, "I'm really worried about Cully. Where do you think he is? I've been to his apartment. Hospitals. Do you have any idea?"

"Hospitals," Kady exclaimed.

"And a policeman came to the hotel. Wanted to know where he was. He had all these questions. He said there was a murder, or something. Vishnu Bhave's son. Remember him?"

"Cully has nothing to do with that," Kady said dismissively. "It's just a coincidence of timing."

"That's what I thought, but I haven't heard from him in two months. That's a long time."

Kady cocked his head and she thought he was going to smile, but he didn't, thank goodness. His expression was so disarming, the most incredible combination of intimate and remote she'd ever seen, she didn't know what to do.

"Is it?" he said.

"Is it what?"

"Is two months a long time?"

Like he was saying how could two months be a long time when twenty years had passed and here are you and here am I and nothing's changed.

The door opened. An airport official stuck his head in, looked around, and said, intensely apologetic, "Oh, I'm so sorry, Minister-sa'ab. I thought you were done," and disappeared.

"Are you holding the plane just so we can talk?" Phoebe asked, aghast. "Why didn't you just call me?"

"I wanted to see you," Kady said, his voice soft.

Phoebe looked out the window, uncomfortable, wishing she was the sort of person who could just go into his arms and make everything easy. "Why, according to my plans, I was supposed to be sailing on the Sound this weekend," she said breezily. It wasn't true. She'd never sailed in her life. Then Kady was beside her, only feet away, and she smelled the faint scent of something cinnamon, so faint she wouldn't have known it was there if she hadn't remembered, and she felt a wind blowing her toward him and knew they'd have to collide and come together, nothing could stop it. He was saying, "I like your hair," and she was saying, "Yes," and he was about to say something else, when someone knocked on the door again and Kady stepped aside, jumped almost, as if he'd been too close to her as well, too close for anyone to see, so she knew he must have been feeling something, too. He said, "Come in."

The official stood at the door. "I'm sorry, sa'ab, but it's the pilot and we can't hold the flight much longer." He left.

Phoebe suddenly dropped in a chair, a wave of sadness flowing over her. She covered her face with her hands.

"What's the matter?" Kady said, concerned.

"I don't know." She stared into the darkness of her palms. "You remind me of the past so much, it's—"

"Oh, Feeb."

"—overwhelming."

"It is for me, too."

"Remember how he used to say, 'Jesus, Feeb,' too?" She brushed her hair off her face and stood up. "I'm all right," she said. "Do I have to go now?"

"In a second."

"Just tell me, quickly. Weren't you afraid of being caught?"

"You mean, the whiskey and all? Of course. He was making all those wild phone calls. Threatening Jiggie. . . ."

"Threatening? . . ."

"Everything was chaos, his job, the police."

"Why'd he threaten Jiggie? Why'd Jiggie come to the house?"

"Calling him, saying that if he didn't treat me better, he'd do something."

"Is that why Jiggie came to the house?"

"I don't know. I don't remember."

"I've forgotten things, too," she said, "but I keep thinking about the house on Golf Links where you and Louis stored the whiskey."

"Don't talk about that house," Kady said.

"I never liked it."

"I didn't, either."

"So you closed down operations after we left?"

"Yes."

The man had returned and was slowly scratching his nails against the door.

"But weren't you afraid they'd blackmail you? Samiji and Kuldip?"

"I took care of them."

"So the Kuldip who called me from your office is the same man as before? He ran things for you and Louis?"

Kady nodded.

"So you're all right?"

"Do you care?" He smiled a little, his eyes seeming only inches away, although they were separated by chairs and a table.

The official outside was scratching at the door.

"I'd better go," she said. She crossed the room. "Coming?"

He didn't move. "Jesus, Feeb," he said, his voice deep and hoarse.

She wondered now if she'd ever see him again and felt distraught at her own confusion. "I have a picture of you. With Cully. You like him, don't you?"

Kady didn't answer. "I suppose I do," he said at last. "How long are you staying?"

"Few more days, I guess. I don't know, really." She turned the door handle.

"Do you think you'll have a chance to call me when you get back?"

"I don't know. If I have time, I guess."

"Yes, if you have time," he said, and with that she knew instinctively he was as confused as she.


Kady watched the plane until it took off and then went back outside, got in the car, and told Samiji to drive.

"Where, sa'ab?"

"Anywhere."

"But, sa'ab . . ."

Kady didn't answer. Samiji took a road that headed west. He looked in the mirror. "Meetings, sa'ab. Meetings."

Kady took off his jacket and rolled up his sleeves. Samiji kept driving, watched as sahib removed his tie and undid some buttons. Kady told him to turn off the road. "Anywhere," he said. "I want to go for a walk."

"Walk, now, sa'ab? No time for walk."

Kady had him stop the car and without a word he got out and walked straight off into the plains, shiny black shoes stirring up dust from the mere pressure of his feet.

Samiji sat in the shade of the car, balanced on the heels of his feet, bottom inches from the ground. Farther out, Suraj did the same, pulled his pants up on his legs to make it easier, balanced on the flat of his feet, knees up, arms out. An Indian can stay that way all day. He looked at the pale brown sky of a horizon that wasn't very far away. Flies landed on his head. Goats grazed nearby, although what they'd be grazing on was unclear because nothing grew out there, the land so parched and inhospitable. Kady just sat and Samiji, too.

After a while small boys who walked the goats came up, cloths tied around their necks and throats to protect them from the dust. They looked at Suraj, came closer, and sat down in positions that gave a good, close view of him, and there they all sat, viewers and the viewed.

Samiji walked out across the desert eventually, carrying a bottle of water. "Sa'ab?"

But sahib didn't notice until the boys said, "Sa'ab." Then he looked up, dazed.

"Do you know what I've done with my life, Samiji?" he asked. "Do you realize what I've done?"

When Kady got back to his office, his mood had turned dark. Vishnu Bhave was still sitting in the reception room and the place was crowded, one man hoping to get a business phone, another with a tax case, they'd been there a week, waiting, no appointment, and they all jumped up, a dozen or so, rushing at him, grasping at his clothes, talking, yelling, waving papers. He shoved them away, his face twisted and upset. He pushed them down and peeled them off while Samiji pulled from the other end. He saw Bhave watching umoved from across the room.

Suraj glared. He despised him. He always had. He went straight in his office and slammed the door.

Bhave overheard orders that Suraj wasn't to be disturbed, and then the phone rang and the secretary said, Oh, Minister-sa'ab's out of station, not to be reached today, and then she called someone and canceled his meeting with Chief Minister Narayan, his boss, because an emergency had come up, she said, but told someone else he was upset by something that happened at the airport. Bhave wondered why Suraj had noticed him at all today, after a trip to the airport, when he hadn't spotted him any of the other days. A tray of food was taken into the office, taken out just the same, untouched, and Bhave heard an angry outburst, Suraj yelling when he was never known to yell at all, and Bhave knew to bide his time and wait.

Inside, Kady picked up a teacup on his desk, one of the beautiful pieces of English china Jiggie had sent from Deeg some time ago. He threw it against a wall. There were more cups remaining, and these too he threw with a hard, tough cast. Not done, with a long low sweep of his arm, he wiped the whole desk clean, so that the tray, pot, books, papers, messages, whole files, cleared the surface and crashed.

Samiji rushed in at the noise, only to flee at a glance.


Samiji sat down outside the door on the floor, his back flat against the panel, and didn't let anyone in all day.


Bhave ate lunch, just like he did here every day, unwrapped his samosa, and bought water from the water seller out in the hall.

Later, for the first time, the receptionist came to him and said would he follow her please to a different waiting room, so he waited in there, where there were soft seats and magazines, designed for people who had appointments, but he still didn't see Kady Suraj until almost dark when everyone else had gone, but for Samiji, still at his post on the floor.

Kady opened the door and asked him to come in. It was after eight.

Kady apologized for making him wait.

Bhave said it was nothing, didn't show he noticed the mess of china on the floor, said he was fortunate so important a man as Suraj would make time for him, but the rudeness, to one as renowned as Vishnu Bhave, was unmistakable.

Five days had passed.

## ❧ 7 ❧

KADY FIRST MET VISHNU BHAVE the same day he met Jiggie Deeg.

He bicycled away from their meeting at the dried-up river bed with the scent of the maharaja's perfume still on his clothes, his voice still ringing in his ears and he went as far from the palace grounds as he could get, then toppled off in the dust and didn't move.

His heart was pounding. His back ached, his eyes hurt, and he didn't know where he was or what Durr looked like or what he'd really done with Jiggie Deeg. He lay there until the sun started to rise and even then the only thing that got him up off the ground was the heat of the sun drying the sides of his mouth and the fact that he had to begin all over again, lunchtime at the palace.

The dining table at Umaid Mahal Palace was forty feet long and seated more people than a bus. What struck Kady right away was that one man, Vishnu Bhave, was nearly navy blue in color and the maharaja, right beside him, nearly white.

He was led in through the back door from the kitchen by the gentleman, Attar Singh. Everyone else was already there, family guests, aides, staff and one solid gold Garuda bird.

The creature, Vishnu's royal mount, had a head as big as a chair, eyes of rubies, feathers made of jewels, and it rose twelve feet from the floor, five feet front to back, so bright and shining Kady had to blink his eyes. It stood right behind the chair where Jiggie Deeg sat at the head of the table. Its golden beak loomed out over his head like an awning, and there was no mistaking the fact that a canopy of wealth and power belonged to those who sat beneath.

Kady saw all this, but no one noticed him at all. Self-conscious, he brushed dust from his jacket and smelled the scent of his own cheap pomade. He vowed to improve himself so that one day he'd belong in here and would sit as high at the table as the man in navy blue.

Then he heard a voice, loud and clear and unmistakable. "That one there." It was the maharaja.

Jiggie had stood up and was pointing down the length of the table to the last seat of all. "You take that one there," he said.

The seat was as far from Jiggie Deeg as a person could get, everyone else positioned above him in rank and stature. The navy blue man smiled arrogantly in Kady's direction.

Kady loathed him on sight and sat down.

It was a seat he came to know well. If the bargain he made with Jiggie Deeg prescribed that the two would never meet, meet they did, year after year, day after day, but Kady Suraj was never assigned another seat, nor was the man in navy blue.


A few weeks later Durr came with him willingly.

Shyam found them an apartment in New Delhi. Attar Singh brought the dowry and supervised as workmen carried it up the stairs, furniture, linen, china, food. Vishnu Bhave brought the art, a wedding gift from the maharaj-sahib to the bride herself.

Kady came up from Deeg alone by bus. He had no one to tell what he was doing and no one to bring along. Durr came by train with Shyam as her escort. Kady met them at the station.

He saw Durr before she saw him, and she was so beautiful he couldn't believe she was meant for him. She was small and round, with tiny feet, and he only saw her take a few steps, from inside the carriage to the stairs leading down, but his breath caught in his throat at the grace of her movement.

Then she looked at him and started to cry.

Kady saw it, not as the deep appreciation that she felt, but as regret over what she had to do, and instead of coming forward to help her down the steps, he backed away and never approached. To do her as little harm as he could, he thought.

The three went to City Hall. Attar Singh and Vishnu Bhave joined them in front of a clerk on the second floor.

The clerk wore shoes and declared it was a "ci-wil marriage," and with that the couple signed their names and went downstairs.

Shyam got a cab, Attar Singh held the door. The bride and groom got in—they still hadn't exchanged a word. Vishnu Bhave looked down his nose at Kady Suraj as if to say, That's as far as you'll ever get, my man. Attar Singh gave the driver rupees to pay the fare and they set off alone.

In the beginning Kady tried to love her. He proceeded slowly to give her time. They kept to separate sides of the bed and talk came shyly. He didn't mind. That was what was done in arranged marriages. But time brought him something he had not expected.

At first it was the saris. Eventually it was the babies. There were too many of both. He thought he'd never seen so many saris in any one room, and if a wife was meant to be a stranger, that was one thing, but the flat brought too much that was unfamiliar.

He adjusted quickly to living in the city and living above other people and other lives. In fact, he enjoyed it. And he adjusted to working in the offices of Deeg and having bank accounts and bills, and he watched as his plans for himself developed.

Gradually he even adjusted to being with a woman, someone with breasts and tiny feet, who washed and cared for a baby and disappeared unclean in a room every few days a month and he even, eventually, grew accustomed to this one's beauty, the gorgeous line of her body as she lifted her arm up, then slowly brought it down to brush her hair—he thought there was nothing so beautiful in all the world—but he couldn't adjust to her.

He knew he was living with the ghost of Jiggie Deeg.

Durr missed Jiggie achingly, and Kady knew it. With each day she loved him more. She hadn't even known who he was until she left Kashmir and traveled down to Delhi, where he sat her in a chair and explained why she had to travel the rest of the way to Deeg in a steamer trunk with holes cut in the sides.

Now her life in Delhi as Mrs. K. T. Keshri Suraj stretched on day after day. She wore one sari, then another, and it never occurred to her that the cloth seemed like arms and limbs to her husband, arms holding her, covering her, having her altogether in a way he could never match.

And so, gradually, what had once been a building thing in Kady, something growing, a touch here, a touch there, the taking of a wife, ceased to build, ceased even to be.

But it wasn't until she was pregnant for the second time that he knew what must have happened.


Kady didn't see Shyam Singh at first. The man didn't come for almost a year. Then one day he was sitting outside waiting for her, and when she came out he handed her a letter from Jiggie Deeg, then opened the door of a waiting taxi so she could ride around and read it in peace.

She was in back, he in front. They didn't talk much except once she asked how Jiggie was, and he told her, "Not very well," and once, how was Yosant, Jiggie's wife, and Shyam said she was fine.

The taxi took her home. There she looked at Shyam with her wide, unblinking orange eyes and said with a sadness that was overwhelming, "Yes, I'll see him."

After that Shyam took her to Jiggie Deeg, sometimes to an apartment, sometimes a hotel, sometimes just a distant park to walk. He always sat in the street outside and waited or took a position far enough away to grant them privacy, but he was always there to take her home, and over time the size of her family increased from one child to two, then three, and then there was one miscarriage, and another, and then a baby who was dead before he was three days old, and then a girl who was dead inside and had to be carved out in a hospital, and after that there were no more because Jiggie said he had to go to Benares and begin his long repentance, but all the ones that were born had the same fair skin as Jiggie Deeg.

## ❦ 8 ❦

KADY SURAJ ENCOUNTERED VISH-
nu Bhave frequently. Wherever Jiggie was, Bhave was not far
away. The little man visited the maharaja daily at Deeg House
and came down to Deeg frequently. During the years of his
employment with Jiggie Deeg, Kady barely concealed his contempt for him, and Bhave in turn never failed to sneer or conde-
scend toward him.

I'm trying to remember how I first heard about Bhave. I know
it was a long time ago, I think when someone visiting my father
said he wanted to buy a piece of art and mentioned Bhave's
name, but my father said, "You have to have an introduction.
No one sees him without an introduction."

So that set him up firmly in my mind. Even my father
couldn't get through to him.

Kitty Chandradas actually saw him once at Jumna Road. It
was years ago, I was just a child. I'd give anything to have been
there, seen Louis and Bhave together, the confluence of those
two men and both their boys. What I'd want to know is how
indebted Louis felt to him, if he did at all. Bhave gave him
identity and a passion. What father or friend can say the same?

Kitty was having tea and later acted as Louis' hostess, when
Bhave came on foot, Anant a toddler at his side. The bearer

wouldn't let them in. Told them to go round the back, this door wasn't for . . . But Bhave wouldn't move, so the bearer finally came in, apologized to Louis and said there was this little man outside. Kitty says Louis went out and brought him back in, the man was only half his size. He ordered tea and cakes, then was adulatory toward him, as if he were the pope, he an acolyte. It was the only time she ever saw him act that way.

The living room was bare. There was only the statue of the great Shiva Nataraj, spectacular the way it dominated the room, so it must have been early on. Cully was only seven or eight.

Cully and Anant were about the same age, and she remembers thinking the boys were a lot alike, although Anant seemed a bit retarded. He hung on his father like a towel draped along his leg. But, then, Cully did the same thing. Or at least tried to, Kitty said. Lean on Louis' legs, sit against him, balance on his shoes, but Louis kept kicking him off.

She remembers that the boys had a fight.

They had started climbing on the arms and legs of the Shiva Nataraj, a natural jungle gym, and they were both up there, hanging like monkeys, when Cully told Anant to get off. Anant didn't move, and Cully repeated his command, said the Shiva was his father's.

Anant said no, the Shiva was *his* father's. They were on the floor tearing at each other, but neither of the fathers moved, although the fight was over them. Kitty was the one who finally got up and pulled the two apart.


Through the years I heard more about Vishnu Bhave. The name itself I loved, Vish knew, Baa vey. He was so prestigious that the fact that Kady Suraj was the one who had introduced Louis to him raised Kady in everyone's estimation. It added to his mystique too, he just the brash, young low caste, if surprisingly prepossessing, employee of Jiggie Deeg's who Louis Guthrie, ranking member of the international business community, had adopted too.

The crucial and remarkable piece of information about Kady and the art and Vishnu Bhave only came years later. I heard it the night of my twenty-first birthday, not long after Louis and Thalia died.

Specifically, the news was that it was Kady who actually got the Shiva Nataraj for Louis and that, furthermore, it was a gift from him.

No one had ever thought Kady had anything to do with it, except for making the connection to Vishnu Bhave. Now it was his gift. It was extraordinary. Whatever the statue was worth then, now it would be hundreds of thousands of dollars, if not millions.

The Nataraj was famous. It was Louis' trademark, the cornerstone of his collection, the only one of all his pieces, he liked to say, he really cared about. Further the statue personified him in everyone's eyes.

It stood four or five feet high, some three feet wide, and it was as imposing as having a cow in your living room. Mere ownership of such a statue made a bigger man of Louis. And the mere giving of it made a bigger man of Kady.

The piece enthralled even me, a teenager then, and for all my youthful lack of interest in the arts, the one time I went to Number Nine Jumna Road with my parents, I was mesmerized, a feeling that added in no small way to the fascination I already had with Louis and his family.

The statue was standing up against a big wall in the living room. Kitty said sometimes it was there, sometimes Louis moved it around and positioned it elsewhere, even in front of the windows, so that it literally glowed in the light, like water with the sun on it. When I arrived, I remember being more interested in Phoebe, wondering if I'd get to see her, talk to her, find out what she was really like, but the bearer, someone named Moosselman, told me she wasn't there.

I didn't believe him. My father had already told me that the girl never shared her father's or mother's life at home, one reason I should sympathize with her. I remember being irritated I wouldn't get to see her, anticipating boredom, and then my mother said to be sure to look at the Shiva Nataraj.

So I did.

It looked huge and solid and awe-inspiring. The four arms and two legs were things in motion, dancing inside a wide circle of flames. "The Lord . . . a mystic dance performs," the Upanishads say, "a cycle of destruction and rebirth."

The god had a writhing cobra in his hair, as well as a human skull and a mermaid that stood for the holy River Ganges. In his right ear he had a man's earring, in the left, a woman's, and he was adorned with necklaces, armlets, bracelets, and anklets, not as an androgynous figure, but as a polished, perfect Indian male. In his right hand he had the drum of creation, another held the fire of destruction, the contrasts of life, one more was uplifted in the sign that means, "Do not fear," and the last, the fourth, was pointed downward toward the dwarf. This was the dwarf of human life, upon whom this greatest of the gods is said to dance for all eternity.

I was so affected by the statue that through the years whenever I was in India I'd read all the books and passages on the Shiva Nataraj, but they told me nothing I didn't already know, or feel, that one and only afternoon.

"It's the clearest image of the activity of God which any art or religion can boast of," one book said. "Our Lord is the Dancer," said another, "dancing to maintain the life of the universe and to give release to those who see Him. All that is destroyed will be reborn. All who want another chance will have it, for if you can only find the dancing foot and the varying steps within you, your fetters shall fall away."

I liked that.

One small book, published in Calcutta and sold here in a bazaar in Old Delhi, had something else to say. It spoke of the "burning ground" and emphasized death as both the fact and the metaphor of the Shiva Nataraj, and I liked it the best of all. It told me the most about Louis and the Guthries.

"Shiva is a destroyer," the quote began, "and he loves the burning ground within the circle of flames, but what does he destroy? Not merely the heavens and the earth, but the ties that bind each separate soul. And where does he dance? Where is this burning ground? It is the crematorium of death, where bodies are cremated, there to burn and fall away, there to turn to dust and mingle with the gods, but there too are the illusions and the wrongs of life burned away and there too in the burning ground are we freed up, amidst the fire and the flames, to live again and be reborn."

To me that was poetry and religion all in one.

I never saw Phoebe that night. I imagined her walking overhead and worried about her, this girl with the blond hair and blue eyes, so alien, it seemed, to India, but to me the epitome of it, living and breathing it as I never would. I saw her and Louis and Kady Suraj as magical and elegant, yet unsettled, their nocturnal roaming about part of the richness and the poverty of the land, its depth and frustrating promise.

The house said it all, so much art it looked inhabited by the gods. Their mystic dance had taken over here.


On the night of my twenty-first birthday, the talk at my house among the group of family friends around the table was about how on earth Kady Suraj from the lower Sudra castes in Deeg had come up with a piece like the Shiva Nataraj and been able to give it as a gift.

Everybody speculated. Did it really come from Kady, or was it from Jiggie Deeg? But, people said, why would Jiggie Deeg give it to Louis Guthrie? They didn't even like each other.

Maybe Jiggie gave it to Kady, someone said, and he in turn gave it to Louis.

But that didn't make sense. Why would Jiggie give it to Kady himself or help him facilitate a friendship? Kady was too low down.

Besides, someone else said, we'd all know if Jiggie Deeg'd had that Shiva Nataraj, and he didn't. Then people got into a debate about the collection down at Deeg; had anyone ever seen the whole thing? Of course not. So how could they know what was in it and what wasn't?

Someone cut through all the brouhaha and took the stage for himself, and what he said was so right, his was the final word. Art in India, he said, is a matter of worship and discretion. All classical art is by definition part and parcel of the Hindu religion, the making and the having and the looking at it, a religious, devotional act. To give a god to an unseemly host was like turning him out in the cold or an act of karma that would do no one any good. Not that the gift of the statue to Louis Guthrie was necessarily an act of religion, he said, but it undoubtedly occurred within that religious and historical context and existed as part of the unknown and the enigmatic that defined it.

So, he declared, "In a word, we'll never know."

That's where the matter stood. For twenty years.

And added immeasurably, no doubt, to the power and charm that succeeded at that point in time from the just dead Louis

Antonine Guthrie to his protégé, K. T. Keshri Suraj.

Who, even at the moment of his friend's death, got his greatest promotion. Head of Deeg Enterprises.


There was one other interesting fact about the Shiva Nataraj that I only discovered years later.

At the very time of that conversation at my house when the statue was an object of such gossip, it disappeared.

At Louis' death his collection went intact to the National Museum of Art. But this one piece was sold by the Guthrie estate to an unidentified buyer, for a sum so large, it reportedly constituted a good measure of the children's inheritance.

It was never seen again.

# ❧ 9 ❧

I SAW A LOT OF CULLY GUTHRIE
the year he came back, at first whenever he came to Delhi and
later, when he couldn't handle Deeg anymore and stayed in
town, all the time. I found him endearing and attractive but
complicated. He had an enormous amount of inner tension and
was profoundly indecisive. He also had a low tolerance for frustration. He had his apartment; he "worked." He presented himself as a professional, someone who intended to settle down in
India and establish himself. I wondered what Phoebe thought
about that. It never occurred to me she didn't know.

His work consisted of three things, cataloging the collection
down in Deeg, formulating his own collection, and, very much
in the amorphous stage, a new idea he had about a book on how
the Shiva Nataraj was depicted throughout history in his role
as a dancer at the cremation grounds.

He had collected hundreds of pictures, Shivas tall and squat,
circles of flames round or oblong. There was an astounding
number of differences to the models but he could explain them
all. He knew not only the history and the iconography, but the
workmanship as well, how the things were actually made, what
they weighed, how they were moved, and what people believed
when they were making them.

The spirituality didn't interest him. He was at heart an academic, he loved the fine print. Phoebe was the one who had an inner preoccupation with the nature of life and death.

I often told him he knew far more about Indian art than his father. I thought that might please him, but, curiously, it didn't. He had no need to better his father or compete with him. He idealized him and was quite touching whenever the subject came up. He specifically loved the whole tradition of the Shiva Nataraj and its role in his father's life.

"I remember where it was," he said once with great emphasis. "That it was in the hall and, another time, in the living room, and remember those windows? A whole row of windows in the living room? It was there once, right in front of them."

What he knew, he declared, was that "it got moved around a lot."


Cully returned to India in September, so it must have been October, early November, when he first flew up to Delhi from Deeg for a long weekend and began to get in touch with people. He paraded it all over that he was Louis Guthrie's son, not that he had to tell anyone, the word got around right away that he was working down in Deeg.

He got into sports right away, and from then on, whenever he was in town, it was tennis, golf, squash, even polo. Sports is all very upper class here, of course, who else has the time and money? Have a gin and bitters, get a workout, chitchat, can you come for dinner? Cully did it beautifully, just eccentric enough to add spice to things, remind people of his father.

But then Cully went private. He had no staying power. They wanted him on the tennis team. He said he couldn't fix his schedule, when, in truth, he had no schedule. Then he was learning polo, but it got so he missed his lessons, and for what? He'd stopped to watch an elephant or gone to see Vishnu Bhave. He was like that. Unreliable.

I realized Cully's plans for India weren't working out, and I began to suspect he was the sort of person whose life never quite goes right. He never took to the work in Deeg. The collection was far too big and he didn't like the place. By Christmas he was staying in Delhi for longer and longer periods, and finally it got like he visited Deeg, not the other way around.

I think he continued to go down largely because of Mirabai.

He said he wasn't romantically drawn to her. They were friends. With her marriage negotiations still not concluded, I thought he identified with her, her limbo matched his own.

Eventually she came to Delhi quite a bit, and he got to see her here on different terms. Once when he knew he was going to be allowed to take her to the movies, with a chaperone, of course, he was as excited as a teenager.

But then I saw them together and my whole perspective changed.

He and the girl were leaving a restaurant, Kady was the chaperon, as it turned out, and as I watched, they all three got in Kady's black Mercedes and took off. Mirabai got in the back, then Cully, too, put his arm up along the seat, the girl not far away, and Kady got in the front with the driver. That's what gave me a jolt. Because it should have been the reverse. Cully should have been in front with the driver, Kady in back with Mirabai. That's the way it's done here, and they all knew it.

I asked Cully about it. He said it was nothing, she was "like a sister."

I knew Louis and Cully had had a fight the last night his parents were alive, January 6th years ago, but I didn't know Louis'd attacked him with the glass, giving him that dreadful wound on his shoulder. I'd seen the scar, a big red worm of a thing, when we went swimming at the Ford Foundation pool, but Cully just said it was an accident and never mentioned Louis.

One day we were at the Red Fort, sitting on the ramparts looking out across the Jumna River to the flats on the other side. He was talking about Kady, who had taken him on a drive that morning to inspect some sewage system, and he was telling me how he'd "adopted" him. He'd said those things before about Kady, and I believed them to be true. But now he said more.

"Not that I need that, of course," he began. "Being adopted. Because I had Louis. My childhood may have been unusual, I'll grant you that, but I always had Louis. He was everything to me. Even his death brought us closer because he was thinking about me. Our fight upset him so much he went out of control

230

in the car, and that's what caused the accident. That's how important I was to him. He didn't always show it very well, but he let me know, and that's what counts. Someone else might have a guilt complex," he went on. "Feel he was to blame for his parents' death, but I feel the opposite. United with him by the death."

Then he said something else, that twenty years before, Kady told him that just before Louis died in Agra, the villagers said Louis was talking about his only son.

If Cully was to be believed, Vishnu Bhave liked him as much as he had his father and was going to help him build a collection.

It was hard to figure. Among other things, I didn't know what was in it for Bhave himself.

Cully talked about getting a big piece from him. He said it was all planned. He even made a point of comparing it to the Shiva Nataraj.

But I had my doubts, and so, given everything I knew and felt about this famous Vishnu Bhave, when Cully suddenly offered to take me to meet him, I was excited.

By the time Cully and I reached Bhave's shop somewhere inside the rabbit warren of streets that was in Tees-he-zari in Old Delhi, the steel grate was pulled down over the front, the place locked up tight. Whatever I expected to find, all I saw was a tiny pinpoint of a place in an alley only a few yards wide.

A cow was asleep outside, sprawled across the street, surrounded by its excrement. A sari store stood on one side, a house on the other, all three buildings with metal rungs that got pulled up or down to set the locks, and I looked at Bhave's place and thought, Louis and Kady Suraj came here? Jiggie Deeg?

I was astonished. This tiny, humble, dirty spot was the point of entry for all this art and beauty?

We peered in through the rungs, but the windows were covered by a thin gauzy curtain, so we couldn't see much except a general whiteness inside.

Why's it so white? I asked.

Cully said a white sheet-covered mattress lay across the whole floor, a combination rug and bed. There wasn't any other furniture. He pointed to the right and said that was where Bhave sat. He sounded almost reverent. He pointed in another direction and said that was where he himself sat, and that first Bhave unwrapped the things, took them out of the cloth in which they were stored, and then Anant, only he called him, "the boy," took the wrapping away. Then Bhave lifted up the object, turned it around and sideways, showing it to you, all sides, holding it to the light, and as Cully talked, it was like he was describing a ritual, this showing of the art. Last, he said, Bhave handed the object to the boy and he was the one who brought it across to you and you got to hold it for yourself, look at it, touch it, turn it, feel it.

"What if it's too big to hold in your hands?" I asked without thinking, the great big Shiva on my mind, and suddenly Cully got flustered. It broke his train of thought, and any sense I'd had of a ritual being explained ended.

He came up with an answer, about how the object was carried into the room and you came over and touched it, and so on, but I realized he didn't know the answer, that he'd never had this experience, never seen it done, had no idea, which certainly left a great doubt in my mind as to how much really good art he'd seen in there.

Cully quickly started talking again, pointed out the door to the rest of the house. "It only has three rooms," he added. "He doesn't even have a phone," and I ached because I could hear him trying to sound authoritative, intimate with this special man, when maybe he barely knew him at all. Maybe he only knew what Phoebe'd told him about the man and there was absolutely nothing real about this collection or his friendship.


We headed back out into the streets. We had reached the slaughterhouse for birds, and I was brushing those tiny white feathers off my dress when Cully touched me on the arm with his elbow.

"See, over there?" he said. "That's him."

Why Cully ever thought I'd pick him out tells you worlds about whatever was going on inside his head, because there were two hundred people where he pointed and I don't think anyone could have figured out which one was Vishnu Bhave.

Finally, through a process of question and answer, I eliminated all one hundred and ninety-nine other possibilities and came down to this one inconspicuous fellow walking along carrying a newspaper.

We were going the same direction as he, he obviously wasn't headed home, and since we had nothing else to do, we just walked along and talked. Whatever Vishnu Bhave was as an art dealer, as a human specimen he was ordinary at best.

He was pathetically thin, almost invisible, whichever way he turned, front, back, or sideways, and his clothes made him indistinguishable from anyone else wearing white shirts and dark pants, or a good fifty percent of Indian males. He had skin as close to the color of navy blue as I can imagine skin being and had curly black hair that stood up straight in ringlets like a child's and was coated with almond oil, so it glistened as though covered with rain.

We followed along. Cully bought an ice from a street vendor and I said, "Oh, you shouldn't. The germs," and he said he was all right, he'd built up his immunity, which was nonsense. Eventually I said, "I thought you said Vishnu Bhave always had his son with him," and he said, "He does," and I said, "Well, where is he now?" and he said . . .

Actually, I don't remember what he said, but he was totally irritated, and I realized that whatever he felt about Vishnu Bhave, his son was another story.

That whatever he said about himself and Louis, he still had plenty of room to feel extraordinarily jealous of a son who was the focus of his father's adoration.


Cully leapt ahead.

I darted after him and was only a few paces behind when he tapped Bhave on the shoulder.

The little man turned in surprise, and then, with Cully towering over him, the two of them wrapped each other up in their arms. Cully lifted him a good foot off the ground, and Bhave had his head back and was laughing, navy blue face and the whitest teeth.

Both of them were clearly transported, so I assumed—how could I think otherwise?—that everything was all fair and square, just the way Cully'd said.

How could I guess Jiggie was paying Bhave to deal with him?

233

# ❧ 10 ❧

IN HIS OFFICE FAR ABOVE RAJ Path overlooking India Gate, Kady didn't offer Bhave tea or even a glass of water. It was getting dark. The art dealer sat in one chair, Kady in another. The room was not well lit. Neither spoke. Bhave recognized a now priceless Ganesha elephant Louis Guthrie had bought from him, and he broke the silence by speaking of it.

"I am pleased the fat Ganesha brings you pleasure, sa'ab."

Suraj tilted his head quickly and sharply to the left. In India it meant a sort of yes.

"And that it now, still, after all these many years, continues to bring you pleasure. It was a wise and knowing choice Guthrie-sa'ab once made, knowing this one piece would go with you always through your very life."

Kady jutted out his face and chin, and then Bhave said something that only had meaning for the two of them.

"I am reminded that it is you, long ago, who was bringing Guthrie-sa'ab the Shiva Nataraj, or so, at least, that was what he was thinking. Do you remember that?"

He waited. Suraj said nothing.

"And you gave him the Shiva Nataraj? And he was believing that it was a very great and special piece? And then—do you remember? or is it too long ago?—he was giving you the Ganesha in return, one of the finest pieces alive. Do you remember all this, or have you forgotten? This odd exchange? Unequal gifts? Time allows us to forget so many things."

He let the remark hang there, ambiguous in its thrust and challenge.

Kady didn't say a word.

"And I am further remembering—"

"You've made your point. Get on with it. What do you want?"

"—that it is some thirty years since Maharaj-sa'ab of Deeg first sent you to me to deliver, was it one small package with a Nandi cow inside? Something that he wanted to make available so that someone else I know who had an interest in these Nandi cows could buy it? While I had known Maharaj-sa'ab some long and pleasant centuries by then, it was my good fortune those days then to make the acquaintance of one so promising as you."

Suraj had started doodling. Outside, the lights were near bright as day, celebrating this heroic part of the city where the viceroys themselves had lived and ruled. The room was warm. The sound of voices came up from the street, one never far from people here.

"But I have to wonder," Bhave said, "if Suraj-sa'ab is knowing these thirty years are not as long as the one month, two weeks, and some unknown number of hours and minutes since my one and only son has departed from my side. . . ."

Suraj had drawn the lines of a woman's face, chin, long hair . . .

"And I wonder if Suraj-sa'ab is knowing what it is for the soul of a father to lose his one and only son. Perhaps he is even thinking about his own one and only—"

"Don't talk about my son," Suraj muttered, not looking up.

"But however old a son gets, he never lives any place else but in his father's heart, and I wonder to myself if Suraj-sa'ab knows," he continued in that singsong voice of his, "that I have no son now, no son at all, no children at all, and that I will have no grandson or great-grandson to pour the oil upon my body and light the fire of my funeral pyre?"

He paused for emphasis, his voice threatening now. "Does he know that?"

"Get on with it. I'll let you say your piece, but what do you want? Or are you just threatening me generally?"

"Does he know that there will be no one to knock at my skull beneath the flames and break it open and release my soul into the afterlife? Does he know that I stand in risk of having no afterlife at all, no rebirth, because I have no son? He himself still has a son," he went on, disingenuously now, for he knew the truth. "Oh lucky, fortunate man you are to have the gods shine on you. You have no fears as to who will set the fire of your funeral pyre and guarantee your rebirth—"

Suraj tapped his pencil hard against the table. "I've let you go on out of some sort of perverse respect for you, old man, but don't you ever speak of my son again. Don't you ever speak to me of a son."

"—who will break your skull beneath the flames and release your soul."

"Did you hear me?"

"You ask if I threaten you. How could I threaten you, Minister-sa'ab? What could a lowly man like me do to one as great as—"

"Just tell me what you want. I'm tired and a little sick. Some days are very long. . . ."

"The police are doing nothing."

"What do you expect them to do?"

"They are doing this and they are doing that, but they are not doing the only thing that will help a father's heart because they have not found the yellow-haired boy."

"There's no proof he did it and you know it." Suraj got up and went over to the window that looked out over Raj Path and the city. He turned around to face Bhave, his hands deep in his pockets. "There's no witness. There's no fingerprint. Your place was open all day long and you know it, so it doesn't matter where the boy is. He has nothing to do with it."

"But where is he?"

"Talk to Jiggie. He'll do anything for you. Maybe he knows."

"I am never wanting to bother Maharaj-sa'ab until I—"

"Then talk to Nasrut Sardar again, the inspector. The metal frame was up all day long. He'll tell you. All the way up."

"He's told me," Bhave said. "I want him to arrest the American."

"It could have been anybody in there and you know it."

"Not anybody," Bhave said. "My neighbor heard a fight."

"She heard an argument."

"It was the afternoon, April second," Bhave persisted,

"twenty-four hours before the body was found, and she saw a man with yellow hair go in my house and she heard him have a fight with my son."

"A lot of foreigners have yellow hair. Maybe she doesn't know the difference, German, Czech, French. The metal frame was up for twenty-four hours before you found the body. Nasrut Sardar has witnesses to that. It could have been anyone."

"It was not anyone. I have a father's complete and utter knowledge. That is the proof I have."

"That's not proof and you know it. So, Cully was there in the afternoon. Or, I should say, maybe he was there. Someone blond was there. That's all you know. Maybe any father would cling to it. I don't know, but there's nothing I can do."

"He's your friend. You're protecting him."

"He's not my friend. I don't even like him very much. His father was my friend. Besides, you're the one who betrayed him, promised to sell him art. Why don't you think about that." He started pacing back and forth.

"Nasrut Sardar said the boy had a long meeting with you the day before the killing."

"I don't recall."

"He told me the boy came in here in this very office and then you went on a long drive and did not come back until—"

"Why don't you think about what you were doing to him? You went to Benares and Jiggie told you what to do with him, didn't he?"

Vishnu Bhave didn't answer.

"Is that why you sold him that horse? Are you proud of what you've done to that family?"

"Louis Guthrie would have been nothing if I had not—"

"You are perverse. He was a better man than you'll ever be."

"I was doing my duty to Maharaj-sa'ab."

"That may be, but that doesn't mean what you've done is any good. A prostitute may do her duty and take money for what she gives and she may be reborn better than any of us, but that doesn't make her a good person."

"Are you implying . . . ?"

"You know exactly what I'm implying."

The two were silent.

"It is your duty to help me," the art dealer said finally. He had started to whine.

237

Suraj flung his arm up in a gesture of dismissal.

"Your duty is to Maharaj-sa'ab and, through him, to me," the man persisted. "You have to help me."

"I have no duty to him and certainly none to the likes of you."

"He's my patron. . . ."

"Then you're the one with duty to him."

"Therefore your duty to him extends to me."

"I have no duty to him or to anyone. I never have."

"You very most certainly did. You were running everywhere for him. You ran like a rabbit, and if I was seeing you once, I was seeing you twice, thrice, running like a rabbit."

"Let me correct myself, old man. If I once had a duty to Maharaj-sa'ab, I'm free of him now and I have been for a long time."

"Free," Bhave smirked. "What do we any of us care for freedom? We only care for belonging. You sound American, like your Mr. Guthrie. We Indians only care for family and community, and you have neither. Freedom is nothing. You're nothing and you know it. The gods beware for you, Minister-sa'ab. You are a man who has shirked his duty his whole life long."

"Don't threaten me, and certainly don't preach."

"It's not a threat, Minister-sa'ab. It's an observation. One anyone could make. Look at your beautiful wife, with the solid-gold altar pieces Maharaj-sa'ab gave her for her wedding. You could say that anyone who had that information would know how much you are alienated from the gods. Anyone who knew as much as I, that is."

His remarks hung in the air. Suraj stood at the windows overlooking the city. Bhave watched him, knowing he had won. A sweeper came in, crouched on all fours like a dog, but when he saw the men, he left.

"All right," said Suraj finally. "I'll call Nasrut Sardar for you, but I'm not doing it because you threaten me. You wouldn't dare talk publicly about what you know because it would hurt Jiggie far more than it would ever hurt me. After I've called Sardar, there's nothing more I can do for you on this case."

"Maybe the girl will help."

"What girl?" Suraj looked up.

"What girl is there? The American sister."

"The American sister?"

"Maybe she knows where he is."

"All right, write her a letter."

"I don't have to write her a letter," Bhave said. "She's right here."

"Here?"

"The boy's landlady notified the police."

"When did she come?"

"I am not knowing."

Suraj shrugged.

"But maybe she knows where he is," the little man said, "and that's why she came. I'll ask her."

"Don't threaten her," Kady said. "She has nothing to do with this."

"She is his sister. She has the very same karma as he."

"She does not," Kady said hotly.

"To me she does," the old man said. "They are the same, one and the same. And maybe he told her where he was going. Maybe he told her what happened. Maybe she knows everything."

"Maybe, maybe, maybe. All you have is maybe, from beginning to end."

❧ II ❦

A FEW DAYS LATER I CALLED
Phoebe in Deeg.

The phone rang at least thirty times. Finally someone picked
it up and I asked if I could speak to "Am-ri-kan memsa'ab." He
told me to wait. I did. I could hear someone in the background
talking, reading a list of sorts. Periodically someone else would
interject a number, like he was counting, but I didn't pay any
attention. I was thinking about the summer heat and wondering
how long we'd have to wait for the rains this year. It was already
so hot I had pretty much stopped eating in the daytime but for
mangoes.

After a while I began to take note of what the man was saying.
I realized he was reading off something about trains and num-
bers of seats and that what they were counting was people.
People who were arriving, hundreds of them.

Then suddenly he said, "Accha. . . ." Done. The final tally, he
declared, was somewhere between three and five hundred people, that was as definite as he could get.

"Coming for what?" I called out into the empty phone. They
didn't hear me, of course, and finally, it must have been about
ten minutes later, my man came back on the line. "Alo?" he said.
"Memsa'ab no here. Out for walking city."

"When's she coming back?"

240

"Not for knowing sure. All time memsa'ab out for walking city."

"Then tell me," I said, "what's the date when all the people are coming? I've forgotten."

He gave me a day some four months off, September.

"And what exactly is going to happen then?" I ventured. "You know, what first, Etcetera?"

"What for always happen," he said, impatient at my ignorance.

"But, you know . . . ?"

"Bridegroom coming up by horse. Maybe elephant. Bride girl Mirabai waiting, taking baths, milk, honey. Same as all time always. Marriage custom not for changing ever."

So the marriage was on, I thought. I hadn't known.


I left my name and number and thought about the marriage. The date seemed a long way off.

Phoebe didn't call. It turned out she never got the message.

I tried her again, but lines were down. I asked around in Delhi for someone who knew Jasdan Singh. Maybe he could call down there and ask about her, but it was the Indian summer and I couldn't come up with anyone, so I had to let it be.


For the first time in years I found myself thinking again about Guthrie, Suraj and Deeg. I thought about Cully, and if Phoebe and Kady had met.

Phoebe eventually talked about the whole thing later in November. That was the time of year when harsh weather reaches northern India. The sun sets early and the nights are long. The sky is clear all day, unless there's fog, and for Phoebe and me this time of year meant the bearers brought us blankets out on the veranda and tucked us in. They themselves wore socks with their sandals and shawls around their necks. We bore it as long as we could outside, then came in and found our spot in the library, full of Jyoti's leather-bound volumes about the British Empire, little Indian there. It was all mahogany and chintz, silver picture frames, and now, in here, she spoke of Kady.

Sometimes when his name came up she stopped talking and the silence said it all.

241

The next thing that happened that summer was that I decided
to go to Deeg myself. It was May 21st, a Friday.

The heat created a kind of vacuum, or maybe I felt a vacuum
emanating from Phoebe herself and the absence of her drew me
down. I made reservations for the Deeg Palace Hotel and was
informed that everything was closed after September 1st for the
wedding of the maharaja's granddaughter. As life would have it,
just before leaving the house, the bearer brought a letter from
Phoebe.

It was short and said little, Cully missing, a body that wasn't
his, had I seen him? She was anxious to see me, sorry not to have
talked, the phones were always out. Nothing about her plans or
what she was doing, just that she was in Deeg, having a wonderful time, loved being back. Might stay a few more weeks in India
before returning home.

A postscript tacked on at the end was about Anant Bhave.
That he'd been "hit in the head and strangled around the
neck." Did I know?

At this very moment Cully was getting a cold. Something
made him sneeze and scratch at his eyes, an allergy, he assumed,
and he had pains in his abdomen and around the rim of his skull.

He was in Delhi. He'd been there all along, since April 2nd,
the day he disappeared.

On May 21st he went to see a doctor. Another doctor, a week
earlier, told him a demon had gotten into his body, he must have
eaten milk or curd inhabited by it, and now the demon was
eating at his blood.

Cully had dismissed that. He did believe in Indian medicine,
however, so when the symptoms persisted, he tried another
doctor.

This doctor was an old, bald man who wore a dhoti, had
streaks of red paste across his forehead, emblems of his daily
worship, and he sat cross-legged on white cotton bedding that
covered the entire floor of his office. His legs were stacked up
one on top of the other like pieces of wood. His office had no
chairs, no table, just matting on the floor and a wooden chest.

Cully liked this doctor from the start. When he opened the

door, the man told him not to move. He then surveyed him closely from head to toe, asked him to turn around and walk up and down the hall outside at a normal speed. Cully did just that.

Cully's circulatory system had been rushing the last few weeks, thumping blood like diesel trucks going through his veins, but from the very moment the doctor looked at him, it began to slow. Even as he walked across the threshold and was told to keep on standing, he saw himself as halfway cured, just by being in the man's presence.

Inside, the doctor told him to take off his shoes and shirt and said he still wanted to watch how he moved, didn't even ask his name or malady. Just watched as Cully walked up and down, bare feet on the matting. Watched his shoulder and his hips, reached out and felt the left shoulder where it sloped down, turned it around a bit in its socket to see if it could move or be realigned. It couldn't.

"That's pretty much where it is," Cully said.

The man tapped at the wormlike scar, like he was making a neurological test to see how it responded to the tapping, then had him bend over, touch his toes, reach around the ankle with his hand, and touch the foot on the other side. Cully could do it.

Finally the doctor had him sit down on the matting and give him his hands. He took first one, then the other, and took his pulses at the wrist, pressing his fingertips against Cully's veins. He said Cully was out of balance and then asked him his symptoms.

Cully was reticent at first, but the more the man listened, the more he began to talk. When he finished, the man's only comment was to observe aloud that Cully had made eye contact.

Cully felt unexpectedly reinforced. He smiled. The man told him, Good, keep on smiling, and proceeded to watch his facial muscles until they started to strain and settle back the way they'd been. "No, keep smiling," he insisted. Cully said it was hard. "Good for mind," the doctor said. "Good for mind. Smiling is for making relaxation."

"I am relaxed," Cully argued. "You saw how I could touch my toes."

But the man insisted, so Cully kept on smiling, then breaking down, smiling, then breaking down, until finally the doctor said he could stop.

Cully had no idea what that was about, except that he'd been shocked by how quickly the smile had turned to hurt, felt nearly like a wound torn in his face, but he couldn't think about it much because then the doctor was asking about his sexual drive and what he ate and what he dreamed, and Cully answered with more candor than he might have done because there was an air of mystery and the exotic here he liked. He ended up pleased he answered so truthfully because, for example, when he said he'd been impotent a number of times these last few weeks, the man nodded knowingly and almost approvingly, not at all surprised.

The doctor asked where the semen was blocked; was it up high or farther down? Cully said it was up high, and that nothing, no amount of manipulation or seduction worked, and again the doctor nodded approvingly, without a trace of surprise, as if he knew Cully already and didn't even have to ask the questions.

He asked was he taking regular oil baths? Cully said yes.

Eating sweet rice and abstaining from chewing betel nut? Yes.

And how had he gotten the scar?

What scar?

The one on his left shoulder.

Cully shrugged. It was an accident.

Accident?

Yes.

Long ago?

Yes.

Very serious all of a sudden, he warned Cully to "take care. Especially toward the end of summer. That time when summer changes into winter, near about September. Watch out. You are susceptible to the change of seasons."

"Take care of what?"

"Of everything. You must not be impatient. You must listen when I talk." He spoke good English, but in a singsong tone.

"I do listen. I'm a very good listener," Cully said.

"Impatience is not good."

"I know."

"Impatience is against law of time. This lifetime is not for impatience, nor is the next or the next."

"I am listening," Cully said, feeling good because he knew he was slow, steady, not impatient at all. "Good for you," he said admiringly to the doctor. "Good for you for figuring me out."

"But you are too quick to anger, isn't it," the doctor said.

"Sometimes," Cully admitted.

"A fierce, intense anger?"

"Sometimes, I suppose. Not too often."

The man had him undress and, with Cully standing, began to feel his body for signs of wind and bile. He pressed around the throat, the back of the head, below the ribs. That's where consciousness lies, he said, "near about the heart. It's not in the head."

"Oh, I know that," Cully said quickly, lying.

Then he had Cully bend over, and when his penis and scrotum were dangling midair, he felt between the penis and the anus, there at the base of the spinal column. Cully said oouch. The doctor checked a few more spots, told Cully to sit down.

When both of them were sitting cross-legged on the bedding, one naked, the other barely dressed, the man took a big breath and announced, "I have diagnosis."

"Good."

"What is wrong is you have undigested karma. Do you understand that?"

"Yes, sir."

"Have you ever suffered any crisis or untoward event? Something with karmic overtones?"

"There was one thing."

"What?"

"Something about my father. He's dead, but on April second I found out he was betrayed," and, according to the precise circumstances, which there was no point going into, he explained, that meant that he himself had been betrayed, too. "It was all by the same set of people, even my sister."

"That's exactly right, most precisely right."

"But what do they have to do with my pains?" Cully asked, confused.

"There's a karmic link-up between you and your father, your sister, and these others. One was a Chinese emperor. Do you know who that could be?"

"That figures."

"You are suffering, aren't you?"

"Yes, sir."

"It's serious karmic disarray. You have to understand that. It's

245

very important. In order to set things right, one has to—"

"You mean do I have actual physical suffering?" Cully interrupted.

"No. Pain in consciousness."

"Because I do have all these physical pains," Cully said enthusiastically. He began to touch his neck, abdomen, lower back. "I knew it was karma."

"But I am speaking of the heart. The pain's in there. Isn't it?"

"Oh, no. The pains are in the neck, back . . ."

"But there's pain to the consciousness?"

"No," Cully insisted.

"No pain in the chest?"

"I have pain there all right," Cully exclaimed, and he pointed at a spot on his big white chest.

The doctor pressed on the spot.

"Oouch."

The doctor moved his finger around some more, said it was serious.

"I know. I know," Cully said impatiently, "but what's the cure?"

"The cure is knowing the cause."

"No, I mean 'the cure.' "

"The question is, what is the cause?"

"No, but what about getting rid of it? It hurts. I can't sleep. I can't have sex. I don't feel good."

The doctor gave a long sigh. "You must first discover the cause," he said, and with that he made a big point of namasteing with his hands way, way up so they were pointed toward where the gods lived and said the cure was to surrender to the pain itself and to the lesson and to the power beyond himself.

"What power?"

"Your community and the gods. They will give you strength."

"I don't have a community."

"Don't you have a family?"

"No."

"Then there's the community of America. There's always community, a person always has community," he said, "a place where he belongs which dictates who he is and what he must do. That place of community may be just you yourself alone, but you have to know it and submerge yourself in it, follow it with your heart. Whatever community or caste it is, it will tell you what to do, and you must take guidance and strength from it. It's the only way to restore harmony, and if you don't restore harmony, you will continue to suffer from imbalance."

"I do have a plan," Cully said.

The doctor said that was good, but it might not be good enough because he had to have "deeper understanding." Then he said, "Feel this?" and reached over and helped Cully press first on his abdomen, then his neck, diaphragm, and groin, and each time said, "There? Feel it?"

Cully said he did. It hurt.

"That is wind and the bile," the doctor said, shaking his head sorrowfully. "They are everywhere." He pressed especially hard on one spot near the navel and said, "Feel it? Feel how it hurts?"

Cully grimaced.

"That's a sign of too much anger," the doctor said. "Very bad sign." It could even be mistaken for demon entry, he went on, but in his opinion it was not that bad as yet. "Did you have a very bad episode recently?" he asked.

"Episode?"

"Of outbreak of anger?"

Cully shrugged. "How long ago?"

The doctor was vague. "Say, one month, two month, one week, two week, April, May."

"Could be, maybe."

The doctor pressed him near the navel again.

Cully winced.

"Take precautions when the seasons change," he said again. "Remember that."

Cully said he'd be all right. His plan would solve everything. He was going to get back at that Chinese emperor.

The doctor shook his head. "Answer is within," he corrected. "There should be no plan for outside. There should only be return to community and to heart. That is best plan."

But Cully was impatient. He pressed the doctor for prescriptions and treatment, said his body couldn't get in the way of what he had to do. It was too important, this plan, a lot rested on it, and he couldn't go around being sick or not being able to get an erection.

The doctor told him he had to be calm and concentrate on

doing the best he could. That was all the gods wanted.

"But what are you going to do?" Cully insisted. "You're the doctor. Why do you think I came here? If I could do it alone, I wouldn't have needed you."

The doctor did a brief exorcism on the spot, in case there were any demons in the vicinity, he said. He had Cully lie down on the matting and rubbed oil, scented water, herbs, and melted butter on his body, said he was evacuating some of the wind and bile. He told Cully it was only a temporary measure, but it would help. He instructed him not to wash it off for two days.

Then he told him to have more oil baths, more rest, employ better posture, and say one certain mantra one hundred and ten times a day for the next thirty-two days.

Cully wrote it down and left.

He felt better.

## ❦ 12 ❦

WHEN I GOT TO DEEG, I VISITED
the Palace Museum and even performed the necessary tourist
ritual of throwing paise in Lake Pichiti for luck, but at teatime
I found myself properly dressed, going down to get a cab. I
never thought of phoning over to arrange a date ahead of time.
That's the way things were done here, even with palaces. One
dropped in.

"Umaid Mahal Palace," I told the driver, Um-eye-id-Mail,
they pronounce it, just like the Taj-Mail in Agra.

The driver refused to take me. Insisted I had to sign up for
tours that went through every morning from ten to one. Finally
I had to get the chief doorman and persuade him that my friend
was staying there and I was expected for tea. "Expected" was
the key word, because he was so concerned that calling over to
check me out would result in someone's ire at him for violating
the rules of hospitality and his duty to Maharaj-sa'ab and his
duty to this and his duty to that, duty on and on, that he decided
to trust me and not even pass the decision on to higher-ups.

"For truth?" he said one last time, wagging his finger at me
like some little stick.

"For truth."

❦

249

Phoebe wasn't there.

A servant asleep on the steps that led up to the main entrance of the palace told me she was out on her bicycle. He took my card, studied it upside down, and led me in through a big, sunlit hallway lined with potted trees, to what I can only think to call a living room. There he told me to sit down. He mentioned as an afterthought that the Am-ri-kan memsa'ab sat there too when she arrived a few weeks back, and with that pronouncement he disappeared, armed with the card where I'd written I was Phoebe and Cully's friend.

The living room was as big as a couple of tennis courts. I sat in an antique French chair. A servant already in place was eyeing me from afar. He was as still as the statues.

I sat and waited. Nothing happened. Some time must have passed. I don't remember much about it, but later, when I talked to Phoebe, she told me she felt electrified in there, waiting for Jasdan to show up. It established in her mind that she was one thing, the Deegs another.

The room was part Louis XIV, the gilt-and-mirrored look, part Victorian, priceless knickknacks cluttered about, and partly, very dramatically, Indian, art with naked breasts and vacant all-seeing eyes, but more than anything it was, simply, massive. There weren't even doors, just archways a good twenty by thirty feet in size that gave off to other rooms, and the walls weren't made of normal stone, but slabs of marble so big Phoebe couldn't even find the cracks to show where one ended and another began. She imagined the hundreds of workmen who'd hoisted these great chunks of rock from the ground, then sat them down so these people could live the way they believed they were meant to live. It would be hard to win against the Deegs, she thought. Even the art was a warning: paintings as big as automobiles showed tens of thousands of warriors lined up behind the flag of Deeg, two lions and a unicorn.

She understood why Cully hadn't prospered here, and, abruptly, she thought of Kady Suraj. This was what he'd taken on. Just exactly this. The power and dispensation of Deeg.

She stood up and started walking around the room, but abruptly, acres away, the servant cleared his throat.

She sat down. Felt trapped. Found herself listening for sounds, there must be people here, but listening for what? Footsteps, laughter, a radio? The voice of Cully's friend, the girl

250

whose marriage negotiations took all year? Where was she? she wondered. Was someone watching her, too?

She tried to imagine living here. It was hard. She couldn't hear anything. Only one small bird, a lime-green parakeet, that had made its way inside, easy, really, a veranda was just off to the side, but now it was flying around the ceiling, unable to get out, batting its wings fiercely.

Cully had left. Kady had left. So had Jiggie. He'd departed for Benares. But did other people leave? And how? Did they just call a cab, or were they trapped forever?

My own reverie was interrupted when I suddenly saw a man who turned out to be Jasdan Singh appear at the other end of the room marching toward me. He was followed by an older man, very much the upper-class gentleman, suit, tie, jacket, trousers. This was my first glimpse of Attar Singh, whose father had been Jiggie's father's prime minister. Jasdan himself was informal, in trousers and a shirt, and the two were coming single file across acres of carpet with their chins jutted forward as if to reach me all the quicker.

Jasdan shook my hand vigorously and with an urgency that was unmistakable asked me if this was all right or would I like to go over to the zenana, "take tea" with the women.

I said this was very pleasant. We sat down. The bearer immediately brought cakes and biscuits, filled our cups. The whole time Jasdan, his face very much like his father's, only better looking because he had decent skin, didn't take his eyes off me. He was swinging his foot madly. I had no idea what was going on, because here was I, total outsider, and there was no reason he should deal with me at all, much less appear so intent.

Next he started waving his hand imperiously. The bearer took off. I had started chatting, anything to allay the tension. Said I knew his father. Charming. So interesting. How was he?

The bearer was leaping across the rug to reach the distant wall, where he promptly sat on the floor next to the other fellow and immediately fell asleep.

"He's renounced," Jasdan said. "Fourth stage of life and all that. Everyone does it. Never see him anymore."

"Emergencies, maybe," I offered, stirring my tea. "You might see him then."

"Absolutely. Right you are," very British and upper class, no Indian inflection in his voice, so he'd lived abroad. Then, with an elaborate gesture to take a cake, he paused, and said, all part of a conspicuous effort to appear casual, "So, tell me, how is our old friend Cully Guthrie?"

My first reaction was complete surprise that Cully figured in all this tension, my second that talking about him was just a blind for something else, and last, that something awful had happened to Cully, so I exclaimed, "No, tell me, what's happened?"

Jasdan peered at me coldly, like some snake or wild animal. "Tell you what?" his thick dark brows, just like Jiggie's, halfway up his forehead, stalking in alarm.

"Tell me about Cully, I guess," I said weakly.

"Exactly. Where is he? I must find him."

"I don't know."

"I thought you did."

"No. Why? Why do you need him?"

"I assumed you did," he insisted angrily.

The silence was total.

Attar Singh heaved his shoulders in a gigantic sigh and settled back, too. "You must excuse us," he said. "We're just worried about the dear boy. This business of the body turning up. Plus the wedding, of course. It's put quite a strain on us. We worry about him endlessly."

I didn't believe him.

Jasdan drank one whole cup of tea straight through. Attar Singh took out a cigarette, tapped it elegantly against a pearly case, then put it away, unused. We waited. Nobody talked. I was bewildered.

"It's this wedding." Jasdan sounded morose. "September ninth. Dreadful commotion all around nowadays. Puts the women in such a tizzy, causes havoc everywhere."

"Yes."

He called the bearer over, told him to pour another cup of tea. He had only to reach a few inches, the man had to walk miles. We waited. When he was finished drinking, he set the cup down and leaned far back on the couch again and looked as though he might take a snooze.

Attar Singh gave me an empathetic grin but showed no sign of pushing Jasdan along. We just waited; no doubt who was in charge here. Finally Jasdan sat straighter, gave me an astoundingly warm smile. Reminded me of Jiggie. "Well," he exclaimed, "enough of that. Can't bother you all day with the trials of putting on a palace wedding, can I?"

He started talking about Delhi society and proceeded to compare notes with me, and I must have passed muster because, putting his cup back on the tray, he launched into talk of the wedding. How he was taking over the hotel for guests, how the ceremony itself would take place in the big palace, which stood empty, there, across the lake.

At a pause, using just the right idiom, I inserted myself. What was the boy's family? I asked. One doesn't speak of individuals here.

He gave the name, a highly prominent business family, one of the richest in the country, but they certainly weren't Rajputs, so I knew right away, very much surprised, this was an intercaste marriage, and not only that, but that it involved two very conservative families, the kind who normally abhor intercaste anything. As businessmen the other family was probably from the lower Bania or Marwari caste. They'd certainly never been entitled to any twenty-one-gun salutes like the Deegs. They weren't even landowners by caste. So, both families had money, but one was Indian royalty and the other was new, brash, entrepreneurial, and low. Interesting, I thought. What had brought them together?

"I must admit it's a tad unusual," Jasdan was saying, "but my father thinks the children are nicely matched."

So it was Jiggie's doing.

"The boy's been up to Oxford and all that, and he's got quite a good thing going in international law and business. So we suspect"—and with that he gestured to include Attar Singh—"that he'll travel, maybe even be quite clever one day. This is all part of the marriage contract, you see. He's very promising. She's to go with him everywhere, travel, entertain. Be quite a good bit of fun, don't you think? Modern and all that, it's the new thing, not produce a son for a good two, three years. My father insisted. The modern approach, you know." But he snorted, and I thought he looked doubtful about the benefits of modern anything. "The boy's sister is getting married this summer, too," he added brightly. "We think a lot of her. Nice girl. Nice family."

"The boy's grades were quite good," Attar Singh interjected with all the assurance of someone who'd seen those grades up close. "We thought they showed a certain . . . I don't know . . . what do you think? Flair?"

"Yes, of course," I said, baffled as to why they were telling me this and why Jasdan had agreed to the marriage in the first place. It was unusual, all of it, both the marriage and their openness with me. Such details are private, family and close friends only, but it didn't require much insight to know Jasdan had had to muster all his sense of duty to go along with his father in this.

I'd heard a lot about marriage negotiations before, the two sides and both their agents, bartering, parceling out factories and properties, if this side would provide such and such, the other would do this and that, exchange of assets and servants, furnishings, even apartments in foreign lands, but none of this could be worked out if they hadn't matched up the children first. Have to catch the girl at just the right age, older nowadays, a few years past menarche at least, stud bulls and a champion bitch. If you cross this with that, you'll get that, even the skin tone was important, and the teeth, to say nothing of astrological forecasts. If you were extraordinarily daring and confident, you might, possibly, with great incentive, cross caste, but nothing could overcome even a hint of sexuality or a scandal in the girl. No amount of money or beauty could compensate for that devastation to the line, children tainted, marriage prospects decimated for a generation or more.

"It's all very complicated," Jasdan was saying, treating me as he never would an Indian woman, sophisticated enough to know I had to be dealt with equally, more like a man, is what he'd have said. "It was our decision, you know."

"What?"

"To put the whole thing off a year."

I had no idea what he was talking about, but I did remember Cully mentioning that the girl had run away to the railway station.

"It was all our doing. The girl had nothing to do with it."

"I see."

"No matter what Cully might have told you."

"Yes." Baffled.

"Then the other side came back to us in April and agreed to everything we wanted. All our terms."

"Yes."

"So we scheduled the thing again. It hadn't ever been really off, there was just a slight gap in negotiations, nothing much, a few weeks, maybe, at the most."

More like a year, I thought, seeing through his lies. "So the marriage was scheduled once, then canceled, and is now scheduled again? Is that it?" I asked.

"I can see Cully talked to you about it. But it's definitely going to take place this time," Jasdan said. "No more postponements, no more nothing. You tell him that. September ninth. You tell him that from me. You hear me? That I said so. Everything is scheduled and our plans are proceeding and nothing is going to get in the way. Nothing."

"But I have no idea where he is. How can I tell him?"

"The postponement was all my father's doing," Jasdan went on. "He'll do anything for that girl."

I could certainly see that.

"He puts her interests first. She's all he cares about anymore. He got this idea in his head down there in Benares that she was too young to get married, and so . . . well, in any case, we put it off a year."

"But that's quite unusual, isn't it?" I said, going along with his lies.

"Not really," he said disingenuously. He leaned back and started to take more tea. Saw his cup was empty, clapped his hand, and the bearer leapt to action. We all waited while the poor man did his duty, then disappeared over to the other side of the room. Jasdan looked more relaxed now, sat back against the couch drinking milky tea. "I might as well be frank," he went on casually. "For all their wealth and prominence, the other side is quite conservative. So my father was absolutely right to hold out for a better contract."

"I see," I said, wondering why he was telling me all this. What did he want from me? What was he after?

"Oh, he got very angry with me. Said the first arrangements I made weren't good enough for Mirabai. Said I should have consulted more with him. He was right, of course. You know our Indian customs, father-son, special duty and all that. He said we had to postpone it. I agreed."

Sure, he agreed, but he'd have married the girl off in a hot minute and not put up with any nonsense about postponements.

Anybody would. Except Jiggie, apparently.

"He did tell us all along," Attar Singh interjected, "to find a modern chap."

"He told me he wouldn't have one of these walking antiques for his Mirabai," Jasdan said, picking up the story. "Someone who won't let his wife outside the door. You know that kind of chap, makes them hide the face, eat in the kitchen away from the men. He said he wouldn't have that. I don't know why. My mother was perfectly happy and she barely left the zenana."

"And so you found the boy?"

"No, you see, it's a little more complex than that. My father has this marvelous chap who works for him, and he sent him up to Delhi to find two, three boys who were suitable. He spent about two months looking into the families. Did a superb job."

"Two months," I exclaimed. "What was he doing all that time?"

"Oh, this and that," Attar Singh interjected with a flourish of his hands.

"Oh," I said innocently, never dreaming Shyam Singh had bribed servants and broken into locked offices, stolen files and more, all pursuant to his duties, and that he'd come up with not two or three candidates, but one.

"What does the girl say?" I asked.

"Mirabai?" Jasdan said with surprise. "What about her?"

"Well, what does she think of this?"

"Why do you want to know about Mirabai?"

Now I was confused all over again. I realized there must be something going on. "Why, because she's the bride," I said helplessly.

"She trusts me implicitly," Jasdan rattled on. "As she must. Duty and all. She's a darling girl."

"Yes."

"At least the other side finally came across. I was rather tired of waiting. We got their letter round about April. They agreed to everything we proposed."

"Proposed the second time around?"

He nodded.

"So, your father knows the boy is more progressive than his family?"

"I guess you could say that," Jasdan answered. "My father insists the old ways of marriage don't work, although they worked perfectly well for him, so I don't know why he should complain. He had a wonderful marriage, was happy with my mother right to the end, but this is what he wants for Mirabai, greater 'compatibility.' That's all he can talk about, compatibility, freedom. You'd think he was from California." He laughed, but it came across as a hollow sound.

"Maybe he wishes he'd had more freedom," I suggested, wondering what was really behind all this. "Maybe he wants the girl to have it."

"But girls don't. That's not the way it's done. Anyway, I was telling you"—Jasdan sounded impatient now—"the upshot of all this is that the other side has agreed the couple can live on their own. They came around to my father's way of thinking. The children will live out." Jasdan bent his head and took on the air of someone speaking in confidence. "Frankly, it was very difficult for them. All the other sons and their families live in the house. That's the way they like it. They have this darling daughter who's getting married in September, too, and according to her contract, she will come home all the time, too. What is our contract finally?" He looked at Attar Singh.

"It went from living in the house," the older man said, "and having a suite of bedrooms up on the second floor to, final negotiations, the couple will have their own house, whatever house we get, in fact, and they only go to the in-laws once a week for lunch and dinner Sunday night. The parents did want both Saturday and Sunday night and lunch every day, but they gave in on that. They agreed to . . . well."

"Agreed to agree," I said pleasantly. "May I meet the girl?" No one answered. The silence was striking.

"May I meet Mirabai?"

"Bless you," Jasdan said finally, "for your interest and all, but she's not here."

"No, she's not here," Attar Singh said.

"The preparations were too much for her," Jasdan said.

"Yes," said Attar Singh.

"She took the train up to stay with my father's sister in the hills in Mussoorie. It's cooler there. Auntie Indore, we call her."

"When will she be back?"

"Oh," Jasdan answered, waving his hand in the air, Indian fashion, pulling a word, like a rabbit, from the atmosphere. "Sometime."

I knew Jasdan had been indiscreet on purpose, that the whole thing, from start to finish, served his purpose. I arrived on his doorstep, opportunity in disguise, and he told me everything, hoping I got his version of the circumstances—specifically why there'd been the delay in negotiations—out to the wider social circles in Delhi where these things mattered.

Because weddings were never postponed.

I was to be his courier, these details not meant to be private, but public as soon as I got back to Delhi and told everyone the blame for the delayed marriage lay with the famous, can-do-no-wrong Jiggie Deeg.

Even a hint that a marriage might not come off implied misdeeds and derelictions on the girl's part. Introduce doubt and wags would say the boy's side was forced to reconsider. So Jiggie had gambled on the girl's future and the family's reputation, in postponing it a year. That was a lot to make one girl happy.

But what I couldn't figure out was why Jasdan was so extraordinarily intense about getting these details out now. Why did it matter? The marriage was all arranged and back on track again.

I told my husband about the conversation. His reaction was more basic than mine. "Why'd he care about Cully? Why is Cully so important?"

He also said Inspector Nasrut Sardar had been to the house, asking if we'd seen Cully Guthrie.

My husband said no, and the man said, was he sure? and my husband said, yes, of course, but why hadn't he asked us before?

Sardar said initially there wasn't much interest in the case. Now Deputy Minister Suraj was involved, so he was going back over old tracks.

"D'you find anything?"

The man spread his hands out in the air hopelessly. But there were no other suspects, he said.

## ❧ 13 ❧

I WAS INVITED BACK TO THE PAL-
ace for dinner at nine. When I arrived everyone was gathered
in a room called the library, so enormous that some thirty-odd
people were lost in it, along with whole tigers and a snow
leopard, two grand pianos back to back. Everyone was clustered
at one end, like a ferry with too many people at the bow, the
women and children huddled together on one side, men on the
other. Phoebe was among the women, and when I saw her I was
dumbfounded.

I was so used to seeing her up against the grayness of New
York or floating around an apartment where she didn't belong,
that she was nothing like I'd imagined. Here she glowed. She
was cloaked in India. She had children all around her, clinging
at her side, and I felt a deep pleasure at seeing her so happy.

I was ushered across the room by Jasdan, introducing me,
saying this was just "family—aunts, uncles, our joint family,
you know, since you are so interested in our Indian ways."

Then Phoebe was clawing her way up out of the sprawl to
reach me. She gave me a great big hug, our bellies separated by
a boy with a diesel truck, but we kept up our embrace and I
could tell she was as happy to see me as I her. She put her hand
along my forehead and brushed my scalp tenderly, like she was
the one who was older and more in charge, and said, heartfelt,

"How are you?" Here in India, there seemed a peace in her there hadn't been before.

We were parted by a tumult of children and the lallis, and after that came dinner, a grand affair. I remembered descriptions from Cully, the Garuda bird, solid-gold plates, one long table with the people who didn't count removed from those who did, the seat at the very top, empty. Phoebe, next to me, sat next to Jasdan, too, and I tried talking to her, but there were too many conversations all around. It was clear no women participated much at this table. Jasdan's wife wasn't even close, we two up here simply because we were Americans.

When I got a chance, I turned to Phoebe and said, "Can we talk afterward?"

Her eyes were suddenly full of tears.

"He'll be all right, Phoebe," I whispered, "I know he will."

Imperceptibly she shook her head. "I don't think he's traveling or anything," she whispered. "I think something's wrong."

After dinner it was so hot everyone went to the roof. It overlooked the lake and the palaces across the way. There were children, adults, servants, lallis, everyone talking, playing, lying on great mattresses of cloth, not a chair in sight. A musician came and played. There were drinks and figs, and always, from first to last, a golden-haired dog who missed his Mirabai.

Eventually Phoebe and I made our way to the side and talked.

Looking back, I see we were setting in motion even then what became the course of our relationship. I see how what started then eventually took us through the long Indian summer and, finally, in the fall, led us out to the shady, shadowy, sunny veranda of Kitty Chandradas' old and sturdy house.

It was that very night, as it turned out, May 21st, that Kady Suraj did something important of his own.

He ate alone, as he often did, in his office at home on Viceroy Circle, not far from Jumna Road. The house, with all its bedrooms and suites, large even for Delhi, servants' quarters out in back, was all lit up. People were waiting in the hall to see him. They came, they often did, invited and uninvited, known, unknown, rich, poor, truly the Indian form of politics. After dinner he took them, one by one, to the office, but afterward, when he was done, instead of going to a party or playing a game of squash as he often did at night, he turned out the lights and sprawled in a chair in the library near the open windows.

It was because of Phoebe.

Every night since he'd been to the airport, he pulled the chair to the windows and stared out at the darkness, restless and melancholy. Tonight his legs were stretched out on a stool. He had taken off his shirt, it was so hot, his feet naked, and he stared out at the garden. Wondered for a bit if Phoebe liked flowers.

He rubbed the bridge of his nose with his fingers, smoked one of his few cigarettes of the day, and finally took up the phone and called the Taj Hotel.

He pretended to be someone else and asked where Phoebe Guthrie was. Did anyone know when she was expected back?

The night manager came on the line, said he had no idea when the woman was coming back, could he take a message? Kady hung up.

Then he called the embassy and, using a deputy's name, managed to get Harriet MacDonald's number from the security guard. He reached her at home and asked if there was anything more to report on Cully Guthrie, Deputy Minister Suraj needed to know tonight. She said no, the male Caucasian body had been cremated, that was all.

And the sister? What had happened to the sister?

She went down to Deeg.

But was she back? the minister wanted to know. When was she coming back?

Harriet said she had no idea, but she was sure she'd hear. Did he want her to let him know?

The man was quiet a long time, and Harriet repeated her question, knew all along it was Suraj on the line, recognized his distinctive voice. "Does he want to know about her?"

No, the man finally said, the minister had no interest in the subject anymore.

But as Kady hung up, he wondered what he would have done had Harriet said, Oh she's right here, want to talk to her? Would he have talked to her? Called her up later? What would he do if she called him?

He put on his shirt, went out to the car park, stepping over servants asleep in the hall. One or two rose to watch him pass.

Outside, there were a number of vehicles, some his own, some the state's, others used by servants or the aides. He was looking for Durr's. It was there, where it always was at night. The car was nondescript. It had taken his wife to many places, but not Benares, or ever Deeg, nor even the hotels and apartments she had visited in her time. The car was not old enough. But if it wasn't a sign of his wife's adultery or his own deprivation, it was, nonetheless, the only sign of his wife he had that night, and Kady needed this reminder of her. She reminded him of who he was.

He opened up the front door of the car and looked in where the driver sat. Then he circled around and opened the back door on the right-hand side and looked down at the spot where she sat. There was an indentation in the cushion.

Samiji called out, did he want anything, sa'ab?

Kady said no, but Samiji came over and stood with him. Kady passed his hand over the vinyl and the back. "I couldn't ever leave her," he said quietly to Samiji. "Not for anyone."

"You are thinking of miss-sa'ab?"

"I suppose."

The rug on the floor was worn, years of little feet and shoes. A handkerchief was on the seat. He picked it up, smelled it, put it back. He might have been looking around her room, so sensitive was his response. But he never went in there, her room, had no idea what was where, cards, pictures, children, jewelry that didn't come from him.

Back inside, Kady sat at his desk and started to write a letter, tearing up paper after paper until he was satisfied. When he finally finished, he pulled out an envelope, stuck in the letter, and licked it shut.

Then, putting on his coat and sandals, he went back to the car park, found Samiji waiting, keys in hand, but he said he'd drive himself tonight, and taking a small Ambassador sedan, drove to Connaught Place. There he found a taxi stand. He walked up and down, looking at the drivers, most of them asleep on the sidewalk or inside on their seats, doors wide open. The monsoons hadn't started yet.

He picked one because he saw how neat the car was, curtains to keep out the sun, pictures of the gods to remind the driver which path was the only path to take. Shaking the man by the shoulder, he woke him up and began to negotiate.

He handed the man the envelope, it was addressed to Cully Guthrie, then gave him a big tip and lengthy instructions on where to go.

The letter itself was unusual: formal, even confessional, and I'm sure Kady would say he was explaining himself to far higher authorities than any Guthrie son could be.

"I have recognized belatedly," the letter began, "that I have a duty to perform.

"But first I wish to apologize for failing to see this right away and being derelict, therefore, in my duty to your father, and to you and your sister as his emissaries. I have been reluctant to interfere with your plans, or frame of mind. I know how serious you are, but I realize now that must not be my concern. Your father was my great good friend, despite what you may think, my duty to him comes first.

"To the point: I must inform you that your sister, Phoebe, has arrived in India. She is looking for you and she is very worried about you. She wants to see you and be with you, do whatever she can to cement your well-being.

"She says she is not staying long, although I am not altogether sure if this is true. You can find her through the palace in Deeg, the Taj Hotel in Delhi, or a woman named Harriet MacDonald at the American embassy. But not through me. I myself do not intend to see her again, so do not try to find her or contact her through me. She is, however, on good terms with the Deegs, so they may be of use to you in this regard.

"I pass this information on to you so that the duty imposed by it is yours, not mine. The decision whether to see her is now strictly yours. I am free of it.

"With all good wishes for your continued well-being and hopes that your physical condition was improved by your visit to the doctor. I hope he proved better than the first. I myself trust him wholeheartedly. I remain, etcetera, etcetera, K. T. Keshri Suraj."

# ❧ 14 ❧

CULLY WAS SITTING IN THE LIV-
ing room of a small but pleasant two-bedroom house on the
outskirts of Delhi. It was called the Garden House. He was
looking out the window at the garden and the fence that obscured the house from public view when something intruded
on his vision.

Was it the sound of the taxi stopping in the street? The movement of the gate itself? He was not sure, but he definitely noticed
when the gate opened and a man in blue-and-white-striped
pajama clothes started walking in toward the house with a white
envelope in his hand.

He watched the man's progress up the walk and listened as,
outside, he called out for a bearer, that's the way it was done
here. Ordinarily Cully might not have paid attention to one man
calling another or strained to hear the outcome of such a trivial
exchange, but now he listened acutely, even rose up on his
elbows on the couch and followed the actual movement of the
letter as it got progressively closer to him.

The bearer entered the room and apologized for interrupting
him, Am-ri-kan-sa'ab did not like to be intruded upon, but Cully
barely noticed. He took the letter, knowing instinctively it was
important because he had no reason to get a piece of mail,
especially one hand-delivered.

He opened the letter, pulling little pieces off the top of the envelope like a mouse might penetrate a box, piece by piece, until the paper inside was visible, then extracted it, remembering, as he always did now, how the doctor had commended him for his patience.

He scanned it. His face gradually got red, color breaking out in blotches on his skin like some systemic illness that hit at certain spots, until his whole face was flushed, even the line of the part in his hair.

As he interpreted it, the letter not only said Phoebe was in India, which was bad enough, it said she was with Kady and the Deegs.

He couldn't believe she was here. India was his, not hers. It had always been his. He imagined the huge triangular shape that extended into the Indian Ocean as some map of land designated all his own, property lines established.

With a kind of shiver he got off the couch as though the couch itself was contagious with her germs. She was some crazy international disease that had tracked him. He had gotten away from one place just to get away from her, because she had gotten in his kitchen, his bedroom, his bureau drawers, closets, even the mattress and the walls, pursuing him as far as jars of jam and toothpaste, things she bought to surround him, and now she had tracked him here, as though she traveled on winds locked onto his smell.

He kicked at the couch, pushed it until it abutted against a wall, then kicked a lamp, chairs, table, and footstool all in the same direction until the items stood together in a corner of the room. He was left standing in the middle of a white room, surrounded outside by a garden and a fence, nothing else in sight, just the sky and India, feeling trapped and literally so besieged that he didn't know what to do, thinking that she was in Deeg. Of all places, she was in Deeg.


Out on the lawn Cully developed his new plan. It was almost the same as before, only now it involved getting away from his sister, too.

A pilgrimage, he said.

❧

He got a taxi and went to Thomas Cook's in Connaught Place, where he stood, May 22nd, in the heat for almost two hours while police tried to move a cow that had fallen asleep on the sidewalk, pressed against the front door. There was another door on the alley, but the clerk who had that key had been dispatched on an errand, so while there were people on the outside waiting to get in, there were also others on the inside waiting to get out.

Police used ropes and sticks, but the animal wouldn't move. It did wake up, however, sat, and chewed, calm unto itself.

Eventually the cow relocated a few feet away, but there it became someone else's problem, and Cully, for one, probably thought no more of it than he had before.

Indian Airlines records had it: a man named C. Guthrie purchased a ticket that day for the 2100-hour flight scheduled to leave the next afternoon, May 23rd, from Palam Airport, Delhi, for Srinagar, Kashmir, with a stopover in Jhelum on the way. "C. Guthrie," paid in cash, rupees, no return required.


Ticket in hand, Cully went straight to the doctor out beyond India Gate and, running up the stairs, barged in. Said he had to have another exorcism before he left.

The doctor said Cully must have misunderstood.

Cully said no, things had gotten worse. He needed a treatment.

The doctor said it wasn't a matter of treatments.

Cully said it was. The other had virtually cured him.

The doctor said no, it was a matter of what he, himself, was doing. The imbalance was his to fix.

"I know, I know," Cully said, "but there is a sister."

## ❧ 15 ❧

EVENTUALLY JUNE BECAME JULY, then August, and what settled in, same as for the Dravidians, Persians, Moghuls and the British, was the intense heat of summer, a period of such potential devastation to the body that lives must have been won and lost all for the sake of a drink of water.

The days are endless in an Indian summer. The sky is white and nothing moves unless it has to. Survival is in question, for animals, plants, people, and cultures, and the only good time is the middle of the night, when the air isn't cool, only slightly less hot, and everyone soaks up darkness and the air.

This year the rains didn't come until the middle of August, which was like putting them off till Christmas.

Until then there was none of that telltale wind that begins to blow from the west, and suddenly one day the trees bend ever so slightly in a different direction and the leaves show their silver backside, and a few days later the ceiling of the sky settles lower and lower until it gets so near, you think it's on the sidewalk and the air is so close and dense, there's almost none of it left to breathe. The humidity starts out so faint that you barely notice, but the wind keeps up and so does an infinitesimal sense of moistness among the dust. Finally the clouds are there, building up across the sky, big, gorgeous, fat, billowing dark clouds full of rain.

This year it was just hot, the endless oppression of heat, God's wrath clear as clear. That's what the Indians think.

Weeks and finally months passed like this, and a lot happened for all of us.

Cully did not return.

Phoebe did, of course, but then she stayed. She did not go back to New York.

Kady too was busy.

Public Works Minister Hari K. Narayan held a press conference in early June and said when he retired the prime minister would have to choose whether to go for reform and innovation on the one hand, which meant Kady Suraj as his successor, or "the same old route."

Kady's renown grew even more.

Mirabai's wedding was still weeks off.

And, unbeknownst to all but a few, Attar Singh started a full-scale search to find Cully and by the last week in May, barely two weeks after Phoebe arrived, he had seventy-five detectives scattered around northern India looking for him. Phoebe remained unaware and uninformed.

Life in Deeg itself slowed. It was the heat. The palace seemed closed down. The family read books and played cards and slept. They emerged in early evening and took rides to all the forts, climbing the hills in caravans of Rolls-Royces. Pushtu was their favorite, the oldest fort in Deeg, and often they didn't leave its rooftop until one might think it was nearly dawn.

Letters from Auntie Indore in Mussoorie in the northern hills were few. The heat, even there, she wrote, was unbearable for her and Mirabai, but no one in Deeg was sympathetic, envying the breeze and coolness that settled on the hills.

In Deeg itself the wind stopped and dust was as thick in the air as underfoot. In the office aides put pots of water around the windows to cool the incoming air, or so they thought.

Cully, for his part, was on the move.

It was partly the demon. A doctor in Srinagar had verified that there had been an invasion and prescribed activity as a curative. He agreed, when Cully asked, that a pilgrimage might work.

Cully had a rhythm, if not a destination. He stayed nowhere for more than a couple of nights and spoke often about his "undigested karma" and the invasion.

Midafternoon, August 11th, the rains had started the day before and Mirabai's wedding was some four weeks off, I told my driver to take me to the house on Bhagwandas Road.

Phoebe had been staying there for three months, at Jasdan's insistence, at Jiggie's sisters. Auntie Indore was the widow of the Maharaja of Indore, so calling her Auntie Indore was like calling her Auntie Philadelphia. She was still in Mussoorie with the bride-to-be. Since her return from Deeg Phoebe had been living in her house alone.

So to speak. She had a lalli named Chumpi whom Jasdan had sent with her from Deeg, as well as the rest of Auntie's staff, some fifteen people, not counting their children, their dependents, and their servants, who all lived in quarters out in back.

I was headed toward the embassy to do more reading in the library, but I had an article on Indian psychology I planned to show Phoebe.

The article talked about how the self in India was not perceived as individual but familial. Family, more than self-identify, was so central that if a man committed suicide, it was likely because he'd failed to perform some duty to his family, and if he showed neuroses, they were invariably diagnosed within this sphere as well.

The self did not develop gradually and assume an identity of its own but emerged, full blown, at birth, within a constellation called the family and, by extension, the community and the caste. It had as its personal attributes obligations to the rest and the knowledge that what shames one shames them all.

I thought the article might help Phoebe understand Kady's resistance to her and his apparent commitment to his family.


Headed down Bhagwandas Road, I assumed Phoebe wouldn't be home and I'd just give the article to some bearer and leave. But the house struck me as so enchanting that day that I just sat in the car with my hand on the door and looked at it.

It was a one-story bungalow nestled under a couple of banyan trees that had grown so large through the years their branches hung down over the windows and the roof. They gave the place a look of being sheltered, cloistered even, under the powerful might of some of nature's greatest trees. It was a beautiful sight, even in the rain, because it was pouring then, causing great clouds of steam to rise off the ground.

I might not have liked the house in another country, seen it as potentially dark and wintry with all that hanging verdure, but in India, where everything is sun and light, even in the rain, and trees with their shade are heaven-sent, it was a jewel, and I sat in the car thinking about it, feeling pleased Phoebe had such a nice spot for herself. It struck me, not for the first time, that she had a far greater gift of luck than her brother, and I wondered again where he was.

Finally I told the driver I'd get out. I had my boots, he'd forgotten his. Neither of us had remembered umbrellas. I knew he'd go in barefoot for me if I wanted, but I just opened the door and dashed up the walkway. I rang the bell and waited. When no one answered I turned the knob and pushed it in, slowly, in case the servant was just now padding on his way. I didn't want to embarrass him. The door moved silently, a heavy thing, thick like the walls, the door of an old house.

As I pushed the door, I gradually saw ever larger portions of a room that was made of clear white stone with occasional grains of gray. I saw furniture, photographs, books, all of it Auntie Indore's, another room opening up across the way, an indoor tree that rose toward the top of the windows as if trying to reach its outdoor brothers just across the glass.

Then I saw Kady Suraj.

He was standing with one shoe on and one shoe off, one foot on the arm of a chair, the other, barefoot, flat against the marble floor, his long brown toes outstretched. He was putting on his shoes, tying the laces, when he looked up and saw me.

He wore nothing but trousers and I could see his belly button, his naked chest and the bushy black hair that ran from his nipples to his pants.

He must have been taken aback at the sight of me, but he just continued to tie the laces, put on the shoe, and then an under-shirt. He said, ever so normally, it all happened in seconds, "Can I get you some tea? Or would you rather have a drink?"

I said, "Nothing, thank you, I've just come to drop off some-thing for Phoebe. I was due at the dentist's ten minutes ago."

"Oh, well, in that case," he said, standing erect, hands in his pocket like he might be talking to a friend and this a home of his. He came over to me at the door, took my envelope and put it on a table where he said Phoebe'd be sure to get it, and slowly, no hurry at all, no fluster or embarrassment, just this great big nearly naked body, or so it seemed, he picked up an umbrella I hadn't seen before and proceeded to walk with me out to the car.

His arm around my waist to hold me in under the umbrella lest I get any wetter than I was, and walking, as I pressed up against him for the shelter, I smelled . . .

Not cinnamon but something French and soft, flowery, not too sweet, jasmine, rose, or ginger root, I don't know, but definitely female. It was lingering in his hair and on his undershirt from a time not too distant in the past when he must have rubbed up against it at its source.

# ❦ 16 ❦

RETURNING TO MAY, WHEN THE
long summer was just underway, my one night in Deeg, Phoebe
and I talked for a long time on the roof of the palace.

She told me she knew no one had told her the truth about her
brother's disappearance. She also said Cully's room at the palace
had been searched.

Phoebe started at the beginning.

How she'd arrived in Deeg and Attar Singh escorted her over
to the zenana, where the women lived. She asked about Cully,
but Singh wouldn't talk, insisted on waiting till they had tea
with Jasdan. After that an old woman opened the door and Attar
Singh wasn't allowed inside, no men were, not even Jiggie Deeg.
The woman took her bag, and upstairs she met a woman named
Chumpi who was assigned to her. From then on Chumpi slept
outside her door, ordered water for her bath, and told her everything about everything, but nothing about Cully.

At least not at first.

Next, Jasdan and Attar Singh summoned her to tea and put
her through an interrogation. Where was Cully? When was she
going to see him? What was he doing? When she asked if he had
stolen anything or done anything, Jasdan said no. Was he mad
Cully hadn't finished the project? No, he didn't care. What was
the matter, then? Nothing, he just wanted to get everything

resolved "so I can stop thinking about your brother and get on with my daughter's marriage. I've got my father's granddaughter to deal with, and if you knew him, you'd know what I meant."

But when she asked if Cully and the girl had a relationship, he got angry and said, "I can't have my daughter making friends with a man, and she knows it."

Cully's room was exactly the way he'd left it, books, papers, clothes, and so on, but no razor, toothbrush, or slippers. Which meant he'd planned to leave and had taken things with him.

She asked them about April 2nd, the last day Cully was there.

It turned out the marriage agreements from "the other side" arrived the week before, and Cully's disappearance occurred within the commotion of signing contracts. Mirabai's brief, if awful, episode of running away as far as the train station the year before was not much talked about, but it wasn't a secret, either, so Phoebe understood the atmosphere of relief. Jasdan insisted the excitement was such no one noticed her brother didn't show up for dinner.

"But how could you miss him?"

"We just did."

And the next day, April 3rd, everyone was so busy helping Mirabai pack because she was getting ready to go visit Auntie Indore in Mussoorie, they still didn't notice.

"Well, when did you notice?"

"Maybe two weeks, maybe one week." The American Embassy rang up to say Cully hadn't been in Delhi, did they know where he was? That was when. His sister from New York was calling, so they tried to figure out how much time had passed since they saw him.

"Then how do you know he left April second?"

Jasdan and Attar Singh shrugged. They just knew, that's all.

"Did you talk to him?"

"We had lunch as usual," Jasdan said. "He was here. He came down from Delhi the night before. It was a normal day. The children must have had school in the morning, Hindi lessons."

"Mirabai, too?"

"Must be," he said. "Same as usual."

"Mirabai hadn't left for Mussoorie yet?"

"No, she hadn't left yet. Attar Singh and I worked here in the office all day. We never saw him."

"He didn't come in?"

"No."

"And you didn't see him morning or afternoon? You didn't have tea?"

"I didn't," Jasdan said. He looked at Attar Singh. "Did you?"

"No."


Chumpi, the old lalli, eventually told Phoebe that Cully came down by plane from Delhi the night of April first and was very upset. At dinner—she was on the floor in the dining room, so she saw—he didn't eat or say a thing. And the next day—

That was the day Mirabai left? Phoebe interrupted, trying to get the sequence of events clear in her mind.

No, no, no, said Chumpi, that was not the day. That was not even close to the day. Mirabai left only a few days ago, "just before you yourself arrived."

"Did you see her leave?"

No, the woman said, no one did. They were told she left quickly with her father.

Then what did happen on April 2nd?

Cully-sa'ab spent a long time in the office with Maharajkumar-sa'ab and Attar Singh-ji. She knew because her second cousin on her mother's side sat outside the door, and he told her they had a fight.

A fight about what?

He didn't know because they were talking English, but it was something about Cully's longtime past dead father.

His father?

Something about his father and Suraj-sa'ab and Maharaj-sa'ab.

What about them?

Chumpi said she didn't know. Something had happened. Cully-sa'ab said Maharaj-sa'ab-Jiggie-sa'ab did something to his father.

But what?

She didn't know. And her cousin didn't know.

What time was this?

In the morning. Her cousin took them tea, and later Cully left.

Chumpi herself saw him outside the palace and followed him down the road. Watched him when he branched out across the field and cut west toward the empty desert. He was swinging his arms the way he did when he was angry.

"How do you know he did that when he was angry?" Phoebe asked.

"Because I saw him do it."

"When?"

"In the garden with Mirabai."

"Why was he angry?"

"I don't know. But they were yelling and when he walked away, his arms were swinging."

"When was this?"

About a week before he disappeared, Chumpi said, the day the letter came from the other side with the marriage agreement. The girl had phoned him, and he had come down to Deeg to see her.

Phoebe asked Jasdan about the fight in his office, but he said, "You can never trust servants. They don't know what they're talking about."

She also asked him again when Mirabai had left, and he said he wasn't exactly clear, but it was about April second.

Phoebe asked Chumpi whether Jasdan had sent Mirabai to Mussoorie in the hills to get her away from Cully.

Chumpi said no, how could he, because Cully-sa'ab was already gone by the time she left.

Was she actually sent away from Deeg? Phoebe persisted.

No, no, no, Chumpi said, peoples was all time always going to Mussoorie in the summer to stay with Auntie Indore, no reason now to have any other reason.

So there was nothing between Cully and Mirabai?

No.

May 24th was Phoebe's last night in Deeg. Unbeknownst to everyone, Cully had flown to Kashmir the day before. She herself was leaving for Delhi in the morning. An epidemic of cholera had been reported in the outlying districts of Deeg, so that day the grounds had started filling up with people coming in to the palace to escape the scourge and get something to eat, and that night was the first time Phoebe suspected her connection with Jiggie Deeg was greater than she thought.

She was sleeping before dinner when she awoke and heard a tumultuous noise outside. Going to the window, she saw thousands of people, villagers in cotton skirts and dhotis, men, women, children, carrying lanterns at the ends of staves, and she instantly knew this was not due to cholera. It was something else. There were too many of them, and they were excited.

She dressed quickly in a long skirt and pastel blouse and went out in the hall, but the zenana was empty, only a sweeper who ran at the sight of her.

Outside, pandemonium greeted her. She crossed the courtyard and went in the main palace, down the central corridor, past canvases as big as couches and marble inlays fit for Moghuls. The hall was empty, but way ahead, where rooms branched out and public events once had taken place, she saw masses of people. At a window she glanced outside and saw the great big silver Rolls-Royce.

For eight years it had not been used, but now it stood in front of the main entrance, flag flying on the front right fender, two lions and a unicorn.

Nearby was another car, a Deeg airport taxi.

Running now, she reached the central core of the palace and at the library with the tigers and snow leopard found servants and people she didn't know pressed in around the door, blocking it. She elbowed her way through them. "Kya hai?"

"Maharaj-sa'ab hai."

The room inside was full, hundreds of people. She pushed her way in farther. Asked why Maharaj-sa'ab was here. Someone said the wedding. She got through so she could see, and there he was, Jiggie Deeg.

Staring at her.

Exactly as if, from across the room, he knew exactly who she

276

was and when she'd arrive, had been waiting for her.

He was seated in the biggest chair in the room, his piercing dark eyes, heavy brows, and ugly yet riveting face made all the more striking by three wide and powerful streaks of yellow paste blazing across his forehead. They were the flags of worship. But his clothing was nondescript, and he had no jewels. He wore a cotton dhoti, same as villagers on the lawns. Phoebe knew at a glance that vanity had lost its hold on him.

The room was a commotion. Children were climbing on him, in his arms and lap, standing beside him on the chair, and around the room people were kneeling, bending, bowing, pressed in tight. Phoebe could tell he'd just arrived, ceremony of obeisance, to a maharaja who wasn't going to return. People were trying to get close enough to kiss his ankles, toes, knees. Phoebe had barely even crossed the threshold before she felt engulfed by the power of his eyes looking at her.

She remembered him coming out of the library twenty years ago, walking down the hall, taking charge of her, except that as he got closer, his face softened from imperious to kind, so that when he finally spoke and said, "This must be the daughter, then. You're Phoebe," he sounded like an uncle.

"Yes," she'd said.

"I've heard a lot about you," he said next. Then he paused. "You know your father's a foolish man. You know that, don't you?" Another pause. "You'll have to be careful."

And she had said, standing her straightest, "It isn't your right to criticize him, and it certainly isn't your right to come in his house and criticize him. Don't ever do that to me again, not anywhere."

Amazing herself as she said it.

But, just as amazingly, he had only smiled at her with great affection and patted her on the back. "Good for you," he said. "I like a girl like that. I like anyone like that. But take care of yourself. You may have to."


Now he held her with his eyes again and lifted his hands and namasted her. She felt honored and singled out.

She stared back, her stomach churning. She was both drawn to him and repulsed; historically he was her opponent because he'd been Kady's and Louis' years before. Abruptly he dropped

277

her from his gaze and she felt another emotion cascade in upon the first.

Discarded, she felt a sense of hurt rise up in her that was so strong she nearly cried out, but he was leaving and everyone was moving, a torrent of people heading toward the door. She pushed against them, wanting to see Jiggie face to face, get more of him before he left, but she got pushed off to the side, and when he passed, some feet away, she could only feel him like a suction cup pulling everything in his sway.

Without warning he turned—he'd known she was there all along—and looked at her again.

What did he want? What was he doing with her? She remembered how he'd touched her father's Shiva Nataraj and how she'd hated him for his presumptuousness. Now she felt the very same thing billowing up in her and glared at him, but he was walking on ahead. She got pulled along with the crowd, only to reach the dining room door, where the masses thinned out and she was thrust ahead with a select few and the door was slammed shut behind her, leaving her in a room as quiet as a closet.

She could hear nothing but the fans. Everyone was already seated. Her heart was pounding. She knew something was happening. She tiptoed to her seat. Sat down. Took her napkin. No one said a word. No one noticed her. A child coughed. Silence. Someone took up a glass to drink. She turned her eyes to look at Jiggie, Jiggie and the Garuda bird. He didn't see her. He was looking at his plate.

An old man in a dhoti was standing beside him. He looked like his dog or pet. He had a fuchsia turban.

The tension in the room was palpable. Servants came with food, bare feet against the rugs. She served herself, couldn't eat. Someone coughed again. Now, here, Jiggie's eyes were old, not blazing and alert as they'd been just seconds before, and in this room he seemed more tired than he had outside, as if days had passed since he'd left the other place and he hadn't slept at all.

He only had rice and yogurt on his plate. He stirred the food slowly with his fingertips, making a ball, which he slid off into his mouth.

Platters of food were served, only to depart, barely touched. The old man in the turban had arms like sticks and a neck like a chicken's but his eyes were enormous. Oversize and brown, they moved all the time. From Jiggie, around the room and back again. She wondered what he did; as if to answer, he started to sing a chant. "You are ash, sa'ab, ash. All is ash. We come from ash, we go to ash. . . ."

No one paid any attention. They didn't look at him, just went on picking at their food. Maybe they'd heard him so many times, it was the same as not hearing at all?

"It is ash, sa'ab, all is ash. We go from ash to ash. . . ."

As if compelled by a great and superior force, Phoebe looked away from Jiggie. She turned her head for the first time far down—

". . . from ash to ash. . . ."

—to the far other end of the table where she hadn't looked before. There was Kady.

Raw silk suit, shirt, tie, more elegant than anyone in the room, and a shadow across his jaw that said he hadn't bothered to shave. He was eating, no hurry. . . .

"Life is creator and destroyer. . . ."

Calm and on his own, just like Jiggie, but so much younger and more handsome. Phoebe knew that somehow, in the time since Jiggie entered this room, he had lost whatever power he had to Kady Suraj, because here Kady had a presence and authority that was undeniable. If Jiggie was infused with pain and suffering, Kady exuded nothing less than monumental triumph.

"It is Shiva, sa'ab. It is the cremation ground of life. . . ."

Jiggie raised his eyes toward Kady Suraj. Was she imagining it, or did his eyes seem exhausted from the mere strain of seeing him? "Shall we talk now, Suraj-sa'ab?" he asked in a quiet voice.

"Just a minute," Kady said lightly, answering Jiggie's English in a low-level Rajasthani Hindi. "I'm not quite done."

Shyam gasped at the insult and looked as though he were ready to leap down the table and grab him by the throat, but Jiggie took his hand and prevented him from moving.

The tension was palpable. Kady kept on eating, yogurt laced with pineapple.

The men hadn't seen each other in years. Phoebe knew it and she knew everyone in the room knew it.

Kady was fixing his coffee, one sugar lump, then another. One swallow, then another, and Phoebe suddenly understood how strong was the neurotic quality of Kady and Jiggie's tie. Her eyes moved from one to the other. Kady was so caught up in the moment, she couldn't get him to notice her. He was still eating, and magnificent.

Finally he put down his cup, wiped his mouth with his napkin, and said, very clearly, very British and upper class now, and certainly polite, "Yes, I think so. Shall we? Is that all right with you?"

Jiggie rose, followed by Attar Singh and Shyam Singh, and, with himself in the lead, the three old men headed out.

Kady was the last to get up. He folded his napkin, put it down, suddenly flashed his eyes to her and just as suddenly looked away, but the look, fleeting as it was, held an exuberance barely contained. He slowly followed the old men out.

Phoebe longed for him to turn around and look at her.

But he didn't. He kept on walking, taking out a cigarette case, and as the three old men were about to disappear through the door, he called out, utter nonchalance, "Maharaj-sa'ab?"

They all three stopped but didn't turn.

"Tell me," he said casually, cocking his head, now tapping a cigarette very precisely against its box. "Tell me, Jiggie, did you enjoy your flight from Benares?"

# ❧ 17 ❧

IN THE MORNING A ROLLS-ROYCE full of women and children took her to the station. There was no sign of Kady or the maharaja. When Phoebe asked the women if the men had really gone, they said yes, they left last night. Jiggie's plane took them both to Delhi, then himself on to Benares. She asked why Jiggie had come, and they said to make plans for Mirabai's marriage. And Kady? To help him. But when she asked why Kady and Maharaj-sa'ab hated each other, they sighed with an air of long experience and said, they didn't. That's just the way it was.

On the train Phoebe and Chumpi settled into a first-class compartment, Chumpi on the floor.

Jasdan had insisted Chumpi go with her. "It is my duty to my guest," he declared. "I cannot let you be alone." It was not such an unusual thing to do, and Phoebe accepted, wondering, though, if the woman was not sent to look for Cully and keep an eye on her.

From her position on the floor Chumpi, her face as creased as an elephant's, pushed her long skirts under her hips and cocked her head to the side like a bird. She even sounded like a bird. She took up no more room than an oversize place mat, and her bangles jingled constantly. They stretched from her wrists up past her elbow, so even the act of breathing seemed to set them off.

The city of Deeg disappeared and the high flat desert of Rajasthan took over. Phoebe stared out the window. She felt disconsolate. They had tried to persuade her to take Indian Airlines, it was quicker and not so hot, but she'd said no. She wanted to see India, feel its heat and soot. After last night, this seemed even more important. India had a portent it hadn't had before. It didn't seem just a coincidence of birth anymore, her link-up with this country. If she had some meaning, however small, for someone as seemingly remote as Jiggie Deeg, then nothing was coincidence.

"The train was hot," Phoebe told me, pouring herself a cup of tea and drinking thirstily while we sat on Kitty Chandradas' veranda. "There was all this diesel soot. I was covered with it, and I kept looking at it, India all over me. I couldn't figure out who I was anymore. India had changed me. I knew Cully wouldn't mind the soot because he fit in, but I didn't know if I did. I knew something else, too. Whatever they said in Deeg about him and Mirabai, I didn't believe them. Maybe they didn't know," she added, "but I did. I knew they were in love."


Kitty's bearer brought us some English biscuits and left. Phoebe commented on how he was wearing a sweater under his uniform and said she had no idea it was turning cold, she hadn't even noticed. Then she watched a dark brown mali gardener weeding out the pool down on the lawn. The man was so skinny, he looked no more than a bundle of twigs; his little daughter was deposited nearby. Who knows, maybe Phoebe wondered how that collection of twigs had sired a child, and maybe the specter of the twigs themselves mirrored her sense of alienation.

"But I like children," she said, apropos of nothing. "I always have. Mirabai had a dog, you know. So I knew right away she had to be different. She'd never even talked to her fiancé. She had his picture. They had to exchange pictures before negotiations could begin, but she lost it. Chumpi said the dog chewed it up. I wondered if Mirabai gave it to him on purpose. I found a short story she wrote. It was in Cully's desk. It was about a girl who joins a circus and travels to Paris and New York and becomes a high-wire trapeze artist. It wasn't very good, but, I mean, is that someone who settles into an arranged marriage with a man she doesn't love, especially when she's fallen in love with someone else?"

Phoebe sounded tired. I wondered if she was getting sick again. She seemed especially weak today.

The train from Deeg cut through the desert hills and hard rock sand with tufts of growth. Phoebe asked Chumpi if women really did fall in love in arranged marriages. Was it that easy?

Must be, said Chumpi, who'd never married or had a child. The womens mostly always did for fall in love. Jasdan's wife had, Jiggie's wife had, and all the others, too, now same as always, nothing changed.

And the men, too? Did they fall in love?

Jasdan did, the old woman said, Jiggie did, this man, that man.

"But what about Kady Suraj?" Phoebe asked. "Did he fall in love with Durr?"

"Must be," Chumpi said. "They all do. For duty."

"So no one ever gets divorced?"

"Ne-ver, ne-ver, ne-ver," Chumpi declared. "Even if no love, no divorce."

"But why not?" Phoebe knew, of course, but she wanted Chumpi to confirm it.

Chumpi didn't have an answer, the idea was so appalling. Finally she said, "Bring ruin to man, to woman, to childrens. What is the good for that?"

Phoebe asked Chumpi to tell her about Suraj, but the woman just shrugged. What could she say?

"Then tell me about him and Jiggie Deeg," Phoebe said. "What do they think about each other?"

"Everything," the woman answered. "They think this way, then that way. Everyone liking Suraj-sa'ab," she added. "Everyone. He is very special mans, is why. Equal to Maharaj-sa'ab."

"Is that why the maharaja doesn't like him?"

"He likes him. I am telling you. He likes him. They are just this way. They have to be."

"Why?"

"Karma, must be." She shrugged again, indifferent to the cause.

283

The journey from Deeg took all night and half the next day. Some three hours short of Delhi the train pulled into Agra, last home and resting place of the Emperor Shah Jehan and his little teenage bride, Mumtaz.

Phoebe stood up abruptly. "Come quick, Chumpi," she said. "I want to see the Taj Mahal."

They found a hotel near the station. The room had no view and little, narrow beds; Chumpi took the floor. They never did get to the Taj, with its two tombs, Mumtaz and Shah Jehan, a white marble building it had taken some twenty thousand men twenty-two years to build. Because Phoebe opened her suitcase, saw her parents' death certificates, which she had brought with her from New York, and promptly forgot everything else.

She opened the envelope. She caught sight of the signature on the first page, "Dr. K. P. Sharma," and immediately put the envelope down.

"Kya hai?" Chumpi asked.

"Get me the phone book."

Chumpi found it under the bed. Phoebe counted out twenty-nine Sharmas, but no K. P.'s and no doctors.

She picked up the death certificates again. They had lain unopened in her suitcase since the day she left New York, just as they had lain in storage twenty years untouched. This time she pulled the pieces of paper all the way out of the envelope.

# ❧ 18 ❧

THE DOCUMENT WAS EMBOSSED IN the lower left hand corner with a round purple seal that identified something called "The Human Actuality and Death Department Bureau, Cantonment Station, Agra General District."

With Chumpi in tow, Phoebe set off by taxi for Cantonment Station where the bureau was located in a large one-time British bungalow. When the car pulled up, Phoebe saw people lying on the grass in various states of sleep or rest, all of them in khaki clothes that identified them as employees of the bureau itself.

Their absence did not seem to make much difference inside, the building visibly taken over by swarms of similarly clothed people, a good portion of them sleeping on the floor.

The building's only apparent contents were paper. Acres of it, yellowed, browned, aged, and stacked high along the walls and in the middle of the rooms. If her arrival came in contrast with the prevailing atmosphere of lethargy and inactivity in the room, no one noticed. Only when Phoebe waited some time at an appropriate desk and coughed in order to get attention did an eye look up in apparent irritation at being interrupted.

"Yes?" a man said unsympathetically, indicating he was already overworked.

Phoebe stated her case, knowing full well every ear in the room, probably the building, was listening. But procedure required that higher-ups be granted the opportunity to defer to the next higher-up, so she—Chumpi was resting by the door—explained her way through a succession of clerks and bosses, going steadily up the ladder until she reached the very top—the man but one room removed from the main door—and finally got to put her case to the Senior Acting Deputy Director himself.

He was a small person, currently drinking tea, and he agreed to locate what she wanted. Although, he pointed out, she had no official status, no authorization, no identity card. No small matters, any of them. Her passport did not count. But she was lucky, he declared, because he had the full authority to grant an exception in her case. He would help her.

She waited for him to ask her why she wanted the name of the outlying district of the town, but he didn't, just told her to wait one minute. She pushed her hair out of her eyes and sat down, held her face up to the fan.

Paper was stacked in every conceivable place, without benefit of shelves or filing system. The attempt to locate documents pertaining to the death of Louis and Thalia Guthrie in Agra District some twenty years before proved a task that required eight clerk-chaprassis the rest of one day and a good part of the next to complete, all in the time-honored process of hunt and peck.

For the first four hours, Phoebe was polite enough to take multiple cups of tea. Later, she leaned her head back against the wall and tried to sleep but couldn't. She only left because the building shut down for the night and because she believed everyone's self-respect was sufficiently at stake that they would resume the search tomorrow.

Just after lunch on the following day, two chaprassis came into the Senior Acting Deputy Director's office carrying armloads of papers that apparently represented the complete documentation for the year in question.

Phoebe knew enough by this time not to suggest that since the date was January 6th, the necessary documents might be near the top, and she just watched as the Senior Acting Deputy Director went through the papers one by one.

Ultimately it was concluded that the files were not there at all, nor was there anything with any reference to the Guthries.

"Try the Police Department, Agra District," the Acting Deputy District Director suggested. "They must be keeping copies of all our files with the official accident reports and the body condition reports."

"But why isn't anything here?"

The man lifted up his arms in a cosmic suggestion of life's mysterious ways. Phoebe thought his analysis very sound.

The police department was worse.

Men recently beaten by police batons cowered in the halls, and others, nearly naked, clung high up to bars in their cells nearby because they didn't want to sit or stand in the excrement on the floor. She overheard discussions about cases that ranged from a ten-year-old being sent to jail for robbery to murder by thugs who held a man and his family captive for three days before killing them, under directions of the man's younger brother, who wanted to inherit the family property for himself. The property consisted of one-sixteenth of an acre of a rocky field.

By the end, two days in total, Phoebe had the same results as before.

No file could be found on the Guthries, no record of their death or accident.

She went back to the hotel and calculated that if there were twenty-nine Sharmas in the telephone book, there were some two hundred and twenty-nine others who had telephones but were not listed—such was the delay in getting into the telephone book—and at least five thousand and ninety-nine others who did not have telephones at all.

She moved into the best hotel in town, because it undoubtedly had the best phone system, and there she went to work. She hired a so-called secretary from the hotel's rosters and put him to work as well. Chumpi slept and watched television with the sound turned off.

Phoebe had no success, but the next afternoon the secretary did. He located a Sharma in the phone book who told him he had a neighbor who had an uncle whose name was Sharma and that he, the other Sharma, was a doctor who had either died or moved to Delhi.

Phoebe called the man back. He said he didn't know any more than he had told the secretary, but he agreed to see her.

The man eventually took her next door and introduced her to

a woman who said she did have an uncle who was a doctor, and his name was K. P. Sharma. But he had never lived in Agra.

"Never?" Phoebe asked.

The niece shook her head. He had always lived in Delhi. But he had a brother who lived in Agra. His name was L. P. Sharma. Maybe she was thinking of him?

Was he a doctor? Phoebe asked.

No, he was a lawyer. Maybe she'd heard of him? Everyone had.

No, Phoebe said politely. She hadn't.

Everyone else had, the woman insisted.

Phoebe showed her the death certificate with the spidery, very legible signature, "Dr. K. P. Sharma, Agra."

The woman shook her head.

Could she see his brother?

Who?

The lawyer, Phoebe said, exasperated. He might know about the accident and the village.

He was dead.

What about Dr. K. P. Sharma himself?

What about him? the niece asked.

"Can I see him?"

"Of course you may be seeing him. Anybody can be seeing him. He is there each and every day. If only you are in Delhi."

Phoebe got the address, there was no phone, and left.

# ❧ 19 ❧

PHOEBE AND CHUMPI WENT TO
the house on Bhagwandas Road. No one was about; Auntie
Indore was still in Mussoorie with Mirabai and none of the
servants were in sight. Chumpi unlocked the door and immediately set off toward the back, yelling who were they, the servants, not to do their duty to memsa'ab, being invisible like
skunks when they should have been at the door to welcome her.

Phoebe followed her in. The place reminded her of Jumna
Road, colonial houses all alike. She imagined Louis walking in,
dark hair and a white suit, "There you are. Jesus, Feeb, where
you been? Get us a drink, will you? That's a girl."

"So soddie, memsa'ab," Chumpi said. "I no here wi-you. You
no like?"

"No, I do."

"You no like. I see. You want hotel instead? Maharaj-sa'ab get
mad."

"No, this is fine. Really. It just gives me memories."

"Ahh-h-h," Chumpi said, indifferent now. "Past, present. All
same."

"I hope not. They better not be."

"Future, too. No matter."

"Chumpi."

"It's for true," the lalli insisted. "You are all time always, past

289

and future, what you were and what you are becoming." She pulled Phoebe to a table where Auntie Indore had photographs. "See?" she said proudly, pointing at the pictures. "All Deegs."

"So I'm the same person I was twenty years ago?"

"Must be."

"And the same person I will be in twenty—"

"Look," Chumpi interrupted, pointing back and forth between herself and the pictures. "This all Deeg. Me, them, same."

"Yes, but if I'm always the same person, what does matter?"

"You no understand. Not same person. But always one child and one old woman in there inside, waiting to come in or out. Look at pictures, memsa'ab. You no looking at pictures."

Phoebe looked. Two stood out, one of Jiggie alone, the other with his granddaughter. She picked up one of him standing near Lake Pichiti.

"Very good," Chumpi declared. "You are having good connection to Maharaj-sa'ab."

"How do you know?" Phoebe put the picture down.

"I am knowing."

"But how?"

"Because why for Cully-sa'ab crosses one, then two oceans to come to Deeg? Must be connection, long time back, this lifetime, other lifetime."

"But that connection is with Cully."

"Same thing, you, your brother. All time, same thing."

"Is that why I picked out his picture?"

"Must be." Chumpi nodded confidently. "Maharaj-sa'ab tell Jasdan-sa'ab to put you here in house."

"How do you know?"

"Everyone knows t-ese tings."

"Why does he want me here?"

"Must be wanting something, must be."

"Well, I know what I want."

Chumpi looked at her with sudden intensity. "What? You tell me."

"I already told you. I told you on the train. I want to feel happy here."

"Just for asking gods for help," Chumpi said matter-of-factly. "They will give you any-ting. That is, if you are not wanting this one one ting too much. Just letting go of all little bits of this and that. Then you will get what you want."

"Letting go?"

"Yes, all little bits."

"And look at what's important?"

"Must be."


Phoebe started seeing Delhi again. That was important. She wanted to reacquaint herself with the girl she'd been before and the city she'd known, tea stalls where they used to eat, the little restaurant-hotels where the three of them would stop for tea and cakes. But it was different in the daylight from what it had been at night twenty years before, so she found Tulsidas, started paying him by the week, and had him take her everywhere. She also looked up a few school friends, some married women now, one divorced, who didn't return her calls. "She doesn't go out, of course," her mother said on the phone.

"Of course," Phoebe said, understanding.

She saw friends of her parents, mostly Louis', and hunted down the orphanage where Thalia had worked, torn down now, an office building in its place. She couldn't find a trace of the servants; no one knew a thing of Kamala, Moosselman, or Samiji. Harriet and me she saw often, dinner, lunch, tea, took Harriet's daughter shopping and to have her hair cut, to an American teenage movie her mother refused to see.

She tried to put Kady out of her mind. She thought of him as a married man who'd never get divorced, so what was the use of an affair?

Once she called his office and left a message. To her relief, he never called back.


She spent a lot of time in Chandni Chowk at Cully's apartment. She cleaned it, brought in food like peanut butter and jelly, pickles, chutney, and biscuits, things that wouldn't spoil. She insisted it was for herself, she liked to munch when she was there.

Thinking about Cully occupied a lot of her time. She read his notebooks and sorted through his drawers, sometimes spent the night there reading and staring at his posters of the gods in light reflected from the street below. She liked the place, even the noise, found it restful. She befriended the children in the building and was always taking them places, giving them rides in taxis and buying sweets, letting their friends come along. She figured out from the landlady that Kady was the one who was paying Cully's rent. She began to take it for granted that Cully was trying to distance himself from her. She didn't like it, but the facts spoke for themselves. Alice reported that no letters had arrived from him in New York.

At his apartment she found a letter wedged in the back of his desk. It was from a museum in Calcutta saying they'd learned of his work with Maharaja Juggernathan Singh and were interested in contracting for his services. Would he please be in touch?

She called them and asked if he had ever written back. He hadn't. She was not surprised.

At the racetrack she located a man he'd written her about. He had a string of thoroughbreds and set up lunch for her with some friends at the Gymkhana Club who could tell her about his early life in Delhi.

She didn't like the men much, felt out of place. They ate the club's green beans and lamb chops and drank imported gin. The black market still prospered, they said.

It wasn't until the end that she asked, so casual they probably didn't even notice, Had he ever said, you know, mentioned he had a sister?

He hadn't.


She visited Number Nine Jumna Road, too, but it was summer, so no one was there to let her in. She stood outside the fence and looked at the house and the banyan trees, found descendants of the same old green geckos who had slithered along the walls when she was there before perched now in the same high places.

The people her father knew were mostly gone, died or moved away, some in the mountains for the summer, Mussoorie, Simla, or Kashmir, lucky no outbreak of trouble there this summer, one could still go up. Those she did see wanted to talk about America and why it was pro-Pakistan when she wanted to ask, What did we seem like as a family? Did I act happy? What was Louis really like?

But they stuck to superficialities, how witty Louis was and

Thalia so dedicated. Phoebe tried to steer them round to deterioration and decay, but they held back. She couldn't blame them,
really. Who'd want to talk about how some man was falling
apart. Oh yes, he kept a gun in his room, didn't you know? Kady
even thought he'd use it on himself.

Sometimes she left a house after tea or lunch, got in the car,
slumped down, and burst into tears, knowing Tulsidas was
watching her in the mirror. But he was the epitome of discretion. She appreciated his concern, the feeling of him sitting in
the front seat worrying about her. One day he brought a big box
of tissues, handed them over the seat, and grinned with so much
pleasure, she stopped crying.

Sometimes on Jumna Road she peered up at the window in
her mother's alcove. A shade had been pulled down against the
summer heat, and to her it began to stand for everything that
had led her to suppress her feelings. She told Tulsidas she
wished she had a camera so she could take a picture of it, look
at it anytime.

"But it's just a window with a shade."

"I know. That's why I want it."


She talked to Tulsidas regularly, often about death and fires.
The subject was something they shared. He, forty-two, had a
grandfather who'd been burned in Benares, on Manikarnika
Ghat itself. The high point of his childhood was being taken
there as eldest son, to witness the funeral. He remembered the
fire, the body, the white shroud, and the untouchables, nearly
black, who tended the body and the fire, carried logs, their faces
white as masks, covered with ash. At the end, they picked up the
bones and ashes, put them in a container, and handed it to his
father. Then they all went down to the riverbank and, with
flowers and oils and chants, sent the leftovers on their way
downstream.

Phoebe asked him what actually happened to the bodies.

He said it depended on how long the fire burned and how hot
it was. But sometimes whole bones were left unburned.

"And everything's thrown in the river? Not just the ashes?"

He nodded.

"But what happens if there's just a fire? Not a funeral. What happens to bones then? Do they burn up?"

"I don't know," he said. He'd never seen a fire like that. "It's just change," he added confidently.

"What is?"

"Death."

"How do you know?"

"Because I've seen my grandfather. He works in a shop over in Old Delhi now."

"What do you mean you've seen him?"

"I have. He's fifteen years old and he has my grandfather's ears."

"They're just similar ears."

"No, memsa'ab, same ears. Exactly same."

Her letters to Alice chronicle a lot of this and talk too of the seeds of a plan to start an export company and sell Indian fabric in the States. But she didn't write Stephen much, and she consciously put off going to Nizamuddin's Tomb.

Dr. Sharma's house was locked and empty.

The stucco bungalow, larger and more prosperous than she expected, was set back from the road by a lawn of its own, in a section of town where mid-level British civil servants used to live in the care of bearers, cooks, and sweeper people.

She was wondering whether to leave a note when a neighbor called from a nearby window, "They're away."

"Who?"

"Doctor-sa'ab and his one bearer only."

"Does anyone ever come by to check the house?"

"Bearer, sometimes."

Phoebe got in the habit of driving by. She brought food and sat on the steps, reading newspapers, writing letters. She always brought the death certificates.

One day a thin old man in a droopy pajama suit and a good dozen rings in one ear was there. He told her Doctor-sa'ab was "having vacation."

She said Doctor-sa'ab had officiated at her parents' death and she wanted to ask him about it. To her relief, the bearer acted as though that were entirely reasonable. He told her the doctor lived alone, his children married, wife renounced. She had gone to Hardwar on the river. "Only me is now all time here."

Phoebe told him her predicament, namely that the death certificates named Agra as the site of death, but that the doctor himself had apparently never been there. "Didn't he ever work in Agra?" she asked. "Just for a while, say, twenty years ago?"

The bearer said he had lived his whole long life in Delhi. He studied the death certificates but said that, except for its signature, it had no connection with Dr. Sharma because he had never worked in Agra. Then, contradicting himself entirely, he made a lengthy distinction between "the source of a man's life," namely, in this case, the Agra of the doctor's youth, and "the living place of that life," namely Delhi, where the man himself had lived.

"Doctor came here just for coll-edge," he said. "He was ne-war leaving Delhi after that."

"So he grew up in Agra and his family went on living in Agra?"

"Exactly what I said."

He invited Phoebe inside to have some water. There was not much to see, clinic and the offices on one side, front room and a kitchen on the other, the rest upstairs. White sheets covered everything; little photographs in wooden frames were tacked to the walls.

Phoebe told him it was very nice, thinking that, indeed, it was, doctors not always prosperous in India. Then she saw a plaque near the door, a date inscribed, twenty years past. "What's that?" she asked.

"Year for doctor owning house."

"Where did the doctor live before that?"

"One werry small place in Old Delhi much too small for having childrens and an office."

"What was it like?"

"Much too werry small, all family sleeping in just one bed, one room."

"Where did he practice then? At a hospital? Clinic?"

"I am not for knowing. I am coming only afterwards. Need for having bearer is here in this place only, having clinic here, nurses, aides, full-time sweepers, too."

She asked him if he knew what happened to bodies that got burned up in a fire. What happened if they didn't all burn? Would they be buried?

He didn't understand what she was talking about.

"I mean," she said, "where would the bodies be now?"

He looked so confused, she dropped it. "He had a brother in Agra?" she asked, ready to try anything.

"One werry fine lawyer brother. Died now long time past, but everyone knows this one big brother. He the big brother and this one here the little brother and him very fine look out for little brother here." The man's pride in all this was enormous. "This little brother most lucky because good fortune always flows from having one big brother—"

"Or sister."

"—and this big brother all time loving these childrens here like his werry own."

"They were his duty."

"Very much. All time thinking duty for little brother and little brother's children. Because he was having no childrens of his own."

She asked if the doctor had ever met Louis and Thalia Guthrie.

The man shook his head and apologized, taking pains she not interpret this as an insult.

Had the doctor heard of Kady Suraj?

No.

Jiggie Deeg?

Of course, he said, who hadn't.

Did the doctor know him personally?

The old man solemnly shook his head, but the lawyer brother, he said with some excitement at the possibility of pleasing her, he might have known him. "He most surely did. Everyone knows Jiggie Deeg."

"But you don't know for sure he did?"

"No."


Little by little Phoebe's attitude toward Kady began to change. The man she liked so intensely at the airport and didn't particularly like in Deeg was replaced in her mind by the friend he'd been from long ago. She began to miss that man and look for him, just as she did for Cully.

One day at Bhagwandas Road she got out six small sheets of paper and taped them to the wall of her room.

Each one had a name. She lined them up opposite the bed. One was for Cully, others for Kady, Samiji, Thalia, Louis, and, last, the Shiva Nataraj.

It was a very peculiar thing to do, she thought, but she didn't mind. They all represented the things she didn't know.

A man who lived in Cully's building told her he helped Cully carry the bronze horse upstairs a few months back, March or early April. She asked who else helped, because the piece was big and heavy, and he said a man who drooled.

"Was that 'Anant'?"

The man said he had no idea, but Cully kicked him out and—

"Kicked him out?"

—threw him down the stairs and yelled at him how they couldn't do the same thing to him they'd done to his father.

He said he asked Cully what was going on, and Cully said, Never mind, made no move to help Anant, lying at the bottom of the stairs. The man himself went down. Anant was bleeding from the head where he had struck the wall, but he was all right. The man helped him up, got him a cab, then, back upstairs, asked Cully-sa'ab once more what was going on.

Cully was knocking at the statue of the horse with a little hammer, listening to the sounds the hammer made.

"What sounds?" Phoebe asked. "Was it hollow?"

"Maybe."

She herself tapped at it, but she couldn't tell.

The next morning Chumpi took her to a temple in Old Delhi and showed her how to pray, Indian style. She said it would help.

One day the landlady told her "the two mens" had been back asking about her brother.

Phoebe knew who they were now, Attar Singh and Shyam Singh, unrelated, but members of the same Rajput caste as Jiggie himself. For the first time she got angry that no one in Deeg had confided in her or told her what was going on.

She hired three small boys to keep an eye out for Cully.

They came to the apartment and proposed she pay them each five rupees a day to watch for Cully. Other boys were doing the very same thing, they said. Didn't she want the service, too?

She paid one rupee and figured out from questioning the boys the other teams belonged to Nasrut Sardar and Attar Singh.

The photo negatives she found in Cully's notebooks back in May turned out to be pictures of Mirabai. They were close-ups, face, dark hair, almond eyes, hands.

The notebooks had passages about how maybe Louis wasn't dead after all, just hiding until he, Cully, could find him and liberate him.

Initially Phoebe found that very strange but, as she read on, it became clear he was talking about the dead man's soul. It was still alive and needed liberating, an idea that was strictly Indian. No son had cracked his skull at a funeral pyre or released his soul into the afterlife. Louis was in limbo.

She realized Cully's idea was not that different from her own. That there was something undone, something specific but unclear about her mother and father that she, or maybe she and Cully, had to do.

She couldn't find the house in Golf Links where they'd stored the whiskey. It had two floors, a garden and a fence that hid it from the road. That's all she remembered, she told Tulsidas, big windows, a door, and trees near a road. She was sure she'd recognize it, but they drove through Golf Links time after time and couldn't find it. This bothered her. If the black market had helped finance her father's life and win Kady his freedom from Jiggie Deeg, it had done much the same for her.

She considered contacting Kady, asking for the address, but didn't.

## ❧ 20 ❧

KADY WAS INCREASINGLY PREOC-
cupied with what his life would have been like without Jiggie
Deeg or Louis Guthrie.

Everything had started to bother him, from the most trivial
to the most important.

One day he impulsively went to Deeg, taking Samiji with him.

In Deeg they hired a cab. Samiji said, "Umaid Mahal Palace,
sa'ab?" but sa'ab said no, and had the cab drive through the
narrow streets of the city, places he hadn't been in over twenty
years. They got out on a street where there were two wells, one
for upper castes, one for lower, but neither worked because
there wasn't enough water.

From there they walked in search of the old mud house where
Suraj had lived and had lain his ear against the door some
twenty-five years ago to listen to Jiggie Deeg talk about a woman
who was having his baby.

Now a woman came out. He talked to her. She said she knew
nothing about a healer who lived there so long ago. She took
them inside, two small rooms, one for animals.

Afterward he was subdued. "You know what that was, don't
you?" he said to Samiji.

"Yes, sa'ab. I knowing everything."

They went to find his village, but it didn't exist anymore; just

299

a few old walls were left. The desert had shifted, the river, too, and what remained looked like artifacts half-buried in the sand. Sa'ab was neither disconsolate nor surprised, but he was very moved. He took some mud from a wall and crumbled it in his hand. "That's all life is," he said, "and I let it get away from me."

"Not everything, sa'ab."

"But a lot, Samiji. I've lost a lot."

He showed Samiji where the fields used to be and the river and how high the waters reached when the floods came. He told him he had a bicycle and was the only boy in the village who ever went to school.

They sat on the edge of what used to be the well. Kady said that in the end—well, there was no end, but when he died—he didn't know what he'd face for coming up so far in station.

Oh, glory, sa'ab.

But sa'ab shook his head.

Samiji understood. The man had violated too much, himself, others.

They went to a tea stall before heading back. Suraj ordered tea with cardamom, cardamom nothing he himself had ever liked, only miss-sa'ab long before.

Samiji sat on the ground, Suraj on a stool. Samiji smelled the cardamom and finally asked, "Is she nice girl? This miss-sa'ab now?"

Suraj nodded.

"Is she like this Cully-sa'ab?"

Suraj gestured toward his head to indicate the hair was the same for both. "She's a woman, Samiji, a woman. And she has a scent," he added. "Something . . . I don't know, but . . ."

"Something nice?"

"Yes."

"But we're not going to see her, sa'ab?"

"How can I?" Suraj looked at him, his face suddenly bleak and pulled. "How can I do that to her? Besides, I don't want to."

Samiji was not entirely sure.

"Sa'ab was not for having any womens anymore," he said eventually. "He stopped. Not that I am knowing everything he does," he added. "I am not knowing this and I am not knowing that, but I am knowing for sure that since that one day when he saw missus-Feeb at the airport, he has not seen one woman."


Attar Singh and Shyam set up an office downstairs in Deeg House in Delhi. They put a map of India on the wall and drew a line stretching from Bombay in the west across to Calcutta in the east, demarcating the north from the south and taking in, above, Delhi, Benares, and all of U.P., as the area where Cully Guthrie was most likely to go. They left out the Punjab because of the Sikh trouble. Jiggie told them to ignore it; he wouldn't go there, but they left in, even farther north, all of Kashmir and Ladakh.

The possibilities were daunting, a triangular-shaped piece of land some 1,260,000 square miles in size, with a 3,535-mile-long coastline.

They checked with passports and immigration right away, so they knew Cully hadn't left the country. Jiggie sent up orders from Benares—this was mid-May, Phoebe had just arrived—to focus on the northern half. Cully spoke Hindi, Jiggie said on the phone from Benares. It made sense he'd stay where he could talk. Attar Singh concurred, but for different reasons. He, who'd gone to Oxford with Jiggie, had looked back over the life of Louis Guthrie in India and determined it all took place in the north. So, he said, would his son's.

But that still left a huge tract of land; the possibility of finding Cully seemed unlikely at best. Nonetheless, they hired detectives across northern India and told them they were searching for Cully in regard to the theft of some art. It occurred, they said, May 11th, the day Phoebe arrived in India.

The search focused on hotels, airplanes, trains, police sheets. Eventually the map had little stars for every place that had been checked and big red pins for places where he'd actually been sighted. Gradually, little bits and pieces of Cully's journey came into shape, most of it in the far north.


The police eventually shut down their investigation, leaving the April 2nd murder of Anant Bhave unsolved.

The press never printed anything about the case, which was

unusual. Murders are not so common here that they're ignored—much less one involving a famous art dealer and a foreigner—but the police never put out any word on it, so the reporters never knew.

Criminal cases that day included twenty-two robberies, four muggings, one drug smuggling, four suspected dowry deaths, seven arrests for illegal shipments of foreign liquor, and one murder that had nothing to do with Anant Bhave. It involved two brothers, Thakur caste.

Who's to say what made the police downplay, even hide, the murder? I assume it was Kady's doing: that he initially bribed people to pay no attention to the case. That's done here. Anything can be done with money. I did determine eventually that in early April he mingled in police circles and told people the murder was a routine mugging with an eye to theft that had gotten out of hand. The case had no importance whatsoever, despite the Bhave name and potential foreign connection, just a coincidence; he knew these people, he said, and the police had to be careful to not allow certain facts to overshadow others. The foreigner, he warned, was one such irrelevancy.

I learned one other thing; it came from the police commissioner himself. He was my next door neighbor's first cousin's husband. He had lunch with Suraj the week after the murder, and Suraj told him explicitly "Jiggie" had no interest in the case, just to make it clear there was no political mileage in settling the case on his behalf.

"I know this Guthrie," he said as well. "He certainly didn't do it."


For Phoebe, the question of Cully became steadily more troublesome.

An art historian at the museum said Cully spent a lot of time studying there whenever he was in Delhi. The official had worked at the British Museum in London and been ostracized by his family for rejecting a position in their bank in order to take up this line of work. That meant he was single and had forfeited all rights to a family; there was no one to arrange his marriage. He said Cully did research in the stacks, looking for derivations of things in Deeg, trying to date objects. He was also interested in the Shiva Nataraj genre of sculpture and was compiling information so he could write a book.

Phoebe said she knew that.

The man said, but did she know Cully threw the research out the day before he disappeared?

She said No.

And that he had been trying to find the bill of sale for the Shiva Nataraj?

Was he trying to find the Shiva itself? Phoebe asked.

The man said, he thought so.

He had other information. Cully had stopped coming to the museum altogether and then, in March, had returned and said he needed to find the derivation of a certain statue of a Mathuran horse. It had only one leg.

She said she'd seen the horse in Cully's apartment in Delhi, but the man told her No, Cully said the piece was in Deeg. There couldn't be two such Mathuran horses.

Indeed, no one had ever heard of any sculpture of a horse coming out of the Mathuran period, much less two.

Phoebe told the man the piece she saw in the apartment looked too big to move. She and I together could barely lift it. And so, she said, if Cully said the piece was in Deeg, in all likelihood it stayed in Deeg.

But that was the problem. Either there were two such horses, or only one, but one was certainly in a third-floor apartment in Chandni Chowk in Delhi.

"You could lift it?" the man asked.

"Yes, barely."

"You and one other woman?"

"It was hard, but we could do it."

The man shook his head. "That's not a good piece."

"What do you mean?"

"It's not good."

"You mean it's false?"

"Must be."

She asked what else he knew about the horse.

Just that Cully bought it from Vishnu Bhave, he said.

The back room of the museum where they talked was filled with old books and stacks of files. "Shall I be honest?" the man said.

"Yes, please, do."

"You are sure? I do not want to be offensive or giving you reason for hating India."

"No, go ahead."

"Then I must tell you that I got rather tired of your brother. You see, he wanted to use these books. Many people want to use these books. We studied his bona fides and they were excellent, even though he never finished his doctorate, but he was clearly someone of promise, and given time, he would finish this thesis. I myself said that and argued for the benefit of having him studying here among us. But by this time now of which I am speaking, I had dismissed him as a serious person."

She called down to Deeg to ask if they knew anything about such a horse in the collection there. Jasdan said he had no idea. Jiggie sent word back from Benares he'd never seen this piece, but that didn't necessarily mean it wasn't there.

I asked her why she didn't see Vishnu Bhave about the horse, but she was adamant. She didn't want to bother him. She finally admitted that she didn't want to hear anything more about the murder.

Attar Singh and Shyam and the others went through every Indian Airlines record since April 2nd and ran their thumbs down as many hotel registers as they could get to. Shyam Singh told them of Cully's attraction to adventure and even the low life, and so, in some cities, they started at the cheapest places and worked their way up from there.

A record for early May, before Phoebe arrived in India, showed that a "C. Guthrie" had taken a round-trip flight from Delhi to Benares and back.

They assumed he'd gone to Benares to see Jiggie. But if that was so, Jiggie never saw him, nor did anyone else they could find. So either he hadn't taken the flight—although he turned in his boarding pass both coming and going—or he had gone, but for what purpose they had absolutely no idea.

They did have a letter, however. It was from Kashmir, addressed to H. H. Maharaj-sahib of Deeg, Deeg Palace, River Ghats, Benares. It was an eight-by-eleven sheet of white paper with nothing on it but six words written in an almost illegible script, right in the middle of the page.

It said, "Just imagine what I am thinking."

Cully hadn't signed it.


As it turned out, Cully, mid-June, was in the Kulu hills, where there was a meadow full of flowers and a little hut. It had no windows, they were broken out, but the shell was there, four walls, roughly square, and a view out across the fields. For a day or so he sat on the floor without going into the meadow.

He thought about the Shiva Nataraj. That the heavy bronze was not heavy enough, that it was hollow through and through. It was made expressly for Louis Llewellyn Guthrie, and Cully knew it. It was definite now, not just his suspicions. No one even denied it anymore. First Louis, and then he himself, had been betrayed by just about everyone Cully could think of.

# ❧ 21 ❧

ON JUNE 8TH, RAY MANSINGH,
head of the All-India Congress party, ran into Kady Suraj in
Bombay and they had a drink at the Taj Hotel, in the lovely old
English bar overlooking the harbor.

Ray came by our house that night on his way home from the
airport. We could tell he was upset. As head of the party and
self-appointed guardian of what should be, he had always re-
sented Kady for his free-wheeling style. He asked if we'd seen
Kady Suraj, when he knew we rarely did, and then, without
even waiting for an answer, said the guy didn't have any stomach for politics anymore and he for damned sure wasn't going
to help him get Narayan's job. "He's worked his whole life to
get this far," he said, "and now he's going to blow the whole
thing. All he wanted to talk about was boats."

"Boats?"

"What's he know about boats? Nothing. So why does he want
to waste time on whether this dhow's from Karachi or the
Sind?"

"If he's been in politics all his life, maybe he's entitled to be
sick and tired of it for once," my husband argued.

"I didn't say he was 'sick and tired of it,' I just said he wasn't
what he used to be. I told him he should line up Jiggie's response
now, ahead of time, just to make sure everything was ready with

the prime minister so that when Narayan retires he gets the position. All Jiggie has to do, for God's sake, is call the P.M."

But Kady was noncommittal, and finally Ray asked him point-blank if he wanted the job.

Kady said he had no idea.


Their conversation ended in an odd way.

An American arms lobbyist came over to Kady at the bar, obviously recognizing him, wanted to buy him a drink, laying the groundwork for future connections.

But Kady had him talk about American attitudes toward divorce.

"Divorce?" I said in surprise.

The lobbyist told him Americans couldn't do without divorce.

Kady asked him about extramarital affairs. What was the attitude?

"Just like here," the American said. "Only at home we don't have to be as discreet. You know," he said, *"have* to."

"But do women accept them?" Kady pressed.

"What do you mean, 'accept'?"

"Do they only get involved because they expect to marry the man?"

"Some do, some don't," the man said. "But most probably want to get married."


Phoebe called me first thing in the morning the next day. She was talking fast. Said she was upset about Cully, India, herself, Nasrut Sardar. He'd been there, it turned out, when she was still having breakfast.

He'd already found her the week before, but this time he had a hand-drawn map showing Bhave's house in Tees-he-zari and the witness's house next door. She said she "tried to call his bluff. I asked him if there were any facts."

He said intuition was his guide. He said if she thought he was bad, Vishnu Bhave was worse. She'd better watch out. The subject of her brother made him crazy, and he probably didn't think much more of her.

She told him she wasn't thrilled by him, either, Nasrut Sardar, that is, and why was he bothering her? Was this murder his hobby?

He said he knew her brother did it.

She said, How do you know?

Because he had "to finish things out."

Finish what out?

Sardar said, "What your father started. One lifetime, then the next. See? Guthrie, Bhave, Guthrie, Bhave. See? The pattern has to have a reason."

She and Harriet met for lunch a few hours later and sat at Harriet's desk in the back of the embassy. Phoebe had calmed down, but she told Harriet under no conditions to let Vishnu Bhave know where she was staying. At Phoebe's request, they ordered food from the commissary: tuna fish on white bread, potato chips with onion and sour cream, Diet Coke, and Oreo cookies. She announced that India was affecting her so much, she had to fill up on America.

"I'm not the same person I was when I arrived," she said. "I'm not even sure if being a human being is important anymore in the scale of things. That's how much India's gotten to me. I think we're like leaves on a tree. I really do. Nothing more, nothing less. Two months ago I never thought things like that. Here, I can't help it. We're born, we grow, we die. Fall on the ground, turn to mulch, and come back to life as a bush or a baby. Did you know Indians believe you have thirteen days between the time you die and the time you're reborn? I'm starting to take this for granted, but it scares me because I don't know who I'll be then when I return to New York."

"Do you believe in reincarnation?"

"I have no idea what I believe," Phoebe said emotionally. "I don't even know if I'm American or Indian. Everything just feels familiar."

"It would," Harriet said. "You were born here."

Afterward Phoebe went over to Cully's apartment and fell asleep on the bed.

The next morning she chatted with the landlady, who said

"the two mens" had been back, now asking if Cully-sa'ab was interested in Kashmir.

Phoebe was so angry, she told the driver to take her over to Deeg House to see Attar Singh and get him to tell what was going on with Cully and Mirabai.

The bearer said he wasn't there. Neither was Shyam. She called down to Deeg. They weren't there, either. Nobody told her—nobody knew—that the men were in Kashmir to trace her brother.


The records showed that on May 23rd two weeks before, Cully had taken flight number 206 to Srinagar, or Sirry—nugger, as the Indians say. There was no indication whether the passenger actually flew to Srinagar itself or got off midway in Jhelum.

Attar Singh located the chief flight attendant at his parents' home in south Delhi, but despite one hundred fifty rupees in bribes, he had no recollection of the American—sought in the theft of a valuable piece of art.

Attar Singh and Shyam Singh headed north themselves the last week in June. Airport officials in Jhelum reported that such a man did not disembark, but in Srinagar some said he did and some said he did not. Beyond that, they were unable to find a single account of a tall yellow-white from the coolies, the taxi drivers, or shikara boatmen. If Cully Guthrie did get off the plane, no one saw him anywhere after that.

The two men put up at Naidu's on the Bund to ensure that no one would recognize them, Attar Singh upstairs, Shyam down among the servants. After six days they had little more information than they had when they arrived.

They headed home, disconsolate, but went to Benares first, as per Jiggie's instructions. Shyam told Jiggie maybe Cully had someone in Srinagar who helped him disappear. Jiggie said, maybe he was right and told Shyam to ask Durr if she'd made her family there available to the boy.

In Delhi Durr, weeping, told him no, of course, she hadn't. How could she? How could Jiggie even imagine she'd put the boy's needs ahead of his?

Shyam comforted her, saying Jiggie was just upset, no need

for him to tell her why, the family was at stake. Afterward Durr went to Kady and cried with him, too.

When he did not seem upset, she realized that he was profoundly and uncharacteristically preoccupied.

Later she brought up the subject of Cully again and asked Kady what was going on, but Kady didn't answer. They were sitting on the stairs, he was going up and she was coming down. Finally he said they had no one to blame but themselves, he and Jiggie and Louis Guthrie. He didn't attribute any blame to her.


Back from Kashmir, Attar Singh learned of Phoebe's visit and invited her to Deeg House for tea.

Phoebe went. She methodically asked about Cully, Mirabai, and the wedding but got nothing back except what she saw as phony concern and shallow candor. Still, just hearing the old man's lies, Phoebe felt more confident.

At least she knew what the stakes were, she told herself.

Then Attar Singh told her Jiggie had asked him to "extend an invitation" to her to visit him should she find herself in Benares.

Phoebe was astonished. "What would I do there?" she asked. "Stay with him or just, you know, come for tea, or something?"

"I suppose that would be clear when you were there," he said, true to the thrust of Maharaj-sa'ab's instructions.

"Shyam won't let up," the letter from Jiggie had said. "Insists I meet with the sister. I've always rather liked her. But to meet her? What do you think? Shall I open the door a wee bit? See what she does? So, be a good fellow, tell her to come by Benares and all that. See what she does. She's as much a part of this as I am, after all."


After tea Attar Singh took her through the building, showed her the inner courtyards and upper balconies. Phoebe let him talk, wondering what he was concealing. He pointed out places where women were allowed to watch activities downstairs, where Deeg Enterprises was located, but he didn't take her near the office with the map of India, and she didn't know the difference.

Sitting for a few minutes in the front salon downstairs before she left, Shyam Singh appeared for the first time, sat right down on the floor, and closed his eyes. Phoebe recognized him from Deeg and wondered why he was here, not in Benares.

"Why do you worry so much about my brother?" she asked Attar Singh at the end. "Why do you keep coming to the apartment to see if he's back?"

"Because he distresses me. I worry for him."

Knowing this was nonsense, Phoebe pressed on. "Why'd you ask the landlady about Kashmir? Do you think he's there?"

"My dear Phoebe," he began kindly, "all foreigners, indeed all Indians, are interested in Kashmir. It's one of the most beautiful places on earth, and I wondered if he might be there."

By now Phoebe knew exactly what was going on.

Leaving Deeg House, she went to the Central Tourist Office in Connaught Place to see if there was a way to find out if her brother was in Kashmir. They said there wasn't. She said what if the trouble between the Muslims and the Hindus broke out again and they had to get the foreigners out; what would they do then? The man said they wouldn't do anything. Besides, didn't she know there were almost no foreigners there anymore?

Phoebe went to the Central Post Office and wrote Cully one letter care of American Express, another poste restante, Srinagar, Kashmir.

Then she wrote two more, to Princess Mirabai Singh of Deeg, American Express and poste restante, Srinagar, Kashmir.

She got post office receipts for her letters, names on each included, and put them all in a separate envelope and addressed it to Jiggie Deeg, Jasdan Singh, Attar Singh, and Shyam Singh, all care of Umaid Mahal Palace, Deeg, Rajasthan.


Still angry, she got in the car. Tulsidas started driving, but after a few minutes she told him to stop.

She got out and walked. He followed along behind. She strode rapidly. Worried, he drove closer and called out to her on the sidewalk, "Deegs much too powerful peoples, memsa'ab. Must be careful."

"I know that," she said irritably.

"Come in car. Safer here."

"I want to walk."

"Much too hot for walking."

She ignored him.

"How about I take you Jumna Road?"

When she was stopped by a cow sleeping on the sidewalk, he cried out urgently, "Coming into car now. Not for being mad at cows or kicking cows."

"I'm not going to kick the cow."

"Then get in car." He opened the door and Phoebe got in. "What you want now?" He started driving slowly. "Something you want?"

"Yes," she said suddenly, and told him to go to a hardware shop, where she bought a flashlight. Then she told Tulsidas, "Nizamuddin's Tomb."

It was a place she'd been only once in her life, with Vikrim Ali Seth, under her, over her, and, most of all, inside her.

# ❧ 22 ❧

WHEN SHE STEPPED INTO THE
darkness of the inner room of Nizamuddin's Tomb and smelled
its slight mustiness, she already had her finger on the button of
the flashlight, and when she pressed it she felt excitement and
anticipation, but impatience, too, waiting for the room to
lighten up.

The button got stuck.

She pushed again and again but couldn't get it to work, and
she suddenly started to cry. She slid down against the wall in
the dark and sat on the floor hunched over her knees, her face
wet in her hands, everything so dark she could see just a grayness to the side that showed where she had come. She sobbed
and sobbed until finally her anger gave way to loss and longing
and pain and an ache inside that hurt so much, she thought she'd
break in half.

She thought of Cully and Louis and Thalia and Kady, and
wanted them all so much, each in different ways, she couldn't
move.

A long time passed. She realized she'd taken Vikrim Ali Seth
in here over someone else far better, just as she had done with
the rest of her life, everything a replacement for what she didn't
have, a foundation and clients instead of a family of her own,
Stephen instead of someone she really loved.

Phoebe wiped her tears and remembered Kady twenty years ago touching her face at the Gymkhana Club.

She pushed the button on the flashlight again.

This time it moved and the room lit up.

There wasn't all that much to see. She shined the light across the marble floors and looked in all the corners, even at the roof, where things that resembled some Asian species of bat fluttered their wings.

The tomb itself, a white marble catafalque, was not disturbing, nor had she expected it to be. She thought of herself as someone who was still and always partly sixteen, partly frozen, but now, sitting in Nizamuddin's Tomb, she got the sense of herself as melting down in the aftermath of anger and coming alive.

It made her feel warm. Her tears were replaced by sweat, and she rubbed it into her cheeks, her nose, her neck. She stood up, wiped leaves off her skirt and blouse, and, seeing a pile of leaves in a corner, went over there and squatted down, waiting for her pee to come.

The flashlight on the floor picked up traces of the liquid as it slid yellow along the leaves and ran out along the marble. The image of what she was doing, bringing light and secreted moisture into this darkened place, was not lost on her. She grabbed a handful of dry leaves, stood, and crumpled them up as much as she could—into ash, is what she thought—and dropped them on the floor.

"Everything passes," she said aloud, "leaves into ash, death into life, past into future." Surely Nizamuddin himself had passed along, too, not even ashes anymore after all these centuries; he'd had at least a dozen lives since then to improve upon himself. She'd had barely twenty years, but she was convinced that if he'd left his body in here so he could move on to something else far better, she herself could do the same thing.

She wondered what would come from being in the presence of this Muslim's death. From death arises life, she thought.

She saw where Vikrim Ali Seth had put his coat down for them to lie upon. It had been cold and hard, she remembered abruptly, not as pleasing as she'd imagined all these years, and she felt a sense of triumph. She sat down on the catafalque and crossed her legs. It felt good. She had the idea that Kady Suraj would understand exactly what she felt, because, once, he

314

had understood everything. Maybe he still did now.

Quite specifically, at that moment and to that moment, Phoebe traces the change in herself. When, for the first time in her adult life, she accepted the fact that someone else besides her brother could understand who she was and be a part of it.

"I can live without Cully," she whispered. "I am more than Cully." She raised her voice a bit. "I don't have to have Cully. There's more than Cully. I love Cully. I do, I do, I love you, Cully, and I miss you, but"—now she was crying again—"but I'm also . . ."

Phoebe stared at the spot where Vikrim Ali Seth had put his coat. She began to imagine everything that could take place there with Kady Suraj, and maybe it was the heat of the room or the sweat on her face or the feeling that came from having peed, but there was no avoiding, not even for Phoebe Llewellyn Guthrie, just exactly what she was feeling and wanting when she thought about Kady Suraj.

# ❧ 23 ❧

SHE WENT HOME AND FOUND A
newspaper article she'd seen that morning that announced that
the next day, June 17th, "K. T. Keshri Suraj" was scheduled to
deliver opening statements at a twelve noon luncheon celebrating the All-India Manufacturers' Association's annual conven-
tion.

She arrived an hour early and was directed to the president's
office.

Identifying herself as the owner of a chain of factories making
small parts for trucks throughout Ohio and New York, here
exploring possibilities of establishing a partnership with an Indian company, she said she'd read about the meeting and wanted
to know if she could attend.

The man agreed, insisted she sit at the head table, and there
she was, napkin in her lap, tali of food in front of her, the only
woman in the room, when the Deputy Minister for Public
Works made a late arrival.

She was introduced to him. They shook hands, Kady gave his
speech, she listened intently, and he left, only to send a bearer
back with a note asking if she would like a ride. She went
outside. He was in the car, Samiji on the sidewalk, smoking a
cigarette, fanning himself with a banana leaf.

Phoebe was so surprised by the sight of him, she started to

316

run, crying his name as if she were ten years old. He was surprised at the sight of her, too, dropped his cigarette, and jumped in her direction. They collided beside the car, hugging, laughing, tears rolling down their faces.

Kady stepped out of the car. "Maybe you'd prefer a cab?" he said.

She sobered instantly, Samiji, too. She got in back, Samiji in front. He rolled up the window separating front from back, and they drove off.

Kady didn't talk to her or look at her. She stared straight ahead. Samiji kept peering at her in the glass, then finally rolled down the window and asked her where she was going. She told him. Kady perused the files in his lap, making notes in the margin, and only looked up when they stopped at Auntie Indore's on Bhagwandas Road.

He mentioned her time in Deeg and said it must have been very pleasurable if she stayed that long.

Yes, it was, she said casually, she loved it. Got out, closed the door, and he drove off, while she and Samiji waved wildly at each other through the increasing distance that separated them.


The next morning a driver arrived at the house with a note asking if she would like to "accompany the Deputy Minister for Public Works on an inspection tour" that afternoon of a series of electrical plants on the outskirts of Delhi. Phoebe wrote back, accepting.

That afternoon an official car showed up with the Deputy Assistant Director for Public Works inside, complete with apologies that the Deputy Minister himself was unexpectedly out of station, and off they went.

The next morning another driver showed up with a similar invitation for that afternoon; again she accepted, took her first quick trip to a tailor to order clothes. Again Kady did not appear.

But the next morning when an invitation came asking her to a buffet dinner that night at the home of a Mr. and Mrs. R. K. Ramanujan, 9:30 P.M., dress optional, car to be provided, she knew he'd be there and accepted immediately. She spent the whole day shopping at boutiques, then sitting against the wall at home with her eyes closed. By the time Kady's aide, Kuldip

Ramchandran, came to pick her up, she was thoroughly relaxed.

She arrived at the Ramanujans' at ten. Kady wasn't there. Dinner was not served until after twelve. Then Kady arrived, greeted the guests, and slowly made his way around to her, just in time to take her elbow and lead her in to dinner.

"Did you enjoy your tour of the manufacturing plants?" he asked.

"Very much."

"It's a notable interest of yours," he said. "Somewhat unexpected."

"Yes."

Kady deposited her to eat with the women, sat on the other side with the men. She saw him ignoring her and understood in Indian terms that it was the biggest compliment he could give her. He was respecting her reputation.

After that he didn't even talk to her, just said good night in time and left.

Kuldip picked her up outside to drive her home, but instead of going to Auntie Indore's as he was supposed to do, he went to an all-night tea stall not far away.

Phoebe recognized Kady's car as they were driving up, a long black Mercedes with Samiji standing outside. Kady was in the back.

Samiji came over to her car, opened the door, and helped her out. She gave him a kiss. "Oh, Samiji," she said, near tears suddenly at being with him again, "seeing you is . . . well, I don't know. But it's the best thing here."

"Yes, missus-Feeb. I am thinking same thing only."

Kady had gotten out, too, his manner formal, polite, his black tie impeccable. He waited while she got in his car, the backseat, then got in, too. He offered her a cinnamon cigarette.

"No, thank you."

They were silent.

"Silly to cry, isn't it," she said.

"No, not at all." He didn't smoke his cigarette, just tapped it against the case and put it away. "You really loved him."

"I guess I did." Phoebe took a deep breath and felt herself taking the Indian air deep into her chest, imagined it heading out into her bloodstream. "I'm surprised to see you here," she said pleasantly. "I assumed you'd gone home."

"I thought it'd be nice to talk. There won't be much chance."

"You were awful at dinner," she laughed, "but I understand."

"This isn't America."

"I know. But maybe we can be friends anyway."

He didn't answer.

She took it to mean he was as ambivalent as she. She looked out the window. There was a tea stall on the sidewalk, closed-up shops, bodies stretched out to sleep. Hot air moved in through the open windows, and she smelled the woodfire burning in the stall. Samiji brought them each a glass of tea. She smelled something deep and woodsy and sweet.

"Cardamom, missus," Samiji said proudly, speaking through the open window. "I am remembering everything."

She smiled at him and drank the tea, heavy with milk and the taste of spice. Samiji sat down outside to wait. The night was silent but for the passing carts and the sound of howling dogs. It reminded her of the past. How often they'd done this very thing, only then there was Louis in between, the scent of whiskey. "You know what?" she said.

"What?"

"I don't think I've ever loved anyone as much as I love Samiji right this very minute. Does that make sense?"

"Yes, of course."

"He's like my father, mother, brother, all wrapped up in one. Does it seem foolish to make so much of him?"

"No, it's nice. Not many people love him here in Delhi. Everyone's up in his village."

"But you do."

"I suppose. But I don't think of it that way. He's part of me. Like my arm."

"That's a lot."

"Yes, I suppose it is." He sipped his tea in silence; so did she.

"I was avoiding you before," Phoebe said. "That didn't seem right. That's why I decided to find you."

Kady didn't say anything.

"Don't you agree? We can at least be friends?"

"Yes, I suppose."

"You know what else?"

"What?" Now he looked across the seat at her and grinned. "You think all the time, don't you?"

"Louis was—"

"Don't you."

319

"What?"

"Think all the time." He was still smiling. "You never stop, do you?"

"No, I do," she said. "Often I'm really calm. Except India's so stimulating my mind just . . ." Her voice drifted off. "About Louis," she began again. "I think it was merciful he died. Do you know how dreadful it might have gotten? He could have . . . well, there were lots of things he could have done. Do you think he'd have shot himself?"

"Not likely."

"You said he had a gun."

"I don't remember."

"That's what you said."

"So do you want to see more of India?" he asked.

Phoebe nodded.

He took up his cigarette again and was tapping it. She knew he'd made a decision of sorts. "Would you like to fly to Allahabad tomorrow? I have to inspect a bridge there and discuss expansion plans for a government project. There's a museum and some old buildings, Moghul. I wouldn't see you much, of course."

"But you would be there? Not your deputy?" she teased.

He smiled. "I have to work, but you could visit these things. There's plenty of room on the plane. I always have a block of seats."

Phoebe didn't know what to say. She both wanted to go with him and didn't. Despite her feelings at Nizamuddin's Tomb, something held her back.

"The river's beautiful there," he was saying, "and you've never been to that part of India. Have you?"

"So you like your work?"

"Very much."

"Isn't it difficult to deal with all the bureaucracy? Hard to get anything done?"

"That's just what I would have said." Kady looked at her.

"What?" she asked. "What are you thinking?"

"Nothing." He paused. She didn't believe him. "Just that it's frustrating," he said. "India is frustrating. It's begun to upset me rather a lot recently. I used to be something of an idealist when you knew me. Thought I could make everything happen, but lately, I don't know, I seem to question the worth of everything.

So did you hear all that?" he asked, laughing suddenly. "Or did you get bored right off?"

"No, I listened totally. I thought it's what you were going to say."

"You can read my mind."

"No," she said. "I just imagine, kind of."

"Then you imagine very well."

She nodded, a trifle awkward at the intimacy, liking it but still feeling her resistance.

"I don't know what I've done all these years," Kady went on. He seemed distracted. It gave her a chance to look at him openly. "A few bridges. Roads, electricity, a thing or two. But I find myself wondering if it's what I was supposed to do."

"You sound very Indian. I'd have to be back for dinner tomorrow night. Is that all right? I'm having dinner with Cully's landlady."

"Whatever for?"

"I slept there last night, too. In his apartment. I miss him, Kady. I tell myself I don't, that I don't need him, but I do. I want to straighten out my relationship with him. I realize I have to. He's obviously avoiding me on purpose. I've been looking for the Golf Links house, too," she added. "I can't find it anywhere. Do you remember the address?"

"Jesus, Feeb."

"There you go again." She shook her head. "Every time you say it, something inside me goes crunch, crunch, and I feel so sad I could cry."

"Then I won't say it. Why are you trying to find the house in Golf Links?" he asked. "There's too much to do to be morbid about the past."

"It's not morbid, and besides . . ."

"Maybe I should forbid it," he went on, "forbid you to—"

"It's my past," she said with emphasis. "More than I ever had of it in New York. No letters, no contact, just everything over, done, kaput. That's no way to . . ."

Her voice drifted off. She knew he heard the resentment.

"So, you want to come to Allahabad?" His voice was soft, as though an apology had been made and accepted.

"If I can be back in time."

They were silent again. Samiji brought more tea, then went back to sit beside Kuldip in the dirt.

"I seem to have spent half my life in the backseat of cars with you," Phoebe said, laughing.

"Things could be worse," he said.


She hadn't mentioned Cully and Mirabai.

Afterward she lay in bed, staring at the seven blank sheets of paper, and told herself she was waiting to see if he would bring it up. She assumed that if she knew the two had run away, so did he.


After Allahabad there was a community meeting the next day with officials in Meerut, a luncheon with the mayor and deputy governor in Bombay several days after that, several quick excursions to sort out problems in places like Kanpur, Patna, Faridabad, and Nagpur. After a couple of weeks, Phoebe's interest in starting a fabric business began to take even more shape, and Kady assigned people on his staff to help her develop plans.


At the same time, Jiggie sent word for Shyam to go back to Kashmir to try again.

After a few days in Srinagar, Shyam found a young Ladakhi who had a car for hire he used to take people the two-hundred-mile, two-day journey across the Himalayas to Ladakh. He identified Cully from a photograph. Said he'd traveled with him for five days, him and his wife.

Ladakh was the remote mountain kingdom, originally part of Tibet, then China, that now belonged to India. The driver said the American called it the farthest place he could get in India. He spoke Hindi better than the girl. Shyam interrupted him at that point and said he had no interest in the girl, just the man. What about him?

He wanted to get to Leh, the driver said, that's all, as fast as possible. He had no idea why Leh, the capital of Ladakh, but as the days went on, he concluded that was just the way the man was. Wanted to get places fast, or thought he did, because then he took five days to do what should have taken only two, and it wasn't because he stopped at the historic monasteries like everyone else did. Never wanted to see the prayer flags or stupas, either, had no interest in anything specific, certainly not the things most tourists came to see.

He claimed he did, the driver went on, talked about monasteries and the art, said he was on a pilgrimage, and she said she was, too, but actually the Ladakhi driver had no idea where they were going and determined she just wanted to do whatever he wanted to do, and that was nothing, so they didn't do anything.

Except walk. The girl brought baskets of fruit and cheese to eat in the car so they wouldn't have to stop for meals, but they stopped anyway, all the time, because it was a moonscape up there, rocks and cliffs, tumultuous colors in sand and granite. They walked into the fields and meadows, looked at the soaring mountain ranges that arched on all sides. They weren't in any hurry, the driver said. They just wanted to be alone.

What did they do? Shyam asked.

The man said well, he could imagine.

Shyam said he didn't want to imagine, he wanted the facts, and he'd paid the money to get them.

So the Ladakhi said they lay down in the high grasses where he couldn't see them. That's what they did. They just wanted privacy. They seemed to talk a lot, too, he said.

It was very leisurely. The first day passed, darkness came, and they spent the night in the inn in Kargil. It was the only place with beds, but there were indications, the Ladakhi said, they didn't sleep in the bed at all. Rugs were laid out on the floor one on top of the other, an Indian form of bedding, and the next day, he said, the man didn't come out at all. A bearer at the inn said he was lying naked on the bedding as if he were sleeping, only he wasn't, he was just staring at the ceiling with his hands behind his head, one sheet tossed around his thighs.

He stayed in the room all day by himself while the girl walked along the river, and he, the Ladakhi, stayed nearby and kept her in sight because he could tell she didn't know what she was doing, certainly not about river water, so powerful that if you put your toe in it, it could take you down. She even asked who did the cooking and could she go swimming and could she buy the jewelry the women wore, turquoise and coral dangling from their ears and nose, chains of it swept up along their forehead like a cap.

He told her yes, if the price was right, and asked her what her husband was doing, and she said, "He has a sister," as if that explained it, but then the American appeared for the first time, now it was night.

She asked him right off if he could buy some jewelry for her, and he said she couldn't buy everything anymore, they had to think about money. But the driver had seen a fat money belt strapped around his waist, when the man was asleep half-dressed in a field.

They stayed in Kargil two nights, the third in a villager's hut where they'd stopped for the afternoon, only when the afternoon lapsed over into dusk, the American still hadn't come out, he'd only gone in to take a nap, and now the host didn't know what to do. He came over to the Ladakhi driver, his family lined up beside him, it was time to come in from the fields, eat and pray, and go to bed. They asked him what to do, but the Ladakhi said he didn't know what to do either.

This man liked to sleep, he said.

He told them to talk to the girl. She sat on the banks of the river, her feet hanging over a rock as she stared into the turquoise water. She'd been there all afternoon waiting for the man to wake up, but they came back up and shook their heads. She didn't speak Ladakhi, they said.

So everyone waited. The driver peered in the doorway, there was no door. They all did. The man was fast asleep. Finally the girl went in, sat beside him on the floor, and rubbed her hand along his arm, up around his chin, neck, ears, he'd never seen anything like it before, and when the man began to rouse, she invited them all to come on in, just like she was the hostess, the hut was hers.

The next morning the American said all he needed was rest, he felt better again, the demon was finally gone, and they all took off for Leh.

When they reached town, the two of them disappeared, hand in hand, sacks on their back, headed right up into the crowd of mountain people who'd come down to market.

Where were they going?

The Ladakhi shook his head.

To the monasteries?

Must be.

And were they in love?

Oh, yes, the Ladakhi said. It was love match, not arranged

marriage, that's for sure. They were of a mind, too, he said. And he thought they had a plan to walk out.

Walk out?

Join a caravan of traders. And walk out over the barren mountain passes, that's what the girl had said, high up where sometimes there isn't even snow and the sun is so hot you freeze. Be on the move with them.

"The farthest he could get," the Ladakhi said.

# ❧ 24 ❧

Phoebe's interest in fabrics became increasingly serious and her vision of it as a business developed steadily. She pushed a desk into Auntie Indore's dining room to make an office and got an Indian lawyer and an Indian business consultant and weighed different options for manufacturing and exporting material. Kady singled out one man on his staff to be her guide through the Indian bureaucracy. She kept in touch with Alice in New York more by fax than telephone, Alice working on finding outlets there, and Phoebe now said she was going to stay in India until the enterprise was under way.

She was seeing less of Kady. After the first rush, his invitations fell off. She understood completely, saw him as backing away, too, and wrote Alice that she was thankful. "Can you imagine how awful it would be to get involved over here with a married man? Besides, he'd take me over completely, he's so attractive. Then where would I be? In a real mess."

But she was the one who arranged with his secretary to see him privately on July 5th.

That day at three o'clock she pulled up to the Imperial Hotel, Samiji already there, waving as she went in.

Inside, the dining room was dark; an old chandelier gave off far too little light for so much space. She saw him across the room and paused. He was staring at the table intently, unmoving, something rigid about him, and she felt her attraction for him lurch both forward and back at the same time. Other tables had been pushed away the night before to make room for dancing, and he was in a banquette with tables set around him like bodyguards. She could tell he was as uneasy as she was.

He saw her. He stood up, formal in a linen suit, and reached out to shake her hand. She namasted instead, not wanting to touch him. She remembered the time at the airport and knew to feel him would only unnerve her more. She sat down, he too, his legs stretched out into the room so that they were at right angles to each other, she with a better view of his ear and shoulder than his face.

Phoebe took a deep breath and, putting her elbows up on the table, leaned in toward him. She could smell the scent of cinnamon about him and see the shine on his face. He looked so attractive, she wanted to lean in farther and caress his face, but instead she blurted out the one line she had rehearsed—"I just wanted to talk"—and then leaned back on her elbows, safe.

Before either could say anything, bearers appeared, one with napkins, one with glasses, another with the menu, and one more, the boss, telling the others what to do.

Phoebe and Kady both burst out laughing.

"Castes," she said.

"Castes and manpower," he said. "No shortage of either." Then he swung his legs in under the table and asked what she wanted to talk about. He was grinning now.

She felt more relaxed, too. "There's so much," she said.

"So much what?" teasing her.

"That I don't know about you. And I decided there was no way to deal with it except directly."

"What's that mean? 'Directly.'"

"You're teasing me."

"Not me. Never."

"Maybe I'll just ask you some questions." She heard herself sounding demure.

"Ask what?" He picked a lemon out of a basket of fruit and fiddled with it.

"I've known you twenty-five years and I don't even know

some very basic things about you. I've been mulling it over. I know it's silly," she added, grinning now, "but I don't even know your favorite color."

"I bet your's pink and mine's supposed to be blue."

"So is blue your favorite color?"

"You're serious?"

"I just think it'd be easier if we talked from time to time. There's no reason not to. We're just friends, after all."

He didn't speak for a while, let her words hang in the silence between them. "Then let me think," he said, toying with the lemon, prodding it with a fingernail. "You know the color of dirt in Deeg?" He dropped the lemon back in the basket. "Sort of a reddish brownish pinkish beige? You see it everywhere?"

She was nodding. She liked it when he didn't look at her because then she could look at him.

"I guess that would be my favorite color," he said. "But put me down in England and my favorite color would be that dark brown, moist color. The color of earth."

"Not the trees?"

"I prefer the browns," he said, "something about the earth itself."

"Because it reminds you of your childhood?"

"Maybe."

"Your village?"

"I don't know. I never thought about it that way."

At that moment precisely Phoebe felt Kady withdraw and knew she had come close to something important to him. "You always said you lived in a village," she persisted, leaning in closer on her elbows, her voice soft. "You said you had brothers and sisters."

"Well, I might have said that, I suppose," he said, covering a lemon with the palms of his hands. He was restless. "It's true."

"But I don't remember you ever seeing them." Even as she talked Phoebe knew what a subterfuge this was because she didn't want to know about his village, she wanted to know everything. "You always talked about going to Deeg, but it was to see Jiggie, not your family."

"Most likely."

Why was she asking this, she thought, when she'd never asked him about the night in Deeg, or his lies or Cully and the girl? Because she didn't dare? Or because it was too intimate? "I guess

328

you don't like me probing," she said. "I can't blame you, really. I'm being awfully pushy."

"I'm just not used to talking much," Kady answered. "All I do is work and think about work. Work, go home, and sleep."

"Does that mean you don't want me to ask questions?"

"Do whatever you like," he said kindly. "I rather like it, actually."

"Why?"

"I don't know. I just do. You're very different."

"From before?"

"No, from anyone." His lips curved up in a halfway smile. "Go on," he said. "I don't mind, really. It's just something I have to sort through myself. I don't know whether to be honest with you and say brown's my favorite color or withdraw a bit. There." He laughed. "Is that frank enough for you?"

"Then, how is your family?" She liked it when he teased her. "When did you last see them?"

"I waited too long."

"For what?" She sensed again this was something important.

"Too long for anything," he said.

"You mean you don't know where they are?"

"That's right."

"You don't know where they are at all?" she asked, horrified at the implications of what he said.

"That's right."

"But how awful," she exclaimed. "What happened to them?"

He didn't speak.

"Kady, tell me. When did you last go back to the village?"

Silence.

"Never?"

"Maybe once or twice."

"Was everyone excited? I can see them, running out, giving you garlands of flowers. They must love you."

Kady didn't answer.

Phoebe waited.

"It was rather quiet when I went," he said finally. She saw his face take on light as he began to talk. It reminded her of the past when she'd watched his face for hours waiting to see that light. "Not too many people," he was saying. "Things had rather changed. I just walked about a bit."

"So you only went there once?"

"I guess, yes, it was only once, now that I think about it."

"Was anyone there?" She watched as he turned the lemon slowly in his large hands. His reserve made him all the more appealing. She liked his awkwardness and knew it made it easier for her to approach him.

"Anyone there? No, there wasn't really. It was rather different than I remembered it. There used to be monkeys, peacocks, even those lizards you always used to talk about. Those green geckos on the walls. As far as I could tell, there was nothing left."

"What had happened?"

"It was empty. I don't imagine anyone but myself had been there in years."

"How awful," she said again. "I'm sorry."

He shrugged. "It's nothing."

"Of course it is."

The bearers reappeared and started putting cloths on the other tables. He looked at her then. "What have you done to your hair? It looks different."

"It's just up on my head today. Kady, what did happen to everyone in the village? Did they move? Die? Where did they go?"

"The water changed," he said. "I suspect that was it. The river was gone. It wasn't there anymore. The well had dried up. Don't look so shocked, Phoebe. That's India."

"But how awful. They're your family."

"They could have all died in a flood, too. It's not awful. Don't keep saying that. It's what happens."

"India's so terrible. I couldn't bear to live here."

"Why? Because water and nature are so much a part of life? How can that be terrible? It's what is. It's the same in America. You just don't notice it as much. Life is short. Or haven't you realized?"

"I do. Don't be so harsh."

"I don't mean to be harsh, but you sound naive."

"It's not naiveté," she said, grinning broadly. "It's total avoidance."

Kady laughed. "That won't get you very far," he said. "But who am I to talk? I can be pretty naive myself. I thought I was helping India. Had this idea about its great future. I gave my life to government. Look what's happened. Nothing. It's the same poverty, corruption, bureaucracy. Nothing's changed, and here am I twenty years older with nothing to show for it. I'm sorry if I sound bitter."

"You sound more shocked than bitter."

"That's right, actually," he said. "I am shocked. It never occurred to me, not one smidgen of it, until I saw you."

"Me?" Phoebe flattened her hand against her chest in surprise. "What do I have to do with it?"

"It took you coming back to show me what I'd done to my life."

"Me?"

"Yes. Nothing else ever got my attention, I guess. Now I've been stuck the last few weeks trying to figure things. I can't get it out of my mind. I don't think I've thought in twenty years, on some level. I've wasted twenty years on nothing, and life's too precious for that."

"I just want the precious part," Phoebe said. "Sometimes I think I'm a leaf."

"Do you now? Well, quite a marvelous leaf."

Phoebe looked away.

"I haven't seen you blush in years."

"I don't blush."

"You certainly are right now."

"Oh, stop it. I don't want any of this."

" 'This' what?"

She didn't answer.

"Okay," he said, drawing back. He took up his lemon again and didn't say anything. Neither did she.

"You want to know what I imagine about you?" she said finally.

"So you do think about me." He grinned at her again.

"I imagine that you—"

"So you do imagine about me?"

"Stop teasing," she heard herself say, despite the fact that she loved that sound in his voice. There was something caressing about it, tender.

"All right," he relented. "I won't ever tease you again."

"I think people miss their family," Phoebe went on firmly, knowing she had to control herself or everything with him would turn into a mess of complications. "That's normal, to miss your family, but I don't think you did. You were too

331

unusual, too different from them. Because even I miss mine," she went on, trying to sound chatty. "I'd like to be able to give them Christmas presents or something. That kind of thing."

"Oh, come now, Feeb," Kady cut in. "That's not true at all."

"Of course it's true."

"You miss them more than that. You're trying to trivialize it so I won't know what you're feeling. But you missed them even when you had them, and you missed every single thing normal family life is all about. And I bet you still do. That's true, now, isn't it. Don't look away. Tell me the truth."

Phoebe looked away.

"Well, there," he said quietly. "I was right. Wasn't I?"

"You don't have to be so mean about it."

"I wasn't. If I hadn't put it that way, you'd have denied the whole thing, wouldn't you? Put up some front."

She nodded.

They heard tourists arguing outside in the corridor about where they were going to go for dinner. They both listened, let the tension subside.

"I had a brother and a sister," Kady said after a while. "She was four years younger than I. She was never very strong. My brother was angry when I left with my father. He knew I wouldn't be back. So did my mother, but she was glad I was going. I don't know what I'd say to them if I saw them again." He paused. "You're right about me being different. Are you always right?" He glanced at her. "I'd like to know if they were alive. I'm sure they're not, though."

Another bearer was making the rounds, and they watched him bring one salt and one pepper shaker, put it on a table and then disappear, gone for another pair.

"You know what I'd really like, Feeb?"

"What?"

"To take care of my mother. There was a typhoid epidemic out that side once, a flood too some years back. So it could have been anything. Cholera, a drought. But I have all this damn money and nothing much to do with it. That's one other way we're alike."

"How?"

"We're both orphans." He stretched out his hand so that it lay near hers, one light, one dark.

"Car crash, fire," Phoebe said, putting her hand in her lap.

"I'm the exact opposite from you. You don't even know what happened to yours."

"But aren't you lucky? If they had to die, wasn't that the right way? However tragic, it was quick and over?"

"But why did they have to die at all?"

"It didn't drag out," he insisted. "It was over."

"What do you mean, 'drag out'?"

"Everything. Anything. There was no trouble, nothing. You could remember them the way they were."

"I suppose."

"You did, didn't you? Remember them the way they were?"

"I suppose. For what it was worth."

"Good."

The conversation about her parents left Phoebe confused. She didn't understand what Kady had been trying to say, but then the bearer came out again with another salt and pepper shaker, and she forgot the subject. "Can I ask another question?"

"Ask me anything, Phoebe. I like being here with you."

"What do you do with your money?"

"Not much." He picked up his knife and used it like a pencil to mark lines on the tablecloth. "That Mercedes?"

She nodded.

"Import taxes alone cost one hundred and seventy percent of the list price."

"No!"

"Now it actually embarrasses me. Never used to, of course. I used to buy everything when I went abroad." He watched the knife. He started twisting it absentmindedly and then said abruptly, "My father didn't even know what happened to me."

"You mean that you're Deputy—"

"No. Way before that. I just took off. That's all. He never even knew I went to get married."

"You had your reasons."

"Greed. . . ."

"It's what you had to do."

"Ambition."

"Don't be so hard on yourself."

"But it's true. You haven't touched your drink," he said.

"I'm not thirsty. So what did you buy with all your money?"
Phoebe wished she had the nerve to be totally honest with him, tell him exactly what she felt.

"Clothes, stereos, televisions," he was saying. "Land, I have a lot of land. Factories, bicycle shops."

"It bores you, doesn't it?"

"Thoroughly. I haven't paid any attention to it in years. But then, I didn't pay attention to anything." He looked at her sharply. "Why'd you really come back? Was it just Cully?"

Phoebe nodded. "He's all I have. Family, I mean."

"I used to like the idea of owning things. Now I'm tired of everything. Have you ever felt that way?"

"Not really."

They were alone in the room now, but for one bearer, standing at attention at the door. "I'll tell you what I do like, though," he went on. "I like work itself, actually. Certain aspects of what I do interest me tremendously, but I don't like having to talk to everybody. I used to, of course, but that was showing off. Now I could be a hermit. I've spent ninety percent of my life being whatever people think I am."

"Oh, Kady, that's not true."

"Sure it is," he said. "Think about it. 'This smart, good-looking fellow, straight from the village, but who, through some perverse twist of fate . . .' I'm sick and tired of it. Although, I suppose it's who I am."

"You could get away."

"That's what I'm thinking about. When I started coming up, I must have transformed myself every day, really, if you think about it. Some days I didn't even know who I was. I'm not sure I know now."

"From a Hindu point of view, what does that do to your duty?"

"Why do you ask that?"

"I'm just curious, that's all. I've been thinking about it."

"But why?"

"It's being back. India's catching, like measles." She grinned.

"There's so much I wish. Jesus, Feeb." He suddenly sounded very intense.

She turned away.

"Feeb . . ."

Kady leaned in across the table toward her, eyes boring in on her. "Do you want to know what I wish?" he whispered.

"No."

"Ask me another question," he said quietly.

"No."

"Ask me about what I think about at night."

"Don't."

"Ask me what I think about in the morning." He was so quiet, she could barely hear him.

"I have to go."

"Ask me what I might, I'm not sure, what I might wish if I were the sort of person who wished things."

His words hung unanswered. Phoebe could hear him breathe, see the rise and fall of his chest. She didn't know what to do. She wanted to lean across the table and touch him, take his hand, but, again, she held back.

Kady stood up abruptly. "Shall we go?"

Phoebe nearly cried out in protest.

He had his wallet, counting rupees. "You okay?"

She nodded mutely, stunned at what they were doing.

"This what you wanted? Talking and all?" He sounded formal, indifferent all of a sudden.

She nodded, drank her water, felt it, full of germs, go down her throat.

Outside in the hot glare of the sun, he asked if she needed a lift. She said no, she had Tulsidas. He said to come talk to him if she needed anything. Anytime, no problem. She said she would, certainly. He said did she have enough to do at night, he could always get her invitations. She said sure, that would be fun, she liked meeting people. With that he left, not even saying good-bye, and Phoebe got in the car, buried her head in her hands, and knew they were both doing the same thing to each other.

# ❧ 25 ❧

THE INVITATIONS CAME. DINNERS
at other people's houses, she Louis Guthrie's daughter, starting an Indian business, Kady the family friend. It all made
sense, but he rarely sat with her or even came in the car with
her. Usually he was late, sometimes he brought an aide. She
enjoyed herself for the most part, though she knew what she
and Kady were doing with each other. His other invitations
continued, too. He took her places when his work was interesting. He said he thought she'd have a good time. She said she
did.

Phoebe had come with no more than a handful of skirts,
one pair of slacks, and some shorts she never wore. Now she
was well on her way toward a closet full of silks, cottons,
some she'd bought, most she designed herself, plotting with
tailors and drawing shape after shape so they could understand.

Her hair had gotten longer, too. At first she cut it every few
weeks at the Oberoi, but by mid-July, two months away from
New York, she'd taken to wearing it long, tied at the back with
ribbons or up around her head in a soft bun, loose strands

hanging at the collar, almost Edwardian. She'd even had sandals made, combining leather with beads and semiprecious stones for night.

She still thought of Cully all the time. His picture was in her purse by day, by her bed at night. So was the one with Kady.


Mirabai's wedding in Deeg was nine weeks away. Everything was on schedule.

On July 6th a delegation from "the other side" arrived at the palace to inspect the plans. They concurred with everything it was their right to concur with, but by the second day they started complaining that the girl wasn't there.

They hadn't expected to see her, of course, except maybe at meals, but they didn't like the fact that she wasn't there.

It belittled the event, the chief uncle said. Worse, it was not the custom. She should have been among the women and children, present but rarely seen up close.

Jiggie was informed.


The detectives got no leads in their search until mid- to late July when Shyam thought of the most obvious thing of all: the art. Then they began working on artistic sites. They started with the most famous and quickly got around to the religious caves of Ellora in Maharashtra State in central India.

Cully was heading south by now and he had been there. They were only a few days behind him.

The south was his destination now. It was not any hotter or drier than it was in the north, but it was different. The language was no longer Hindi. In Ellora it was still a derivative, but as you went farther south all connection with Hindi ceased and other languages took over, as different from Hindi as Russian from English.

In the south the people were darker and more Negroid, descended from the Dravidian stock native to India. The north was marked by inbreeding, Aryans, Moghuls, British, all of the Indo-European race. The Dravidians were the primal people, but Cully was not among them yet.

He had just stated his intention of getting as deep into the south as he could get.

Ellora was on the cusp.


Samiji was upset.

He knew what sa'ab was doing. He'd known ever since Cully arrived in India September the year before and a month later Durr found him asleep, drunk, on the steps at Viceroy Circle. Cully awoke long enough to tell her he'd been hired down in Deeg for the art, then Suraj came to the doorstep, picked him up, and carried him up the stairs to bed, just as he'd done twenty years ago the day the boy's parents died. Only now he noted bitterly that Jiggie'd hired him. Jiggie wanted everyone in his control; why not Cully, too?

The next day Suraj-sa'ab had him on the plane back to Deeg, telling him he had to do his work down there, it was his job, his responsibility, he could come back anytime.

But sa'ab had sounded strange. Samiji recognized it straight off, and from then on Cully came back to Viceroy Circle again and again. Sa'ab took him places, found him the apartment, introduced him to Vishnu Bhave, and Samiji knew what was happening.

He listened as Suraj talked to him about Deeg, asked so many questions—oh, my God, not one, not two, but two hundred—and Cully answered every one of them. He talked about Deeg all the time. Samiji hadn't heard so much of Deeg in years, and he didn't like it.

Suraj was interested in the girl.

How old she was and that Jiggie had given her a dog and that she'd run away as far as the train station but that marriage negotiations were still going on anyway. Why? he wondered. Because she'd run away to the train station, Cully said, and it caused great problems with the other side. The bartering was intense, both sides wanted the other, had their own specific reasons, the Deegs wanted the boy's modernity and independence, the others wanted the renown, but neither would relent, the issue was the girl's uncertain character.

Samiji watched and listened. Suraj and Cully talked and talked, Suraj took him to lunch and dinner, on trip after trip, doing, in fact, the same thing he was doing with the sister now, except with the sister everything was different.

"With her he was just being taken up in the flow of the river," Samiji said, "the way the river flows and you are in the werry river and have no choice of getting out, even if you are a werry good swimmer, and you struggle and struggle and struggle, but the flow of the mighty water is just too great, and who are you, one werry man, to overcome it?"

# ❧ 26 ❧

THE RAINS STILL DIDN'T COME.
The heat was intense. Phoebe's interests expanded to include
rugs, shawls, linens, and tablecloths, items for export. She saw
the Chandradas' socially and Mr. Smith, who'd been Louis'
CEO, but Dr. K. P. Sharma, who had signed the death certificates, was away.

The bearer there told her a letter had come saying he'd started
a pilgrimage to a holy spot near the source of the Ganges and
wouldn't be back until next month.

He also told her that the older brother, the one who was dead,
had been lawyer to Jiggie Deeg.

One day Phoebe had lunch with Harriet. She talked about
how much she loved India.

That afternoon she went to the bank, and, strange how things
work, she spent two hours in line waiting while one man did
this, another did that, one caste for each job, one to stamp,
another to pull out a drawer, on and on, a million different
functions, a caste for each, until a week had passed, it seemed,
and she was still no closer to the money order that had come
from Alice.

Then, after two hours had passed, a new fellow suddenly

showed up on the other side of the window. Asked had she been taken care of? The last chap had gone for tea, what did memsa'ab want?

Phoebe started to scream. Goddamn it, I've been waiting two hours! but it didn't do a bit of good, no one even looked at her.

After that she promoted Tulsidas and gave him chores.

One was to go to the bank. He understood perfectly.

No one who was anyone ever went to the bank, he said.

Phoebe relaxed by going to the temple Chumpi had shown her. It was a run-down place in Old Delhi where the tiles were crooked. She sat at the back, and the Brahmans, naked to the waist but for the cord tied around their backs, chanted, *"Ram, Ram, Shiva, Ram. Rama nam satya hai."* The name of God is the only truth there is.

Phoebe listened, never once imagining Kady was there, but just being quiet and alone in the midst of these Indian sounds made her feel they were together. She imagined him taking her deeper and deeper into India, an inner place where she'd been, yet never been, and sometimes she hated it and sometimes she loved it, but he was always there.

On July 15th they were in Aligarh. They'd gone for a Muslim celebration, Kady representing the Prime Minister. They were seated at a dais under a tent erected in a cricket field. Their seats were angled toward the stage, still empty but for a microphone and pictures of Gandhi and Nehruji. Crowds were milling around in front of them, women on one side, men the other. The men came up to shake Kady's hand, but there was no getting around the fact that it was rude of the Deputy Minister to sit down so early, so most people steered clear of him, which was what he wanted.

Phoebe told him that the night before, Jyoti Chandradas had said he'd seen Cully on Rani Jhansi Road.

"When?" Kady asked.

"He was asleep on the sidewalk."

"When?" Kady asked again. The ceremony on stage was already an hour and forty minutes late.

She said in April or May. His driver stopped to buy a glass

of water, and he saw him on the sidewalk, sound asleep, head on his arm.

"Why didn't he talk to him?"

"He didn't know we were looking for him. He asked about the wedding, too," she added.

Kady didn't say, What wedding? He only said, "Mirabai's?"

So, to a tickle of anxiety in her chest, Phoebe asked him about Mirabai.

But right then a man namasted Kady, and he returned the greeting much too quickly.

"Do you know her well?" Phoebe asked.

"Quite well."

"How?"

Jasdan had him act as her chaperon from time to time in Delhi, he said. But he didn't mention Cully.

Neither did she. Knowing she was treading on sensitive ground, she asked what had happened with Jiggie.

Oh, he said, that was a long time ago, but she said, "No, I mean, just the other night. Why did he send for you in Deeg?"

A man got up on the stage, tinkered with the microphone, and then started to play an accordion. No one listened. The women began to sit down on the sheets on their side of the tent. Little children in their skirts and short shorts were sitting, too. A few of the bigger boys were allowed on the men's side.

Phoebe felt tense, afraid Kady was going to avoid her questions but relieved she'd finally brought the subject out in the open.

"Jiggie thought I might know where Cully was," Kady said in a low voice.

"But you didn't."

"No."

"And why," she asked above the music, "does he care where Cully is?"

"Because Cully is with Mirabai. She ran away the week you arrived."

Phoebe knew Kady was looking at her, but she forced herself to go on watching the accordion player.

"She ran away the day before they found the body. She got to the Palace Hotel in Deeg, got a cab, and made it to the train. They met in Agra."

Phoebe could feel Cully, he was lying down somewhere, hot,

maybe barefoot, because she suddenly felt herself grow hot and was conscious of her feet, bare, out of their sandals, beneath the table.

"He sent Jiggie pictures of them at the Taj Mahal," Kady was saying. "They were kissing. For God's sake, Feeb, can't you even look at me?"

She turned.

His face looked angry. "Damn it, this is me talking to you. I'm telling you something."

"Something you should have told me months ago."

"Then get angry, or say something. Tell me what you think. Don't just ignore me."

"I knew it."

"You knew it, goddamn it, you did not."

"I did too. Don't 'goddamn' me. I figured it out ages ago."

"You figured it out."

"I did."

"So you knew I hadn't told you that?"

"That's right."

"Why didn't you say anything?"

"Why didn't you?"

"You were testing me."

"Maybe I was," she said.

"Don't you trust me?"

"Why should I? You can't have it both ways, Kady. You can't hold out on me and then expect me to trust you. If you want to know the truth, I've started trusting you less and less. Because I didn't know why you weren't telling me things. And because a couple of times you've actually lied."

Kady took up his glass of water and swallowed it at a gulp.

"So he sent Jiggie pictures?" Phoebe continued.

"And a letter, asking what 'this' would do to the wedding. He said Jiggie deserved a scandal and he hoped it ruined them."

"Why on earth would he say that?" Phoebe asked. "I can't imagine him saying that. That sounds vindictive."

"Maybe he didn't like the marriage plans."

"And they deserve a scandal for that? It doesn't make sense. What's going on?"

The accordion player had started to sing. His berry-stained teeth were as red as his gums, his song about a girl who hoped to meet her lover at a well.

343

"Who can say what was going through his mind," Kady said. "I certainly don't know."

"He must have talked to you."

"Not much."

"You're still not telling me something. I know you too well, Kady. You may not like it, but it's true. I knew at the airport you weren't telling me the truth."

"What do you mean?"

"You've told me a lot of lies. You said you'd been in Calcutta. You weren't."

Kady looked out at the crowd. She could see his profile now, the big nose, high forehead, black hair laced with a little gray.

"You're still not talking to me. You're avoiding something."

"I'm not really," Kady said. "I'm just thinking. This is so complex," he exclaimed suddenly.

"Who else knows she's run away with him?"

"No one."

"Where do you stand in all this? If you won't tell me, I have to ask you. Do you want them to find her, or do you want the scandal, too?"

Kady shut his eyes and didn't move.

"Tell me," Phoebe pressed. "Do you really want to sit there with your eyes closed? You think you won't have to answer me if you do that? That I'll just go away?"

Kady opened his eyes but still didn't say anything.

"You want the scandal, don't you."

"I don't know."

"Oh, Kady," Phoebe whispered urgently, leaning toward him. "What is it? What's the matter?"

He didn't look at her.

"Please tell me what's going on."

He didn't answer.

"Please."

"I thought it's what I wanted. If they ran away, I thought it was a way to get back at Jiggie after all these years. The scandal and everything. So I encouraged their relationship, hoping something like this would happen." He sounded anguished.

"And now?" Phoebe wanted to put her hand on his back and soothe him.

"I don't know what I want anymore. And I'm not going to look at you. I'm not. This is difficult for me. I've never had a

344

relationship like this with anyone in my life."

"Relationship like what?"

"You think I don't want to touch you, love you?"

There was another accordion player on the stage now, a duet. Phoebe didn't know what to do. She loved what Kady had said, but she felt upset and knew he was, too. She drank some coconut milk and felt it trickle down her throat. "Maybe if they find her in time, it can still be covered up." She fanned herself with her hand and didn't know if she was mad at Kady or simply mad at herself for resisting him and him, too, for resisting her.

"She's obviously not a virgin," he said.

"What's that have to do with it? Nobody'd have to know."

"They'd find out soon enough. It'd still be a scandal, even if she came back and went through with the marriage." His voice sounded tired all of a sudden. "The other side could get a huge sum of money out of Jiggie, breach of contract and all that. Word would get out."

"And if they don't find her, the wedding will be postponed and all eight zillion people who were invited will . . . Oh, Kady," she whispered. "What a mess. Jiggie must be devastated."

"If I know him, he's got something in the works. He always does. Jesus, Feeb. How'd we get in this spot?"

"What spot?"

"This one. Right now. You and me."

"If no else knows she's run away . . ."

"Now you're ignoring me."

"I can't think about what 'could' be. We have to accept what is. Tell me, please, who else knows she's run away."

"Jasdan, his wife, Jiggie, Attar Singh, and Shyam."

"Then how do you know?"

They looked straight at each other and didn't speak.

Someone started testing the microphone on the stage. People were sitting down.

"How, Kady?"

Gradually his eyes lost focus until she knew he wasn't seeing her.

A man approached the podium.

"Tell me the truth. Have you known it ever since I've been here?"

"The ceremony is about to begin."

"Then whisper."

"He sent me pictures from Agra, too," Kady finally said.

Phoebe didn't speak.

"Say something," he urged.

"I can't. I'm too hurt."

His eyes tracked every movement in her face. "I got them May 12th, the day you arrived."

"Before you saw me at the airport?"

"Before I saw you at the airport. It's why I didn't want to see you. Still don't. I've been lying to you all along."

"Do you know where he is now?"

"Not anymore."

"But you didn't tell me when you did."

"Jesus, Feeb."

"But you didn't."

"Do you know how upset about this I've been?"

"About Cully."

"No, goddamn it," he said, eyes suddenly blazing. "About you."

"What do you mean?"

"You. My life is a sham from start to finish."

"I don't understand," she whispered.

"No," he said. "I know you don't. But it's why I lied."

"Why?"

"Because I never tell the truth."

"About anything?"

"No, of course not. Just about the important things." He sounded disgusted.

The man on the stage was welcoming everyone to Aligarh.

"I told myself you'd only worry more if you knew," Kady said. "I thought I did it for you."

"But it was just because it was hard."

"That's absolutely right," he said. "It was hard. I couldn't face it, the utter complexity of it all, and so I didn't tell you."

Phoebe could feel him pulling away from her, like a giant wave ebbing out to sea. He looked the same, big shoulders, brown face, white eyes, but he had withdrawn.

Children appeared in front of them and started making their way to the stage. They were fidgeting with their clothes, fancy veils and gauzy silks, cooler in the heat.

"Jesus, Feeb," Kady finally whispered. "I'm sorry about this. Say something to me."

"You didn't want me to get involved in what was happening. Mirabai running away, Jiggie. You didn't know what I'd do. How I'd interfere."

"Can you read everyone's mind?" He smiled.

"Don't joke. This is serious."

"Of course it's serious. What do you think I think it is?"

"I have to tell you something."

"You have a lie, too?" He grinned suddenly.

"Stop it. I have to tell you something so you'll understand me clearly. I really hate being left out. I hate it more than anything in the world because it makes me feel like I'm back on Jumna Road and I'm unloved and unlovable all over again."

Kady took her hand under the table where no one could see. "What are you trying to say?"

"Just listen to me," she said, pulling her hand away. "I know I'm going home soon. . . ."

"When?"

"I don't know. That isn't the point."

"It sure is the point."

"Will you listen to me."

"Yes."

"It's this." Phoebe was very quiet. "I want you to know—"

"I can barely hear you. All this noise."

"I want you to know"—she was staring down at her hands—"that I care about you as much as anyone I've ever known, and it's really hard when I think you don't trust me or want to tell me the truth. I need to know what's going on." She felt tears in her eyes. "This is my life, too. You don't have to tell me whatever happened with Jiggie a thousand years ago. Strictly speaking, that's none of my business, but the rest of it is, and I don't care if it's good or bad, I want to know and understand."

Kady didn't speak. She felt his presence, an expression on his face for other people, but his eyes, only for her.

"I know there's more you aren't telling me," she went on. "I feel there's a lot. About everything. About, I don't know what about. But I feel this silence inside you. Please, share it with me." She moved her chair closer to him. "I'm not mad at you. I'm not," she whispered, almost in his ear, so close she could kiss his cheek. "I knew about Cully and Mirabai all along. That's why I'm not mad. It's my fault, too. I had the information and

347

I ignored it. Because I didn't want Cully to come between us."
She paused. "I still don't."

Kady looked at her. "He already has."

"He doesn't have to anymore."

A man was speaking at the podium in Urdu.

"Do you have anything to say?" Phoebe whispered.

He shook his head sorrowfully. "I can't, darling. I have to think."

"Then I'll meet you in the car when the ceremony's over," Phoebe said, and got up and walked away.


Kady didn't say anything in the car and not on the plane, either. He was deep in thought.

Back in Delhi, his invitations kept coming every morning, only now she sent them back with a note to remind Minister-sahib about their conversation in Aligarh. She wanted an answer, she said.

Meanwhile she went on with her work. She avoided the temple, associated it too much with him, but she started going to Rani Jhansi Road, asking shopkeepers if they'd seen a man with yellow hair and blue eyes, a left shoulder sloping down. She thought it was unlikely Cully was still here and assumed he was away with Mirabai, but it gave her a concrete way to express her concern for Cully, as well as keep her mind off Kady.

Rani Jhansi was a business district. Everyone she asked about Cully had nothing to say, except one old man who opened doors for people coming in and out, and he told her, There was one, he had the same yellow hair as you? and she said yes, and he said, When he woke up he got on a bus.

So after that in her desperation she took to riding the bus, up and down Rani Jhansi Road, but all it did was belch out diesel smoke through the inner streets of northern Delhi, and she finally figured that she could ride for the rest of her life and still not find her brother because the road and the street could have taken him anywhere.

So she kept on roaming the streets herself, seeking out places where hippies went in their shorts and torn-off blue jeans, the way Cully looked, she thought. Most were European, beards and hair in braids, but none of them knew Cully

Guthrie or someone with such yellow hair. She bought them drinks and food, even started asking about someone else who was missing, too, a male Caucasian about his same size, the body that had stretched out navy blue and pink on the far shores of the Jumna River, but he, poor fellow, brought no sign of recognition either.

## ❧ 27 ❧

PHOEBE FINALLY MISSED KADY so much, she accepted an invitation for a dinner party at some friends of his. She had figured out that although Kady couldn't tell the truth yet, he was learning, and changing, and for the time being that was good enough for her.

After that they began to meet again at other people's houses, sit around tables set with linen cloths, buffets on a lawn, and she would hear his voice talking about work and politics, the monsoons that hadn't come when this was monsoon season, the heat stifling.

She sensed, through it all, that something important was happening to her and to him as well.

The next time Stephen called from New York, she had Chumpi say she wasn't there. It was the first time she'd ever done that.

One night she imagined a pillow on the bed was Kady and she saw how he would be, naked arms and legs. She picked up the phone and tried Alice in New York, but the lines were out, all she got was static, couldn't even hear the operator, knew that in calling she was trying to reaffirm who she was, or used to be, in the face of what was becoming something overwhelmingly Indian in her mind.

At a dinner on the 24th Kady was wearing a dhoti—most men did that night, it was too hot for anything else—and when she sat down on a bench outside, he kept on standing, no one else out on the lawn just then. They had gotten used to the silence of being together. They'd done it so often over the last two months, there was something intimate about it now, just being together, quiet, alone, no questions asked, two people who had known each other for a long, long time.

That night Kady sat down beside her. His arm was inches from her own, his in homespun khaddar cloth, hers pale and bare, and she abruptly felt all her breath and life focused there on her arm. Heat was emanating off him like a radiator, compounded by the night's heat and the faintest scent of cinnamon. She felt even her breath clogged in her throat, a tension due to the nearness of him, and she stood it as long as she could, until finally she couldn't bear it anymore and she got up.

"I have to go home, Kady."

He rubbed his arm, the one that she had left, and said, "But what is your home? A place of Auntie Indore's?"

"I can't stand the heat anymore. There's no air. I can't breathe."

"Don't you want more than what you have?"

"Yes, if you want to know the truth, I want more, a lot more. I want more than my parents had and more than Cully has and far more than I had."

"Then why are you leaving?"

"Because something's not right, and I don't know what it is. Why don't you tell me what's going on?"

"I have."

"That's not true. Why did you tell me you were out of town?"

"When?"

"At the airport. The very first day."

"It was something to say," he said. "I don't know. I don't remember."

"Then what is going on, and where is Cully? It's been months, for God's sake. Why can't you talk to me?"

"I think he's scared by Anant's murder," Kady said. "I think he's running from it. I've done everything I can to squash interest in it with the police, but—"

"He has nothing to do with it."

"I know, but I think it's what's keeping him away. He's hiding with Mirabai and he doesn't know what to do."

"What's keeping him away from me?"

"He doesn't know you're here."

"He does," she said. "I know he knows."


Two nights later, on July 26th, some Qawwalli singers gave a concert on the lawn after a dinner party and everyone sat around on sheets, the ground as warm as the air. Above, peacocks were swinging from the trees, their tails hanging down like blankets on a line. She and Kady sat on the ground in back, leaning against a chair that had been positioned under the trees so tendrils of growing things had come up around its legs and over the back, turning it into a thing of nature. "I know he knows I'm here," she said, so low no one would overhear.

"Maybe he's having a hard time. If coming here means you're facing the past . . ."

"Why are you so protective of him?"

"I'm just telling you what I think's happening. He's probably had to face the past these last few months. We all have."

"You too?"

"Haven't you heard a goddamned thing I've said to you? Of course me too. I've been one way for so long, I don't know how to be different. That's why it's hard for me to be with you. Maybe he's avoiding you. You're the one who had Louis and he didn't. Maybe he resents it."

"Did he tell you this?"

"Not in so many words. It was just my impression."

"You knew him for almost a year. Why aren't you more definite when you talk about him?"

"Maybe I don't want to hurt your feelings."

"Nothing can hurt them. What did you do with him all that time? How much did you see him?"

"I'll talk about him all you want," Kady said. "What do you want to know?"

"Everything."

"I think being back was much worse for him than for you. He feels more alone than you ever could. You, at least, have him."

352

"Just tell me one thing. How could you push them together that much?"

"I explained that to you. Besides, they didn't need me to push them together."

"But he's not right for her. She has no capacity to understand how complicated he is. That's probably why he's attracted to her. She's safe. She doesn't threaten him."

"You sound as conservative as Jiggie."

"Do I sound jealous, too?" She laughed.

"I can tell you one thing I haven't said before. He asked Jasdan if he could marry her. It was April second, the day he disappeared. Jasdan turned him down. Cully knew he would, but it gave him a reason to get even madder. I'm not defending what I did with him and Mirabai," Kady added. "I'm saying my role was minor. They're two strong-willed—"

"Did you help her run away, too? Will you tell me the truth about that?"

"I was trying to do whatever I could to make him feel better."

"Do you see how you never answer my questions? You slide out from under them."

"How could I help her? I was in Delhi."

"Did you give her the money?"

"No."

"I don't believe you."

"I gave her money all along," he relented. "She never had any money to buy things, so I gave it to her. What's wrong with that?"

"Do you know how she spent it? If she used it to pay for the cab and buy the train ticket?"

"I never paid any attention to how she spent it. I was just trying to help them both, help Cully especially feel better about himself. Put a different gloss on his relationship with Louis."

"Conceal the truth of what Louis really felt, you mean."

"He was desperate here. Nothing worked. None of his expectations were panning out, and even if they were irrational to begin with, they were all he had. Jesus, Feeb, if being back's hard on you, imagine what—"

"Have you seen the horse?"

"That horse is nothing and he knew it all along. He was testing Bhave from the very start."

"Are you saying it's fake?"

353

"I have no idea. I assume it is."

"So, Bhave deals in fakes?"

"Sometimes."

"But that's shocking."

"Well, India is shocking."

They were quiet.

"But Louis was the hardest thing for him to deal with," Kady said after a while. "Cully had all these notions about them being joined in death, and he had to give them up."

"Why?"

"Bear with me. Don't rush me. I'm trying to tell you something. I saw him the first of April. Then he went to Deeg and had a fight with Jasdan. He came back to Delhi very upset about your father's death."

"Not Thalia's?"

"No, Louis'. I haven't seen him since. That's all there is to it. That's all I can tell you."

"So you never saw him after Anant was killed?"

"No. I was just trying to help him. I felt it was my duty to Louis." Kady sounded tired. "I'm telling you the truth. I haven't seen him. No one has."

"Then why do I feel . . . ?"

"It's all so complicated. Two kids have run away. She's in a lot of trouble. They both are. But why do you insist on making it your burden, too? Why does it matter to you?" His eyes were questioning. "It's not your life. If anyone else is involved, it's Jiggie and me. What's it have to do with you? Your life is in New York, your work. . . ."

"But it's Cully. He's all I've had. And what? Anant is nothing? Just a coincidence?"

"Cully . . ."

"But what if he did? I'd rather know the truth."

"The truth. . . ." Kady stood up abruptly and walked away, farther into the garden.

She followed him. "What?"

"Nothing." He pushed her away with his arm.

She followed him. "What is it?"

"It's this business about you and the truth. Why did you have to come back to India?" She was standing a few feet away from him. "Why all this obsession with the truth? The truth for one person is—"

"That's not so and you know it."

"You should let go of Cully."

"I just want to find him. Then go on with my life."

"And me, Feeb. What about me?"

They were silent.

"What about you?" Phoebe asked quietly.

"I don't know what you're doing here. You keep saying you're going home, but then you stay longer and longer."

She held out her hands in his direction. "Granny said India was our 'home.' She also said New York was home. I don't know where I belong or even what India means to me. I'm trying to find out."

"And that's all?"

She didn't answer.

"Is it?"

"No."

"Then what is it?"

"I do have to go home sometime, and I don't want to leave too much behind. I couldn't stand that again."


Soon after, Kady's secretary called her at Bhagwandas Road and said the Deputy Minister had to see her immediately.

She went right in, sat down. He shut the door and sat down, too, looked at her with such intensity she looked away. Then he asked why she had come to India.

"I mean, really," he said.

" 'Really'?"

"Of course," he exclaimed, and with that he pushed all the papers straight off his desk on the floor.

"Because I needed to find Cully," she said.

He waved his hand, impatient.

"Put my relationship with him on a more realistic level."

"No, I mean more than that," he stressed. "Tell me. I have to understand. Why did you come, and why have you stayed so goddamn long?"

"Because, if you really want to know, I lived in New York for twenty years and never knew what I was doing or what my life meant, if it meant anything at all. All I did was live in my grandmother's apartment, look after Cully, work my ass off, and see my friends, and one day I realized that I had a nice life and

I was a nice person, but in twenty more years, I'd have the same nice life and be the same nice person and still not know one more thing about myself. Unless I came back here and faced everything."

"Then why don't you stay with me tonight? Face things with me?"

Phoebe felt a surge of panic.

"Will you?" He looked at her with such tenderness he was almost in tears, his head moving back and forth ever so slightly. "You know there's nothing between me and Durr. Will you please come be with me, so we can do these things together, face your life and mine? Will you?"

Phoebe let her head bow.

"Phoebe."

Then, ever so slightly, she let it shake.

"But why not, darling?"

"Because," she mumbled, eyes closed, "I'm so scared I could die. Falling in love is the hardest thing I've ever done."

"Then die with me."

She clutched her hands to her breast to soothe the pain inside. "I'm too afraid of going home without you," she whispered. "I thought for a while I could do it, but I can't. I can't be without you again." She stood up, walked out of the room, and went downstairs, where she found Tulsidas and had him take her home.


The next day Phoebe took a plane to Calcutta and caught a Piper Cub that flew down the coast to Puri.

There she lay on the beach, white sand and a blue sea, an old English hotel that had wide windows and gauzy curtains, but the next morning she abruptly caught the same plane and came right back.

She telephoned Durr Suraj.


"This is Phoebe Guthrie," she said on the phone. "I've been back in India to visit. Do you remember me? We met a long time ago? I was only sixteen, at a wedding, and you . . ."

The woman drew in her breath. Phoebe had no idea if she knew about her and Kady or not. "Of course I remember you,"

356

Durr exclaimed, and then, at Phoebe's urging, she agreed to tea that afternoon.

At four-thirty Phoebe came up the long driveway to the house at Viceroy Circle. She was surprised at how elegant it was. She rang the bell and Durr came to the door, not too tall, older, still beautiful. Phoebe felt the pull of her orange eyes like an undertow that insistently sucked her in. Without thinking, she took the woman in her arms and, holding her tight, felt tears leak from her eyes.

Durr hugged her back. "There, there," she mumbled. "It's all right. Everything's all right. Of course I remember you." She pulled away. "What a life you had; how could I ever get it out of my werry mind."

Phoebe straightened up, embarrassed. "I don't know what that was all about," she said, laughing and wiping her eyes. "I just felt overwhelmed. Funny the things you think of, my mother, Cully. I guess you know he's . . ."

"Yes," said Durr, and drew her in.

They sat in the living room, sparsely furnished and simple. Servants ran in and out, tea, trays, little potatoes wrapped in dough, sweets made of pomegranate. Durr took her on a tour downstairs, showed her the living room, dining room, all of it a bit too empty, and then they went back to sit. There was no evidence of Kady at all, except in the number of chairs and phones everywhere, pads of paper, pens, pencils.

Durr pointed to a closed door. "That's his office," she said. "There."

No need to identify him any more than that, the pronoun sufficed.

That was when Phoebe knew she knew.

Durr pressed her with questions: Had she missed India? Had her grandmother looked out for her? Had she fitted in back there or did she belong right here? Her marriage, husband, her work . . . Phoebe answered as best she could.

"You must be wondering about us, too." Durr looked Phoebe full in the face, orange eyes as bright as bulbs.

"I do wonder about you," Phoebe heard herself say. "I wonder about a great many things."

"Tell me what they are."

"I want to know where he was born and why he is so unhappy." Her voice was slow and measured. "I want to know

357

what he thinks about. What he feels. What he feels about his children. Where you were born. How you met. How he met Jiggie. Why he hates him, what has happened to him all these years." Phoebe stopped, looking Durr full in the face. "I want to know everything."

"That's what I thought," Durr answered. She poured more tea and fixed herself on the couch with cushions. "Well," she began, "he was born in Deeg, in a little willage not too werry far from the palace. As a child he had four brothers and three sisters, but by the time he was only just ten he had only one brother and one sister, they had all just died, of this and that, and the grief made it an unhappy place to be. He went to school until he was twelve, or maybe it was thirteen, I am not knowing that for sure." She paused. "Do you want to hear more?"

Phoebe nodded.

"His father was a healer, and by the time this man he left and went to Deeg to make his service there, Kady was old enough to go with him and get employ, too, so he is not ever, I am thinking, going back to his willage or seeing his family or that one brother and one sister, because he had ambitions even then for the werry things his life was not prepared to give him."

"And that was politics?"

"Always, always, always. Politics and ambition. What he would do, electricity, water, everything, anything, for all these Indian peoples. So many Indian peoples, and I am thinking he has them all as his werry own family, since he has no family of his own. It's all time always the only thing he has on his mind."

"What about you?"

"I was born in Kashmir. Have you been there?"

Phoebe shook her head, knowing Durr must be forty years old, but she looked ageless and her eyes had a tenderness Phoebe didn't think she'd ever seen in any other set of eyes, even Kady's.

"It's the most beautiful place in all of India," Durr was saying. "You must be having him to take you there sometime. I was the last of seven sisters and no brothers, and so I was always knowing I must be having no opportunity."

"Wasn't it difficult? Knowing that?"

"No," Durr said, "life is what it is, isn't it? That is what Kady has always told me. He is the wisest of the wise people, aren't you finding that? And he has all time told me that life is allotted to us and we must make the best of what we have, not snivel about this and that, and one thing is sure, and that is that I am not sniveling, never once, not since I am knowing Kady, and maybe the gods will notice that and give me the benefit in my next life."

"He doesn't snivel, either."

"No, he doesn't," Durr said. "He surely doesn't. I was a burden to my parents, and they are having to get rid of me." She paused. "I was having only one thing that the gods had given me."

"Your eyes."

"Yes. So Kady and I had an arranged marriage. All marriages in India are arranged, you must be knowing that. That's all there was to it."

"That's all?"

"For sure."

Phoebe looked at her, unconvinced.

The bearer returned noiselessly with another plate of things. Durr shooed him away.

"That's how they got rid of you?" Phoebe asked. "The marriage? How'd they pay the dowry?"

"I can't tell you any more."

"But you can't leave it at that. You've barely told me anything. I could have learned all that in the newspapers."

"Then maybe you should be learning it in the—"

"Was the marriage arranged by your father and Kady's father? Just tell me that."

"No," Durr said. "It wasn't."

"Then who arranged it?"

"It was not being an ordinary marriage in the beginning and it was never being ordinary afterwards and that is why my husband is the way he is. Don't you think he's all time sad and different from the other peoples?"

"Sometimes, he's sad, yes, but . . ."

Durr looked at her curiously.

"I love it when he laughs."

"Well, that is werry good, and it says werry much for you, but don't forget the sadness or the reason why. You are always wanting to know the reason why. This is not Indian. Indians have no interest in why because they know all time why. Because it is. But, just this once, I will tell you why he is different. Because of his marriage. There is one other reason I can tell you,

359

too, and that is that for all that he is gaining in his life, all these werry big and important things, he is losing everything else."

"Everything?" Suddenly Phoebe felt terrifically scared. "What?"

"What does a man want?"

"I don't know."

"Of course you do," Durr said. "Maybe you are just not wanting to think about this one thing, but I am knowing what he has lost."

"You mean you. That's what you mean, isn't it," Phoebe said suddenly. "He lost you."

"I can't tell you what it is. I am doing my duty to you as his friend by talking to you. But this other is his, his privacy all alone, and if you are not knowing, then I am not the one telling you."

"That isn't right."

"What isn't right?"

"He didn't lose you. He never had you. That's it. Isn't it? That's what he never had. A wife. Who else knows?" she whispered, looking around at the servants' door.

"In India everything is either for all the world to know or only one, two persons. Something werry secret."

"Like no one knows about Mirabai?" Phoebe said.

Durr didn't answer. Phoebe knew she was listening for signs of servants and moving doors. "Like no one knows about Mirabai?"

"More so." But Durr didn't even say the words, she just moved her lips, no sound at all.

Phoebe felt her heart thumping. "And the children?"

Durr didn't say a word, orange eyes wide open with honesty; Phoebe missed Kady so much, she was afraid she might lose him forever. She remembered blindingly what it was like to get on that plane twenty years ago, no one there ever after except her brother, and she knew she didn't want to be without Kady Suraj again in her whole life, whatever it meant to her.

Durr knew. "You want him very much?"

Phoebe nodded imperceptibly. Then she looked around the room. "Do you ever go out?" she whispered. "You never went out."

"You never saw me," Durr said, as if to say that someone else did.

360

Phoebe looked at her questioningly. "But you saw someone else? A man? The same man you told me about years ago. That's it, isn't it. That's why Kady never had you."

Durr started talking, her voice neutral. "Yes, I am going to see my childrens. All the time my childrens, and there is this one priest in one temple I am visiting werry often because I am having this paining in my heart that only the gods can lighten and so I must be with them often, these gods of mine, sometimes I yearn to be with them all the time, and I have sometimes this one teacher of singing because I am still always after all these years liking my music lessons."

"So you don't see this man anymore," Phoebe said. "But it makes you sad and so you go to the temple and pray and sing and you think about this person when you sing, don't you?" Her tone was hurried, intense. "You love him, don't you? But it's over, isn't it, your love affair, and you're alone, except for your children. You're not happy, either. That's what you're telling me, isn't it."

Durr nodded.

"Except that he is happy. Kady. I know he is. He's happy with me. But what does Jiggie Deeg have to do with all of this? Why did he come to the house after my parents died?"

Durr was silent.

"He never even knew my father," Phoebe rushed on, still in a whisper. "Why did Kady bring him?"

"Then asking Kady only."

"I did."

"What did he say?"

"He said he didn't remember."

"Then I can't say, either."

"Why does he hate Jiggie Deeg?"

"Ask him."

"I've tried."

"Someone might not even be knowing the hate is still there," Durr said, "but I know it. I am seeing it, smelling it, like his cigarettes, and let me telling you, this hating is the one thing you must worry about. He cares about this man, too, very much, maybe even sometimes loves him, but the hate is still there, too, and it is the one and only one thing you must worry about."

"But why does he hate him at all?"

"It is not mine to tell."

"Why did Kady give Louis the Shiva Nataraj?"

"I can't tell you these things."

"But I want to know. It was my house and my parents and their death and—"

"But it's not yours alone."

"This is all about you, isn't it?" Phoebe said. "All about you."

"Some of it."

"And Jiggie Deeg. He's the man my father saw you with. He's the one you told me about at the wedding. He was in the restaurant and my father saw you and afterwards he followed you down the street and that's when he came to your apartment and met Kady."

"I can't say."

"You married Kady, but you spent your whole life with Jiggie Deeg. Didn't you. And my father knew. That's why he threatened Jiggie, and maybe Jiggie was scared of him."

"I can't say."

"But, please tell me. I want to know," Phoebe rushed on. "Please. You asked me if I had any questions and I do. Please."

"I asked you if you had any questions about Kady."

"But now I want to know about my mother and my father."


At the door Durr took her in her arms and held her tight. "Coming back anytime," she said.

"But you won't tell me any more."

"And take good care of him."

"Who?" Phoebe asked.

"My husband."

# ❧ 28 ❧

EARLY THAT EVENING A CAR CAME to Bhagwandas Road with a note from Kady. "I'll wait until tomorrow," it said. "Then I want to see you."

But that very night he came to the house in one of his little Fiat cars. It was nearly dawn, August 10th, the sky was filling up with light, and he went up the steps and rang the bell. A bearer finally came, half-asleep, and Kady saw Chumpi getting up from her spot on the floor. He asked for memsahib, please for bringing memsahib. When Phoebe came out in a dressing gown, tying up the ties, he said, "Come for a drive with me."

She didn't answer.

"Come on," he said. "Have you seen the sky? The clouds are incredible and the rains are coming. We won't get through the night without them."

"But it's almost morning."

"All the better. Come out and see. It's beautiful."

"Just a minute." She went back inside to dress.

She came out in a skirt and T-shirt, sneakers and no socks. They got in his car, windows down, and drove out into the darkness that was compounded now by the great dark clouds low slung over the city, huge imposing shapes of gray and blue.

Everywhere along the sidewalks and the roads people had gotten up too and were standing, looking at the sky. The lights of the city, getting paler in the traces of the dawn, reflected upon the clouds, which hung heavy, waiting for some internal combustion that would explode them and send the waters down.

Kady drove slowly through the streets. They barely talked, a little about the sky and the rain, once about a man who was half naked out in the street, his arms uplifted, yearning for the rains to come.

Kady asked, was she all right? She said yes. He asked, had her trip been good? and she said yes, especially the beach. He asked what she thought of Durr and she said, "She was great," and he said, "Yes."

He had his arm out the window, resting on the sill, so did she, the heat in the air dense. There was something else, not moisture yet, but anticipation. She was breathing through her mouth, her lips open, throat clogged. He wore a dress shirt, the sleeves rolled up, old trousers frayed around the edges and some sandals, leather, that showed his long brown toes, and the scent was flowers and ginger root, something that hovered in the airlessness.

The thunder began, a vast noise that started somewhere else and traveled as fast as could be, bringing its awesome sound over the city and the car, and then rumbled out until it disappeared. As the real light of dawn finally arrived, only to go nowhere because the sun was locked in the sky behind the impenetrable shield of navy blue and black, Kady brought the car to a stop along the edges of a meadow. The clouds were like the largest armies in the world positioning themselves for battle, stretched out for miles across the sky, line after line of them. He shut off the motor, and they listened to the thunder.

"It can't be much longer now," he said.

"No."

"It's been such a long, long time."

"Yes."

"I can't wait any longer." He looked at her now. "I waited as long as I could."

"So did I."

"I tried to stop. I tried," he said.

"But what are we going to do?"

364

"It doesn't matter. But I can't wait. Jesus, Feeb, not any longer."

"Neither can I."

"Then let's get out, get out of the car."

"Now?"

And he said, "Yes."

But their words were drowned out by a clap of thunder that
was directly overhead and the sound of lightning as it cut across
the sky above the meadow, a jagged sword, sharp as any instrument. She opened her door. He did, too. Came around to her
side and took her out and stood in front of her looking down at
her. He laid his hands along the side of her face, and then his
body fit in along the length of hers, legs and stomach, thighs, all,
and he wrapped his arms around her and kissed her, their lips
barely touching, getting the feel of her. Slowly he pushed her
back against the car to kiss her more, harder, until the two of
them were flat against each other, the heat of the air slowly
moved by a sly little breeze that rustled up, brushing against
their arms and legs. The rains started, pouring over their heads,
but there wasn't any room between their bodies for the rain to
go, so it just splashed over and around them.

They were wet, soaked through, rain flowing over their lips
and mouths. He kissed her on and on, not letting up except to
wind his arms tight around her back, she the same, hands against
his shirt, neck, back, hair, everything wet and cool and hot and
clean, and when he moved his lips from hers, he mumbled,
"Jesus, Feeb," against her hair, "Jesus, Feeb," and then kissed
her again, and again, hard, then soft, breathing so deep that she
thought he was taking her all the way into his throat and
beyond. Finally they just stood there, interwoven, her foot
wrapped around his ankle, as all around them people celebrated
the rain. He kept taking in more of her, licking the rain off her
skin, her neck, her shoulder, and they stood that way, sometimes
kissing, sometimes not, lips traveling to the ears and neck, and
even farther down, his hands up along her breasts and thighs.

He whispered against her hair, "Let's go to Auntie Indore's,
Feeb. Let's go now."

# PART FOUR

**❧ I ❧**

THE NEXT DAY THEY NEVER LEFT
the room. About noon Chumpi scratched on the door and said
there was tea outside, but they didn't move to get it. A few hours
later she came back, scratching again, saying she had fruit and
cakes this time, tea and filtered water, and Kady pulled the tray
in. They had it on the bed, sitting up against the pillows, until
Phoebe spilled tea on her chest and he began to lick it off, finding
crumbs and bits of jam as he covered the whole terrain.

The windows were open, curtains pulled across, and when
they finished they lay back on the sheets again; he barely let her
go, still had his arms around her. "Hear the birds?" she said, and
he grinned with pleasure, birds cawing in the yard, even pecking on the windowsills as if trying to join them in the room.
They were cool from so much sweating, and he moved to put
his head on her stomach, stretched his legs out, resting his feet
against the wall behind the bed so that he looked like a narrow
walkway across a chasm, her own white body part of the land
he was attaching to.

The rains stopped for the first time, it was in midafternoon,
and they could feel the effects of the steam outside rising up out
of the ground. It got so humid Phoebe climbed off the bed to find
a rubber band and pull her hair up off her head, but at the last
minute he did it for her. Sat up naked on his knees on the bed

beside her, took the band and gathered her hair up in his hands, so engrossed in the feel of it, she knew it was something he had thought of often in the weeks before. When he finished she took his hands in hers and kissed them like a mother might kiss a child, each finger, knuckle, the palms themselves.

That night she said, "You don't want to go home to Viceroy Circle?"

"No," he said, "I don't."

The following day was the same. They were never more than a few inches apart. Once he sang an Indian love song, a couple of lines was all, he was so embarrassed and off key. Then he insisted, for recompense, on seeing a love letter she had mentioned she had written him, so she found it crumpled in the drawer and gave it to him. Her face was buried in his stomach while he read.

Chumpi left a new set of sheets outside the door, so they fixed the bed eventually. But she also left the newspapers, edition after edition all day long, as Samiji brought them by. Samiji came with messages from the office too and piled them outside the door, but when they took in the trays of food and tea, they left his deposits there, untouched.

They heard his car outside, coming and going, and several times his voice in the hall with Chumpi. Finally Phoebe asked Kady what he was going to do, and he got up off the bed, naked, went out in the foyer, empty now, and said, "See?" She was watching, and he pushed everything far out into the room with his foot, a pile of things now standing isolated in the middle of the marble floor outside.

The next day, the 12th, it was still raining and the streets were starting to flood. No surprise about that. It happened every year. But after lunch the electricity went off.

It flickered first, a warning, on and off several times, as if telling them, Quick, get candles, lamps, and batteries, and then, sure enough, the fan started to go slower and slower and they could hear it *whoosh* each time it went round, and then it came to a halt, stunning in its silence.

Phoebe and Kady stared up at it. "It's like the world," she said.

"Stopped," he said. "But for how long?"

"As long as we want?"

"We can always hope."

Around three he went out to the phone in the foyer and tried to call the office. He dialed several times, but the lines were down.

There was no one in the house but them by now. Chumpi had told the servants to go, even the sweepers, they were to come back once a day. The pile of things was still in the middle of the floor, and all Samiji did now when he came by was add things to it, files, messages, a couple of written reports. He sat outside in the car or talked to Chumpi in the kitchen, said once in a loud voice they could hear that he had let it be known in the office sahib was "taking small vacation."

Later that night they went for a walk, and Phoebe mentioned Durr for the first time. "Won't she worry where you are?" she asked.

Kady shook his head.

"She knows where you are. Right?"

"Right."

They walked side by side, the way Indians do, never touching, and when they came to a hippie sitting on the side of the road, Phoebe stopped. "Are you all right?" she asked the boy. It was lightly raining, but very dark. He had a pack and some bedding that was wet.

"Yes," he said.

"You have money for food or something?"

"Enough."

They went on. "I wonder where he is," she said.

Kady didn't say anything.

"You don't know," she said declaratively, and Kady said, no, he didn't, but she registered that he didn't say it very loud.

By the next day a good part of the city was flooded and people were beginning to worry about cholera. You always worry about cholera in Delhi in the summer, except, maybe, over on our side of town. The phones were out, electricity failed, and the rain continued, deluges, really. It came down so hard that it

371

seemed literally poured from the sky, bathtubs unplugged, dams broken.

There were bodies in the street. Phoebe saw two people, drowned at intersections, life and death mere trifles, just something for gods to do or undo, but for her, this presence of death was unnerving.

The dust disappeared. It was just plain gone, and in its place was the scent of the land itself, earth and deep red clay, and mere breathing made Phoebe feel ecstatic. One morning they were walking outside Nizamuddin's Tomb and she looked up at the sky, briefly blue and clear. "Look at that," she cried. "Don't you feel like you've taken a hat off your head?"

"What do you mean?"

"You take it all for granted, don't you. You don't even see that bowl that hangs down over your head all the time, and it's really just the sky?"

"No, I guess I don't," he said. "But I don't take you for granted. Not for a second."

"Maybe you should," she teased. "But isn't it beautiful?"

Until the clouds roll in again, she thought, and then it was still beautiful, only in a different way.

That night she had a bad dream. She didn't know what it was about, just knew she woke up sweating and afraid. Her heart was pounding, her emotions in a panic. She imagined mosquitoes hatching. She listened to them. They were in the room. She sat up in bed, not afraid of the mosquitoes, but of death and dying, separation and the loss. She touched Kady for reassurance, put her hand on his stomach, felt how it rose and fell as he breathed, but even then she imagined the mosquitoes. They were festering outside in pools of stagnant water, in the streets, lawns, gutters, doors, multiplying, danger everywhere.

She went over to the window and peered out, thought about sores on the face of the land, India, with these pools, muck and menace, illness and decay. "Kady," she whispered urgently, getting back in bed.

He didn't move.

She touched him again, pushed him gently on the side. "Wake up." He rolled toward her and curled his arm around her. "I want to talk to you. About India." She lay down alongside him, squirming underneath his arm. "Kady," she murmured again, her voice trembling.

But he still didn't move, and all she heard was the mosquitoes. She wondered if life was good or bad. Was it all relentless and you were zapped in the end by bugs or the elements, water or disease, life one big terrifying ordeal, haphazard at the best, disaster at its worst? Tulsidas had seen someone hit by a rickshaw, then beaten to death afterward by someone who mistook him for a man who'd kicked his cow.

She put her arms on Kady's chest and pulled herself up so that she was halfway on top of him, her face burrowing in his neck. He was the only exception, she thought. The only thing of good. "Kady," she cried suddenly.

He woke up abruptly. "What is it?"

She pushed her head into his neck. "Don't you hate India sometimes?"

"No."

"I know I'm being irrational, but how can you stand it? Heat, floods, that man. He was beaten to death, Kady, beaten to death." She was crying.

He rubbed his hand down along her head and back, soothing. "Everything's all right," he murmured.

"But how can you stand it?" She lifted her head.

"It's a typical Indian summer, darling." He shifted on the bed so that she was beside him, her head on his shoulder, leg across his thigh. "That's all. It's India."

"But you never know when it'll get you, accident, a beating, flood, disease. One of these mosquitoes could—"

"But this is real life, Feeb, and it can't be a whole lot different anywhere. A taxicab runs you over, earthquakes, cancer. Not that I'm any great expert on happiness, but isn't that what makes everything else worthwhile? It does to me."

"But I wonder so much. I can't stop my mind. I know it's impossible but I want to know what will happen. I want to know about everything, when I'll die, when you'll die, when . . . just everything. I think all the time, about Durr and what am I doing and what's going to happen when this is over. What's going to happen to us?"

"That's what we'll find out."

"But don't you want to know right now?"

"No. Because we can't know right now."

"We could decide," she said.

"Is that what you want?" he asked, kissing her hair.

"I guess not."

"Then let's just wait and see."

"But we can't live in Auntie Indore's house forever. And sometimes I feel like I'm just a leaf and I don't like feeling so small and—"

"Oh, Feeb."

"—and I hate the heat and the rain."

"No, you don't."

"But I do. I know it's childish of me, but I feel you can't get away from it."

"You don't want to."

"Maybe I do. Maybe it's too hard for me and—"

"It's not too hard for you. You're one of the strongest people I've ever known."

"Maybe I should just leave now."

He squeezed her. "Jesus, Feeb, I love you."

"But why doesn't all this bother you?"

"Because I don't expect it to be any different."

"Why not?"

"Because that's life. That's just exactly what it is. And you shouldn't expect it to be any different either."

"I want it to be different," she persisted.

"You can't 'want' that."

"But I do. Sometimes I think I just can't stand all the anxiety. Fear and confusion."

"But you do, don't you?"

"I guess. It's so easy for you."

"It wasn't always. I've gone mad a million times trying to sort myself out," he said. "You can't go through what I have and not want to find meaning in it. Finally a leper taught me everything I believe. He lived right outside the gate, a place where Durr and I once lived. Every day I had to pass him on my way in and out of the house. Sometimes if he was asleep, I literally had to step over him. It got so I thought about him all the time. I sent the servants out with food . . ."

"That was nice," Phoebe said, sitting up in bed to listen.

"But I kept thinking, What do I do with him? How do I incorporate this into my life? Why was he there and me here? It took me a while to realize I couldn't change the situation. I couldn't make him go away, but I couldn't forget him, either. I finally realized the question was not so much whether I was going to have compassion for him, or respect him, but whether I was going to grow from the experience of having him in my life."

"What happened?"

"One day I sent the servants out to make a tarpaulin cover for him, the monsoons had started. I ended up going out to do it myself, and I suddenly realized he was no different from me. It sounds so simple, but it wasn't. He didn't, quote, deserve to be a leper. I wasn't better than him because I had a good face and he didn't. We were the same and he was a leper just because he was. That's the way it was. We get what we get and the question is, what do we do with it?"

"What do we do?"

"I try to understand that I have a connection to the leper and the mosquitoes and the bodies in the street. I think that's all there is to it."

"That's all?" she asked uncertainly. "It sounds so vague."

"It is vague. But for me that's what answers my questions. It's what allows me to feel sometimes that I rise above the outward circumstances of life and find a larger vision. I think that's why the gods put it in the mix," he added.

"Put what in the mix?"

"The good and the bad. Precisely so we have to try to figure them out and do exactly what we're doing now." Kady paused. "But I like it," he said, smiling at Phoebe. "Before you, it was one of the few things that really gave me comfort and purpose."


It was the wedding season, floods and romance, death and renewal. At night you could hear trumpets and horns and those whiny violins, wedding parties all across town. It was like the Fourth of July every night, searchlights, noise, and fireworks.

Down in Deeg, the notion of romance took a different turn.

The chief uncle from the other side was summoned, an unofficial visit all alone.

He was put up in a guest room on the men's side of the palace and made to wait, finally brought to the office where Jasdan and Attar Singh were waiting, Shyam with some papers in his hand.

Jasdan told Shyam to lay the papers on the desk, in front of the uncle's eyes.

No one could help but see the papers were copies of doctor's records or that the name on top was the name of the uncle's niece, she the girl awaiting marriage in a few weeks' time, sister to the groom of Mirabai.

That the doctor was a gynecologist was enough in itself.

Because why would a virgin girl have need of a gynecologist? Much less see the doctor twice.

A good deal of talking ensued. Jasdan did not get to the point fast, but the gist of it was not complex. During the previous year Shyam Singh became friends of a bearer in the other side's house in Delhi, and eventually this bearer told him that a very great and true friendship had developed between this girl and her affianced.

The emissary must have turned pale at this point.

And Shyam, true and loyal servant that he was, had no choice but to pay a discreet visit to this girl's doctor's office. He got her records, no need to say it was the middle of the night, had them photocopied, and the next night he put them back.

Jasdan lifted up one sheet of paper from the pile and handed it to the emissary.

It was a prescription order for a diaphragm.

"We didn't choose to act at that time," Jasdan said as the uncle read. "What is discreet can remain discreet. But now . . ." He paused. "There is this. It is not discreet."

He picked up another sheet. Handed it across. A three-day-old report, similarly acquired. The girl was pregnant, eight weeks in.

The uncle didn't even look at it. "But her fiancé is the father," he protested, halfhearted at best.

Jasdan shrugged. Given the scandal seven months from now, he said, the parent was irrelevant. He had "no choice but to consider cancellation of Mirabai's wedding."

No need to say if one wedding was canceled, the other would be canceled, too, the word out, scandal unleashed.

The uncle asked him to negotiate.

Jasdan said no.

The uncle pleaded, but Jasdan sent him back to his room, only to receive a handwritten letter a few hours later saying the man had consulted his brother, the girl's father, on the phone, and they proposed a cash settlement to the Deegs of $250,000.

Jasdan summoned the man back and said it was not a question of money, but of honor.

Then what did he want?

Attar Singh, speaking now for Jiggie Deeg, was ready. He said they proposed, first, a further loosening of the marriage contract to give Mirabai and her affianced even greater independence from the family—to distance them from the upcoming scandal, was the way he put it—and, second, that the two marriages in question, Mirabai's and the sister's, be scaled down in size and splendor and the preliminary ceremonies eliminated altogether—ceremonies at which the girls' presence was required—so as to reduce public awareness of the Deegs' linkage to these people.

The emissary gulped but agreed. Said his side insisted on making the cash offering anyway to show their good intentions, and Jasdan said the Deegs would be only too happy to accept.

Shyam was sent to Delhi.

The next day he returned with $250,000, cash, in a brown cloth sack.

# ❧ 2 ❦

ON AUGUST 19TH, NINE DAYS
after Kady moved into Bhagwandas Road, three things happened.

The chief uncle returned to Deeg, bearing gifts and offerings,
to officially make the apology and to announce his side would
not request a meeting with Mirabai. Not yet, he warned, retaliation upon retaliation.

Vishnu Bhave boarded the Delhi-Calcutta Express, third class
reserved, a ticket for Benares, some twenty-one hours away.

The sky was clear, breezes were astir, no rain forecast, and
among the throngs of people who set out to walk in Connaught
Place, enjoy the air, and exult in the gods' blessings was Minister
of Public Works Hari K. Narayan.

He chose late morning, the busiest time of all.

The day before, Samiji drove Kady to the office. Phoebe
stayed at home and had a bath, did her exercises, looked without
interest at telephone messages that had accumulated, including
one from Harriet saying Vishnu Bhave had asked for her again.
She eventually got dressed and, with a sudden sense of purpose,
had Tulsidas drive her over to Dr. K. P. Sharma's house.

The bearer there had taken off the white sheets that covered the furniture and was washing the windows. "Soon, memsa'ab, soon," he said. "Doctor coming home soon for surely now. Must be."

Then she went back to Bhagwandas Road and lay down on the bed. She missed Kady with an intensity that was unnerving. When Kady returned he sat down beside her. "I couldn't do it," he said. "I couldn't stay there and I couldn't stay away."

"I went to see Dr. Sharma."

"Let's take a trip."

"He wasn't there."

"Who?"

"Dr. Sharma."

"Who's he?"

"Someone I know."

Kady brushed the hair off her face. "Let's go somewhere. I don't want to do another thing in the world but be with you."

"But what about your job?"

"Never mind about that. Let's go right now."


Kady sent Samiji to Viceroy Circle to get some things; she packed, too. From the beginning they set their minds on Kashmir, the most beautiful place in India. "It'd be safe now," he said, but they didn't really consider the outbreaks of communal fighting there or the presence of soldiers, never mentioned Durr or Cully or what else was going on outside their lives.


The next morning they said good-bye to Chumpi and Samiji. They caught a cab for the railway station, bought tickets, berths for two, no first class or air-conditioning, the best was third class reserved, exactly as they knew, and they were just about to board the train when they saw the newspaper.

The paper wallah was walking up ahead, and he turned to avoid stepping on a leper, otherwise they'd have missed the headline tacked up on the board he carried.

EXTRA EXTRA

NARAYAN HEART ATTACK IN CONNAUGHT PLACE

EXPIRES ON SPOT

Kady grabbed her arm; they sprinted ahead. He gave the man the first bill he found and held the paper out so they both could read.

The words were plastered across the top of the page.

At eleven-thirty that morning, less than two hours before, Chief Minister of Public Works Hari K. Narayan had "suffered a heart attack whilst walking in the crush of people in Connaught Place and expired on the spot."

The second paragraph said there had been a riot "of no small proportions."

The third, that a doctor "attending Narayan said he died, embarrassingly, of suffocation."

The heart attack, apparently, was mild and had nothing to do with the actual cause of death.

Kady dropped the paper.

The paper wallah picked it up and tried to give it back to him. Kady pushed him away, took Phoebe fiercely by the arm, and pulled her toward the train. "Let's go."

She followed.

The conductor was announcing the final call. The coolie had their seats. Kady gave him money and sat her down by the window, himself in the middle. It was just a bench, wooden, flat, and narrow, right angles to the wall. There were eight minutes to go before departure. His profile was calm but set. She wondered what he was thinking. Her heart beat rapidly. She waited for him to look at his watch, but he didn't. Could he actually let his future fall away, just like that?

People faced them from the other bench inches across. They didn't recognize him. They were mesmerized by her instead.

Kady opened his sack, got out a book, leaned back against the wall, one leg up on the other so that the ankle rested on his knee. He had on old trousers, shirt, belt, sandals, and he was perspiring more than usual, tiny drops of water slowly making their way down the side of his face, little moving pieces of reflected light against the dark. She wanted to reach up and wipe them off. The place was noisy with hawkers, coolies, children selling tea, mothers begging with their babies. With a jolt, the engine started turning, seats shaking with some inner turmoil. Kady didn't move, just kept on reading.

Phoebe got her book, too, put it on her lap, but she couldn't concentrate. She turned a page. Another page, she hadn't read a word. The engine was going faster. In a second the train would move. Was this really what he wanted? Ending it all like this?

Then came a giant sound of steam released from the inner bowels of the train itself. It signaled motion at last and that the getting away was here. Then, only then, did Kady look at her.

He smiled. Just a bit, but it was a smile nonetheless, kept small for privacy. "Ready to go?" he asked.

"You sure you want to handle it this way?"

He nodded, reached over, and fingered her hair.

"Take the consequences?"

"I love the consequences."

"No, I'm serious."

"So am I. I know exactly what I'm doing." He took her hand and held it up against his cheek while the eyes across the way opened wide in full amazement.

They got a houseboat on Nagin Lake. It was private, no tourists anymore; from every room they could look up into the pink-and-blue mountains that rose like cliffs from the edge of the valley and the water itself. Around them were fields, a wooden bridge, some other boats, and a solitary mountain peak topped by a deserted fort that stood dark in the morning light, red at sunset. They swam, walked, went fishing in the streams, took *shikaras* up and down the waterways, and talked about everything now, Cully, Mirabai, Durr, if not themselves or what lay ahead. What hadn't been said was only minor.

That's what Phoebe thought.

Days passed. She picked up her letters to Cully and Mirabai at the post office and the tourist bureau and threw them out. She and Kady agreed that even as the wedding date in Deeg was getting closer, it seemed farther away to them.

When she woke in the middle of the night, she hung on to him and even his heartbeat became a reminder of the future, everything uncertain and unresolved.

❧

One day they were hiking in the hills, a guide was leading the way, and they stopped for lunch at a lonely spot where they could see distant peaks covered with snow. In the beginning they didn't talk much. It was too beautiful and still. Nearby melted snow trickled through the grass. There was a little mountain stream and she stuck her bare feet in the frigid water.

She asked him to explain more thoroughly why the bargain he made with Jiggie turned out so bad. Why it wasn't just a variation on an arranged marriage. A marriage of convenience, however difficult. Why it was worse than that.

"Let's not talk about that," Kady said.

"No, let's. Please."

They were silent for a long time. "I told Louis about it," he began finally, speaking in a low voice that sounded creaky and slow, like a door opening. "But he knew anyway. Figured it out somehow just from the looks of things, the contradictions in our lives, and of course, he'd seen her with Jiggie. I was standing in the apartment. Durr came in. He followed. After that he was always warning me. Saying I'd pay for it one day if I didn't get free of Jiggie. But I didn't get free of him. Whatever I've told you, I didn't."

"But you said—"

"I know what I said. Believe me, it wasn't true. It's worse now than it was then, too," he went on. "I was greedy then. Now I'm not. Now I'm just trapped."

Phoebe pulled her legs out of the water and turned so she could put her hand on his thigh, the warmth of her getting through to him, she hoped.

"Jiggie and I had everything mapped out," he said, tracing little routes in the earth with a stick. "It was a contract. We planned for every contingency. I knew he was ruthless. Cunning. I tried to think of everything. So I'd have him under control. That's what I thought. But we never took the basic thing into account."

"Neither of us faced how much they loved each other. That's right," he said. "I should have known the contract wouldn't work." He looked up at her. "Neither one of us did our duty, don't you see? He said he'd never see her again. I promised to love her. We both simply broke the agreement." Kady paused. "I intended to love her. I really did."

"But you do love her."

382

"Now I do. Very much. But, you see, as soon as I met her everything started to go wrong, and, of course, Jiggie never did let her go. He couldn't, but if he'd ever come to me, even once, and said, 'I can't let her go. I love her too much. Do you think it would be all right if I kept on seeing her?' I'd have said yes, fine. Because I understood, really. I did. I do. But he never did that, and now our whole lives have passed—"

"Not our whole lives."

"—and look where we are." He was staring across the faraway abyss of land toward the highest mountains in the world where mammoth sheets of jagged ice spread halfway across the sky.

Phoebe moved her hands along his leg as if to say, over and over, an affirmation, that she loved him, all was well.

"I met her the first time at the train station," he said. "Attar Singh brought her up to Delhi. I must have looked bloody ridiculous in my new clothes. But I thought I looked great, and when she stepped off the train, she lifted her sari to let me see her face and I namasted her . . . you know, my hands up. . . ." He looked at her.

Phoebe nodded.

"And . . . you see, she came down the steps." His hands made a motion downward. "Attar Singh helped her down, and then she lifted her sari off her face." Now he made a lifting motion with his hands. "I couldn't believe how beautiful she was. She was showing me her face. I couldn't believe she did that. She didn't have to show it to me. We weren't married, and I almost went into a state of worship, she was so beautiful, but then she started to cry. Now I know it was because she was so moved by what we were doing and my willingness to help her. But I had no idea then, and the only thing that crossed my mind was that she was devastated looking at me, missing Jiggie, her life ruined because of me. And she did miss Jiggie, of course she did, but I just saw that she was crying."

"You saw rejection."

"Yes, I suppose that's it. I thought she couldn't bear the sight of me."

"How awful."

"Yes, it was, actually. It was only a misunderstanding, but I never knew it, not for years. I couldn't forget her crying. I thought about it every day. By the time I understood, it was too late. Years too late."

"It made it hard for you to love anyone else."

"I suppose."

"Or trust. You never fell in love with anyone else."

Kady shook his head. "Never. I never committed myself to anything," he said with disgust, "except myself."

"And India."

"I just closed down. I could feel it. I didn't pay any attention to her. I focused on my work. I tried to understand what I'd done. Not just hate Jiggie, you see, but understand. The more time went on, the bigger it seemed. This thing we'd done. This bargain. A bargain for life and death, really, if you see what I mean. But my intentions were right," he went on. "I even loved their child. It wasn't born yet, of course, but I imagined it. Ever since I heard Jiggie and my father saying it was too late for an abortion, I knew I could love it."

Phoebe kissed him on the cheek.

"I thought of it as a lost child. A child crawls away from its village, gets lost. Someone else comes across it, say a herd of camels are passing through and the shepherds find it. I thought about that a lot, before I even met her. Had this idea in my mind that it was a lost baby, only I'd found the mother, too, wasn't I the lucky one? I didn't mind, really, that it wasn't mine. But that's because I assumed she'd have plenty more and they'd be, well, all . . ." He looked at Phoebe. "You understand?"

"They'd all be yours."

"Yes."

She gripped his hand.

"Then one day I saw Shyam Singh," he said.

"What was he doing?"

"Nothing."

She waited.

"He was just walking away from the apartment building. That's all. We'd been married about a year then. He had the same turban. Same color, at least. Barefoot. He's always barefoot. Jiggie used to give him sandals, said he couldn't go places with him if he didn't wear shoes, but he never wore them so he finally stopped. Jiggie said you couldn't change a leopard's spots. I told him it depended on the leopard."

"What about Shyam?"

"I tried to think, were there were any shops he could have been going to? There weren't. He'd come for her. I knew it the

384

second I saw him. I didn't say anything to her."

"And she didn't mention it."

"I hired someone to keep a lookout. A boy. A week later, couldn't have been much longer, Shyam came back. She went out with him, they got a cab, came back several hours later. He paid the driver. Took her to the door, left her, didn't come inside."

"Were you seeing Jiggie much in those days?"

"When he was in Delhi, he came to the offices. That's all. But he never paid any attention to me then. Why should he? I was no one. A servant, dark one at that. He never even noticed me at all until Louis came along and I started to, well, you know, change. Change rather dramatically, I guess that was it. He'd never expected it. I remember the first time I saw him looking at me in the office. He just plain stared. Rather rude, actually, but he couldn't help it. I had some clothes Louis'd got me. I acted like I was the same, but everything had changed and I knew it and he knew it. You know how you can feel tension in a room?" He smiled. "Well, it was like that. It was rather great, actually. I loved it. Louis was frightfully excited. Asked everything. How Jiggie looked? Did he stare at me? Say anything? I didn't even know you then. That's when Jiggie began to get scared," he went on. "He had Shyam follow me. Everything was changing and he knew it. He was scared he was losing his hold on me, afraid I'd abandon Durr, not need his patronage anymore, now that I had Louis, and that she'd suffer. Everything was for her in his mind. For Durr. That's why I respect him finally. He does have a heart, in spite of everything."

"My father said he was insecure."

"He is, in his own damned way. But he loves Durr. There's nothing worse than for a woman to be divorced here. You know that. He was tremendously worried for her."

"I know." She thought of Durr down on Viceroy Circle, a woman who had a husband she was always going to have.

"Jiggie was afraid Louis would make me see I could get along without him," Kady was saying. "Or without her. He was very threatened by your father. Didn't understand him at all, how much he loved art. Me, at least he understood. I suspect he hated Louis more than anyone in his whole life. Quite an honor, that," he said wryly, "to be hated so much by Jiggie Deeg."

"Then why did he allow you and Louis to be friends?"

"By the time I saw Shyam Singh," Kady said, "the second baby had already started."

"Why did he allow it?" Phoebe asked again.

"We were already friends. How could he stop it?"

"But Jiggie is so powerful, he can probably do anything."

"Yes and no."

"So he let you be friends? As simple as that?"

"Why not?"

"It doesn't sound like him. And why did he come to Jumna Road?"

"He's always gotten his way."

"Not with Mirabai, he hasn't."

"But he did with me and Louis."

"Why did he come to the house?" Phoebe persisted. "Why did he allow you to be friends?"

"Durr never—"

"Kady, you haven't answered my questions. Twice now."

"Do you want me to tell you about Durr and the children?"

"No. I want to know . . ." Phoebe leaned back on her hips. "I get uncomfortable when you don't answer my questions."

"Jiggie threatened me, that's what he did. He said that if I stayed friends with Louis, he'd be watching every second and . . . You know. That kind of thing."

"What kind of thing?"

"Emotional blackmail."

"I still don't understand."

"Damn it," Kady said. "Let it go. I've told you everything."

"But if he hated Louis more than anyone . . . ?"

"Let it go."

"He's asked me to come visit him in Benares," Phoebe said abruptly.

"Well, don't you bloody go!" Kady exclaimed.

"I probably won't," she said, not wanting to argue.

"I don't want you to."

You can't stop me, Phoebe thought. "But I may go," she said aloud. "I haven't decided yet."

"He's unscrupulous and cunning."

"What could he want with me?"

"Who knows."

They were silent. Phoebe knew she'd do whatever she wanted

to do, no matter what Kady said, but the memory of his intensity stuck with her.

"Jiggie studied your father, that's what happened," Kady went on. "He had Shyam check him out, and he decided he could always find a way to control him if he had to."

"You're being vague."

"I am?"

"Why can't you tell me exactly what happened? I always get the feeling you haven't told me everything. Just like at the airport."

"Can I postpone talking about this? Can I get back to it in a minute?"

"Why not now?"

"Because I'm not ready. I don't know why, but I'm not. This is hard for me. You're right, I do keep things back, a lot of them, and I don't like it, but I have to go at my own pace. Just be patient." He laughed. "That's like telling a monkey not to eat a banana, isn't it."

Phoebe grinned.

"So it's a deal?"

"Deal. You were saying that Durr was having another baby," Phoebe prompted.

"She never did tell me about it," Kady said. "Maybe she knew I knew. She just got bigger and bigger."

"What happened before that? The first year?"

"Nothing."

"Nothing."

"That's just it," he said glumly. "That's where I broke the contract. I didn't fulfill my duty as a husband."

"You sound so Indian. You mean you didn't sleep with her."

"I didn't even touch her. She was never mine. I couldn't. After a while it never even occurred to me."

"What's so wrong with the fact you never slept with her? I see it as extraordinarily human and understandable, under the circumstances."

"But you're not Indian. You don't know what it means. It was my duty as a husband to sleep with her. If I'd fulfilled my duty, she would have done hers. She'd have been a true wife and the children . . . None of this would have happened. They'd have been mine, some of them. And I'd have had my honor. Things wouldn't have gotten so far out of hand. If even one of them was mine. My God, it's gotten so complicated. I've completed my obligations as a father. Found them husbands and wives, paid their dowries. I did what had to be done. But it still doesn't change the basic thing. That they're his."

"As long as no one knows . . ."

"They don't know." Kady laughed suddenly, a miserable laugh. "It's all very Indian. You won't like it."

"Why do you keep saying that? I don't hate things that are Indian. They just frustrate me sometimes."

"It all comes back to secrets," Kady said. "They don't know their father. They assume it's me, and all they know is that, whatever I've done for them, I don't see them, have no interest in them, never have. They attribute it to my work, but when I approached Jiggie and made this bargain, I set in motion a whole abomination of things. Don't you understand? They're the victims. I've denied them the most important duty a child has: to honor and respect his father."

"Does it lessen your guilt to know Jiggie did the same thing?"

Kady didn't hear. "The child has to give obedience to his father, take care of him, and eventually, when he dies, the eldest son is the one who liberates his soul into the afterlife. I've violated all that. I've denied these people their true karmic role. They have no way to build their karma through a father."

"Maybe that's precisely their fate. You alone aren't responsible for it. And if you believe that about children, what do you think will happen to you if . . . well . . . you don't have a child to crack your skull?"

"There's that, too," Kady said, "but I don't care about that."

"Why not? I could give you a child. We could do that."

"You know you won't stay with me."

"You're the one who's not free. You won't leave Durr."

"And you won't stay if we're not married. I've always known that. I knew it at the airport. It's one reason I didn't want to have anything to do with you."

"And I've always known you wouldn't leave her."

"I can't," he said.

"I know. And I can't live here and have children and not be married. I can't be such an outsider. Not for the rest of my life."

"I can't divorce her. I won't do that to her. Oh, Feeb." He pulled her on the grass with him and lay on top of her. He started kissing her eyes, ears, cheeks, his hands holding her face. "But it's not the end," he said into her hair. "Not yet."

He held her so tight, it seemed he thought it was.


After a while he moved away from her and sat up. "Shall I tell you about the bargain now? How it affected everyone?"

"Yes."

"You're even caught up in it."

"Me?"

"And your father and Cully." Kady took a deep breath and seemed almost to hold it, a swimmer preparing for one high dive. "Jiggie made me give Louis the Shiva Nataraj," he said. "It wasn't a gift. It was a way for him to control us."

"And it was false, wasn't it?"

"How do you know?" Kady said in surprise.

"Because Louis moved it around the room and out in the hall. It was always in a different place."

"Cully said the same thing. That it moved."

"And you knew it was false."

"Of course I knew. Jiggie said he wanted me to give Louis something. I said what? He told me. Point-blank. That it was fake. I said I wouldn't. He didn't even bother to argue with me. Just left the room, told Shyam to set it up. Jiggie knew I had no choice. No choice at all, because I still wanted what only he could give me." He looked away from her, head in his hands. "Cully said the whole thing was one betrayal after another, and he was right. But it hurt me, too. Do you know how many times I went in your house all those years? Once, twice, maybe. That's all. I tried to pretend the Shiva didn't exist. I tried to blot it out of my mind, but how can you blot out the Shiva Nataraj? The dance of life?" He laughed derisively. "I tried to tell myself it didn't matter. That Louis didn't know, so it didn't matter. But it did. It was like the business with Durr. Everything was false. And secret. In the end Jiggie came to Delhi and went right over there and told him."

"That's why he was at the house."

"He told Louis to stop threatening him. Louis was saying he'd tell everyone about Durr. He wanted Jiggie to let me go. Jiggie didn't want to. He had refused me. I was going to leave anyway, but Louis started calling him and saying if he didn't let me go, he'd tell everyone about Durr. So Jiggie came up and told him what he'd do. No uncertain words. Told him Bhave worked for him. Told him Bhave made the Shiva. That it was fake. Do you know what Louis must have felt?" Kady bent over, his head almost to his knees. "Remember how he used to talk about it?" his voice hoarse.

He sat up, took a deep breath, and held it a second. "There's more. It gets even worse. After Jiggie left your house, Louis called me." Kady was looking straight at her. "I was in Deeg. Remember?"

"Yes."

"He knew I was there. But I didn't come to the phone. The bearers came up to the room over and over again, and said Guthrie-sa'ab was on the phone, 'Guthrie-sa'ab, sa'ab,' but I said no, I wouldn't talk to him. I couldn't do it. I just lay on the bed and wouldn't even open the door. I didn't know what on earth I could say to him. I was so ashamed I could die."

"And you think that was what made him so depressed and strange?"

"Of course," Kady said harshly. "What else could it do? Cheer him up? Of course it upset him. It destroyed him."

"You're not saying you're responsible for the accident?"

"Of course I was. Partly. I just lay on that damn bed. Kept looking at my watch. I don't know what I'd have done if . . ." He stopped.

"If what?"

"Shyam finally came up. That night. Woke me up. I told him to go away. It was the middle of the night. But he insisted. Told me Samiji was on the phone."

"Calling about the accident."

"Shyam said I had to come to the phone. Something was wrong. You see why I don't tell the truth about these things?" Kady shuddered. "I've told a million lies every day of my life."

"I think I can understand," Phoebe said tentatively.

"Do you? How can you? Jiggie is devilishly smart," he went on. "I'll give him that. Can you imagine what it must have been like for Louis? No money, no statue, drunk, his wife driving him slowly crazy, his prize possession false, and on top of that, I don't even come to the phone?"

"You have to let go of it, Kady. It's over."

390

"But what do *you* think? Don't you mind?"

Phoebe thought for a long time. "No," she said finally, "I don't. Not if you're telling me everything now. I can understand why you did what you did. It seems so long ago. Now it's just you and me."

"No," Kady said abruptly, his voice angry.

"No what?" Phoebe exclaimed.

"I haven't told you everything."

"My God, Kady. I can't stand this coming out in dribs and drabs. Either tell me flat out whatever you have to tell me, or that's it. I can't go on like this."

"I let Cully and Mirabai stay at the Garden House. They were there in May when you arrived."

Phoebe stared at him hard and then drew away. A long time passed. She fiddled with things on the ground, looked across at the distant mountaintop, tried all the while to adjust her mind again to incorporate one more set of facts and lies.

Finally she stood up. "Come on," she said. "We have to go back."

"What about . . . ?"

"We have to go on from here," she said. "I don't mind what you did about the Shiva, but I do mind you not telling me about Cully. I mind a lot, but I'll get over it. The thing is I do understand what you're struggling against. I don't particularly like it, but it means a lot to me that you finally told me the truth. I'm angry, and hurt," she said flatly, "but I don't take it personally. I guess that's why I can be so sanguine about it." She took his hand. "Come on," she said again. "I'll get over it."

"Cully won't. He was shattered by the information about the Shiva."

"You told him April first, didn't you."

"And then he went to Deeg to confront Attar Singh. He told him the truth, too. Then he ran away. I can't say I blame him, really, he felt completely betrayed."

"But why haven't you told me any of this?"

"I'm truly sorry, darling. First, it didn't even occur to me. I am so walled off, you can see that now, I couldn't break through. That was at the beginning. Then, you see, I was afraid to, afraid of what'd you think of me. Not very admirable, I grant you."

Phoebe squeezed his hand. "We'll work it out," she said.
"You sure?"
"We'll try. We'll find a way out somehow."


But he didn't say what happened to the Shiva Nataraj or tell
her he bought the Garden House twenty years ago to shelter it.

# ❧ 3 ❧

CULLY AND MIRABAI WERE HEADing south when the train stopped in Nagpur, the center of the subcontinent. Their destination was Madras and Trivandrum, due south. They were seated, third class reserved, waiting for their journey to proceed, when Cully suddenly jammed his finger down on a railway map. "We can go to Ellora," he exclaimed. "It's Shiva's home and it's not far away. I didn't realize how close it was."

They stayed in the station overnight, waiting for the next train to Ellora. They slept on the floor like everyone else. Mirabai was used to this by now, and as they lay down Cully whispered that he felt "really happy." She said she was, too, and they fell asleep holding hands.

The next morning they caught the train that headed west. At the little town near Ellora, Mirabai did what she always did nowadays. When they got off the train, she stepped down ahead of him, then reached back and took his hand. He needed help in the downward step. He had to know she was there, or else he got nervous. Recently, at Konarak after they left Calcutta and began the journey south, she left him to wander around the temple grounds. He stayed where she left him.

When she came back he was staring up at the great Wheel of Life, a circular carving that spoke of karmic truth, and shaking all over as if he were ill.

393

Mirabai didn't know what to do. He was sitting on a boulder, he hadn't seen her. She took one look at his face and felt for the first time the mad inner rush and chaos of who he was. That look only took a second, but she still had time to remember school-book pictures of skeletons and the nervous system, blood routes and the heart, and she took in his body not as it looked from the outside, khakis and a shirt, but as it was on the inside, everything pushing toward some horrible collision or stampede, but for the mystical, if fragile, order that somehow kept it still intact.

She started to call his name, run to him, but instead went slowly so as not to frighten him. She reached the rock, sat down, and put her hand gently on his back and left it there, heard him take a deep breath, without even looking at her, and begin to relax.

He gripped her hand, and as he let the breath out, she imagined it contaminated with all the toxins that commingled with his flesh and blood. "Breathe again," she whispered. He did, and she felt his tension ease, pounds of weight falling off as he adjusted to her being back. She pulled him in closer to her.

"You were gone so long," he said. "I didn't know where you were."

"You knew I'd be back."

"But I didn't know when."

"I'm here now and I won't leave you."

They sat in silence, her arm around his back.

Finally Cully said, "See that?" He gestured in the general direction of the intricately carved Wheel.

Mirabai looked. He slid off the rock, taking her with him, and went up to the Wheel, where he pointed to the exact intersection between one spoke and the outer rim. "See that?" he said, eager now.

"Yes."

"That's where I am. Right there exactly. See that spot?"

"Yes."

"I mean, exactly. Right there?"

"Intersections are bad."

"But do you see it?"

"They're endings. The flow is broken. Even the changing of seasons is dangerous."

"Well, that's where I am," Cully said, "but I'm headed there."
He pointed triumphantly toward the topmost spoke of the

Wheel. "That's where he is," he said powerfully. "Jiggie Deeg. And I'm going to be the one to bring him down. I'll do it for Louis."


Three months later Mirabai showed up at Kitty Chandradas' where Phoebe was staying. It was mid-November. The sky was heavy and white. There was a dense fog and the air was cold. The newspapers had asked people to contribute firewood and cooking oil so the poor wouldn't freeze to death, and Phoebe had told Tulsidas that morning to buy some wood and take it over to the collection point in Old Delhi. She said any little bit might help, but invariably there'd be word in the papers tomorrow of more deaths and malnutrition. Phoebe said it was all so damn sad and deep here in India, living itself a profound act of survival. Tulsidas came back and told her most of the people contributing supplies were the poor themselves. "Of course," she said. "The rich don't see it."

The bearer had made us a fire in the library and brought us tea with cardamom. She and I were talking. It was late afternoon. She was beginning to feel a whole lot better. She had found some nail polish and put it on. Now she held out her hand and asked me how it looked, shy, a child trying for the first time. But I could understand. A lot had happened.

Then the doorbell rang. I thought it might be Kitty herself, forgotten her key, so I went to the door, and there was Mirabai.

I knew her at a glance. She was only a little thing, standing pale and serious in the swirls of clouds. She barely reached my shoulder, and as the fog moved around her in great sweeping eddies, only her head stood out. She had big eyes, pale skin, wonderful lips, and thick black hair braided in a single strand that hung down her back. She wore a coat, scarf, sari.

"May I come in?"

"Of course," I said, catching a glimpse of her hand laden with a heavy emerald wedding ring. Chumpi, the servant, was standing farther down on the steps, a blanket wrapped around her shoulders.

"Daddy gave her to me as a wedding present," Mirabai said by way of explanation, and she came in, the lalli at her heels like a dog.

"May I take your coat?"

"Yes, please." Her voice was young and virginal, the singsong sound of girls in India who've been to private school and English is their mother tongue. "I know I'm not expected," she said, "but I'd like to see his sister."

She was taking off her coat, and I watched, fascinated. There was an aura about her. Her skin glowed, as if there were a light behind the surface, and she had a still and quiet confidence. The bearer came and she handed him her coat, turned to me. "Will you tell her I'm here? Please say I want to tell her what happened with her brother. It's my duty." And with that, she sat down in the waiting area and proceeded to remove first one glove, then the other, calm, relaxed, sitting perfectly straight.

"I'll go tell her."

The girl nodded. As though she were giving me permission to leave.


In August they got a room at the dak bungalow in Ellora. Cully sent her into town to buy the longest tape measure she could find, she told us in her little, girlish voice, and in the morning he took her to the caves. They started at the most distant site. Inside it was dark and shadowy, the only light came from the opening. He had her hold one end of the tape, him the other, and on their hands and knees they worked their way across the giant temple room that had been carved out of the interior of the hills, measuring.

He was the most intense Mirabai'd ever seen. He didn't even look at the carvings, just stayed close to the ground, pulling the tape its mere three feet at a time, wordless, methodical, keeping track of the numbers on a tablet. Statues lined the sides, carved by monks and religious wanderers eleven centuries ago. It was a peopled world inside these caves, it wasn't empty at all, but she knew that for Cully it was just himself alone and whatever was going on inside his head.

When they finished it was so late, they had to grope their way out, where it was cooler, if that's the word when the temperature's three digits high. Mirabai fell back against the hillside. "I can't do it again," she said. "Not even for you. I just can't."

The next day she waited outside the caves, sitting in the brush. Inside he had started drawing the statues. She didn't like it here. The land bore no resemblance to the land she knew up north. There was growth everywhere, bushes and high grass that reached to her thighs and waist and clung like thorns to her sari. She wondered if Cully was right, that the south where they were headed was another world, and this was a warning of how bad it'd be.

At dusk he came out. His knees were bleeding, his legs scratched, and he could barely stand the glare of the sky. "I didn't know if you were here," he said.

"Of course I'm here. I'll always be here."

Day after day he kept on with his drawing and measuring. She made him lunch and bought a pail for water. She nearly wept at the sight of him some days when blood trickled down his legs, his skin embedded with dust and flies, caked on, in the heat, like icing.

One night he sat outside the temple caves, exhausted, and pulled her toward him. "I have to talk to you," he began. "I love my father. I owe him this. Do you understand?"

Mirabai nodded.

"I feel like he's here with me." Cully nuzzled his face against her hair. "I think about him, remember him, feel close to him. He needs someone who doesn't let him down."

He talked about the caves, which were carved out of the hillside in the ninth century and meant to duplicate the mountain that lay thousands of miles away in the north of India and Tibet. That was Shiva's real home, he said, the real Mount Kailash on the top of the frozen world. That's where he lived when he wasn't visiting cremation grounds and burning sites, summoning his awful power to destroy things so that, miraculously, he could give them life again.

"Down here is the closest I've ever been able to get to him," he said.

"To Louis or the god?"

"To both."

"Do you worship Shiva, then?"

"Oh, no," Cully answered clearly. "But I feel him. He's my link to Louis."


Phoebe listened, transfixed. Her eyes never moved from Mirabai's face, and for much of the time she felt a sensational ache of jealousy.

397

Her yellow hair came down just below her ears by now, or at least parts did, the rest stuck up straight on top like a boy's, and the physical therapy had brought her arm back to normal so she could move it again. The doctor the other day said the inner wounds were probably just about healed by now, healed and sealed, as well as they ever would be, he'd said, and she had said, "That's all right. I don't want to be the same again. I want to be different."

Now she sat on the lounge chair listening to little Mirabai, an American in an English room with an Indian girl who spoke less Hindi than she, hearing this girl talk about the Lord God Shiva, who she knew less about than the American listening.

It was disturbing to Phoebe. No wonder she didn't know where she belonged, she thought to herself, India or New York. The talk of Shiva seemed intensely personal, he, her rival, with both her father and her brother.

When the girl excused herself to go to the bathroom, Phoebe asked breathlessly, "What do you think of her?"

"I like her."

"Do you think she'll explain why Cully changed toward me so much?"

"Ask her."

"I intend to."

The girl came back. She was so little, she did seem like a child, but the thick silk sari was a bright salmon color, and as she walked across the room, it rippled like a million lights and gave great depth to her. "Are you feeling better?" she asked, sitting down.

"Yes."

"I'm sure you'll get well. My grandfather says you're rather amazingly appealing. He knew I loved my dog," she added as an afterthought.

"What about your dog?" Phoebe asked, despite her desire to probe more serious things.

"I was more worried about my dog than anything else," the girl said. "Whether the lallis were taking care of him. Whether they let him sleep on my bed or shunted him out to the back, or killed him."

"Killed him?"

"Yes. Cully said they wouldn't. I said they would." The girl paused and her eyes went dreamy. "Cully loved how I loved my

398

dog. Even that I had a dog. It's unusual for an Indian girl, you know. I wanted to take him with us, but he said I couldn't. So I took a picture instead. Every night I kissed the picture. Then I asked Cully if he wanted to kiss it, too. He always said no. Then I kissed the dog once again and put the picture down." Mirabai paused. "He very much wanted his version of your father's death to be true," she said. "He loved the idea that your father was so upset about their fight that he crashed the car and died. It's very Indian, you know, to want to be on someone's mind when he dies. Because your last thoughts affect your next life, you know, and he believed they would be close in their next life."

"Did he lie to you about what happened with Anant?" Phoebe asked.

"No. He told me everything. He even told me he wanted to hurt my grandfather."

"Didn't that bother you?"

"No. It was between them. I understood. It had nothing to do with me."

Phoebe let it pass. "Did he tell you about your grandfather and the fake Shiva and what he made Kady do?"

"Yes. But I didn't believe what he said about Anant. He was too happy. We were both happy. Living in the Garden House. I was cooking. He was eating. When we went back to Deeg we were going to get married."

"Didn't you know he was sick mentally?"

The girl shook her head.

"I did," Phoebe said. "I always sensed it, but I denied it to myself."


Mirabai said that one night she and Cully sat outside on the veranda of the dak bungalow and talked straight through till morning. That was when Mirabai finally got it clear in her mind that one set of things had happened January sixth, twenty years before, and another, not so very different, happened April first and second.

She said that during that time Kady told Cully the truth about the Shiva Nataraj, Cully returned to Deeg to see Attar Singh, who was so old he knew Louis Guthrie himself and could tell him what had happened way back then. Then he went back to Delhi.

Where he found Anant.

## ❧ 4 ❧

He pressed the doorbell at Vishnu Bhave's. The grill was up and curtains were flapping in the breeze but no one answered. He peered inside. The heat of summer had already started, it was April 2nd, and when he stepped inside he felt the air dense and hot about his head. The place was empty. He was so disappointed, he pounded his fist against the wall and nearly burst into tears. "Dammit, Louis," he cried. "He's not here!"

Then he heard someone start laughing inside. He knew it was Anant and suddenly the fact that Anant was in one of the inner rooms of his father's house gave him a power over Cully that nearly made Cully gag.

He doubled over. His stomach was in agony. Anant started to laugh even louder, laughing because of him, Cully knew, and in frustration, he pounded on the wall, trying to stamp out the laughter, and the memories of Kady and Attar Singh too.

Inside, Anant began talking to him. "Cully-sa'ab," he said derisively. He sounded simple-minded, he always did. Cully felt full of the putrid stuff of Kady and Attar Singh's revelations, betrayal and confusion and, oddly, that Anant was retarded had always pleased him, but now it bothered him. It gave the man strength, the two of them more equal, Anant's imperviousness to reality eerie now when he spoke the awful words of truth.

400

"You are not worth a valuable piece of art," the man was saying. He was gaining steam, pushed on no doubt by his father's contempt for Cully too. Cully heard him moving in the kitchen. He was eating lunch.

Of course the Shiva was false, Anant was saying. The Mathuran horse was false too. He didn't deserve a real statue any more than his father had. Who did he think he was, to think he could have anything of value.

His Hindi words kept on coming. "Who are you? Nothing. The Shiva is fake. Your father was fake." Cully couldn't shut him out.

Now Anant was coming toward the door to the front room. He had stuck his fingers in tomato curry and red skins were all over his hands. Still blabbering about how his father had destroyed the Guthries, he stood in the doorway, the white floor matting between them, holding his hands out like a witch's teasing tools and grinning at the tall American.

Cully gagged. He smelled the curry. He lifted his hands in rage and started to yell.

Later he couldn't remember what he said, just that his yelling took over and Anant's laughter and talking ceased and that the sudden smell of India, cumin and coriander, tomato-based, brought out his anger as the words alone had not.

It all happened in seconds. Anant was standing there with his red hands, seemingly unaware of whatever it was he saw or didn't see in Cully's looming face. Then Cully, far bigger, was hitting him, harder and harder, delighting as the head flapped like a balloon and the laughter stopped and the hands dripped their tomato skins about the poor man's hair as he tried helplessly to protect himself from Cully's strength.

Maybe it was that, Cully said later to Mirabai. Maybe that touch of red inspired him and drew him on, made him hit Anant all the harder. Because he flung the dark brown head against the inner walls and doorways and felt powerful and creative, decorating spatially with his force. Then, one final touch before the wet of so much blood scared him into running, he clamped his hands about Anant's skinny brown neck and squeezed.

It gave him an exhilarating sense of power and fulfillment he'd never felt before.

Mirabai started to cry. "It was awful," she said, "but all he really wanted was to be loved. I gave him all my love, but it was never enough."

The girl's description reeled in Phoebe's mind.

"I even washed his legs and feet," Mirabai went on. "At Ellora they were covered with cuts, and I washed them with my bare hands."

Phoebe kept seeing the tomato skins and poor Anant.

"Cully said why bother to wash his wounds? If he'd been alone, he would have let them be. But I don't think any of this would have happened if he'd been alone. There would have been no Ladakh, no Ellora. We never would have gone to Madras."

"Are you implying it's because of me?" Phoebe cut in. "That I caused it? Caused the murder?"

"No, never that," Mirabai cried. "But he would have left Mr. Vishnu Bhave's house and gone to his apartment, or maybe to the Garden House. Maybe he wouldn't have been so angry. Maybe he wouldn't have run away. Or the police would have come and gotten him." She stopped. "Instead," she said sadly, "he remembered me. I think the idea of being with me brought him hope."

"Will you tell me more of the truth about my brother and me?"

Mirabai looked away.

"Please."

"You want to know more?" the girl asked.

"You know I do."

"There wasn't any running water in Ellora. We had a stall outside our room, with a hole in the floor."

"I don't care about that," Phoebe blurted out. Her impatience felt like Cully's nausea, rising.

"There was a well out back," Mirabai persisted, "Cully said it would go dry. I said maybe not, but he said all wells went dry."

Phoebe kept silent and tried to breathe. She felt her tension subside in the silence. Closing her eyes, her vision of Cully and the tomato skins receded and she saw little Mirabai and her salmon-colored sari. A surge of appreciation for the woman's gentleness swept through her. She took in a couple of deep breaths. "I'm sorry," she said, smiling a little. "I want to hear everything you have to say. Some of it's just hard for me. Do you understand?"

"I do."

"Please tell me whatever you have to tell me, but sometime please help me understand why he turned against me." Phoebe picked at her hair, all its different lengths. "I don't know what you're going to tell me," she went on. It could be awful. I have to be strong."

The girl looked away.

"Can I pour you some more tea?"

"No, thank you," said Mirabai.

"Biscuits? Samosa?"

"No thanks."

"I want to give you something."

"I love you," the girl said with the glimmer of a smile.

"You do?" Phoebe asked, aghast.

"You're Cully's."

"Hardly."

"But you are."

They were silent for a long time. Outside, the fog pressed in through the rhododendron trees and swirled up around the window like steam attracted to the heat. "He never even liked Samiji," Phoebe said. "Or this ayah we had. He never really liked anyone."

"Except you."

"Maybe for a while. But not even our grandmother." Phoebe stared at her hands, determined not to cry. "When we were little I used to come home late. I always tiptoed so I wouldn't wake my mother, but I was really worried about Cully. I always wanted to see him. I secretly wanted to wake him up and say, Hi, I'm home. Half the time he was asleep at the window, waiting for me. And I'd go over and kneel down beside him, put my face on his. He was about ten or twelve, maybe. Then I picked him up and put him in bed. Sometimes I got in with him and fell asleep beside him, holding him. I'd kiss his hair and pray he'd be all right." She looked up. "You see," she said, "I never thought he was going to be all right."

Phoebe stopped. Tears were running down her face. She brushed them away. "I miss him so much," she said. "Even now. Despite everything. He sent me a picture in New York, you know. It was him and Kady."

"Yes, I took it."

"They were on Raj Path and Kady's arm was around his shoulder. Remember?"

"Yes."

"At first I couldn't even look at the picture. I put it in a drawer. You know why?"

The girl shook her head.

"Because I felt left out. You've no idea. I stuffed it in down in a drawer and forgot it. I thought he was telling me, 'You don't count. You have been replaced.' And I was right. Only Kady wasn't the replacement."

"No," Mirabai said quietly. "I was."


Sometimes Mirabai would talk just so he could listen. Sometimes she sang, or held him, his head in her lap. When the monsoons finally broke and the rain poured in against them, they were huddled on the veranda in the dark, and it was the last time they were happy.

A few nights later he cried. She was rubbing his back and he buried his face in the bed. She pulled him across her lap like a child and he clung to her, weeping, tears flowing down his face. "You love me, don't you?" he said. "Please say you love me." She said she loved him, but he went right on crying.

The next day he slept. In the morning he went back out to the caves.

"He was on a pilgrimage," she told Phoebe. "We have this custom in India where you make a pilgrimage to a sacred spot. The harder it is to get to, the deeper it is for you in your spiritual journey inside. Sometimes, if there's no faraway place at hand, you can just walk round and around a temple instead, you know, round and around, a hundred times or more, or you can set yourself a difficult task to accomplish, one that has special meaning for you, and it all serves the same purpose. I think that is what your brother was doing. The true purpose of a pilgrimage in our country is to cleanse the soul and liberate it. I don't think he found that fulfillment with me or inside Ellora caves. I don't think with him it worked."

The day he announced they were leaving the caves to head on south to Madras, Mirabai said she knew she had to ask for help.

She found some paper and an envelope and wrote the only person she could trust.

The letter arrived at Viceroy Circle in New Delhi, where Durr saw it first.

"We couldn't have done it without Kady," the girl said. "It's as simple as that. He helped us with everything. When Cully wrote me in April, asking me to meet him in Agra, I called Kady to ask him what to do, and he said it was up to me. It was my life. He said my grandfather would understand. That he did the same thing once, what he wanted, even when it wasn't right, and it ended up affecting his whole life. I said running away could affect the whole family, and he said what my grandfather did affected the family, too, and that I shouldn't worry, the family wasn't my responsibility. It was my grandfather's. Later he helped me again. When my grandfather came to Deeg in June he had Kady call me. Kady didn't tell him where we were, with his friends in Ladakh. He said my grandfather wanted me to come home, but that I should do what I wanted, so I told my grandfather we wanted to get married and we wouldn't come home until he agreed. He said never." The girl paused. "Isn't this what Kady himself has told you?"

"Yes," Phoebe murmured. "Now tell me about Cully." She paused. "What did he say about me?"

"Nothing."

"But he must have."

"He didn't mention you."

"But he must have. You were together for months."

"Is it that you want me to try to remember things I can't remember?" the young woman asked.

"You've remembered everything else."

"I've tried my best."

"I'm his sister. I want to know what he said about me. I'm sure you—"

"I do understand," Mirabai said. "There was one time. It was when he first arrived in Deeg. He said he had a sister. He seemed to admire you. It didn't occur to me he didn't."

"What about after that?"

The woman shrugged.

405

"Nothing? Last summer he didn't talk about me?"

"No."

"What about when Kady's letter arrived? When he learned I was in India?"

"He never mentioned you," Mirabai repeated. "He never said your name."

"Wasn't he happy, or something, just a bit? To know I was here?"

Mirabai paused, and Phoebe understood. She was lying.

"Didn't he?"

"No." The young woman was quiet for a long time. "I would have to say it was the reverse."

"Reverse what? What do you mean?"

"He said he didn't like you being in this country."

"What do you mean, 'in this country'?"

"He said you had no right to follow him. He said you weren't on his side and that you had joined up with Kady and my grandfather against him."

" 'Joined up.' "

"We had our plans. We were going to stay at Kady's Garden House until my grandfather came around to our views. That's what we had arranged with Kady. After you came, Cully changed his plans. Then everything was to get away from you. Not even Kady knew where we were then. That's when Cully's sickness started."

"It didn't start because of one letter."

"It did. He changed after that."

"He'd already killed somebody by then, for God's sake! It wasn't my fault."

"He said he couldn't be in the same room with you."

"He wasn't in the same room with me."

"Or in the same city. Same country. He said he left America to get away from you because he couldn't live with you around."

"I don't believe you."

"He said you wouldn't let him eat things."

"What things?"

"Eggs, mayonnaise. I don't know."

"I told him about cholesterol. That's all."

"He said you wouldn't let him eat them."

"I bought them for him, for God's sake. I put them in his icebox."

"He said you were testing him. You wanted to see if he ate them."

"I didn't even know if he ate them or—"

"I'm sorry to tell you these things. I know you don't like what I say, but you are a very persistent person. According to our Indian custom, we wait for the things we want, and if they don't happen, then they don't happen."

"You're the one who ran away. Where's the waiting in that?"

"None. I did the wrong thing."

"You were just trying to get what you wanted."

"That was not the right thing for me to want. If I was meant to be with Cully, my grandfather would have arranged it or—"

"If hell freezes over, he'd arrange it."

"Or I should have approached him properly. I should have gotten more information. I should have done a lot of things, but not what I did. I should have waited."

"How long am I supposed to wait?" Phoebe asked, tired all of a sudden.

"Wait for what?" Mirabai asked.

"To know what I'm supposed to do. I have to decide whether to go to New York or stay here. How am I supposed to know what to do?"

"You have to wait longer."

"But I have waited."

"When the time's right, you'll know."

"But, please, explain it to me. I really want to know. How will I know what to do?"

"When it's right, you'll know," Mirabai said. "There won't be any doubt. Whereas five minutes before you had nothing but doubt."

"Then what's changed?"

"Maybe someone will say something. Maybe you'll think of something, something so little you'll barely notice, but afterwards everything's different. You'll know."

## ❧ 5 ❧

Two days after Cully and
Mirabai left Ellora, a detective working out of Bombay called
Attar Singh and said he had information someone of Cully's
description had been at the caves.

Attar Singh chartered a plane and went down. The bearer at
the dak bungalow told him about the American and the girl and
said that when they left, they were going to Nagpur, then heading south.

On September 1st, the wedding now eight days away, Jiggie
phoned Jasdan and directed him to tell the other side Mirabai
was sick.

Jasdan did.

The chief uncle countered by saying that in order for the
wedding to proceed, under the new conditions that were difficult all around, he wanted proof the girl didn't have something
contagious or unpleasant.

Jasdan had said, assuredly, he'd want the same thing, who
wouldn't? It was just that the girl was so truly comfortable up
in Mussoorie in the hills with her auntie who was taking care
of her that he didn't want to move her, and he, poor father, who
was about to lose a daughter forever, he was torn between wanting the girl to be with him and leaving her nice and happy

where she wanted to be. Of course, her mother was there, too, with Auntie in Mussoorie. She had gone up ages ago, because after all, he said, what girl doesn't want her mother beside her when she's sick and about to be a bride, and what mother doesn't want to be with her daughter?

The other side was unmoved. That was all very fine, they said, but they wanted proof of the illness.


Vishnu Bhave was not to be put off, either.

When he reached Benares he told Maharaj-sahib he wanted the American's life in exchange for his son, Anant.

Maharaj-sahib said how could he do that?

Bhave said he was concerned what the other side would do if they discovered what Jiggie had done some twenty-five years before and how Jasdan was not Maharaj-sahib's only son and how the line of Deeg could be threatened by children from a caste far lower than their own.


Bhave had already sent Phoebe a letter, care of Harriet MacDonald at the embassy. She forwarded it to Bhagwandas Road.

Why was she avoiding him? Bhave wrote, he who was so very good friend for her father?

"I am calling each and every week to get your address, and they are telling to me they do not know where you are. Do you think I am believing this, what they are saying?

"You must be knowing just one thing only I will tell to you. I can be finding you any time I am wanting. Are you not knowing this already? Are you thinking the one and only one reason I am not seeing you is because I am not knowing how to find you? That one simple person like yourself can escape from me?

"Instead it is only because I am occupied with some other program just now and have not made decision how to make use of you. But you, he, your brother, it is all same thing to me. I am not caring. I am not caring one bit. One or the other, you are same to me, exactly in every which way same to me. I am thinking only of my son and I am thinking if I am not finding one of you to make fair and equal exchange for my son, then I am finding other.

"One thing only. You must be believing that when I am

wanting you, I will be just right there, in your presence only. I will be looking at you and you will be looking at me, and you will not be once more able to avoid me. If you are wanting to go to the left, then I will be going to the left. If you are wanting to go to the right, then I will be going to the right. It will be just like that only."

In Kashmir, Kady told Phoebe there was even more.

He told her the Shiva Nataraj had never been sold.

He said he himself had bought it from her father's estate and put it in a house he had on the outskirts of Delhi. He said it was still there and that he'd shown it to her brother, and Mirabai, and that he'd written Cully there, at the Garden House, to say she herself had arrived in Delhi, on and on, more, how he'd telephoned them in Ladakh for Jiggie that night in Deeg, but Mirabai told her grandfather they wouldn't come home.

This time he said he told her everything.

Again Phoebe sorted out her response. She told him she didn't like his lies or his protective attitude toward her, or toward himself, or that he used things to shield himself from who or what he was. But she said her love for him was great enough to deal with this and that his increasing openness proved he was continuing to change.

Privately, however, Phoebe saw how encrusted were the lies and truths that peeled away from Kady Suraj. She knew that if she had her journey to make to get to him, this was his to get to her, through the layers of nearly geological encrustations of secrecy and resistance.

On an even deeper level, though, she knew it wasn't a matter of whether she liked or didn't like what he'd done, but how much her love could take. For a man she knew she couldn't marry, she didn't know whether love was worth the agony.

Oddly, she determined that one of the most disturbing things of all was what he revealed about the source of her money. That so much of it, hers and Cully's, had come from him and his purchase of the Shiva Nataraj.

She didn't know how she could adjust to the extraordinary complexity that underlay her life.

At the same time Cully and Mirabai arrived in Madras and took up residence in a three-story walk-up hotel not far from the downtown center.

Detectives were not that far away. They were fanning out across the south in cities hooked up with the railway line.

For the first time Jasdan and the others had a glimpse of hope.

The wedding was little more than a week away. All they needed was the bride.

On August 31st a plane was sent to Benares to get Maharaj-sahib Juggernathan Singh and bring him back to Delhi. It was a formal occasion. Jasdan Singh and Attar Singh were among the ones on board.

When they landed in Delhi, the runway at Palam Airport was crowded with officials, friends, and diplomats. Afterward they all went in to town, a cavalcade of cars, trucks, and taxicabs, and Deeg House was thrown open, just like the old days. Jiggie took the microphone set in place for him and announced the occasion was his granddaughter's wedding.

The bride herself was so traditional, he laughingly told the crowd, she wouldn't even come out of her hiding place with his sister up in the Mussoorie hills. But nothing would keep him away, he said.

The wedding was nine days off.

After that there were numerous affairs. Luncheons, dinners, one long tea, all to honor the other side. Deputy Home Minister K. T. Keshri Suraj's wife came to all events, inevitable, given the association between her husband and the host, and so too did dozens and dozens from the other side and anyone who was anyone.

And so too did the Delhi Police Commissioner.

The commissioner was a tall man, new to his position, and he didn't know Jiggie Deeg had long made use of Delhi police, since the days of Guthrie and Suraj and what they did on Golf Links Road.

So he was innocent when he considered himself lucky to be

right here in the slightly decaying, old stone mansion set in the English-Moghul design, walking in around the courtyards and the fountains.

The commissioner had no notion—nor did anyone else among the crowd, except the woman with the orange eyes—that Jiggie had arranged the whole thing, from first to last, three days' worth, just to placate the other side and involve enough people so that it was plausible to involve him, too.

And to see Durr, of course. Always Durr.

In Kashmir, it was September 3rd. Samiji appeared.

He was sitting in the doorway of the houseboat when Phoebe and Kady came home. He wore his khaki uniform, proper shoes for once, and when they came up the path leading from the road, he was sitting so tensely, Phoebe knew at a glance something was wrong. "Is Cully dead?" she cried out as he stood up and namasted.

Kady stared, his eyes gone cold as ice.

"What is it?" she said.

"Kumari-sa'ab Durr-sa'ab telling me bring tese tings from office," Samiji said to her. "I have sack, missus. See?" He held one up.

"Get over here," Kady said angrily, startling Phoebe with his tone. "Get off that boat."

"Soddie, sa'ab, not my fault, truly not."

"Get off the boat."

Samiji darted into the boat, disappeared, then reemerged. "Soddie, sa'ab," he said, "so, so soddie, truly soddie." He scurried across the boards to shore, passing them without a glance, then plopped down in the bushes where the Muslim family that owned the boat lived and ate.

Kady disappeared inside. She heard him in the bedroom.

She boarded the boat herself and went to the porch at the far end. She knew everything had changed.

A kingfisher was flying in low over the water. She watched it swoop down, swallow a fish, and she listened for Kady in the bedroom. She couldn't hear him. It was late afternoon. A muezzin was calling from a mosque nearby. This was the end. She knew it. The world had slunk in quietly and done its work,

Samiji its delegate. Dusk was coming, too. She could see the high pink-and-blue clouds that meant night was settling in over the valley of Kashmir. She wondered where the clouds had come from, pink and blue, little pieces of a boy and girl, Cully and herself. She felt Cully's presence. He was always close to her, but now she imagined him in her arms, a little boy, asleep. No matter that he didn't want to see her, she still loved him.

The continent was big enough for both of them, Phoebe thought, north, south, east, west, there was plenty of room. Dr. Sharma was in her mind, too. He had no face, just earrings like his bearer's, and she remembered Louis, too, with black patent-leather shoes and a gun.

Phoebe watched, the world pressing in on her. She knew she was adjusting to the fact that everything was over. She saw a heron flying south and thought her brother was somewhere in that direction, refusing to come to her.

She still couldn't hear Kady. The world had reached him, too, the future taunting both of them. She longed to grasp his hand, tell him if Durr had done it with Jiggie, she could do it with him, align her life with his. But it wasn't true. Maybe in America with an American. But not in India. She wanted to belong. She wanted it all locked up solid and real, with paper and pens and official stamps, total proof she, Phoebe, had a home where she belonged and a person to whom she belonged.


She found Kady in the bedroom. He was lying against the pillows, his eyes distant and unclear. "What are you doing?" she asked.

He held up a book.

"Reading?"

He nodded.

"What about Samiji?"

He shrugged, indifferent. "It's just office business. I'll see him later. Come," he said, standing up. "Let's have tea."

That night Kady didn't leave the boat and Samiji didn't board. Every time she woke up, she saw Samiji sitting in his spot underneath the tree, uniform, mustache, hair that was too long, a family of his own somewhere off in the village where he was born. She wanted to run to him, ask him what was happening, but didn't. She just watched him from her darkened window and wondered what he knew.

Why had he worn the red burgundy scarf twenty years ago? The Kashmiri scarf, so fine that Louis had bought it for himself? Why was he standing in the living room January 6th, with Kady and Jiggie Deeg, when he was never meant to leave the kitchen or the hall?

And why, if Jiggie Deeg had come to Jumna Road once, did he come back a second time?

And why, most of all, why did Kady distance himself from her the second Samiji appeared?


The next morning Samiji was gone.

The bearer said he'd gone to the airport. Phoebe was relieved until she found his sack. It was on Kady's side of the bed.

It held two envelopes, both empty, the letters gone.

She looked for the letters in Kady's drawers and the pockets of his clothes, under the pillows and behind the curtains, even in the trash and the shallow waters of the lake, but she couldn't find them.

Both envelopes had been sent to "K. T. Keshri Suraj" at his Delhi home. One was postmarked Ellora and written in handwriting she didn't know, a schoolgirlish kind of script.

The other was from her brother. The postmark said Madras.

Up near the stamp on one was a message written in Hindi. She took it to the Muslim bearer and asked him what it said. Kady was asleep in the bedroom. The bearer said he couldn't read Hindi or even Urdu. He took it to a friend and then came back.

He told her it wasn't much.

"But what's it say?"

"It says, 'Shall I give him what he asks? Have Samiji tell me what to do.'"

"But who wrote it?" Phoebe asked. "Who's it from?"

"It's signed with a woman's name," the Muslim said. "A Kashmiri name. You know it?"

Yes, Phoebe said, she did.

Durr.

❧

414

She put the envelopes back in the sack, and later, when Kady woke up, she sat beside him on the bed and asked what Samiji wanted. She traced her finger up along his face and around the outlines of his mouth.

He barely looked at her. "Office stuff," he said again. "It's nothing."

She asked why Samiji had gone, her finger running down his arm to the tip of a finger, then back up to the wrist and down again to another fingertip. Then she went to his breastplate and the chest, did the same thing there, moving out along each vertebra until she reached his pants. He looked at her.

"I told him to visit his village," he said, and put his hands on her arms to encourage what she was doing. Her fingers kept on moving down. "I told him to take some time off." He leaned back on the bed, his mouth open, and started to take off his clothes. Phoebe kept her fingers working on his body and thought about how this business with the letters was the very last lie that she could take, the very last one, but how right now, this very minute, she would get exactly what she wanted.

One last time.


The next day she told him to go fishing without her, that she wasn't in the mood, and he set off with a boatman in a shikara headed toward the forest streams.

She stood on the porch and watched them disappear, wondering if he would come back, know he shouldn't leave her alone, not today of all days. But he did, so she went inside and packed.

She told the Muslim to give him a letter and tell him she had seen the envelopes Durr had sent. Then she went to the airport.

"Kady," the letter said. "There's no point in staying to talk to you. You'll just charm me again, or try to, and whether that would keep me here with you or not, I don't know. I'm afraid it might, so it's better this way. I'm off. Samiji and the letters are the last straw. I can't do it anymore. Know you're not confiding in me. What else have you kept from me? Anything important? I can only imagine.

"I've spent a lot of time the last few weeks trying to understand your lies. I really have. I know they're part of all you're trying to shed in order to become a different person, and I know they're hard to give up because they're part of what you've been,

415

but I don't like them. They don't make a very good basis for a relationship.

"If you still think you're trying to protect me with them, first, they don't protect me, and second, that's not what I want. I've never wanted to be protected, although I know I haven't always wanted to face things and I've taken my own sweet time dealing with things emotionally, but the fact remains, I am dealing with them now and I want the truth.

"It's time for me to do it by myself. Whatever 'it' is. Sort things out. Learn the truth. If there's any 'truth' out there to learn. But just go out and do it on my own. Understand myself.

"I do love you, though. That's the problem. I love you very much, more than I've ever loved anyone in my life."


On the plane, she was oddly calm. Everything seemed clear. She was going to find Samiji. Start there. He would tell her something. Then she'd follow it where it went, "the werry river," as he would say.

She was struck, though, heading south, by what she now knew about her brother and her father. They both had their false statues, and both their lives were twisted up with Jiggie Deeg and his onetime, part-time, full-time dazzling enigma of a protégé, whose allegiance was perpetually and endlessly unclear.


When she got to Delhi it was hot and humid. Steam was rising off the pavement and mosquitoes were omnipresent. It was perfect, she thought, the real world in full force. She went to Bhagwandas Road. There was no electricity or running water in the house, and before she even got the pails to take a bath or wash her face, she did what Chumpi told her to do.

She sat down.

Chumpi gave her the letter from Vishnu Bhave, which she stuck in her purse to read later, and the day's paper.

Chumpi had opened it to an inside page and folded it so that a single item had some prominence. It was so small, Phoebe might never have seen it.

FOREIGNER WANTED IN MURDER, the headline read.

The story was two sentences long.

The police had issued a warrant for the arrest of Cullen Guthrie, American, of Chandni Chowk, Delhi, in the May second murder of Anant Bhave.

The deceased lived in Tees-he-zari District, Delhi.

Phoebe stared at the paper. For the first time she knew that Cully was a murderer. Not a doubt in her mind.

## ❧ 6 ❧

PHOEBE RAN TO HER ROOM AND
sat on the end of the bed. "Please," she whispered, panicked, "let
Cully be all right." She felt she had to protect him, but she didn't
know how. She visualized Cully in Vishnu Bhave's house, ex-
ploding in anger, not against herself or Louis, as he should have
done, but against someone whose only sin was to have the very
thing he wanted most. "Damn you, Louis," she said aloud.
"Damn you."

She pressed her hands against her temple. "Please," she whispered, "let me know what to do."

Finally she got up and went out in the foyer, newspaper in
hand. Chumpi was sitting against the wall. "Do you know
where Samiji is?" Phoebe asked.

The woman shook her head.

"Do you know where Maharaj-sa'ab is?"

The woman shook her head.

"But he's here, isn't he? He came to Delhi, didn't he?"

Chumpi didn't answer.

"Didn't he?" Her voice was rising.

"Is possible."

"Why can't you tell me?" Phoebe yelled. "You won't betray
them by doing that."

Chumpi looked away.

418

Phoebe told her to get Tulsidas and bring him back.

"Why for?" Chumpi asked, sullen.

"Because I said so. That's why."

"What are you going to do?"

"I'm going to the police and then I'm going to find Samiji. You can tell them that. Tell Jiggie. I don't care who knows what I'm doing. Tell Jiggie I'm not afraid of him."

As soon as Chumpi left, Phoebe went to the desk in the dining room and sat down to use the phone. Her heart was pounding. She called Nasrut Sardar in Tees-he-zari Police Station.

A man in his office said he'd gone to Calcutta to take care of his mother.

She asked when he was coming back. He said he didn't know, "maybe one, two weeks, months."

"Do you know anything about the Anant Bhave murder case?"

"Why not?"

"Do you know why they put out an arrest warrant now?"

"I am not at liberty to say."

"But do they have a lot of manpower assigned to it?"

"I am not at—"

"But do they?"

"What is this case you mention?"

"You don't know anything about it, do you?" Phoebe said, and she slammed the phone down. Then she called Harriet.

Harriet said the embassy had nothing to do with murder. It was "strictly an internal matter. It's up to the Indians."

"How much trouble d'you think he's in?"

"It's hard to say. They'd have to find him first."

"But they will," Phoebe said. "I know they will. The way he looks, he couldn't hide. Not if the police really wanted him. That's what I want to know. How much they want him."

"It must be bad if they put out a warrant."

"Not necessarily," Phoebe argued. "It could be a pro forma thing."

"It's certainly bad if they get him. Indian jails are among the worst in the world."

"But maybe it's not a big case," Phoebe said. "It was only two sentences. It didn't say anything about him working for Jiggie Deeg. There was no mention of Vishnu Bhave, Kady, anything."

"Do you want me to get you a lawyer?"

"No. If it's not a big case and they don't have a lot of manpower on it, maybe Cully can just disappear."

"But he can't leave the country," Harriet said. "They check passports on this kind of thing. Although I suppose he could get out another way. People certainly do. He'd only need a boat."

"Can you find out how big a case it is? I know Jiggie's behind this."

"I already planned to, but there's no reason the police'll tell us anything. You have to realize that. Not without a personal contact, something behind the scenes."

"Does anyone in the embassy have a contact?"

"You. You have the best."

"He's in Kashmir. Can you do it?" Phoebe pressed.

"I'll certainly try. But it may take some time. None of us knows the police. They're a remote bunch. Difficult. But calm down. Nothing's happened yet."

"I can't just wait around. I have to find out what this means for him."

"There's nothing you can do. You have to be patient."

Phoebe sat at the desk and imagined Kady on his way back to Delhi. She could call him, he could find out anything. He could probably even get Cully off. Or Jiggie could. You could do anything here with money and connections.

In the end she went to the kitchen, where Chumpi had filled some pails with water, and, taking one, went in the bathroom and washed. She took a while. Then she dressed as elegantly, if simply, as possible, skirt, blouse, hair up on her head, earrings dangling at her ears.

She looked good.


Police headquarters were located in a pale gray building in a corner of New Delhi not far from Connaught Place. The commissioner was on the second floor. Phoebe told his secretary she was a friend of Jiggie Deeg's.

The woman told her she'd have to wait, but the commissioner came right out and ushered her in. He was obsequious, took her hand, and complimented her on her looks.

She told him who she was and said she wanted to know what

new information had tied her brother to the Tees-he-zari murder, why an arrest warrant was put out now when it wasn't before.

"Did Deeg-sa'ab send you?"

No, she said, but Jiggie told her how helpful the commissioner had been to him.

This seemed to please the man. "Then I'm at liberty to tell you," he said in a low voice. "Frankly, we have no new information on this killing. I am sorry for your brother. I am just trying to help Maharaj-sa'ab with his most difficult situation. He has so much feeling of kindness and respect for this one Vishnu Bhave, I am making decision to put out this one warrant as my personal and special effort to help my good friend help his good friend Bhave with his tragedy. It is like that," the man said, straightening up. "We must help our friends, isn't it?"

"But Maharaj-sa'ab doesn't want any publicity about the murder. It might reveal my brother's connections to Deeg and embarrass the family."

The man looked disturbed. "This is true," he said. "But Mr. Jiggie Deeg has some problems with this Mr. Bhave, and this Mr. Bhave has some very strong concerns about your brother. Maharaj-sa'ab is trusting me with his confidence," he said proudly, "and with his encouragement, I am seeing it as my role to help by issuing a werry small and not werry interesting warrant. We are both hoping, Mr. Jiggie Deeg and I, this will make Mr. Bhave happy."

"Does this mean the case doesn't have any priority?"

The commissioner shrugged. "My people in Tees-he-zari have it," he said. "I do not know what they are doing."

"I know you don't care about my brother. Why should you? But I do. Are a lot of people trying to find him? That's what I want to know."

"I have no idea what they do in this Tees-he-zari. I am sorry, but you are asking a lot of questions." He stood up.

Phoebe stood up, too.

"I can only tell you this, missus. This Mr. Deeg-sa'ab's concern for his friend Mr. Vishnu Bhave is so great, I am happy to do him this one small favor."

❧

Outside, she found a man with a cart selling tea. She bought a glass and sat down on the steps of the building. She told herself she had to think, otherwise she wouldn't do Cully any good. She put her handkerchief in her tea and proceeded to wash her face with it.

She bought another glass and a pakora, but the pakora was so old that she didn't dare eat it. She handed it to a beggar. Another beggar showed up and another. She gave them money and was about to give them even more when she remembered that not all Indians were as corrupt as the man upstairs, not as indifferent as he was, either, and she suddenly began looking for a taxicab.

But she couldn't find one, so she got a cycle rickshaw and told the pedaler to go to Old Delhi, to Tees-he-zari Station.

He stopped in the middle of the street and looked back at her. "Tees-he-zari?"

"Yes."

"You don't want to go there, memsa'ab."

"Yes, I do," she said, wiping sweat off her face. "It's all right."

He shook his head.

"I'm expected. Really."

"Is not any place for—"

"Really."

"My one cousin went there and he never came back."

"I have an appointment."

## ❧ 7 ❧

TEES-HE-ZARI WAS A LONG LOW
building, police, courts, and jail all in one, set back behind a
wall. The streets outside were clogged with people. Lawyers
were dressed in black. Most of the others were barely dressed
at all, they were so poor. There was a little parking lot in front,
but it was so dense with cars and rickshaws the driver had to let
her off a block away. He asked did she want him to wait? She
said no.

He asked did she want him to come in with her? She said no,
and he said not to make anyone angry, because they kept you
there, people got lost that way.

She headed in through the crowds, but when she turned back
she saw him sitting on the wheels of his contraption watching
her.

The sun was beating down and the humidity felt near as high
as the temperature. She couldn't even get in the building at first.
The entrance was so crowded with people coming and going,
some not moving at all, determined to wait right there, she had
to clutch her bag and jab with her elbows to carve a path. She
had planned to ask who was in charge, but she felt dwarfed by
the mob, and any preference she might get due to sex or color
meant nothing at all, the struggle was so extreme.

Suddenly she burst through and got into the building itself, only to feel abruptly plunged into the inner-core maelstrom of the universe.

The place was horrible.

She could hardly breathe or see. It was like the insides of a beehive that had decomposed. There were people everywhere, walking, sitting, eating, huddled on the floor, the ground so alive she tripped, legs and arms beneath her, lawyers and their suppli-cants. Everything was colored golden brown, not a hint of light, bulbs so low she had to squint. Sweat was stinging at her eyes, and the stench so great, urine and the body parts, she thought she couldn't stand it. The place seemed not just filthy but an-cient, and she imagined that centuries of life had compacted down to produce this awful alchemy of the so-called lower courts of justice.

Corridors stretched up and down the building like strands of dirty yarn, offices, courts, police, and cells on the sides, and everywhere noise echoed, a million hapless souls. Screams ema-nated literally from the walls, the stones themselves alive in anguish, and the thought of how much worse the jails and cells would be, sunk away somewhere inside this maze, was so horri-fying to Phoebe, she imagined death far better.

She came to a single window carved in the wall and stopped to look outside. Across the inner courtyard there were dozens of windows with thick crossbars. It was the jail. Scores, hun-dreds, of naked male arms flailed out in the sunshine, the men inside urging their extremities alone to make some desperate escape from this hell where they were caught.

Phoebe gasped. She felt perilously akin to them. The compari-son did not seem irrational. They could hold her here in Tees-he-zari, force her to help them until they found her brother.

She kept walking, looking for someone in the crowds who seemed in charge or a sign that spelled out "Homicide." There were almost no women. Officials were everywhere, police or prosecutors, more like military men to her with their khaki uniforms and hard block shoes that looked like weapons in themselves. One kick would stun and bruise. But the guns were the worst, at their waist or in their hands. Even the truncheons seemed huge, whole branches of trees that had been molded down to fit a hand. It didn't take much to imagine the limitations of English law or how brutality could be unleashed; just shut the door and let it swing.

The brown walls stank and dripped with some mixture of humidity and excretion. She was wary of everyone. She'd never felt this way before. In America there was invariably a face that promised warmth or recognition, and in India it was the same. There might be menace of a cosmic kind, life as fragile as a breath of air, but the people themselves were rarely the culprits.

Here it was different. There was no privacy, hostility everywhere, no allies, not for anyone, and in her female whiteness she felt acutely vulnerable against this dark swarm of male life.

She slumped to make herself less conspicuous and kept on going. She peered into all the open doors and thought the files almost worst of all. There were stacks of them everywhere, six, twelve feet high, thin manila things, papers sticking out. She saw them as so many helpless lives, lost on tops of tables. The looks that came back to her were menacing and cold, men staring at her not with interest or sexuality, but power. It was so disconcerting Phoebe never stopped to ask her way or get directions.

She just kept heading upward, assuming she'd eventually find a chief or boss. That some rooms were courts where the spoken tongue was English and lawyers wore British wigs was no relief from tension and hostility because there was barely a word she understood, and it only increased her impression that in here, at the core of the earth, there was nothing to trust or rely upon.

She wished she had Tulsidas with her, but she kept on going, hall after hall, floor after floor, an hour must have passed. Despite her anxiety, after a while Phoebe began to realize that, in truth, she was remarkably unafraid.

Intimidated, yes, but that was almost all.

The top floor brought a change.

The offices were slightly bigger, the smell a little less offensive. She chose one that looked the most important, it certainly was the biggest and least crowded, and she paused before it, trying to summon, not courage, but a message that would work.

A swarm of people clustered outside the doorway. They all had pieces of paper in their hands and were waving them into the room to get attention. Phoebe pushed her way through them and went inside.

Instantly the occupants looked at her, clerks and two officials, their eyes like darts that hit the mark, pinning her to the wall.

"What on earth are you doing here?"

She couldn't tell who'd spoken. The two officials were on opposite sides of the room, both seated at desks they dwarfed, the circumference of their chests so big they looked like extensions of the desks themselves. They were loaded with medals, but the power of their presence alone proclaimed their importance more than any decoration.

Two clerk-chaprassis, cowed and half their size, moved files back and forth around the room like some human conveyor belt.

The windows were open, but the room stood dark and airless and dirty. A fan slogged above. Files were piled up along the walls.

"I want to talk to somebody in charge," Phoebe said clearly, and looked back and forth between the two men, realizing the one with more medals was very odd. He viewed her with the most interest, but she could barely face him without grimacing.

He had strange skin that was shiny and smooth as glass, and he had no eyelashes. The other one just looked mean, a heavy mustache and big eyebrows that slashed across his forehead.

"I said, What on God's good earth are you doing here?"

It was the one who had no eyelashes who spoke, but then, with one long final look, he just lowered his head and went back to work.

Relieved, Phoebe focused on the one with the mustache.

The people at the doorway had stopped waving their papers. A clerk brought her a chair but set it back against a wall, out of the line of traffic. Maybe he knew something because as soon as she sat down, three officers pushed their way through the doorway and strode into the middle of the room, dragging a man in handcuffs.

The man with no lashes and the strange skin told the prisoner to stand up and ordered the men to take off his handcuffs. Done, the officers started talking so fast and loud, she could barely understand, except to know they were making a report.

Abruptly Phoebe stood up. She didn't want to wait, and besides, she knew if she did, she'd lose whatever advantage she had.

She made her way around the group to the mean-looking official with the mustache. "I need some help," she said.

The room suddenly went silent. The man didn't say anything.

"You have a murder warrant out against my brother. I saw it in today's paper. I'd like to know more about it. If it's possible for you to talk about it, that is." She spoke clearly and slowly.

426

"I know you don't usually discuss these things, but I'm worried about him." She paused. The man seemed irritated but slightly baffled, as though he'd never met a woman before. "His name is Cully Guthrie," she went on. "It's the Anant Bhave case. I'd feel better knowing more about the situation."

The man narrowed his eyes impatiently.

"It was in today's paper," she went on. "Look." She brought the paper out of her bag and put it on his desk.

He glanced down at it, then back at her.

"Do you know the one I'm talking about?"

No response.

She shuddered. "I'm trying to . . ." Her voice petered out. The fan circled slowly above. Sweat was slipping down her face. She ignored it. "Do any of you know about the case?" She looked around. "Can you suggest where else I could go?" she asked no one in particular.

Then—she felt it before she even saw it happening—the ugly man stood up. Slowly he rose to his full height. He towered over her. She felt physically overwhelmed. He simply stood there, silent, announcing his command.

Phoebe turned to face him squarely. She realized, somehow, that he'd been aware of her all along, even when he was dealing with the other people. She saw scars running down his neck into his chest. They looked like giant worms. It reminded her of Jiggie Deeg. His hands were on his hips, the hands scarred, too, two fingers gone, and his hair grew far back from his forehead.

Involuntarily she turned away, looked down at the prisoner, then back at the man.

His eyes were like dark grapes. He didn't say anything, just pinned his gaze on her and didn't move. She didn't know why. He was about her age, he had clean fingernails—were they polished?—hands the size of baseball mitts, but an expensive watch and a uniform so perfectly pressed he almost looked like a gentleman. Without lashes, though, his eyes seemed not only naked but merciless. She'd never seen anyone so ugly.

"How may I help you?"

His voice was surprisingly normal, the accent English and refined. She was taken aback. She willed herself to seem calm, knowing he'd been taking the measure of her and she had to maintain whatever it was that had gotten his attention. "There's a warrant out for my brother's arrest," she said. "I saw it in this morning's paper. I want to know more about it."

"What about it?"

"As much as you can tell me."

"Are you here to tell me he's innocent and to let him go?"

"Do you have him, then?"

"Is that what you want to know? If we have him?"

"No, I want to know about the case in general. I don't know if he's innocent or not. I don't even know where he is."

His face was completely expressionless.

"Do you have him?" she repeated.

He didn't answer. His dark eyes didn't move off her face, as if completely immune from any social restraints against staring, and she imagined that whatever had given him the scars and malformation had freed him up from everything else as well. She felt intensely uncomfortable. "I told you what I want to know."

"If you're not going to beg me to let him go, then why don't you say you'll take us to him?" The man paused. "Try that," he said. "That's what people usually do. Say you'll do it in return for leniency."

"I just want to know about the case," Phoebe said. It seemed vital he understand her. "I can't take you to him because I don't have any idea where he is. Except I don't think he's in Delhi anymore."

The man still hadn't moved his eyes off her.

"And I'm not here to beg for anything, except maybe information, and I don't think I'm actually begging for that. I'm just asking."

"Nor do we," he said.

"What?"

"Think he's in Delhi. There was a sighting in Nagpur."

"Nagpur? The last I heard he was in Ladakh."

"He has friends there, I suppose? In Nagpur?"

"Not that I know of."

"I want to find him," the official said. "Most urgently."

"I understand that. But I don't know where he is."

"It means nothing to me that he's American or has a sister or important friends. I know all about these friends, but I don't care. He murdered someone most viciously. That's all that counts down here. No one can do anything to me anymore. As

428

you might imagine," he added dryly, "I am not so easily intimidated."

"But I can't help you," Phoebe said. "I don't think I would, even if I could. But I can't anyway, so it isn't a question. You can help me, though," she emphasized. "I've been here three and a half months. I've been looking for him. I knew about the murder, but I didn't think you had a case against him. Do you know very much about it?"

The man shook his head, but she couldn't tell from the way he did it if it was a yes or no or maybe.

Suddenly one of the officers in the middle of the room started talking. The official waved the group of them away and turned back to her. The men were gone. "He is your older brother or your younger brother?"

"I'm thirty-six," she said. "Is that what you want to know?"

"I want to know where he is." The room was quiet. The two clerk-chaprassis had gone, too, and now the other official left as well. Phoebe realized it was just the two of them now. "I want to know how serious it is."

"Is murder not serious to you, then?"

"Of course it is," she said, "but I want to know how serious police interest is in his case."

"It's very serious. Do you think it would be anything else?" He started tapping on a low stack of files on his table, and suddenly Phoebe knew Cully's file was among them, Cullen Llewellyn Guthrie. She stared at the pile. It was the closest she'd come to him so far.

"Yes?"

She looked up, scared by her knowledge Cully was so close.

"What are you afraid of?"

"Nothing." She blinked. He was just across the desk from her.

"I can see you are afraid."

"It's those files."

"What about them?"

"You have Cully in there, don't you."

"Yes. Right on top."

Phoebe felt very vulnerable.

"So your younger brother is a murderer," he said.

"I don't know that."

"I do."

"You don't have proof. Nasrut Sardar said there was no evidence against him and I went to the police commissioner this morning and he said there was no evidence."

"What else did he tell you?"

"He didn't," she said. "I want to know what it means."

"What what means? Are you always so confusing?"

"That there's an arrest warrant against him," she said. "Does that change everything?"

"Change what?" His eyes still never moved from her.

Phoebe didn't feel naked or humiliated, just challenged. She was conscious of this as one of the most difficult moments in her life. She had no idea what was at stake. She stood up straighter—saw he noticed—and summoned everything she had, but in his relentless gaze she felt her hair wet around her neck and her blouse clinging to her back. Moisture ran between her legs and her sandals stuck to her feet. She suddenly felt dirty and tired, stripped. "I just want to know if you're using a lot of manpower to find him." She listened to her voice sound weaker and knew the intensity had gotten to her.

"Is that what the police commissioner said?"

"He said he wasn't involved. He said you handled it here at Tees-he-zari."

"Why do you ask all these questions?"

"Why do you?" she challenged directly, but without vigor.

"Answer me."

"Because I want to know."

"Why didn't you stay in your hotel and call someone? Call the embassy. Call your friends. Get them to ask?"

"I told you. Because I wanted to know."

"But why did you come here?" he pressed. "Here."

"I told you," she repeated, but suddenly she knew why he was bothering with her so long. Because he was interested. Because . . .

"People never come here. So why did you?"

"People come all the time," she said, pointing toward the people outside lying on the floor.

"But not people like you," he said. "Why did you think you could get anything accomplished here?"

"I didn't think that. I just wanted to find out more, and I thought this was the only way to do it."

"He's a murderer."

"He's my brother."

"Why do you want to know about manpower?"

"Because it will tell me what chance he has of getting caught. If he gets caught, I'm afraid he won't let me know." Phoebe heard her voice running ahead of her, saying things she hadn't known she felt. "That's why. He won't tell me. He won't contact me. Can you? That's what I want. Can you make sure you tell me if you catch him? Shall I write my name and address down on a piece of paper?"

Her voice petered out altogether. She clutched her face with her hand, suddenly afraid she was going to cry. "He's very angry," she murmured.

"What?"

"I said he's very angry at me."

"Talk louder. Do you think it's easy to hear in here? Do you think this is a drawing room or something?"

That was preposterous. Phoebe turned away. What was he doing? Her mouth was dry and she wanted to sit down.

"I'm talking to you."

"I know that." Her back ached and her head hurt. She felt like she was being interrogated.

"Who is this brother?"

"I told you. He's Cully Guthrie. The one in the newspaper, the one—"

"I know who he is. He killed Anant Bhave. I asked who is he."

What was he doing with her? What did he mean, 'drawing room'? A man like that didn't visit drawing rooms. People would run and hide. She brushed her hands over her face and hair. There were plenty of disfigured people in India, but they were all in the streets. You never met one up close. Even Jiggie was nothing like this. This man seemed impenetrable and alien, and he made her feel nothing in India was what she thought it was. She felt intensely that Tees-he-zari was the pit of the universe and he its spokesman and commandant.

But for all that, Phoebe had the overpowering desire to ask him why he spoke such good English and why he talked of drawing rooms. "He's my brother," she cried out. "What else can I tell you?" She started to shiver. Her extraordinary arrogance in coming to Tees-he-zari stunned her. "He studies art history," she murmured, almost stuttering now. "I wish he didn't. I wish he'd come back to New York and be with me."

"And who are you?"

Suddenly Phoebe smiled. Inexplicably she relaxed so much she let her head fall down to her chest. "I'm nobody," she said. "Nobody."

The man didn't move an inch, but Phoebe knew incontrovertibly he was surprised by what she'd done, her smile and even the small collapse.

"Nobody's nobody," he said. "Not even here. Stand up straight."

"Can I sit down?"

He went over to the chair and held the back for her.

"Thank you," she said, sitting. "Thank you very much." That's when she realized that for him, just like her, something was going on in here that had nothing to do with Cully Guthrie or a murder case.

"Please answer me," he said. "Who are you? What do you do?"

"I work," she said. "I live in New York. I came here to find Cully. He was missing. I'm his only relative, you see. We're orphans, and I was worried about him. I still am."

He poured a glass of water from the pitcher on his desk and handed it across to her.

"Oh, thank you." She drank it although it was nearly the color of tea and put it back on the desk.

"Not afraid of germs?"

"You can't be afraid all the time."

"Just sometimes?"

"Yes, sometimes. I was born in India," she added without thinking.

"Do you speak Hindi, then?"

"Not as good as your English. Please, will you just tell me if it's an important case? That's all I want to know. So I can calculate what his position is. What might happen to him. Then I won't bother you about anything else."

The man sat down at his desk. He started leafing through the file.

She felt a change come over him.

"Why do you expect me to tell you the truth?"

It must have been a burn, she thought, looking at him. Some terrible fire. She wondered if his skin had lost its sense of touch and what it'd be like to feel it.

"Answer me."

432

She jumped. "I'm sorry. I got distracted."

"I can imagine."

The grapelike eyes looked at her, and she realized he knew exactly what she was thinking. She gave him the hint of a smile. "What was the question?"

"Forget the question." He went back to the files. "It was a fire," he said then, not lifting his head.

Phoebe held her breath.

"I was eighteen."

"How awful." She spoke slowly. "Did your whole body burn?"

"No. Some good parts are left, what one might call important parts."

She couldn't believe what he was telling her. This seemed the most intimate conversation she'd ever had. "My parents died in a fire, too," she said. "I was sixteen."

He cocked his head, interested.

"I have their death certificates. I'm trying to find out what happened. So I can forget about it, I think."

"I can tell you what it was like," he said. "It hurt."

"But at least you didn't die."

"No," he said, but his tone suggested there was some doubt.

"What happened?"

"It was a house."

"Were you going to school, then? Did you have an education? Is that why you speak such good English?"

"You answer my question," he said. "Then maybe I'll answer yours." He sounded almost seductive.

Phoebe was spellbound. There was moisture all over her body, armpits, legs, vagina, everything awash in sweat and dirt, and she thought that even Kady had never seen her as dirty as she was right now.

"Answer me," he said again, with the same hint of softness.

"What was the question? I'm sorry, I keep thinking about you."

"I asked you why you expect me to tell you the truth."

"Because telling the truth is no easier and no harder than telling a lie." He didn't seem so ugly anymore. "And because the truth means a lot to me. I believe in telling the truth. It represents someone's effort to be honest and communicative."

The man's hands lay like plates on top of the files, dozens of lives at his fingertips. He didn't move, just looked at her, impenetrable, and she was conscious of looking back. But he still didn't seek out anything but her face. She didn't know why. She almost wanted him to see the rest of her, her body. She imagined standing up and turning around.

"Do you have your passport?"

"Yes. Do you want it?"

"No." He shook his head. His profile was Indian, a straight nose, lips that were big and nicely shaped. He lives in a cage made of branchlike scars, she thought. She looked at his hands. They had no wedding ring. Not all men in India wore wedding rings, she thought. But most who spoke such good English did.

Phoebe wondered how much time had passed and if her encounter with this man was truly as unusual as she thought. "What happened to your family?" she asked. "Your parents?"

"I don't see them anymore."

"Why not?"

"It seemed better that way. I don't see anyone." He paused. "No," he said.

"No what?"

"No, the case is not important."

Phoebe breathed. She saw him look at her chest, as if to watch her breathe, then take in the shape of her, her breasts and arms, even down to her waist, and then come back to her face. She had the feeling he'd never looked at a woman like her before and knew intuitively that he found her beautiful.

Abruptly he turned away. She knew he was embarrassed, and she was conscious for the first time that she liked him. "So you don't have a lot of people hunting for him?"

He looked back at her.

"You don't have a national warrant out for him?"

His mouth opened, slowly and methodically, and then stopped, stayed in position, the lips apart. Phoebe sensed that something had changed yet again.

"You haven't made it a top priority?" Did he come from an upper-class family? Was that it? He'd had an education, even spoken English at home, and had a future, even a marriage, all laid out, but then the fire happened and he was so disfigured, he was banished and rejected? India did that. Sold its rejects, people who didn't fit were shunted out to protect the ones who did. Or

434

had the man banished himself? That's what he'd implied. Farmed himself out to the lowliest of the low down here in Tees-he-zari. This was the drawing room, she realized, a drawing room for the two of them. He knew it before she did.

They were standing on the two sides of the desk, Cully in between.

She leaned forward. "Please."

"What search or effort there may have been"—she could barely hear him, he talked so low—"there will not be anymore. Because of you."

She was drawn right into his eyes now. "Where did you learn such good English?" she whispered. "Where do you come from?"

He looked down at his desk. He picked up a pen and held it, as if prepared to write. "Do you like it here?" he asked, almost in a whisper. "Do you enjoy yourself in this room?"

She opened her mouth but didn't speak.

One clerk-chaprassi had come back and was waving his hand at her again, urging her to leave.

"Do you?" the man said to her. "Most people do not choose to come in here. This place, Tees-he-zari, is not . . ." The sentence remained unfinished.

She didn't move. He was vulnerable and not, she saw with extraordinary surprise, unkind. For the first time his eyes, those little grapes, looked accessible and barely, just barely, warm.

"I would say—do you want to know what I would say?" He was whispering now.

Phoebe nodded and leaned closer.

"I would say that you should take what information I have given you and leave."

She waited.

"Quickly."

"But—"

"Before I change my mind."

"But . . ."

She saw that something in him was slipping back over to the way he'd been before. "Please," she whispered. "Just tell me your name."

"No."

"But I can find it out. Easily. I have friends."

"Then find it out."

"But what if I want to ask you something else?"

"You won't."

"But I might."

"Go," he said. "I don't know exactly what I have done."

## 8

BACK AT BHAGWANDAS ROAD, Tulsidas was sitting on the front steps.

Phoebe thanked him for coming and asked if he could wait. She said she had to rest.

He said yes but followed her to the door. Her mind was so full of the man she had left behind, she tried to ignore him, but he came inside the house and she finally asked him what was the matter.

"Chumpi say tell you she go back Deeg House," he said. "I am driving Chumpi there, memsa'ab."

"That's all right."

"But I sorry sorry for going to Deeg House."

"It's okay," she said. "There's nothing wrong with going there."

He followed her when she went in the kitchen. "Chumpi not coming back."

Phoebe drank some filtered water.

"She say they own her, memsa'ab. They give her werry much money." He was frowning. "You know this, memsa'ab? Werry much money?"

"I know. But what's the matter, Tulsidas? What's bothering you?"

"So werry much money, memsa'ab."

437

"Do you want money, too? Is that it?"

He shook his head, but she didn't believe him. "Everybody needs money, Tulsidas. It's okay." She headed for the bedroom. "We're going to look for Samiji," she said at the doorway, "but not now. Can you wait?"

"Yes, fine, any-ting."

Inside the room, she closed the door and lay down on her bed. She forgot Tulsidas, overwhelmed by the man at Tees-he-zari. She could hear the sound of his voice and feel the presence of his body. She realized again she didn't even know his name, but that, fantastically and improbably, they were friends forever. She kept thinking about him, the embodiment of something awful, but wonderful. She'd never been so repulsed yet attracted in all her life. She felt exhausted. The awareness she'd gone to Tees-he-zari and come out with what she wanted seemed incredible. But after a while she noticed something else, too.

That she wanted to bring him out of Tees-he-zari and save him, protect him from whatever it was that drove him there in the first place.

Phoebe jumped up and looked at herself in the mirror. Her long blond hair was falling about her face, and her skin was sweaty but vibrant; it looked beautiful and alive, even to her. "You have to stop this," she said, staring at the image staring back. "That's what you've done your whole life with Cully. Focused on him and tried to save him, and forgotten everything else."

She went in the bathroom and poured the buckets in the tub, thinking Kady would know who the man was and tell her what had happened.

She got in the bath. "You mustn't rescue people anymore," she said aloud. "Your responsibility is to yourself and to what you can do, and if you can go to Tees-he-zari, you don't have to run from anything anymore."


Tulsidas put water in the car to cool the engine down and they set out.

Samiji was not at the office on Raj Path, or at Kady's house, nor was Durr or anyone. The servants in the back said they hadn't seen him. The chowkidar next door said maybe he'd gone

438

to the bazaar, so they drove there. There was no black Mercedes and no sign of Samiji.

Phoebe got back in the car. She felt so tired her body ached.

Tulsidas watched her in the mirror. "Try kumari-sa'ab one more time?"

"Sure," she said, "why not."

When they reached Viceroy Circle again, she knocked. There was still no answer. She was tempted to go home, forget Samiji for now, sleep instead, but she heard a noise. Durr had opened a window upstairs and was peering down at them.

Neither woman spoke. Then Durr said, "One minute only. I'll come down and give you tea."

Durr only opened the door a little bit, her body framed by the walls itself.

"I don't want tea, thank you," Phoebe said. "I'm looking for Samiji. And my brother. Do you know where they are?"

Durr didn't answer.

"Do you?"

The woman shook her head.

"Please, I know you must."

"I cannot betray my husband."

"I didn't ask you to betray him. I just asked where Samiji was." But you have betrayed him, Phoebe thought to herself, all along.

Durr dropped her head. "I can't tell you," she said. "It's not my place."

Phoebe gripped the woman's hand. The door opened. "Durr, I have to find Samiji," she said. "He'll tell me where Cully is. I absolutely have to find him. I've put it off too long."

"Is Kady back, too?"

"I don't know."

"Is everything all right?"

"Yes and no, I don't know. It's complicated. I left him in Kashmir."

"If my husband said he loves you, he does."

"I know."

"And that would come before everything else." She was pleading for him.

"But he's not telling me the truth."

"Maybe you are not understanding him."

"He's lied to me over and over again."

"He will have his reasons."

"I don't care about his reasons anymore. I need to find Cully and try to resolve things with him. I need to know what has gone on in my own life. I stopped everything because of Kady, but now I can't anymore. There are things I have to do."

"He never loved anyone but you."

"I still need to find my brother."

"I am not knowing where he is, Samiji either. I saw him this morning, and after that I am not knowing where he went."

Phoebe didn't believe her. She said good-bye and went down the driveway, but she felt terrible. She turned around and went back to Durr, who was still standing at the door. "I'm sorry for all this," she said, putting her arms around the woman and hugging her tight. She smelled the scent of flowers in her hair and talcum powder.

"You're so tired," Durr said, holding Phoebe close.

"Oh, Durr," Phoebe murmured, her face nestled in her hair. "Do you know how much I've always loved you?"

"Me? Why?"

"Because you were so wonderful to me at that wedding. Do you remember?" She held her arms in her hands tightly. "You made me feel the way my mother never did. I felt so cared for."

"But it was long ago."

"That doesn't matter."

"It only lasted a minute."

"So far," Phoebe said, smiling, "it's lasted a lifetime."

"Kady was worried about you."

Phoebe dropped her hands. "He's still worried about me. I wish he'd stop."

"Forget about your brother," Durr said. "He's no good anymore. I am telling you."

"He's still my brother."

"Did you see the newspaper?"

"Yes." Phoebe started to leave. "I love you," she said. "Thank you for everything. That's all I wanted to say. Just thank you."

She kissed Durr on her cheek and went back down the path to the car. As they drove away the driver said, "What are we doing now, memsa'ab?"

"We're going on a journey."

"But it is coming late. Nighttime."

"Can you go with me?"

"Yes, any-ting."

"Then we're going to Brinj."

"What is this Brinj?"

"It's Samiji's village. It's up in U.P. State."

"But where is this?"

"Don't worry," Phoebe said. "I've been there before, a long time ago."

They stopped at Bhagwandas Road long enough for Phoebe to find a map and put some things in a suitcase. Tulsidas asked to make a phone call. Phoebe was surprised but said yes. In the kitchen she put filtered water in a bottle and tried to overhear him on the phone but couldn't and then forgot. Tired as she was, she knew the drive to Brinj would do her good.

They got on the Grand Trunk Road and headed northeast, toward the land just below the foothills that rose up into the lowlands of Nepal. The road was crowded, India on the move, full of animals and vehicles, people on foot and beast and trucks that went far faster than they were meant to do, mowing down chickens, goats, anything. The car window was open. Hot air blew in, and toward nightfall the sky grew pink, with high white clouds and swarms of crows.

Phoebe understood why she was so exhausted. It was the weight of all she'd become, the new shape of her life. She knew she was no longer the woman with one brother who'd boarded a plane for India almost four months ago.

She knew what her life really was and always had been: something twisted in among interwoven lives, skeins of wool that turned in and around each other so that her life wasn't just Jumna Road and Granny's place and one beloved brother, but Durr and Kady and Jiggie Deeg and even children whose names she barely knew, and they were all of them, three families and three generations, as ingrained in her as if termites had burrowed in for decades along a wall and left their tracks.

All because of ancient acts of love and kindness, greed and fear.

Phoebe listened to imaginary voices. Had Jiggie apologized and said, I'm sorry, but I really love her? Had Kady said, Look what Jiggie wants me to do, give you a false Shiva? Isn't he mad?

And had Louis himself laughed, My God, do you believe what Kady's done? Then everything might have been different.

Tulsidas found a dak bungalow for the night, and they set out again in the morning. The road went from Kabul in the west straight through Afghanistan across the subcontinent all the way to Calcutta in the east. But Brinj was not that far.

It was just a little village where, once, a long time ago, Phoebe had gotten sick and a doctor had treated her with ground-up flies and Cully had said: What did it matter? She was "nearly Indian anyway."


The wedding was only a few days away. Jiggie was still in Delhi, but down in Deeg the Deeg Palace Hotel was empty, the paying guests gone, and the old palace across the lake had been cleaned out, squirrels removed, beds repaired, everything washed and redecorated. Artists were painting gods on the walls, others bringing in furniture and ornaments, the priests were ensconced.

At Umaid Mahal Palace itself, the cooking had begun. The dowry was in place, hundreds of saris and trunks of things waiting for the in-laws to accept and take away. Upstairs on the top floor of the zenana, the rooms were full with women, except for the ones that belonged to Mirabai and her mother.

They lay empty, and that the bride was not back from Mussoorie in the hills was something no one discussed. To even mention it was to give appalling credence to the worries, and for once not even the servants talked. The bride's absence was a nonevent, a nonfact; but, inexorably, time kept moving.

Jiggie stayed in Delhi so as to feel it less. That's what he told his son and Attar Singh, but, in truth, he stayed to see his Durr.

Attar Singh waited in Deeg. The other side had already started to arrive, and he was tempted to say, Oh, Mirabai's right up in her room, see? It's the one on the very top of the zenana where you can see the curtains fluttering.

Actually, he was hopeful, not because the sister on the other side was pregnant and beginning to show, but because the Guthrie girl had come back to Delhi and the driver Tulsidas had phoned to say now they were headed for Brinj.

So the sister knew something they did not.

He and Shyam were waiting by the phones, one in Delhi, the

other in Deeg, and he figured they would know where Mirabai was as soon as Phoebe did.

The driver had been paid to call.


Kady in Kashmir came back from fishing. It had been a long day. He read the note from Phoebe, crumpled it up, and threw it away, only to retrieve it and spread it out on the bed to read again. One thing kept going through his mind. Why, if they weren't going to be together, if she wouldn't live with him and he wouldn't marry her, why did he have to tell her what he still hadn't said?

He took off his clothes but for the white shorts that served as underpants, and then, conscious that he was about to do something very Indian, he climbed up on the roof of the boat and, taking off the shorts, lay down flat on his stomach in the warm sun of midafternoon. He'd never done this before, although he'd seen many a yogi spread himself to the elements, but now it was he himself prone to sun and sky, seeking the nourishment of whatever came and went, good and bad.

He had his head on his arms, his belly on the wood, and he let time pass. He felt how the sun and air was stripping away the sham of his lies and the persona that couldn't reveal itself. A second day came and still he barely moved, except when he had to urinate. He felt himself disappearing, the sun and the air reaching through to his inner bones and cells, boring away at the flesh bit by bit and reducing all to its barest simplicities until nothing remained but calcium.

He imagined Phoebe's thirst for knowledge as part of the sun and air, and he understood what she was doing to him, both the challenge and the lure of her.

But still, despite his efforts, he mostly felt a kind of desperation that the soul that had kindled him for all these years and lifetimes had brought him no further than this, still so locked in his past he couldn't break through to her.

# ❧ 9 ❧

CULLY AND MIRABAI WERE STAY-
ing in a walk-up hotel on the third floor overlooking an alley.
They had a balcony and some windows, but the place looked
very dark to Samiji.

The door wasn't even locked. He turned the handle and
walked in.

Darkness and heat. The fan was going, but there wasn't any
air.

The building across the street abutted the hotel, and the room
seemed closed off to him. He squinted, but the only thing he
could make out was something white. It turned out to be sheets
drying outside the window on ropes strung across the alley.

He closed the door and looked around. Shelves, table, bed,
chair, floor made of white tiles that had come from England. It
was an old place. Then he saw the girl.

She was sitting on the floor, her back pressed up against the
wall, knees to her chest, sari same color as the walls, a shiny blue,
and her arms were clasped tight around her legs and stomach.

She raised her head. She knew who he was.

"Where's Cully?" he asked.

He expected her to get up, but she put her face back down on
her knees and didn't answer.

"Where is he?" he repeated.

"In the bathroom." She didn't move.

He went to the bathroom.

Cully was lying down full length in a tub with claw feet. He looked all white and yellowish under the water, just a spot of dark where hair stood out between his legs. Samiji wasn't conscious of being quiet, but he didn't make a sound, just stood in the doorway, the sack Durr had given him in his hands.

Cully began to move. Without looking at Samiji, he stood up in the bath, straight as a soldier, and climbed out, barely changing his posture. His big lean thighs and broad chest seemed ramrod stiff.

Samiji had never seen anything as big or white as he was. He was tempted to leave, give him privacy, but instead he watched, fascinated, not sure if Cully even knew he was there.

Cully proceeded to get dressed.

There was still no sign he knew Samiji was there, a short man with a mustache, trousers, and a shirt sharing the room with him.

Cully had his pants on. He bent over and let the water out of the tub and started folding the towel. It took some time because he pressed it on both sides as though he were ironing it, put it across the bar on the wall, only to rearrange it until it was lined up straight. Then he started to comb his hair, pulling hard and deep through the strands. He looked at the comb and pulled out thick strands of hair and rolled them in a yellow-white ball, which he kept in his hand the whole time.

"Sa'ab?" said Samiji.

No answer.

"Sa'ab?"

"I'm not dressed yet."

"Aacha." Samiji stepped back, sat down on the floor, and leaned up against the wall.

The girl was across the room from him. She faced away from the window and the balcony so that all she looked at were the wall and the bed.

Samiji studied the room and saw how everything was all lined up, sandals along wall, toes in a line, shirts folded on the shelf. Even her saris were perfectly in order, the jewelry, too, a string of pearls and an emerald necklace laid out on the table, parallel lines together.

He knew Cully had done the arranging. "Can I get you some

445

tea?" he whispered so Cully wouldn't hear.

She shook her head.

"Please do me this one favor and allow me to do my duty?"

"It isn't time." She kept her voice low. "We have tea at four-fifteen. It used to be five. But he wanted to make it earlier."

"Aacha." He knew he had to call Phoebe.

Cully spoke. "Where is it?"

His voice was strong and unexpected. He had come out of the bathroom and was standing, feet apart, hands clasped behind his back, wearing pants, no shoes or shirt.

"Where is it?" he repeated. "The money."

"I have it, sa'ab." Samiji stood up and picked up the sack. "Right here only." He lifted the bag high. It was heavy and full.

"Put it down."

Samiji put it on a chair.

"On the table."

Samiji put it on the table, next to the pearls and emeralds, careful to align it with the edge of the table. Then he stepped back.

Cully went over and rearranged the necklaces in their perfect position, then returned to his spot near the bathroom door. "Is everything in it?"

"Just as you said, sa'ab. Kumari-sa'ab is putting everything there, much money."

"Why didn't he come?"

"He's out of station. He gave orders only." Samiji looked at the girl reassuringly. "Can I be getting you some tea, sa'ab?" He made his voice servile.

"In a few minutes."

Samiji sat down again on the floor. He shielded his eyes so he didn't appear to see anything.

Mirabai started folding saris on the shelf that were already folded before.

Cully stood motionless outside the bathroom. "Why did it take you so long to get here?"

"Me, sa'ab?"

"Suraj didn't know what to do, did he? It's just like I said, Mirabai. He'll do anything to hurt me. If it weren't for him turning Bhave against me, I'd have my collection by now."

Mirabai nodded.

"He feels guilty about what he did to my father, though. I'll give him that."

"Yes," she said.

"I bet he didn't give you the full amount I asked for. Did he?"

"I am not knowing, sa'ab."

"Did he tell you to find out what my plans were, too?"

"No, sa'ab. Not one ting."

"I'll have to warn the clerk. Tell him not to let anyone up. There's people who do that, you know," he said to Mirabai.

"Yes."

"Beat you up. Do anything someone like Kady tells them. You just hire them. Did he say he was going to tell Jiggie where I was?"

"He is not saying, sa'ab. But he has not told him before."

"Have you seen my sister, too? What's she doing?" He still hadn't moved, standing in the doorway like a soldier.

"I am not knowing, sa'ab. I am not privvy to tese tings, but I am thinking maybe she has made one trip to Kashmir only."

"Of course," Cully exclaimed. "See?" he said to Mirabai. "What'd I tell you? That's what she does. She follows me, tries to check up on me. I went to Kashmir, she goes to Kashmir. What else?"

Samiji shrugged.

"Where is she staying? What hotel?"

"With Auntie Indore," Samiji said. "On Bhagwandas Road."

Mirabai put her face down against her knees, and Samiji knew she had started to cry.

"That's perfect," Cully said vehemently. "She can wrap any-one around her finger. Of course she'd want a house. Hotel's not good enough for her. Or my apartment. Of course she wouldn't stay there. She gets people to do anything she wants. It's her hair. They all love it, don't they?"

He was looking at Mirabai, but Samiji said, "Oh, yes, must be. Same hair for you too only, sa'ab."

"She had my father wrapped around her finger from day one," he said. "Some girls are like that. They can get their fathers to do anything."

Mirabai was crying harder now. Samiji could hear her.

"They get everything they want," Cully was saying. "I mean everything."

447

At four-fifteen Samiji went out to buy tea and brought it back to the room. He was supposed to go to Delhi, he already had his plane ticket, but instead he sat down on the floor again. No one paid any attention to him. Cully lay on the bed. The girl sat on the same spot on the floor. She drank her tea, watched the fan. Samiji watched it, too. The air was hot.

Later it rained, and afterward Samiji went outside again and bought them food. Cully asked for cutlets, said you couldn't tell with Indian food. Sometimes it was poisoned.

Samiji bought the newspapers too and fixed them so that Mirabai would see the article about the arrest warrant. Cully barely moved from the bed.

Samiji spent the night outside the door in the hallway. He slept, but he kept getting up to use the phone. Durr told him Kady wasn't back yet, but Phoebe had returned and was looking for him. He called Bhagwandas Road, but there was no answer. He kept trying every few hours. One time when he got up, Cully was crying.

He opened the door carefully and peeked in. He was on one side of the bed, the girl on the other, wrapped up in her sari tight as a mummy, eyes closed. Cully was facing the other way, and the noise he made wasn't sobs, exactly, just a murmuring that seemed like an odd form of breathing, it was so steady.

Samiji felt sorry for him and remembered how the mother, Thalia-sa'ab, had ignored the boy even as she berated her husband. He could barely recall what the woman looked like, just that her hair was thin and she had legs that were almost blue, they were so white. Cully, poor thing, looked like her, and he thought that was why Guthrie-sahib had never liked him.

He sat back down outside the door and put his ear up against the wall. He heard the tortured sounds of Cully moaning.

He even sounded like his mother, Samiji thought. Because he had heard her, too, inside the alcove where she lived, eating chocolates and crying.

## ❧ 10 ❧

BRINJ WAS SOME TWO HUNDRED huts spread out along the edge of a creek that stretched through the bottom of a small valley. The town itself was poor, no automobiles or electricity, animals that looked nearly starved, people not much better. Cows and goats were sleeping in the street when Phoebe arrived, and she saw a couple of stalls selling tea and tobacco and bottled drinks. The few larger buildings housed the doctor, the lawyer, shops for canned goods and cloth. She remembered it all. There was a repair stall for bicycles and bullock carts, one telephone on an outside wall, the post office, and, along the edge of the road, people sitting on the ground with piles of grains in front of them to sell.

The dirt road in was narrow and by the time Tulsidas stopped the car, in late morning the day after they had left, what looked like the whole town rushed out to see them. From the first look of things, Phoebe knew Samiji wasn't there.

When she opened her door the crowd, with their little bodies and dark eyes, pressed in around her, asked questions and fingered her skirt. She said she was looking for Samiji Jabu Mal—did they know where he was? And right away they all set off, her in tow, children attached to nearly every finger.

Her eyes sought out everything in this little village that, surprisingly, was so familiar after all these years, and despite all

449

that was on her mind, she felt an unexpected pleasure. Brinj seemed part of her, that was the curious thing, the buildings, the layout, the turns in the creek. It recalled a time when everything had been right with Cully and they'd visited here together. She remembered they'd slept, those few nights so long ago, with their heads against each other, her arm flopped across his back.

She looked in at the doctor, his place wide open to the street, and could tell he was a different man from the one she'd known before. This one was too young. He had a woman inside and was looking at her teeth. Phoebe paused and watched, the children jumped and chattered at her edge, and saw herself sitting there years ago. "You're nearly Indian anyway," Cully had said.

"He was right," she exclaimed aloud, realizing how simple everything could be. She laughed. "I'm half Indian and half American," she said in English.

"Yes, yes," the children cried back in their Hindi chatter.

"The answer's so easy, but I never knew it."

"Hahn," they exclaimed, delighted by her voice.

"Bet you didn't know that I belong half in one place"—she tweaked noses and caught others by the ear—"half in another?" She picked up a child and swung him round. "Did you know that?" she asked. "That I belong here and in Am-ri-ka, too?"

"Am-ri-ka," they cried in unison.

"What do you think?" she said, Hindi now. "Shall we find Samiji Jabu Mal?" They all cheered and said, Why not? Just follow us. But she knew Samiji wasn't there. They meant his place, she thought, or his family, not him. Because he was probably back in Delhi where he had been all along. Otherwise she'd have seen him by now.

He had brothers and sisters here, nieces, nephews, and even a wife and children who benefited from the salary he sent back every month. Years before, the family huts had been small, bare ground for floor, and Phoebe expected it to be better now. She expected his family and she expected signs of prosperity. She had even told herself not to be surprised if there was something like a television set that couldn't be plugged in because there was no electricity.

But she was not prepared for the one thing she saw: and that was a car.

It was not clean or in fine repair. It was covered with dust and nicks, and the back fender was bent, and it had its name, "Samiji

Jabu Mal," painted right across it, even words in English painted underneath: "Taxi Car for Hire." But there was no getting around the fact that it was a very old white Ford car that had never been broken or burned at all.

Phoebe felt her knees go limp. Had the children and the crowd not pressed around her, she might have fallen, but their momentum kept her going. She stared at this apparition she'd imagined a million times before, charred and smashed, so melted down in her mind it was no larger than a child's blackened cart.

Phoebe had imagined many things for the fate of this one important car, but in all her thoughts and fancies, she had never once imagined it whole and fine, untouched by fire or accident.

She got back to Delhi late at night. She had barely fallen asleep when the phone rang. She stumbled out of bed to get it.

It was Samiji. She knew immediately something was wrong, so she couldn't ask what she was longing to; knew, instead, if it'd waited twenty years, another few minutes, or hours, wouldn't matter.

He was talking Hindi and he called her "Feeb-ji," just two syllables, as he had so many years before, so she knew it had to do with Cully. He told her he had found them, he didn't even use their names, but she knew who he meant, and he said she had to come right down because her brother was werry sick, he wasn't right at all, and he had to tell her because it was her duty to take care of him, and she had to come and make "de-ci-she-yons," because he, Cully, couldn't.

She asked where he was and was not really surprised when Samiji said Madras, the farthest place from her there was. It seemed fitting Cully had gone there, and the one word, the city alone, told her all over again how much he'd changed. Or, maybe, hadn't changed at all. "I'll come right down," she said. "I'll be there in the morning."

"Is plane at eight o'clock."

"Don't hang up," she said, and suddenly, unexpectedly, she felt a wave of longing for Kady Suraj. "Tell me what's going on."

Samiji didn't actually have a great deal to say. Only that Cully-sahib looked much too big and white, and Mirabai was reduced, he used the word in Hindi for something that is lesser than it was before. Phoebe understood completely. "I'd trust you with my right arm," she said apropos of nothing, knowing fully that Samiji would never do anything to hurt her, so if he'd owned a white Ford car for twenty years now, he would have had it with no other purpose in mind than to help her.

And protect her.

But that still didn't answer her questions about the car. Or the people who'd been inside it twenty years before.


The plane to Madras didn't leave Palam Airport for two hours after its scheduled departure. First the pilot didn't show up and they had to find a replacement. Then a government official called to say he was having lunch and wanted the plane to wait. So it was nearly two in the afternoon when Phoebe landed in the south.

When she finally reached the hotel, the clerk in the lobby told her the room number and pointed up through the inner tunnel of the building toward the skylight far above. He seemed amazed by her appearance. Phoebe knew it was her hair, the color so astounding a sight for India, and as she began the upward climb, she pushed the hair out of her eyes and realized that in a few minutes she'd be together with her brother and there'd be two yellow-white heads in the same room.

Although she'd prepared herself for this moment, at least she thought she had—worked out how it would be to face the resentment she had come to accept, even understand—the thought of having two such heads of hair together overwhelmed her with such feelings of loss she sat down on the steps.

After a few minutes she wiped her eyes with her skirt, breathing deeply until her abdomen was full of air and it felt . . . not easy, it could never be easy to face what lay ahead, but right to proceed with what she had to do.

She started climbing again. One flight, another. It was dark in the hall, high ceilings and old tiles, so old and reminiscent of another era, she smiled to herself. She was walking back in time, she thought, akin to going into Brinj. Then she stood outside their door.

She raised her hand, held it in the air. Told herself she was listening for sounds, but, in fact, she was postponing what had to be—how different this was from what she'd thought when she left New York four months ago—then she knocked.

She knew Samiji had said he wouldn't tell Cully she was coming, but still she wondered if Cully, even now, despite everything, knew she was there.

It was so. He did.

Because when Samiji opened the door and stepped back out of sight, there was Cully framed in the doorway, pants and no shirt, barefoot, looking right at her, and she knew he'd known it was she the second he heard her knock. He said, "So you had to follow me here, too? Can't you leave me bloody well alone?"

## ❧ II ❧

His coldness stunned her. Every instinct told her to go slow. She stared and he stared back. He looked big, she thought. There was a dull expression on his face, like his flesh was made of wax and had never seen the sun, and she knew, clearer than she ever had before, that his triumphant return to India had been a catastrophe.

She felt herself go flushed, then pale, but she allowed herself the makings of a gentle smile. Cully seemed unprepared himself, all he could do to absorb her presence.

She could tell the room was dark and airy, had a balcony. She didn't see Mirabai. She went in through the doorway, heading for her brother, propelled to hug him, but an overpowering sense of rationality and control held her back.

He was standing vacantly in front of her. His white skin seemed so akin to the male Caucasian body stretched out in the morgue, it was like, in some peculiar metaphor, he'd been Cully all along, dead and out of touch. She shut the door, slow and easy. Where was Mirabai? Whole chunks of his hair had fallen out. She could see the scalp and she felt a sudden panic; he was medically ill. She had to force herself not to look down at his one big toe because she knew it would make her feel so achingly sad she'd burst into tears in front of him. Then she said stilly, "How are you? I'm so glad"—not happy, be neutral—"to see you."

454

"You had to come here, too? To India?" He turned and walked over to a chair, where he plopped down hard, and sat facing the alley, spread out on the furniture in a twisted position that left him looking like a giant angry slug.

Phoebe looked at him in agony. His back was big and splotchy; it had been gorgeous. "I'm glad to see you," she said again, noticing patches on his back that stood out like sores about to burst.

"You can't let me be?"

"I've missed you."

"Do what I want for once?" His voice took on a plaintive tone, and he sounded like a child. "I don't want you."

"I know." Soothing.

"But I don't."

"I know."

"Don't you ever have enough?"

He sounded just like Thalia, the thin voice when she complained and nagged at Louis. Phoebe remembered how Louis linked them in his mind, his wife and son, and she recognized the expression on her brother's face as pain. She wanted to reach out, make it disappear, but she couldn't move. The wrecked history of their lives seemed to fill the room. Then she spotted Mirabai.

The girl was huddled on the floor almost behind her in a corner. Phoebe watched her, appalled at how depressed she looked. Concern for her now crowded into her already jumbled mind.

She wanted to shake Cully and snap him out of it, fix the girl, and make everything all better. Tell them both how lucky they were, it wasn't all bad, they had each other, after all, and they had others, too, they had love, the gods be thanked; but she knew that was just simplistic pap, the situation much too serious.

Cully started to moan and kept on moaning. She watched the veins throbbing on his shoulders like worms and wondered exactly what to do, both for him and Mirabai. His red blotches had spread, and she imagined they were things alive, his flesh contaminated by some internal toxin that was her.

"You didn't even let me tie my shoes," he said, mumbling now. "It was my birthday, too. You didn't even remember."

Phoebe had no idea what he was talking about.

"You just went ahead and tied them."

455

What had he remembered? What resentment had he stored for years? It was hard for her to fathom.

"You wouldn't even let me do it myself." He was picking threads from a hole in his pants; his hands looked enormous. "I said I wanted to stay in the room. I said it, didn't I?"

"Yes." Was he talking about the time they'd rearranged the room so that the two beds were at opposite ends?

"You knew that's what I wanted, to be with you. I told you I didn't want to be alone."

He was speaking through clenched teeth, his voice familiar because this was the tone he'd used against Granny and the landlord, others, for years.

"I told you I didn't want to move to the other room," he said. "You said that was fine. You said I could stay with you."

"You did," she said. "We just rearranged the furniture." She heard water dripping in the bathroom. In New York he took too many baths, and she said wasn't it a waste of water? And he said he was dirty, and she said, How can you be dirty four times a day?

"But why'd you have to move the bed?"

"Cully, I love you so much."

"Why couldn't you just leave everything the way it was?"

"I love you more than anyone."

"I liked it the way it was, the two beds, the—"

"Remember that summer when I drove to camp and brought you home?" She took a step closer. "You hadn't called, but I knew you wanted to leave? That you'd had enough? I didn't even tell Granny, just came and got you? It was after breakfast and you saw me and you just got in the car and we drove away? Remember that?"

He didn't answer.

"There's a plane to New York tonight. Another tomorrow. We could get either one you want. Anything you want, I just want to be with you." But did she? Was that really true anymore?

"You still don't want me to do anything, do you?" Cully said. "You don't care about my collection, my work. All you care about is what you want."

"Shall I get us tickets?"

"What tickets?"

"For New York."

He turned back toward the alley. She felt a profound sadness emanating out of him. It reminded her of Louis at the end, when everything was falling apart around him. She felt a sense of panic rising in her but she suppressed it. Should she leave? Stay? Trust him to Samiji?

She saw the newspapers and glanced at Samiji. He shook his head. Cully didn't know about the arrest warrant.

"We can go out to Long Island and lie in the sun," she said. He shrank away, closer to the alley.

"We'll take those big towels down to the beach. We can eat lobsters and boil corn. Cook them on the hibachi, if you want, but you have to light the fire. . . . Cully?"

He didn't speak.

"I can never get the charcoal burning. You have to do it." Tears were rolling down her face. "Cully?" she whispered.

Outside in the alley someone had started to sing, about love and a wishing well. The tears spilled into her mouth. She shivered.

Samiji cleared his throat and jolted her back to the present. He gestured toward the girl, whose eyes looked so sunken and dark Phoebe suddenly felt frightened for her. "Mirabai," she said urgently. "Do you want to come for a walk? We can get some tea?"

The girl nodded gratefully.

Phoebe blew her nose. Cully didn't move. The girl had gotten up.

"Sa'ab?" It was Samiji.

"Hahn jee?"

"Can bibiji be getting your tea and crackers? It is just now time." He sounded submissive and servile. Phoebe realized he was trying to distract her brother.

"It's too early for tea."

"But I am thinking, sa'ab, that this waiting until four o'clock like we are doing nowadays makes this teatime one little bit too late. What are you thinking?"

Mirabai tiptoed across the floor toward the door.

"Are you maybe thinking, sa'ab, we shall have tea now? On the early side, that is true, but then having one more tea before dinnertime? It is up to you, of course, you are boss." He wagged his head, watching Mirabai out of the corner of his eye. "But I am thinking it is time now only to make this one change. If it

457

is not working, you can change it back tomorrow to old way."

"That's true," Cully said, serious and thoughtful.

The girl had reached the door.

"Exactly right, sa'ab. Just what I am thinking. Let the memsa'abs go. I will stay right here with you, because, really, it is woman's work for getting tea, isn't it."

Cully looked at the women vaguely and nodded. Phoebe opened the door. "I'll see you in a few minutes, then," she said.

Cully turned away. Mirabai slipped out, then Phoebe, too, shutting the door behind them.


Outside, Phoebe headed for a park up ahead. The girl was beside her. Her skin looked even more sallow in the bright light. Phoebe took her hand and held it tight. "I'm sorry you've had such a hard time," she said. "It must have turned out very differently than you hoped."

"Yes."

"My brother's a wonderful person, but I don't think he's in good shape. You know that, don't you."

"Yes."

"Has he been like this for long?"

"Yes."

Phoebe could barely hear her.

"Thank you for coming," Mirabai said.

"Do you want to go home now?" Phoebe asked. "Do you think it's time?"

"Yes."

"Would you like me to arrange it?"

"Yes, please."

"Shall I pay for it, too? I can if it makes it more convenient for you."

"I don't have any money left." Mirabai's voice sounded hoarse from disuse.

Phoebe put her arm around the girl's shoulder and drew her in closer so they walked together like a couple or a woman and her child. "You want to go to Delhi, don't you?" she said, still reeling inside from the vision of her brother.

"You mean Delhi, not Deeg?"

"No, actually, I just meant the airport. Delhi airport, instead of Bombay or something."

"Yes."

"And after that?" Phoebe said. "Do you know what you want to do?"

The girl didn't answer.

They kept walking abreast, except that the street was so crowded, they had to swerve around animals and people.

"Where's my grandfather?" Mirabai asked.

"He was in Delhi yesterday."

"I'm supposed to be getting married September ninth."

"I know."

"Does the other side know what I've done?"

"Your father told everyone you were in Mussoorie with Auntie Indore."

"What's happened to my dog?"

"I don't know. Nothing. What's the matter with your dog?"

"I'm afraid they hurt him."

"Oh, they wouldn't."

"My grandfather would."

"What do you want to do?"

"I want to see him. I think he'll understand."

"I doubt it," Phoebe said dryly.

"No, he will," the girl said urgently. "Kady said he would."

"Yes."

Inside the park, they sat down on a bench. "Kady knows my grandfather better than anyone," the girl was saying. "I want to see my grandfather. I want to go to Deeg House."


They returned to the hotel. Cully was lying on the bed. Phoebe went over and sat next to him. He turned his head away so he wouldn't have to see her. She put her hand on his arm. "Is there anything I can do?"

Behind her she heard Mirabai getting her things together. Samiji was watching.

Cully didn't answer.

"Do you know what you're going to do?" she asked. "Where you'll go?" Someone outside was singing in the alley again. "The police are looking for the person who killed Anant. Do you know that?"

Cully didn't respond. He didn't even seem to register her words.

459

"They think you killed him," she said. He still didn't move. Didn't he care about the police? Know Mirabai was leaving? Or wasn't he conscious of anything? "I'm going to leave, I guess," she said tentatively. "Samiji, you'll stay here?"

"Definitely, miss-sa'ab."

Mirabai was holding her duffel. It was small.

"Shall I just leave, Cully?" Phoebe said. "Go back to Delhi?"

Still no answer.

"There's something I have to do there. Otherwise, maybe, I don't know, maybe I wouldn't leave you. Maybe I'd get a room here. But I have to do something. There's someone I have to see. It has to do with Louis and Thalia." He didn't react. "It's important. Afterwards I'll come back if you want me to." She paused. "We can talk on the phone. The police think you had something to do with Anant, though, so whatever you do, be careful. Okay? Can you hear me?"

No answer.

"You've helped me a lot, Cully. Thank you for that." She paused. "You know what the Buddhists say: Your enemy is your best teacher. Although I don't think of you as my enemy."

He still didn't say anything.

"But I know you're mad at me."

He was silent.

Samiji shrugged. Mirabai had tears in her eyes.

Phoebe bent over and kissed Cully's shoulder and then, almost involuntarily, brought her hand up and wiped it across his face, moving the hair off his forehead tenderly. He shrank down into the pillow.

She stood up. "If you want me," she said through her tears, "I'll either be at Auntie Indore's or the Taj. . . ."

"I don't want you."

She backed away.

Mirabai was at the bed, kissing Cully on the cheek. "I love you," she said. "I'll always love you, but I'm going home. I have to go home."

Phoebe went out in the hall, then Mirabai, too, both of them suddenly gone, heading down the stairs. Inside, Samiji watched the body on the bed, not knowing if Cully realized they had left. But suddenly Cully leapt upright on the mattress and ran across the room and out into the hall. "Mirabai . . . come back," he yelled through the stairwell.

There was just the echo of his cry and the sound, somewhere, of footsteps descending.

"Mirabai," he yelled again.

The two were leaving the hotel and walking out into the street. The girl heard her name, "Mirrrr-aaaaahhhhhh-baiiiiiiiii," echoing off the tiles that stretched from the lobby to the skylight far above. Phoebe heard him, too, his voice reaching out into the street, and the last thing she heard was him crying, "I'll get you. You've taken everything I ever had. But why did you have to take her, too?"

## ❧ 12 ❧

ON THAT DAY, SEPTEMBER 5TH, I
was in Mussoorie in the hills staying with some friends. The
days were long and and beautiful. Blue skies stretched from
the Himalayas at our backs out across to the plains at our feet.
In the distance to the south, the blue turned into dust and our
longest, farthest view was of the white that covered India. One
had a sense of relief looking out. Up here we were protected
and aloof, but nothing could obscure the knowledge that inevitably you had to go down, descend, as it were, to the reality of
India.

My time was all very leisurely. I took naps, walked in the hills,
wrote my son. I thought about Phoebe a lot.

When I left Delhi there'd been no answer at her house, Bhagwandas Road closed. I imagined she and Kady were happy and
content. That is, until I heard the news of the death of Hari K.
Narayan and learned of Kady's debacle. That he wasn't in town.
Didn't show for the funeral, his own peculiar version of political
suicide. I only hoped it was what he wanted, but I could imagine
the distress he was going through.

The servants heard the news on the radio in the kitchen and
brought it out to us in the drawing room. Everyone speculated
as to where Suraj was and what was the matter; Indians don't

462

do things this way. Not show up for funerals, be so blatant with their disrespect.

On the 6th my friend and I drove down to Delhi. The plains were hot and humid. We were slowed by a storm halfway back. Whole villages were nearly flooded, water, the source of life, so destructive, and I knew I was emotionally back in the confusing maelstrom of India.

You can never be absolutely serene out here. That's what Phoebe, finally, has taught me.

She says that's why you try so hard to find an inner calmness, a way to understand it all. You have to, she says. How else can you deal with all the poverty and the sheer horror of life around you? She talks about this a lot now. Says that in India you either have to think deeply or not at all. She says here she has learned that you can't control your life, so you have to find some source within yourself and mine it.

It unfolds endlessly, she says, and teaches you.


Delhi was suffocating. Whatever the temperature was, the humidity was higher. I had no idea yet that Phoebe herself had come and gone, that she'd found Cully and a car, that Kady was alone in Kashmir, or that Jiggie was in Delhi, tormented by the approaching marriage and the specter of what he himself had done, the bargain he had made.

The wedding itself, three days away, was what expressly drew me back. The prospect of being a witness either to a wedding or a nonwedding was too interesting to miss. I didn't know which would be more spectacular.

Home, I took special efforts with the house, airing it out, lest dampness become a problem later on. I called over to Bhagwandas Road, but there wasn't any answer. Harriet told me about the arrest warrant and that the police were, oddly, first very interested in the case, then not at all. Inexplicable, she said.

She didn't know where Phoebe was. She wanted to tell her about the police.

As to the wedding itself, all I knew was that it hadn't been canceled. But that didn't necessarily mean anything; Indians would stage circuses to conceal a scandal. At least I had seen the girl before. That meant I could try to catch a glimpse of the bride's face behind her veil, if there was a bride, and see if they'd substituted a stand-in for the day in order to give themselves more time to find her. They could hope the groom himself would never see beyond the veil, and at the last minute maybe he could be persuaded to leave her at home for a few more days.

A stand-in could win them extra time.

# ❧ 13 ❧

ON THE 7TH KADY CALLED. HE asked if I'd seen or heard from Phoebe.

No. Hadn't he?

"She left me a note," he said, "but I can't make out her handwriting." I didn't believe him for a second.

"Oh," I said, "rotten luck. Can I give her a message if she calls?"

"Thanks awfully. Not to bother. But you're sure you don't know where she is? I've called everywhere."

"No, and it's no bother, either," I said, anything to keep him on the line. But I needn't have worried, because suddenly he blurted out:

"She's very difficult for me, you know. I love her so goddamn much, but I'm not good at this, really."

"Oh, I'm sure you are."

"I'd do anything for her, but instead I've hurt her."

"Have you told her this?"

"Yes, but it's hard for Indians to talk about these things. Americans are different." He sounded forlorn.

He was just about to board the plane in Kashmir for Delhi. Phoebe, at the same time, had just returned from Madras. It was late in the afternoon, nearly dusk, and she was across town standing with Durr and Mirabai in the living room at Viceroy Circle.

Tulsidas was at the door outside, he'd met them at the airport, and Phoebe was asking Durr if Mirabai could stay there until she arranged someplace else for her to go. The wedding was two days away.

Durr said yes and suggested the girl come upstairs and have a bath, she must be tired from so much traveling. No one had mentioned traveling or even given the girl a name, but Durr had figured it out the minute they walked inside. As Phoebe left, the bath water upstairs was running and Mirabai was being entertained by a woman she thought of only as Kady's wife and Phoebe's friend, not as the woman who had started it all.

Durr must have had time to make a call, because when Phoebe pulled into the big courtyard in front of Deeg House, Jiggie and Shyam were out in front waiting for her. Both were barefoot. Jiggie namasted her so deeply, Phoebe knew he knew Mirabai had returned.

"Come right in," he said as if they had talked yesterday when, in fact, they hadn't talked in twenty years. He looked old, dark furrows across his face. He was thinner, too, and as they went back in under the shadows of the giant palm trees, she thought his spirit had ebbed. Unexpectedly, she felt sorry for him.

He directed her toward a small, nondescript room with faded chairs and cheap tables. His sandals were lying on the floor, books as well. He gestured for her to sit. She leaned back against the cushions and tried to relax.

Tea had been made. He handed her a cup. Shyam was sitting on the floor.

Phoebe drank the whole cup. Jiggie filled it up again, his own untouched.

Finally she sat up straight. "Thank you," she said. "I needed that. Shall I proceed?"

"Whenever you're ready, yes, please do. We're eager to hear from you."

"I flew down to Madras this morning and spent the afternoon with them. She came back with me."

"Thank you." Jiggie brought his hands up and namasted her. Shyam didn't move.

"She seems all right," Phoebe went on. "Tired, of course, and she doesn't look well, but other than that, I think she's all right. I think it was probably very difficult for her, the whole experience."

As she talked, Phoebe found Jiggie strangely vulnerable. He didn't seem vital, proud, or cunning anymore, just rather unattractive.

He handed her another cup of tea. She took it, wondered if this aspect of him was real or designed to manipulate her feelings. She remembered Kady's warnings not to trust him. She wanted to ask him questions about January 6th but decided not to. She couldn't want anything from him.

"Do you think you could keep talking?" he said.

His words jolted her. Somehow they gave her the impression that, for whatever reason, he respected her, and this worried her. Respect was not a feeling Jiggie Deeg enjoyed.

She drank tea to give herself time, looked at the pockmarks that disappeared down his back, and felt her wariness return. He reminded her of the commandant in Tees-he-zari, but she wondered if Jiggie shared his hidden kindness. "I'm very tired," she said aloud.

"No wonder. You've been busy."

"Mirabai had a lot to say," she began, "but the gist of it is that she's willing to go through with the wedding."

"Willing," Jiggie exclaimed.

"Yes. She has certain conditions."

"She has conditions!" He lifted his eyebrows in anger.

"I think you'll find this experience has changed her. I think she's matured a good deal."

"She damn well should."

"She wants you to give her money," Phoebe went on. "She wants enough money in her own name, in banks here and abroad, so she can always be independent."

"She doesn't need to worry about being divorced," Jiggie said confidently. "I've already taken care of that. They won't dare now."

"She still wants the money."

"But they can't divorce her. I know too much about the family."

Phoebe just looked at him.

"How much money does she want?" he finally asked.

467

"She hasn't figured it out exactly. But a lot."

"That's your idea, isn't it."

"The specifics are mine. The ideas are hers." Phoebe paused. "She assumes you've hurt her dog. She wants me to find out if you have."

Jiggie looked at Shyam.

Shyam moved his head hard to the left and jutted his chin out sharply. It meant "Yes."

Phoebe drew in a breath of air.

"Don't be sentimental," Jiggie cut in coldly. "What's a dog?"

"Then why'd you kill it?"

"Is she pregnant?"

"Why did you kill the dog? What good's that do?"

"Is she?"

"I don't know."

"Well, what do you think?"

"Her last period was a week ago. She won't know for another three weeks."

"So we could say it was her husband's baby," Jiggie speculated.

"Not if it's blond and blue-eyed." Any impression she'd had about Jiggie's humility was gone.

Shyam said something in Rajasthani Hindi.

"What else is going on with this girl?" Jiggie asked.

"She thinks you understand what she did. Kady told her you risked the family honor, too. She doesn't know the details, but she knows what it means."

"It doesn't mean a thing."

"She thinks it does. She knows what you did could ruin her chances of getting married just as much as her running away. She assumes you'll do whatever's necessary now to save the situation with her marriage."

Jiggie looked angry.

"She knows you don't have any choice."

"That's for me to decide. Of course I have a choice."

Phoebe didn't like him. "She has more conditions," she went on.

"This is all your doing," Jiggie said hotly.

"She's prepared to suffer the consequences."

"Then let her come to Benares and see the consequences. I'm

bloody angry with that girl. Let her look at all those widows, divorcées, spinsters. See if she likes it."

"It's not a matter of what she likes. It's what she's prepared to do. I admire her, by the way," she added. "She has a lot of courage. As part of the dowry," Phoebe went on, "she wants you to transfer ownership of the Deeg Palace Hotel to her and her fiancé."

"I absolutely will not."

"Not to the in-laws, as people usually do, but to her and the boy."

"Let her talk all she wants. That's my prize possession."

"She wants it specified as a wedding present, so the financial and emotional implications of making them a joint team, independent of his family or yours, will solidify her position in the marriage and compensate if any rumors get out about her running away."

"What if there's a baby?"

"There won't be. I'd be very surprised if there was anything between her and my brother the last few weeks."

"What else is there?"

"It's just as I told you, if she's going through with the marriage, she wants to have a strong position and not be the typical Indian wife."

"This is your influence."

"No, it's not. It's yours."

He didn't hear her. "Then that brother of yours."

"She said to tell you she learned it from you."

"Me?" Jiggie exclaimed, but he did not sound altogether displeased.

"Shall I tell her you agree?"

"Tell her I have to think. And you?" he added suddenly.

Phoebe's heart clenched in abrupt anxiety.

"How was your trip to Kashmir?"

She didn't answer. "Inconclusive," she said at last, wary.

"And Brinj?"

So Tulsidas had talked. "Interesting."

"And your brother?"

"He's not well."

"I could have told you that a year ago."

"Not twenty years ago?" What was he getting at?

"In all honesty, Miss Phoebe Guthrie, it was you yourself who caught my attention twenty years ago."

Phoebe looked at her watch with pretended disinterest. "What do I tell Mirabai? It's getting late and I have something I have to do tonight." See Dr. Sharma, she thought.

"Tell her I have to think," Jiggie said. "He and I have to talk." He pointed to Shyam.

Shyam began talking in Rajasthani Hindi. Phoebe waited.

Finally Jiggie looked at her. "He says I have no choice but to do what she says. He says, What happens next?"

"She'll fly to Deeg with you tomorrow if you put all this in writing and give one copy to me and another to Durr. Before you leave."

"I see your hand in all of this."

"My hand, but it's her character. That's what I'm supposed to tell you. That this is all your doing. She believes she ran away with Cully because of you. You put it in place by hiring Cully and making her the kind of girl she is. She's very willful. She also believes that a good part of Cully's sickness is because of you, too, what you did to his father, to him, that horse you had Bhave sell him, the Shiva, her dog, everything. That it's all your doing and your karma—"

"Hers, too," Jiggie interrupted harshly. "And your damned father's."

"You picked Cully for the job in Deeg, and she knows it. She says you trained her all along to be strong but didn't give her any room to be strong when the time came. You took the marriage out of her hands."

"What does she expect?"

"You trained her to be different. You should have treated her differently when it came to marriage. And bringing Cully to Deeg, you miscalculated what could happen between them." Phoebe couldn't stop. "Apparently it never occurs to you that things have a life of their own. It was just like with my father. You didn't calculate what betrayal would do to him any more than you did with Cully."

"And what'd it do to him?"

"It drove him mad," Phoebe said hotly. "What'd you think it'd do? You know about betrayals. You create them. You deal in them."

"Really, Miss Phoebe Guthrie." Jiggie smiled in derision.

"You set my father up so you'd be able to destroy him if it was convenient."

"You are disturbed. I can tell this is not a good time for you."

"You set him up and pulled him down," Phoebe went on, "just so you could control Kady."

"And what did it do to you?"

"Me?" Suddenly Phoebe felt confused.

"Yes, you." He said it offhandedly. "What'd this 'fake' statue do to you?"

"Nothing."

"Are you rather sure about that?" Jiggie leaned back in his chair.

Phoebe disliked him intensely. "The statue means nothing to me, except for what it did to Louis."

"What about your college education?"

"What about it?"

"And this foundation of yours, what do you call it, 'Guthrie and Guthrie'? Rather an odd name."

Phoebe felt herself getting cold. "What about it?"

"Did you ever think of calling it 'Guthrie and Deeg'?"

She stared at him.

"Did you? It has rather a nice ring to it, don't you think? I like it, rather. That Shiva may have been all very fake, but your father's estate brought in a good bit of money for you. It was sold to a very rich man. You didn't know that, did you?"

"I did too. Kady bought it."

"A very, very rich man," he went on without stopping, "who just happened to be in a good mood. He had rather a feeling of affection for this Guthrie girl. She was more bankrupt and dispossessed than she knew. She and her brother. She had no idea how bad things were and this man was kindly disposed to do something about it."

Phoebe knew what was coming. Inside she felt herself reeling and wanted to get away, be on her own, but something kept her glued to her chair.

"He rather liked her," Jiggie continued apace. "Maybe it was her spirit. Maybe he was rather bothered it would be crushed by all the adversity and he didn't want her to be impoverished as well, nobody wants to be poor, so he bought everything the family had to sell. Bought the Shiva, too. You didn't know that, did you?" he taunted her. "For great whopping amounts of

471

money it wasn't worth. Not even if it was real, was it worth it. He paid more for it than it'd be worth today."

Phoebe's eyes narrowed in fury, and when her voice came out it was thin and cold. "I know why you bought it," she said. "It had nothing to do with your mood. You'd killed my father and mother, just as if you were driving that car, you killed them, and you wanted to balance it out with something good. That was it, wasn't it? Charity's easy if you're rich, isn't it. Set the balance right, wasn't that it?"

"I paid an astronomical sum that went right straight into your bank accounts at Morgan Guaranty Trust, number Ten Wall Street, New York, New York, and then, because I was still in a good mood, I bought your father's house and I bought his furniture and I bought his land. I spent far more for these piddling things than they were worth, and all that money went right straight across to Morgan Guaranty, too."

"And you barely even felt the pinch, did you?" Phoebe said. "A couple of necklaces at the most."

"It was a tidy sum," Jiggie said casually. "For children whose father was bankrupt, in debt, in danger of being arrested—"

"He was dead," Phoebe interrupted. "He burned up in a fire. And you bought all that, not because you were in a good mood, but because that's what you do. You get control of people any way you can, because, who knows, one day you might need them. That's the way you operate. What do you want me to do now? Feel beholden to you? Feel guilty? Miserable? Or is it just a whole lot simpler than that and all you want is to undercut me because of what I've done with Mirabai and Kady? I stood up to you in my father's house, and sure, you liked my spirit, but it threatened you too and that was your way of dealing with it. You put your hooks in something and you feel better. It's automatically lessened in your eyes. You had all those Guthries right where you wanted them. Didn't you? Right down there under your thumb where you could squeeze them, any old time you wanted.

"Well, personally," Phoebe said, standing up, "I don't feel all that squeezed."

# ❧ 14 ❧

OUTSIDE, IT WAS ALMOST DARK. The rains for the day had come and gone, and now pink clouds filled the sky and the air was clear. Phoebe had Tulsidas take her to Bhagwandas Road. There she called Mirabai and told her everything was worked out, but that she should call Deeg House herself and make sure he remembered about writing things down; Jiggie was upset when she left and maybe he forgot. She didn't tell Mirabai about the dog. Let Jiggie, she thought angrily.

Afterward she went through the house and opened windows. The place was empty and airless. She went in her room and sat on a chair, knew she had to find another place to live. She didn't even think about whether it would be in Delhi or New York, just that she had to get a place that had nothing to do with Jiggie or Kady, anyone but herself. But even as she realized she was thinking about the future, she knew the past wasn't done.

There was still the white Ford car and seeing Dr. K. P. Sharma.

She decided to visit him in the morning. It was too late now.

She sent Tulsidas home and went in the bathroom, looked in the mirror, at her great mop of hair. Why had she survived, she thought, when Cully didn't? Why had she come out all right? She stared at her face, pulled her eyelids, stretched her ears, even

473

inspected her teeth. Where did her strength come from? She looked closer in the glass. She felt less angry. She certainly didn't look Indian, she thought with a grin.

But maybe that's what it was.

A recessive Indian gene. Thousands of years old, a source of strength.

The phone rang.

She went over, sat on the floor, and picked up the receiver. She knew who it was. "Hi," she said flatly.

"Hi."

There was a long silence. Neither talked. She could hear him breathing. Having him so close, she knew she loved him, but that she couldn't be with him anymore.

"I just got back," he said. "Durr told me about Mirabai. What happened with Jiggie?"

"He told me about the money, where it came from." Her voice was emotionless. "My money." She didn't even feel angry with Kady, just numb, and finished.

Kady was silent. "You didn't know Louis lost everything?"

"How could I? I thought you were both rich. That that's what the black market was all about. I didn't pay any attention to his gambling. Besides, you told me you had the Shiva. Remember?"

There was silence on the line as her words sank in.

"Can I see you?"

"Not tonight," she said.

"I've been trying to call you for days. Where've you been?"

"It's a long story."

"I have to see you."

"Where are you?"

"The Garden House. I've been thinking nonstop since you left, and you're right. Everything you said in the letter was right. But I didn't understand that you had to know. It didn't occur to me, really. I thought it didn't matter, because it was over, the past."

"I'm going to bed."

"Then can I come over in the morning? I have some things to tell you."

"I have something to do in the morning."

"What?"

"I went to Brinj. I saw the car."

Kady's silence was total. She couldn't even hear him breathe,

474

he was so quiet. "That's what I want to talk to you about. That's why I want to see you. Let me come over right now."

"No. I'm doing this on my own."

"Doing what? What are you doing tomorrow?"

"I have their death certificates. I know the doctor's name. I'm going to see him."

She told him about her trip to Agra. He listened in silence. She could hear the traffic outside, bells and wooden wheels.

"Then hear it from me, Feeb. Not the doctor. I decided in Kashmir I had to tell you."

"You should have decided that a long time ago."

"You're right. I desperately want to work it out with you."

"You say that every time."

"Yes, I do," he said, "but every single time I have worked it out. As best as I could. I've changed in the last few months more than I have in my whole life."

"That's true," she said reluctantly. "But you've had twenty years to tell me."

"Time only started for me this summer. With you, Phoebe. You want everything from me, but I can't do it overnight. I don't know how to be intimate. I'm having to learn. Please, see me before you see Sharma."

"You even remember his name."

"It's you and I that are at stake now. It's the rest of our lives. That's what this is all about. You and me."

"No," Phoebe said, "it's about me and my parents."

## ❧ 15 ❧

WHEN THE KNOCKING AT THE
door started, Phoebe woke up. She knew it was Kady, so she lay
there, listening to him and the sound of the trees outside brushing up against the roof. She looked at the curtains blowing out
into the room; there was a strong wind. Then the knock came
again, more insistent. She only had a T-shirt on, so she got up
and found a clean skirt and underpants, slipped on her sandals,
and brushed at her hair with her hands, wondering if she and
Kady could ever work it out.

But at the door it was someone else, very dark in a white shirt
and khaki trousers, and even as she opened the door she'd had
a premonition. She screamed and tried to shut the door, but he
pushed his arm through the opening and struggled with her.
She remembered Vishnu Bhave and his threatening letter and
pushed against the door all the harder, but the man clasped her
around the wrist.

"Stop it," he said in Hindi, wrestling with her now to get her
arm back down to her side. "I'm come from Suraj-sa'ab." She
didn't believe him and tried to pull away, but he didn't let go.
For all his shorter stature, he was stronger than she by far, and
he finally got her arm back behind her and held her tight. "Calm
down, memsa'ab," he said urgently. "I only have a letter for you
from sa'ab himself."

476

Phoebe relaxed a little, but he still didn't let go, as if afraid of her himself. "Let me just show it to you," he said.

She wrestled her arm free, her mind dazed with fear and the pain in her wrist. Breathing hard and wishing Tulsidas were there, she watched cautiously as he got a letter out of his pants pocket and held it up before her. Her name was on the front. She recognized the writing.

"I've never seen you before," she said accusingly.

"Soddie."

She took the letter and watched as the man retreated back a step and took a servile pose. "Why didn't he send Samiji?"

"I don't know."

"Or come himself, if he had to. This is ridiculous. It's the middle of the night." Her breath came easier now; her anger increased. "How dare you fight with me like that."

"You fighting first, memsa'ab. Me only here to give letter."

"Then why did you grab my arm?"

"Because you were shutting door. Reading letter now is best thing, I think."

Keeping her eye on him, Phoebe turned on a light. The letter was thick. "What do you do for him?" she asked accusingly.

"Some things," the man said evasively.

"Step outside while I read the letter."

"Sa'ab wants answer."

"Then maybe I'll give you an answer."

She shut the door behind him and opened the letter.

"Dear Phoebe," it began. "I know it will sound bizarre, but before you see Dr. Sharma, please do one thing for me. I've been thinking about it all night. It's very important. There's something I want you to see. You'll understand when you do. It'll make everything clearer, answer some of your questions about me.

"Will you go with this man now? Before you see Sharma? He's very trustworthy, and I'll meet you there. Wait for me."

Phoebe opened the door and looked outside. It was dark. There was a nondescript car in the driveway. "What does he want?" she asked the man in Hindi.

He quickly stamped out a cigarette. "Only that I take you to this one place only."

"What place?"

"Not so far."

477

"But where?" she persisted.

"Other side of the river."

Phoebe gasped. "The other side of the . . ."

"Yes, miss."

"But . . ." That was where the male Caucasian body had been.

"I think you will help sa'ab by coming."

"Help him?" she exclaimed. "When he's frightened me in the middle of the night? What time is it?"

"Must be four, five, roundabout."


The car drove for what seemed like a long time. She was in the back, he the front. He asked if he could smoke, she said no. Eventually the road got bumpy, and she felt a shift in the wind and a reduction in the noise outside. As the car crossed the river, she wondered what the connection was between Kady and the long-ago body that brought her to India. Had someone killed that man, and was he bringing her to the place to tell her who? But how could that be? It was too preposterous.

Thoughts were spewing wildly in her mind. What Kady had to show her, and why the white Ford car had never burned, what had really happened to her parents. Phoebe told herself to calm down, just calm down, that was enough. Kady loved her, whatever she felt, and nothing really bad was going to happen.

She slowly felt a kind of peace spread through her chest and she willed herself to follow it. She knew she had to be calm to face whatever was up ahead and beyond that, only a few hours away, Sharma himself.

She opened her windows all the way and smelled the scent of rain. She breathed in deeply, telling herself this was life, just life, calm down, everything would be all right. She wished Kady had come himself, but she knew, truthfully, that she probably wouldn't have gone with him. The letter alone had a power he wouldn't have.

In the end the car stopped at one of the prefabricated warehouses that lined the other side of the river. The man shut off the engine. She could make out the empty fields up ahead in the darkness. She knew exactly where they were, a stretch of land she'd passed in May on her way to the male Caucasian body. The buildings had been here long before, twenty years ago, when they were new and she was young.

She got out, the man, too. Everything was still. In the distance she heard the beat of a chowkidar's stick hitting the ground.

The man spoke. "He's deaf," he said, and she thought, Only in India, a deaf watchman.

They crossed the street. The man had a flashlight. He unlocked a door and held it open for her. She went inside, with only the narrow beam of light to guide her. The man kept the light small, focused on the floor immediately in front of them so she couldn't see anything else in the darkness.

"What is this?" she asked.

He didn't speak.

"Can I have the light?"

"In a minute." He directed her forward. Finally she could make out a small chair, a table, some bananas, water and a box of crackers, a charpoy bed with a cotton comforter over it, and, of all things, a chamber pot. She realized, preposterously, that Kady had set this up for her. She had no idea what was going on, but from the sight of the things, she reluctantly felt his kindness reaching out to her amid the strangeness of the circumstances. "What's happening?" she asked the man in Hindi.

"He says for you to stay here." The man sounded apologetic.

"Stay here?" Phoebe exclaimed. "When's he coming? Are you leaving?"

"I wait outside. I be here all the time."

"But what's in here? What does he want me to do?"

"You will see. You can have light."

"Thanks a lot," she said sarcastically, but when she reached for it, he held it away. He shut off the flashlight, put it down on the table, and, in the darkness, walked away. Next there was a metal sound as the door opened and a vast, thundering echo as it slammed shut. She was alone.


She didn't reach for the flashlight immediately. She tried to feel Kady's presence and determine just how angry she was with him, or whether, in fact, she was still angry.

Angry, yes, but curious, too, so she tried to relax, feel what was happening around her here in this darkness where Kady had brought her. First she felt a sense of space. It surrounded her, spreading out about her indefinitely. She knew exactly where the flashlight was, but she didn't reach for it. She wanted to adjust to the darkness because she knew that was what Kady had arranged, and she felt willing to let him get his way.

She whistled to measure the room's size. She got an echo and realized the place was even larger than she'd thought. It was pitch black, and, picking up the flashlight but not turning it on, she set out gingerly into the darkness, conscious she was standing up to Kady in some small way by not turning on the light. She went without interruption for some distance, then hit her shoulder against something.

She reached out and touched it with her hands as though she were blind.

It was a carton box that came up to her knees. She fingered it more and determined it was stapled shut.

She turned on the light and saw before her, like a solid wall, dozens, hundreds, of cartons. They loomed above her head and spread out to the right and left, going back to the far end of the warehouse.

Phoebe reeled at the sight. The smell of the boxes themselves almost overcame her, something faintly chemical and industrial. She started clawing at one, trying to pry it open. It was stapled so tight she couldn't make the ends budge, but finally, taking full note of just how obsessed she was and knowing exactly why, she pried loose an end and slipped her hand inside.

A bottle.

More bottles.

She wrenched back the sides of the carton and pulled out a bottle so aggressively that she almost dropped it.

Johnny Walker Red Label.

These were bottles of whiskey that weren't Indian and weren't meant to be.

Features of her personal history, they were contraband.


Phoebe lay on the cot and stared at the ceiling she couldn't see, thinking about corruption and payoffs, black markets, and illegality. She heard Louis telling her to count the boxes and Kady asking, wasn't he scared? and Louis saying, no, it gave things an edge.

Her past lay in the darkness around her whiskey and contraband, and Kady Suraj. But it wasn't the past to Kady, and that's what he wanted her to know.

She imagined him planning this, knowing she'd see the boxes and open them. She knew it was his own odd way of trying to break even further out of the limbo where he'd been his whole life, stuck in his own ambivalence and enigma.

Phoebe imagined she could smell the whiskey. She groped for the box of crackers, opened it, and ate one. She said, "Louis?" but there was no reply.

"Louis?" she tried again.

She remembered him. Then the darkness overwhelmed her and she realized she was inside the inner terrain of Kady Suraj. He seemed to stretch acres around her, a giant, never-ending blackness. "You didn't stop the black market, did you," she said aloud, her voice reverberating against the walls of the metal building. "You told me at the airport you did. But you didn't. You just moved from Golf Links to the riverside and went on being in danger for twenty years."

Phoebe caught her breath, appalled at the anxiety he must have felt. He didn't need the money. His thirst for wealth expired long ago. So why hadn't he stopped?

Oh, Kady, she thought. Is that how stuck you've been?

She wondered when he would come here to see her, how long he'd let her think. He told her at the airport he'd given the business to Kuldip. But he hadn't. And he hadn't left Jiggie. He hadn't shut down the black market. But he hadn't stayed in Golf Links.

Why not?

The secrecy was palpable. The room had no light, no windows, sheer high walls, this locked-up inner core of Kady Suraj, what he and Jiggie Deeg and Durr, but mostly he himself, had made of him in the time since his friend died and a sixteen-year-old girl went to America, taking with them, father and daughter, in death and departure, his past, present, and future, leaving him all alone.


She fell asleep.

When she woke up she was dreaming about the Garden House she'd never seen and imagining it at the end of a long tunnel that stretched for miles. She realized she'd heard something.

There it was, a long way away, at the far end of the room. She didn't hear it again, but after a while she realized someone was there, just as still as she.

Phoebe didn't move on the bed, just stared in that direction and imagined the person staring back. She wondered if it was Kady and what he was doing there, and tried to understand. He's not ready to talk to me, she thought. She considered using the flashlight, but she was intrigued by now, ever more certain it was Kady himself, and her anger with him so forgotten in the enormity of what she'd discovered here that she was willing to go along with what he had set up.

She relaxed, not afraid, not even irritated, just very conscious of Kady Suraj.

Then there was a faint speck of red light. It went on, then off, on and off again, a slow, unhurried rhythm: Kady's cigarette. Subtly, it let her know something very serious was going on with him.

She began to feel anxious, afraid he was about to be arrested and he knew it, or that something else, awful, was going to happen. Gradually, though, the calmness of his smoking told her to let him be, let him work it out his way. This was his setup, his plan, and she thought enough of him to go along with it, whatever the future would be. She trusted him.

Eventually something came in along the air. It was a smell that was faintly, inescapably and, finally, very intimately, one thing and one thing only and that was cinnamon.


When she woke up she knew it was morning even before she opened her eyes because she heard a truck passing on the road. She heard a door open, saw cracks of light and the driver coming toward her.

"Sa'ab says you can go."

"Where is he?"

"I no idea."

"He was here."

The man shrugged.

"Is he outside?"

"Just you go now."

The man left. Phoebe heard a car drive away. She was all alone again.

She stood up, calculated there were between seventy and

seventy-five boxes and that the room itself was almost one block long. At the far end she saw another door and the chair where Kady'd been.

She gazed out into this odd incarnation of what her past had been and felt strangely moved. She imagined Louis out there and remembered the excitement of it all, running down streets with the two of them, Kady and her father, waving her arms to feel the wind, her life swooped up and carried along by these two men.

Outside, Phoebe stood in the shadow of the warehouse and tried to figure out what to do. She knew Kady would come get her. She had no idea what she'd say to him.

The road was empty, no taxis, nothing. She breathed deeply. The air felt clean, although it was hot and muggy. Rain clouds appeared on the horizon.

She saw a car coming down the road toward her. It approached slowly, Kady's old Fiat, and, just before it reached her, pulled off into the bushes on the side of the road.

"Come on," Kady called out the window. "Get in."

She didn't move.

"I'll take you to Sharma's house. Isn't that where you want to go?"

"Yes."

"Okay, then, come on."

She started to cross the street, then stopped.

"There's trucks. It'd be pretty silly to go through all this and then get run over." He got out and went around the car to the passenger side, opening the door for her. "I'm sorry," he said, throwing up his hands in a gesture of helplessness. "I had to do that. It was the only way I could think of letting you know. To tell you face to face felt impossible."

"But that man scared me to death trying to get in the house. And why did you just sit there last night?"

"You saw me?"

"Of course I saw you," Phoebe said angrily. "You think I'd be asleep? How do you know I'm not afraid of the dark?"

"Come on," he said, tapping the roof of the car. "We can't stay here all day."

Phoebe got in.

"What's the address?" Kady asked from his seat.

She told him.

He started up the engine. "But I won't wait for you there," he said as the car set off. "Afterwards, it's up to you. I know I've been a complete ass about everything, and Sharma's only going to confirm it. But you know," he said, smiling grimly, "showing you the warehouse was the only sensible thing I've done all summer. I should have done it three months ago."

They were headed back across the Jumna River, windows wide open.

"Don't ever do something like that again," Phoebe said after a while. "Send someone to my house in the middle of the night, leave me for hours in the dark. I may understand, but I don't like it. And why did you come in there last night? Why didn't you say something?" She glanced at him. His hair wasn't combed and he hadn't shaved, but he seemed completely relaxed, almost at peace.

"Just to say good-bye, I expect."

"To me?"

"Oh no," he said, throwing her a quick smile. "I hope not."

"Then to what?"

"To everything, really. I turned it over to Kuldip."

"You told me you'd already done that. At the airport. It obviously wasn't the truth, no more than anything else was true."

"I did it in Kashmir."

"Kashmir?" she asked in surprise.

"The day we climbed the mountain. Remember when we were walking home and I said I had to make a phone call? You bought a cold drink? I was calling him."

"When did you move operations from Golf Links to the warehouse?"

"Right after you left. Right after they died."

"Does Jiggie know?"

"Does Jiggie know," he said sarcastically. "He showed up at the warehouse the day I moved everything in. Said he wanted to be sure of everything so he could keep the police informed."

"He doesn't ever stop, does he."

"No," Kady said, "but neither did I."

❧

When they reached Dr. Sharma's, Kady turned off the engine. No one was in sight. "Who'd have thought everything would come down to this."

"What do you mean?"

"I barely remember what he looks like. Tall, maybe? And he kept talking about how many children he had to take care of. He wasn't very subtle about what he wanted. But neither were we, I suppose. I've never been here before."

"I used to eat lunch over there when I was waiting for him." Phoebe pointed toward a corner of the veranda. "In the afternoon there's no sun. Sometimes his bearer brought me water."

"As far as I'm concerned, it's better for you to learn about this now than when you were a child. It's nothing a child should have to handle. You'll see. Although, knowing you, you'll disagree with me. But I certainly should have told you in June."

"Why didn't you?"

Kady didn't answer. He pulled at his lips as if to shape the words. "Bear with me," he said. "I'm not very good at explaining these sorts of things. At first," he said, "it didn't occur to me. The whole thing was over. I didn't think it meant much anymore, and even though having you back—"

"And Cully."

"—made me think about it, I was so unaccustomed to saying anything particularly truthful about myself that it never really occurred to me to. It just seemed over. Besides," he added, "it was so linked up with my own devastating private life, I couldn't talk about it. Does that make any sense?"

"Yes," she said, but she looked away from him.

"Then I fell in love with you, all over again, and it was stunning because it was absolutely familiar, wanting you, but knowing, just like before, that I couldn't have you. Only this time it was because of the lies. I didn't want to be with you because of all the lies. You're a wonderful woman, Phoebe, but you've put me through hell."

"What do you think you've put me through?" she retorted. "You have a totally one-sided view of this. All you've done is lie to me and manipulate me, and the biggest lie is probably right over there with Dr. Sharma. If I weren't so numbed by last night, I'd be furious with you. I'd no more be sitting in this car than—"

"That day at the airport was the worst day in my life."

"Why?" she asked, curious despite herself.

"Everything I'd repressed for twenty years exploded in my face."

"But you went on lying."

"You're absolutely right, and if you weren't so goddamned tenacious, I'd probably still be lying." He reached in his trousers and got some money.

She took it.

"For the taxi. In you go now. I've done everything wrong, but it was all I could do." Kady paused. "You know where to find me if you want me."

"The Garden House?"

He nodded.

"Not Durr's."

"No."

"But I don't know where it is." Her hand was on the doorknob.

Kady wrote the address on some paper. "There's no phone."

"What are you going to do now?" Unexpectedly, she didn't want to leave.

"I don't know. Samiji's back."

"And Cully?"

"I don't know."

"Are you going to the wedding tonight?"

"I don't want to talk anymore. This is too serious. I know what's waiting for you in there." He gestured toward the house. "You don't. If you still want to see me after this, we can talk all you want."

"But what are you going to do about work?"

"Never mind about that now."

Phoebe opened the door and got out, started slowly toward the house.

Kady revved up the motor, leaned his head out the window. "Take care of yourself," he said, smiling that halfway smile. "I must confess to feeling awfully sad."

"I'm as confused as you."

"But I'm not confused anymore. In an odd way, I've never felt better in my life. Will you remember one thing? I did everything because I love you." He nodded toward the house. "Even then," he said, "twenty years ago, when you had your first pair of high-heeled shoes. Remember?"

"Yes."

"I didn't know if I was supposed to be your brother or your lover. Did you know Jiggie had you followed?"

"When?"

"Then. Shyam followed you."

"But why? I was only sixteen."

"Because I was in love with you."

Phoebe stared at him dumbly.

"Durr told him, and he had Shyam following you whenever you weren't with me and Louis."

Phoebe felt her skull cracking open and air *whoosh* around inside.

"He saw you go to Nizamuddin's Tomb with Vikrim Ali Seth."

Her eyes widened. "He came inside?" she asked, aghast.

Suddenly Kady got out of the car and drew her over to the shade underneath a tree. "There's one thing," he said, squeezing her hands tight. "When Sharma tells you what happened in Golf Links . . ."

"Golf Links."

"Just remember that Jiggie had already told me about Vikrim Ali Seth."

Phoebe was shaking her head. "I can't take any more."

"You have to remember this."

"But I can't. I can't do another thing."

"Just remember he told me about Vikrim Ali Seth as soon as you got home that night. I was in Deeg and he walked into my bedroom and woke me up and told me everything, and so, the next night, the night . . . you know . . . when we got to Golf Links . . ."

"Not Agra? But they died in Agra."

"You have to remember I still loved you and wanted to protect you, no matter what you did with Vikrim Ali Seth."

"I don't understand a thing," Phoebe said angrily. "Let go of me and stop this. I hate it." She wrestled her way out of his arms. "Let me be."

Kady grabbed her arms and shook her. "Listen to me," he growled.

"No."

"If you could sleep with him, goddamn it, not me, then I knew I had to get you away from here. From me and Jiggie and India. You had to start over someplace else that wasn't decadent and awful."

"But you said you were going to leave him yourself," Phoebe said. "Do you know how terrible it is getting little scraps of information about your life? Just stop telling me these things. I can't stand it."

"I did tell Jiggie I was going to leave him. Two seconds after he told me about you and Vikrim Ali Seth. He expected me to get mad at you, but instead I yelled at him and said I didn't want one more thing from him. Not one. It was over. Done. No marriage, no bargain, no nothing."

"No black market?"

"Nothing."

"Then why didn't you?"

Kady turned away from her, his hands plowing roughly through his hair. "Because it turned out I was wrong. There was one more thing I needed from Jiggie. I just didn't know it yet."

"What was it?"

"That's what he's going to tell you." Kady pointed toward the house.

Phoebe turned around.

A man was standing on Dr. Sharma's porch. He was tall and thin, leaning on a cane and wearing a dhoti, with little wire glasses on the end of his nose.

Phoebe heard Kady get in the car. She began walking toward the man.

"Just remember," Kady called out, "we were at the end of the line. All of us. I thought I was doing everything for you."

# ❧ 16 ❧

SHE GOT CLOSER TO THE HOUSE.
Dr. Sharma watched her.

The grass on the lawn had turned green, and birds were drinking from a gutter that had backed up somewhere and was overflowing so that a good part of the lawn had turned to a shallow bath. Her feet were dark with mud. She remembers noticing her clothes were dirty and telling herself she had to remember the date because this was going to be an important day.

But mostly she was conscious of Dr. Sharma himself, looking vaguely professorial, standing on the veranda with his cane and little glasses.

She remembers thinking he would know who she was because she'd discussed the death certificates with his bearer. The closer she got, the more she liked his face. There was something simple but intelligent about it, a broad high forehead and a strong yet troubled look, as though he understood they were linked by the one thing in his life he had done that was wrong.

She proceeded across the wet lawn, sure he was reliving what he'd done all those years before. I've been troubled by it, too, she thought, so has Kady and Cully; we're all contaminated by what happened, whatever it was. But she still knew that whatever the doctor told her, it would only help.

"Good morning, Dr. Sharma."

"Good morning." His voice was distant and noncommittal, not what she'd expected.

"Do you think I can come up and talk to you for a minute?" Polite she was, and circumspect.

He took a step backward.

"Your bearer told me you were away. I've been here to see you many times. I'm sure he mentioned it."

She started going up the steps. He turned toward the screen. The bearer opened the door and the doctor went in, half to get away from her, she thought, but she followed him inside.

The room was cool and veiled, curtains covering the windows. The doctor ordered her a drink. The bearer disappeared, and suddenly it was only the two of them in a not very big room. Phoebe felt consumed with the desire to know what had happened twenty years ago, but she realized he still hadn't said anything or even acknowledged her.

She watched the curtains stirring in a breeze, and she saw the same family pictures on the tables. She remembers wondering if he was seeing them too and telling himself that he'd done it for them, his family, whatever it was he'd done, because he wanted a nice house and a nice life, but it was only for them, he didn't care for himself. She wondered if that was true. Were people ever corrupt only for other people? Not themselves?

The doctor jolted her back by asking her to sit. She decided he was trying to get the feel of her, an American with yellow hair and dirty feet and a dirty skirt, so she switched to Hindi and, talking slowly, said she'd been born in India and had lived here for sixteen years until she went back to New York to be with her grandmother.

"Does everybody in America have a television set?"

The question threw her. "Listen, Dr. Sharma," she said, speaking English, "can I ask you some questions?"

"Oh, yes, anything for a guest to our very country." He tapped his cane on the floor, disconcerting her.

"You must be knowing," he was saying, "Indians are most hospitable peoples in this very world and—"

"Yes. It's a wonderful quality."

"It is what God tells us to do. We are only God's servant, this one time and every time, in all our lifetimes."

"Dr. Sharma." She leaned forward. "I believe we have some mutual friends."

"Oh, yes, must be."

"Mr. Jiggie Deeg and Kady Suraj."

"Jiggie Deeg, yes, most good friends with my elder brother. Everyone is knowing of this one great man."

"My parents died twenty years ago, Dr. Sharma. I think you signed their death certificates." This wasn't how she'd planned to start at all.

"Death is only life in the making—"

"You—"

"—and we must all"—rocking back and forth—"awaken to the life ahead."

"Yes, but I am interested in death. I want to know about my parents' deaths."

"We must be thinking of life only as a phase of transition."

"I don't care about life," Phoebe blurted out, nearly bursting with frustration. "I want to know about death."

"But the two are only one and same, just now one, just now other, life and death becoming other."

"They died, Dr. Sharma," Phoebe cried out, so intensely that the man opened his eyes in shock. "They stopped breathing. They died. You're a doctor. You know what that means."

"Must be."

"I want to know how they died. I was told it was a car crash in Agra. That the crash killed four or five villagers and some cows and turned into a great big fire. Only the thing was, the car didn't burn up, and you didn't live in Agra. Something happened here in Delhi, in Golf Links. You signed Agra death certificates here in Delhi."

There was a glimmer of light in the old man's eyes, and Phoebe knew that, however strange she seemed to him, he had locked back on to twenty years ago, the one thing they had in common.

"They died," she said, slowing down. "It was January sixth, twenty years ago."

Nothing moved, chair, cane.

"You signed the death certificates. I want to know what happened."

There was a long silence. Then, slowly, his body began to

rock, the chair, too, and she knew she'd lost him all over again. "I want to know about it," she said, but she knew he wasn't going to tell her. "Two Caucasians. A car crash, Golf Links. You must remember. You even remembered the man who drove me here. You recognized him."

"What is it you are wanting to know?" he asked.

"I want to know what happened to my parents."

"But you were just now saying it was twenty years ago. What is this wanting of the past? The past is gone, turned into the future. Already the present is passing."

"Don't give me that," Phoebe cried, pressing her hands against her head.

"Maybe if you have been coming one day sooner." The doctor stood up. "Five, ten years, maybe. Then maybe I am remembering. Now I am not remembering anything. I am an old man." He turned toward the door.

Phoebe didn't move.

"You must go," he insisted.

She stood up.

"I have nothing to tell you. It must be another Dr. Sharma."


Outside, Phoebe sat down hard on the veranda steps, drew her legs to her body, and stared at her feet. Grime had wedged between her toes and crusted along the edges of her sandals. There was little traffic in the street outside. She propped her head in her hands and watched the gutter overflowing and the clouds approach. After a while it began to rain, a slow drizzle. She stretched out her legs to get them wet. Her blue skirt turned a darker blue, a puddle of water grew in her lap. She cupped her hands in it and tossed the water up into her face and hair.

The bearer tiptoed out. He had a glass of steaming milky tea.

"Here, missus." He handed it to her and darted back inside.

Phoebe drank the tea thirstily, put the glass down by her feet, watched it fill with rain, then drank that, too. She had no idea how much time passed, but at some point she realized she was being watched again and she turned around.

The bearer came up to her. "My master has one question."

She glanced at the house. The doctor was peering out.

"He is just now wanting to know this one thing only. Why is this one matter not important but so important?"

"Why?" Phoebe exclaimed, talking to the doctor. "Because it's everything. It's this great big dark black pit. My parents disappeared. They didn't say good-bye. They didn't say they were going out. They just got in the car and went, and I didn't know where they were going or why. All I did was stand at the window and watch. I knew they were going forever. I knew something was wrong, but I didn't know what it was. To this day I don't know what it was. No one will tell me. I don't know where the car went or how they died.

"Unless I've known it all along," she said, "and that's why it's this pit. I didn't want to know. But now I do. And no one will tell me. I want to know the truth, Dr. Sharma," she cried. "With all my heart, I want to know the truth. My heart. . . ."

"Your heart?" The doctor came to her side. "Why didn't you tell me it was a matter of the heart?"

"I did," Phoebe said weakly.

"No," he said, taking her hand and drawing her toward the door. "You were telling me what I must do. But you never told me why. If it is a matter of the heart, then I myself will be telling you everything there is to tell."

## ❧ 17 ❧

"I AM SLEEPING VERY SOUNDLY IN this place where I am living," the doctor began. "There is only me and my childrens and my wife and this one motor scooter that I am having, and there is this loud pounding on my door one night. We are living not one, not two, but three stories up from above the ground, and at the door, now three stories up, is this one shopkeeper which I am knowing which delivers telephone messages to me, I pay him one, two rupees."

Phoebe had taken off her wet clothes in the bathroom and was sitting on the couch shrouded in a bedspread. She had a towel around her head and her feet in a pail of water. That she looked and felt like an invalid was deeply satisfying to her because, although she barely knew these two old men, she felt their kindness now as something she greatly needed.

"So I am going down the street to this one shopkeeper's, so late and cold it is, this is winter now, and I am wishing I had my scarf, the wind is blowing oh, so hard. On the telephone it is my brother in Agra yelling at me why did I take so long? My brother is this lawyer who works for Mr. Jiggie Deeg, and he is telling me to be quiet and not talk, although I have not yet said one word, not one word, and then he is telling this is my one chance, that he has provided for me this one big chance, and that there is only this one small favor I must do. Then everything in

494

my life will change and I will be rich man, oh, so very rich man. He says it is only one small thing, but it must be secret.

"He has this one big friend, he says, and he cannot tell me who he is, but I am knowing in my heart right away he is speaking of Mr. Jiggie Deeg himself. This man, he says, has just now been telephoning to him. This man tells him that he too has just received one phone call from some personage in Delhi, and there is true emergency.

"Then he waits, my brother, for me to get one pencil, and I inform the shopkeeper to leave me alone because this is private"—only he pronounced it "pri-watt"—"between me and my one brother, and the shopkeeper leaves. My brother tells me to write down this address for Golf Links. I say I have never been to Golf Links. He tells me never mind, go there now and wait for this man, he will be coming soon and tell me everything, not to worry, it is just a matter of his very own plane which is bringing him up to Delhi in a jiffy. He says too that I must be waiting for this one other person, a second person, and I say 'Who?' and he says, 'One clerk-chaprassi who will arrive from Agra.'

"And I say, 'Why must I wait for some clerk-chaprassi from Agra?' and he says, just do what his friend tells me to do because he himself cannot be saying more on the telephone, but I say, 'Tell me, tell me,' and he does.

"He says there is something 'to dispose of.'

"He does not tell me what it is, but I am coming to know it is not garbage and it is not old clothes, it is something far more precious. He tells me there can be no police at this Golf Links and no delay, and everything is in my hands because only a doctor can put this right. He says it is all for childrens. He says there must be no delay in settling the estate in-wolved because there are childrens. His big friend in Deeg has these two concerns, he says. One is the police and the other is these childrens.

"And I say, 'Are these childrens to be protected from the police?' and he is telling no, not exactly, but they must never know this situation has occurred and I must fix it so they may never know, and fix it so all affairs in-wolved can get settled in a jiffy and there is no botheration from police or surely they will come to know, these childrens, and all in my heart I understand because I have childrens, too."

Phoebe was leaning across her knees toward the doctor, his

words, like minute cells, going deep inside her.

"Then he tells to me that I must wait for this clerk-chaprassi from Agra because . . ." The doctor paused. "Because he will bring death certificates for me to sign."

Sharma paused.

"That," he said solemnly, "is when I am knowing for sure this is a matter of departure.

"Then my brother explains this whole bus-i-ness to me. He says he has been able to locate blank and unused death certificates for Agra, but there is no doctor which he knows and trusts the way he knows and trusts his little brother, a doctor who can stamp them and seal them and take them to the municipality to perform the registration."

"But I looked for them in Agra," Phoebe interrupted. "They weren't there."

"Wait only," Dr. Sharma said firmly. "It is my duty to tell you every single thing there is to tell, and I am doing that, piece by piece, little by little."

"Sorry."

"So, I say to my brother that death certificates for Agra do not work for Delhi. He says they will. He says I am to register them in Delhi and the authorities will accept them because they only check license number of the doctor, nothing else, what does it matter? Delhi, Agra? This is only fine print, and that is what all he is telling his friend, Maharaj-sahib. That doctor is what he needs, doctor can fix his problem, doctor and his stamp. Then death can be registered anywhere, no matter, and estate can be settled with not one hesitation or interference from police.

"But I am not liking this, and I say to my brother, 'I must be doing this with the death certificate one time?' because until then I am thinking there is only one of these certificates, and I do not want to wi-olate even one piece of paper that has to do with death and the departure from this life, just as I would not want to wi-olate the coming of life, but my brother says, 'No. There are two. There are two times you must be doing this,' and I am knowing at just that moment that in all this life and even into the next, I will have difficulty because I have interfered with a true and proper departure. And I am knowing for certain that these deaths will remain unfinished and unresolved for a long time to come."

"Why didn't you refuse?"

"Because I was summoned," the man said simply. "There was no choice."

So Dr. Sharma walked back down the street to his little apartment where his wife and children were sleeping, and he found the rubber stamp that had his name and license number embossed on it and he put it in his pocket and went out into the night, leaving the motor scooter behind because it was the most precious thing he had and he didn't want to risk it in this terrible and complicated event.

He walked until he found a cycle rickshaw. He woke the driver and told him to take him to Golf Links. He got to the house before the others did. He knew right away which house it was, because the lights were on, when there weren't any lights in the other houses, and there were two cars outside, one Indian, the other a white Ford with the doors wide open into the street in a way that doors aren't meant to be hanging out. It was the first thing he saw that warned him that something was not right at all, something he hadn't even imagined, because the car itself looked as if it were screaming, doors, like mouths, open with its yells, and he knew all over again what a terrible bargain he had made.

"So you went in?"

"Miss-sa'ab, maybe . . ." He hesitated.

"No, tell me. I want to know."

"I knocked and knocked, and . . ."

"What happened?"

The door opened a couple of inches, no more, and a short man with a face that was slightly larger on one side than the other peered out at him and said, "Yes?"

"I am the one."

"The one?"

"My brother is this one lawyer in Agra."

"You are the doctor?"

"Yes."

Samiji slowly opened the door, standing behind it so the doctor couldn't see him, until, finally, the door was wide open, the doctor was inside, and there was nothing for Samiji to do but close the door. That's when Sharma saw him full figure and saw his clothes were covered from top to bottom with great splotches of blood. His hands were covered, too, the palms full of blood. The doctor stared at him in horror.

"Your brother didn't tell you?" the man said.

"Just there are two deaths."

Samiji shut the door. The place was quiet. Sharma could see the foyer and the living room, empty but for carton boxes. "Where's . . . ?"

"Upstairs."

"What . . . ?"

"Didn't he tell you anything?" The man turned away, holding his hands out from his body. "I'm not in charge. You have to wait. I can't tell you." He disappeared up the stairs.

After a while the man came back, his face troubled and intense. "Maybe you are wanting to come up?"

"Anything."

"Then you come up. I am telling you." He sounded different now. "I am only driver, but it is my duty to be in charge, just now when no one else is here. This is my de-si-shi-un."

Sharma understood the situation exactly.

They went upstairs, and on the landing they turned right.

Ahead was a room that wasn't very big, ceiling slanted down on the sides, a child's room at one time. In the middle there was a large pool of blood and the body of a male Caucasian, his back to them, who had fallen over headfirst into a pile of carton boxes and was resting there, midair, embracing the boxes themselves.

His dark hair was barely tousled, and from his position near the door, Sharma could see his eyes were wide open and his face was ashen. He might have been a mannequin, arms in space; there was no sign of damage or injury anywhere, just, in the pool of blood, proof that, somewhere, his body had a monumental leak.

The blood itself was so dark it was almost black. It shone in the reflection of a light bulb overhead.

Sharma could see a second set of legs underneath the first, Caucasian, too, wearing shoes that could only be a woman's, and that the shoes were pointing out, whereas the man's feet were pointing in. The woman had toppled over backward and been nearly crushed by the larger weight of what had fallen on top of her. They rested, in death, facing each other in this weird embrace that was getting ever colder and more awful as their bodies hardened and settled in to the shape the gods must have wanted them to have.

Sharma clasped his hand across his mouth and contained a wave of nausea.

A gun was on the floor. It had an attachment that took away the sound. From his position Sharma looked at the bodies for signs of bullet holes, but there were none. Neither body, as far as he could see—he couldn't see the woman's face or torso—even looked injured.

"You see?" Samiji said. "You see what awful thing has brought you to this wretched place? Death as miserable as this?"


Sharma hadn't spoken in some time. Phoebe hadn't moved. It was still raining outside; wind was blowing against the windows. She was chewing on her thumb. Her hair, drying, had come out from under the towel and was falling down, yellow clumps that hadn't been brushed standing out around her face.

"Are you all right?" the doctor asked.

She looked up, dazed.

"You want some tea?"

"No, this is fine."

"I mean . . ."

"This is what I want," she said. "It's a relief. I promise. I feel relieved." But her voice was flat, a monotone, and her skin was pale even for someone whose skin was white.

"You said to give you each and every detail."

"I know."

"I am only trying to be of service."

"No, this is perfect. Really." Her voice trailed off. "What did he look like?"

"Like he was dead. Nothing moved. Not one thing. The fingers stay out, like this." He showed her. "This is sign of death. Anyone can see it."

499

"He was my father."

"Yes."

"And my mother."

"Yes."

"I have a brother."

"Yes, I remember."

"What was he wearing?"

"Trousers and one shirt."

"And she?"

"Some dress," he said. "Maybe blue with red-and-green stripes."

"I know the one." Phoebe looked up with a trace of life. "A plaid dress with a belt at the waist and a bow at the neck?"

"Must be."

"A tailor made it," she said. "He came to the house. The bow was my idea. I said . . ." She stopped.

"What did you say?"

"I just said a bow would look pretty, and she said, did I think so? That's all. I don't remember much," Phoebe added, almost whispering. "Sometimes I don't even remember what she looked like."

The rain rattled against the windows. The doctor waited.

"It explains the car, too," she said.

"What car?"

"And why no one gave me straight answers. They never did." She looked up again. "No one ever told us anything. Just that it happened in Agra."

"And so it is becoming this dark deep pit."

"No," she said. "The pit was my mother. I could never understand why my mother went with him that night. I never understood, so I finally made myself stop thinking about her."

He waited, not knowing what she was talking about.

"Tell me the truth," she said. "I don't want anything but the truth."

The rain was tapping harder at the windowpanes. The room was filled with other people's photographs and a prosperity that stemmed from her parents' death. So she was linked with the doctor, too, she thought, thread upon thread of entanglement. "He killed her, didn't he?" she said finally, her eyes steady. "That's what happened, isn't it? My father killed my mother."

Sharma nodded, one tiny movement of his head.

Phoebe shivered, a jolt that went through her body, shoulders, torso, legs, and feet, a quake along the fault lines. "He killed her," she murmured, her face gone truly white. "That's what no one wanted us to know."

"Must be."

She clutched her stomach with her arms.

"Can I get you something?"

"They'd have told us if he killed himself. This was what they couldn't say."

"Must be."

"He must have been really sick. He must have . . ." Phoebe didn't finish the sentence, just held her stomach and started taking in great breaths of air.

"Maybe just you lie down for one minute."

She held herself in solitary embrace. Her breathing began to ease. "He shot her," she said, "and then he shot himself. That was his solution. He couldn't leave her. But he could kill her. Why couldn't he just leave her?"

"I'm so sorry to tell you."

"It's all right. But, you know, I never thought that's what happened. It never even crossed my mind. Not once."

"Truly sorry."

"I thought about everything else. That she might have died in a different kind of accident, or . . . I don't know what. But never that. The truth is," she went on, "I didn't think." She chewed on her thumb. "We were probably still sitting at the window."

"What window?"

"Cully and I. We had a window in our room. We were probably sitting there. I fixed his shoulder, he had a cut, and then we were sitting there. Kneeling, really. You had to kneel down and put your elbows up on the windowsill. It was cold. I remember. Do you think we were still there?"

Sharma didn't answer.

"Afterwards I looked for the gun," she went on. "I looked everywhere the next day, but I couldn't find it. I even looked under his bed. I thought, maybe, he had, you know . . ."

"Shot himself?"

Phoebe pulled the bedspread higher around her neck. "But I couldn't think about her."

"You are not letting yourself think this horrible thing."

"It was an old dress," Phoebe said. "The plaid one. What happened to it? What happened to her wedding ring? And the shoes?"

"Same thing only that happened to her body," the doctor said. "Same thing that all time always happens to bodies."


Flies were dancing in the blood. He hadn't seen them before. Now he realized there were dozens, scores, materialized out of nowhere in the winter air to feast on death. He started shooing them away, then stopped. It was no use. There were too many. Samiji, against the wall, had closed his eyes.

The doctor could hear the wind, a tree brushing up against the roof. It was cold. He wished he had his scarf. He noticed the window shades had been pulled down and that they were covered with bloody handprints, prints too big to be the woman's, and the man's hands, he saw, were hanging down, pink and clean. "He wasn't thinking," he said aloud.

"Who?"

"This man. You only are pulling those down, isn't it." He pointed toward the window shades.

The driver shook his head.

"I know," the doctor said. "I know everything. Your hands are bloody. Those are your prints. He wasn't thinking, this man. Not one bit." Sharma felt angry suddenly. "He should have closed them first thing. Isn't he caring if neighbors see? Doesn't he understand this thing what he is doing? Doesn't he even think about his childrens? If they are finding out?"

Samiji put his hands over his ears.

"This I am telling you," Sharma insisted.

"No." The driver sounded anguished.

"I must say truth."

"He was a good man, truly he was. Something happened to him."

"But he isn't even pulling shades down. This one thing only he could do."

Samiji started to cry. He rubbed his hands in his eyes, smeared blood over his face.

Sharma watched him.

"He was my master," the man mumbled. "I drive him every

which way, all time always. I am belonging to him and his childrens."

Sharma patted the man on the shoulder, his anger dissipated, and led him down the hall to the bathroom. There he propped him up on the sink and threw cold water on his face and hands until the blood was gone.

Back in the room, Sharma asked him what had happened.

"I cannot reveal," Samiji said.

"It's all right. I have to know."

"I was in one car. They were in the other. I followed them from this one big house where they live. I cannot let them be alone."

"Why?"

"I cannot say."

"It's all right. Tell me."

"He was not well. I am knowing this, and I am all time always worrying for him. He is unhappy. He has misfortunes. Oh, so many, just these last few days even. One, two, three, so many things. Here at this house, he parks. I park. He is telling me to wait outside. He tells me not to come in. There is something he has to do. And so I am waiting. But they do not come out."

"Yes?"

"Still they are not coming out. She was not one for liking to be outside her house, she is very Indian woman in this matter, and so I am knowing she is not liking to be there with him. I am coming inside finally, for her, I am thinking, but I am not hearing anything, so I come upstairs."

"Yes."

"He was very good man," Samiji said, wagging his head sorrowfully from side to side. "Truly he was."

"You tried to move the bodies, didn't you."

"No."

"It's all right. I can tell. That's how you got bloody. You wanted to find the bullet holes."

"No."

Sharma went over to the bodies and, taking hold of the dead man's sleeve, pulled him out far enough to get a look at the woman's hidden face. "Oh," he said, understanding.

Behind him, Samiji covered his eyes in shame.

The doctor let go of the sleeve, and the body descended back into the spot where it had died.

"What was it? Tell me."

Her face was incomplete. A good part of the left side was gone, a bullet had removed it. The other side was already black and blue, and the eye, the only eye, looked as though someone had pounded it with his fist. There was nearly nothing left of it.

"Then why didn't she tip over when he hit her? Fall off the boxes?"
"She was standing up."
"When he hit her?"
"She probably fell, but he kept on hitting her. Then he was having her sit down. She was sitting on edge of boxes when he is shooting her. It is not natural position, the way she is sitting, I am sorry to say. She cannot have been entirely and completely comfortable sitting in this way, and so I am knowing he has told her to sit very, very straight while he does this one thing only to her. I am truly sorry."
"So she just watched?" Phoebe asked, aghast. "She knew what was going to happen?"
"Must be."
"But she was a good person. Or I think she was, until her misery twisted her and made her cruel."
"Must be. Mothers are the universe."
"What happened?" Phoebe asked. "Tell me."
"He is shooting her and she falls backwards, but her legs are staying up. In the very same position she is having when she is sitting. She is frozen, maybe."
"So she knew what was going to happen?"
"Must be."
"And didn't try to get away."
"Must be. I am seeing no bruise marks. The big man, when he came, the man who brought you in the car, he had me look and look. He tells me to discover every single thing I can about these bodies and what has happened. I tell him the man hit her in the eye and then—"

"So she just sat there while he shot her?"

"Must be. Otherwise she would be having different position, this one, that one, so many different positions, they are all possible."

"And so he just shot her? Point-blank?"

"Must be."

"But how did she look? Was she screaming? Scared?"

"The face did not show any one thing except that she was not scared, I can say that to you, there was not any expression of fear, and she was not screaming. That all was werry clear. She must have been werry strong and serious person," he said with admiration. "The shooting must have been something that did not altogether displease her."


Dr. Sharma let the man's body descend back into position. It felt cold to his touch; it had already started to harden. Samiji, against the wall, had begun to groan again, a low guttural sound that didn't let up.

Sharma looked toward the ceiling and along the eaves, searching for the souls of the two Caucasian bodies. They would be there, he knew, waiting for transition.

Samiji glanced at him, understood, and looked up, too.

They were silent, knowing they were not alone, even if there was nothing, expressly, there to see.

"I called the punditji," Samiji said. "They are coming sometime now, one hour, two hours. Prayers, prashad. Is fitting, I am thinking. But is not my idea. His one friend is telling me all what to do."

"Maybe they've learned," the doctor said, looking at the bodies again.

"Yes."

"And the next lifetime will be better."

"You think?"

"Is possible."


"Learned what?" Phoebe asked.

"Maybe they didn't pay attention," the doctor said.

"Pay attention to what?"

"To anything," he answered. "Maybe she has not been paying

505

attention through many lifetimes, and this has happened to make her take notice at last. Maybe he—"

"I don't understand."

"The gods exact their price. This is price. Very great one. Maybe now these peoples are learning from so big a lesson as this."

"But learned what?"

"Who's to know?" the doctor said. "Each and every one of us has something he must learn. Only he can know exactly what it is."

# ❧ 18 ❧

THEY HEARD A CAR PULL UP OUT-
side and went downstairs. Samiji unlocked the door and let two
people in. Sharma stood back and watched.

The first was a short man with a pockmarked face wearing
trousers and an astrakhan coat that came to below his knees. He
barely talked. The other was a man so imposing in his suit and
sweater that Sharma automatically bowed in deep respect and
knew he had finally met Maharaja Juggernathan Bisamillah Rajender Bahadur Singh.

This one, the man he mistakenly assumed to be the maharaja,
paid attention only to Samiji. "Where are they?" he asked.

"Upstairs."

The maharaja ran up two stairs at a time, the driver following,
saying, "Slowly, sa'ab, slowly." At the top he turned the wrong
way. The driver had to call him back. "This way, sa'ab, this
way," and the maharaja wheeled around and strode back and
there, at the doorway, stopped and swayed as he stared inside.
"Oh, my God," he said over and over again, hands frozen in the
air.

The other, little man had no such temerity. He pushed past
the maharaja and went in, looking down at the bodies like a
policeman. "Have to clean the floor," he said right off. "Walls,
too."

Sharma watched from the hall and assumed he knew precisely what was going on. That was the maharaja's father: his tone and manner were so preemptive and controlling. But no maharaja could have a living father, he realized, so he determined he was his uncle.

As Sharma watched, the uncle waved his hand over the bodies in a gesture of dismissal, retreated to the wall, and proceeded to lean back against it in a position so utterly relaxed and indifferent, one leg up along the other, that Sharma gasped aloud. The man produced a cigarette and took a long and noisy drag.

Everyone stared at him, aghast. His nephew narrowed his eyes and watched him. "You really are disgusting," he said.

The uncle ignored him.

"You appall me. You revolt me."

The uncle smoked, indifferent. "You'll have to wash this up," he said.

"Don't you have any respect?" his nephew said. "Doesn't anyone mean anything to you?"

"Oh, yes," the man said, smiling broadly, "and you know her well."

Sharma stared back and forth between them. He was mesmerized by the antagonism, even as he had no idea what they were talking about.

"You'll have to get the pails out of the jeep," the uncle was saying, talking to Samiji now. "Wash down everything, walls, doorknobs. Get rid of the flies. The carton boxes, too. You know where you want them taken yet?"

His nephew shook his head.

"You want them gone, though, don't you?"

To Sharma everything was clear: the two were inextricably bonded, yet deeply estranged. It made perfect sense. He'd figured it out completely. The maharaja's father had died young, everyone knew that, he himself now remembered the day the man had died because all the Agra papers had it, the Maharaja of Deeg dead, his heir was only six, and he had no mother, either. Sharma assumed from the look of things that the uncle had stepped in and assumed a parental role, but something had gone badly wrong.

It made perfect sense. It was all in the nature of relationships, father, son, uncle, son, same thing.

The tall maharaja hung in the doorway, staring at the bodies. Finally he straightened up, put his hands on his hips, and was suddenly so altogether in command and impressive to behold, Sharma imagined him leading elephants and troops. He turned to Samiji. "He say anything to you?" he asked. "Anything at all?"

"He told me not to come inside, sa'ab."

"What else?"

"I say to him, 'Don't go in there,' but he say he know what all he's doing. He say he know everything, sa'ab, and he has everything all fixed up, and I say, 'But it's not the way, it's not the way.' I am begging and pleading, sa'ab. I am out of car. I am on sidewalk. I am pulling on his right hand and I am pulling on his left hand, but he is saying everything will be all right. And I say no matter about job, no matter about Shiva, no matter even about you, sa'ab, his one friend, because I am knowing everything, sa'ab, so sorry to say, I know all what has happened. I tell him he can go to America or to mountains, and everything will pass over and go away. I tell him, 'Go to mountains, sa'ab, go and take some rest,' but he says, 'No, no, no.' Just this. No, no, no. He say only for me to get rid of Shiva."

"That was all he cared about?" the tall maharaja exclaimed.

"Must be, maybe," the driver said.

"He didn't say anything about the children?"

"No, sa'ab. Not one thing. I beg and plead for him to let missus go and to give me gun, and he say, 'What gun?' and I say, 'I saw you put it in your pocket when missus is getting in car, but he say he is going to scare her only, that is all, he has had enough. He say that again, 'enough, enough,' many times, and so I let him go, sa'ab. He is my master. It is my duty. I tried to stop him, but then I must be letting go."

At that point Sharma felt the stirring of his own duty to his lawyer brother, and he approached the maharaja and said that if timing was important because of the estate and the childrens, then they better hurry quickly and move the bodies or they wouldn't be able to move them at all, no crematorium would take them, rigor mortis was setting in.

"You're Dr. Sharma," the maharaja said, looking at him for the first time.

"Yes, Maharaj-sa'ab."

From the side of the room the uncle chortled with pleasure.

After that they were busy. The driver brought in pails, mops, tarpaulins, ropes, and rags, from the jeep outside, and he and the maharaja tried to pull the bodies apart. It was difficult. The couple had hardened into a rigid shape, interlocking pieces of a puzzle.

Sharma decided he had to help. Even though only untouchables were supposed to touch bodies, he knew this was a matter beyond all caste. He took one of the woman's arms, and with all three pulling, they got the two apart. The uncle watched.

"What else was my father wearing?" Phoebe interrupted. "Didn't he have a burgundy red Kashmiri scarf?"

"Yes, he was having one scarf."

"Was it burgundy red?"

"Yes."

"What happened to it?"

When the bodies were finally separated, the driver reached in, pulled the scarf off the dead man, and wrapped it around his neck.

"He's got a hell of a nerve," the uncle said with contempt.

"You think this doesn't change everything?" the tall man said. "It'll affect you, too."

"Nonsense."

"You wait."

The uncle laughed. "Never."

They got the man's body on the tarpaulin, but it was still curled up in a fetal position. They pushed down hard on his legs, arms, and neck and eventually got him to be flat.

The wound then was clear: a single shot under the left arm, straight into the heart.

The woman's body remained alone on the boxes in a position not unlike her husband's, arms and knees up. She had been shot three times at close range, chest, face, and upper arm, with the shot to the arm apparently the first because her other hand had grabbed it in response, as if to stop the pain, but her mouth was closed, no teeth or tongue exposed, no scream, the lips set and waiting.

"What was the tall man like?" Phoebe asked. "What did he say? Do?"

"He was mother, father, son. He was everything in this loss. He had so much feeling, I am worried for him. I am wanting to help him, help the childrens, the driver. Wanting to do anything, there is so much e-mo-shun in this room."

Afterward they sat on the floor in the hallway. They were covered with blood. The maharaja had stripped off his suit, down to the shirt-sleeves, everything stained with blood.

They had cleaned the room, carried pails of water to and from the bath, scrubbed everything down. The boxes had been pushed out into the hall, the bodies wrapped in tarpaulins.

Finally the tall maharaja turned to Sharma. "You know what you have to do?"

"Wait for this clerk-chaprassi from Agra, Maharaj-sa'ab."

"He'll be here any minute," the tall man said. "I want you to write they were killed in Agra. In an accident."

"What kind of accident?"

"I'm not sure. Say it was a fire of some kind, an explosion. Make it a fiery explosion. So there's nothing left."

"A car crash?"

"That's a good idea," the man said. "They drove down to Agra and had a car crash that led to a fiery explosion. How's that?"

"But why must it be Agra, Maharaj-sa'ab?"

"Because it's far from Delhi."

"But—"

"There is a daughter."

"But—"

"It can't be in Delhi," the maharaja said firmly. "That's all there is to it. It's simpler this way. She'll want to see the site, see the car. She's curious. She won't let up. If it's in Agra, she won't be able to. It's too far away. Besides, this'll answer all her questions. A car crash, a fire. Thank you for being so concerned, but we'll do it my way."

Now the driver spoke, voicing his confusion, too. "I don't understand, sa'ab," he said, the red burgundy scarf wrapped around his neck. "How can you not be telling truth to missus Feeb?"

The uncle answered. "This way the children'll get his life insurance," he explained. "At least they'll have that and whatever else I can put together. . . ."

"You?" his nephew asked in surprise.

"I like children, too, you know," the uncle said, tapping his fingers against the boxes. "You should get these out of here today," he said to his nephew. "Soon as possible."

"I know that."

"Is all this worth it?" he asked, looking at the maharaja. "Are you really doing this for the girl, or did you decide not to leave me after all? You couldn't lose both patrons all at once? Was that it? So you decided to stick with me? Is that what happened? You could have removed the boxes before the police came, you know. They'd never know the difference. Then you wouldn't have needed me at all. If the police asked questions, you could say you had no idea why he came here. You could even leave the bodies until they rotted and the neighbors complained about the smell. But it's too late now, isn't it?" He paused. "So?" he said. "Is it worth it this way? To be so beholden to me?"


"What'd he answer?"

"He didn't," Sharma answered. "The maharaja is not saying one thing."


At about four in the morning two holy men arrived. They were all downstairs by then, waiting. They had brushed their hair, washed, and changed. The maharaja had brought extra sets of clothes. Louis's body was downstairs, but not Thalia's, her face too mutilated to be seen.

The holy men were bare-chested despite the cold. They had

Brahmin threads around their shoulders, ashes in their hair. One was barefoot, the other wore sandals. They carried pots of oil and ash. The face was uncovered.

First they lifted the body onto a white cloth they had brought and sprinkled it with cow dung. The soul needed assistance in its transition to another world. Then they sat down cross-legged at Louis Guthrie's head. The maharaja, the driver, and the doctor sat close, the uncle back on the stairs. The holy men dropped oil in the dead man's mouth to purify his body, put flowers around his head and betel leaves between his lips. The holy men began chanting, now alone, now together, dropped water on the man's white face, painted it with ash and oil, and drew three streaks across the forehead, the ash a sign of Shiva dancing on the burning grounds.

At the end the holy men brought in a litter, two long poles fastened with wood and straw, and laid the body on it. Then they bound the man's two thumbs together. That was the way. Then they opened his mouth and put wet rice in it, so hunger and thirst would be satisfied until he got where he was going.

The woman upstairs remained unassisted. Her journey might be harder as a consequence, but she was still going wherever she was going and no holy men, or Shiva dancing, could affect the way of that. Nothing could except the soul and its intent, and that was determined the moment she died, when she set her lips and did whatever she did inside, thought whatever thoughts she thought.


The holy men left. The clerk-chaprassi from Agra came. The sky outside was still dark. At the door the clerk handed Samiji an envelope sealed with drops of red wax. "One contract from lawyer Sharma-sa'ab in Agra," he announced.

Samiji took it and closed the door. The man hadn't even stepped inside.

Sharma, the doctor, wrote that Louis Antonine Guthrie and Thalia Louise Guthrie were killed in a car crash in Agra that led to a fiery explosion.

Then he stamped the papers with his seal and license number.

Dawn finally came.

The maharaja called the municipality and ordered a hearse. Then he called the Electric Crematorium and arranged for an early appointment, there was no family or son, could the thing be done right away?

The uncle prepared to leave. "Well, at least I don't have to say good-bye," he said as he namasted his nephew. "I know I'll be seeing you again."

His jeep started up, and the others, standing inside, listened as it took off. The place was now quiet. Even the wind had stopped.

Sharma wondered if the souls were still present, waiting to go with the bodies, or if they'd already left. He doubted that. Souls usually left early only when they wanted to be with their loved ones someplace else, but in this case he thought that was unlikely. Nothing that had happened here suggested there was much concern with love, except on the maharaja's part.

In a while the hearse came. The bodies were carried outside and put in the back.

Sharma showed the driver of the van the death certificates. He barely looked at them, for he was looking at the maharaja's gift of money instead, and left.

Then Samiji and the maharaja got in the Indian car, the front seat, Sharma himself took the back and they pulled away from the house. They followed the hearse.

Suddenly the maharaja told the driver to stop.

He got out and ran back to the white Ford car. Shut first one door, then the other, and this time when they drove away, they all looked back at the Ford. Sharma wondered if they were thinking the same:

That the maharaja had, when he shut the doors, silenced the only screams there'd been to mourn these two sad and sorry deaths.


The crematorium was a one-story brick building with a wide veranda. It overlooked the Jumna River, not far from the spot where the male Caucasian later lay. It was surrounded by a green lawn with flowers around the border.

They parked outside near the hearse and filed into the one big hall inside, just the three of them, the bodies had gone ahead.

They sat alone in the front row, row upon row of empty seats behind them, and as they watched, an employee opened the door of the large oven on the side. First, with the help of the men

514

from the hearse, he lifted Louis' body in, then Thalia's, so that one lay on top of the other, very unusual, but the maharaja had given him two thousand-rupee notes to do just that.

Sharma heard the door click shut.

The fire inside got going fast. Reflections of the flames inside leapt out into the room and shone bright red. Sharma imagined he could feel the heat, but he couldn't. He couldn't smell anything, either, and he thought longingly of the place down the river where bodies usually were burned, on piles of wood laden with saffron and oil.

Here there was only electricity and a roof, no sky or smells or open air, not even a body to see, no eldest son to approach, hammer in hand, and crack the skull so his father could soar to the heavens to await his next descent.

And no Doms, either, the untouchables who lived and worked the funeral ghats and did the tapping at the skull for those who had no son to do the deed.


At the end dark smoke curled up from the single chimney outside. It rose high above the crematorium, one long straight line of ashes. A breeze took it out across the Jumna River to the other side, where the land was flat and barren and only the poorest of the poor lived and died.

A few days later Kady retrieved the ashes. Going down to the ghats, he emptied the urns in the water.


"Thank you for telling me," Phoebe said. Her voice cracked, but she did not cry.

# ❦ 19 ❦

PHOEBE WENT OUTSIDE. IT WAS
still raining and the wind was blowing hard. Dr. Sharma had
given her an umbrella, asked if she'd be all right. She said yes.

Outside, the street gray and empty, she didn't know where to
go. She pushed ahead through the rain, face down, holding the
umbrella in front of her. The storm was lashing. She stared at
her feet, a blur.

She remembers feeling light-headed, numb. She thought of
Kady but didn't want to see him. Of Alice in New York, even
Stephen, his brown hair and familiar face. She started to run,
steadily, but with no destination and not much speed. She felt
achingly alone. India seemed strange. She didn't know where
she was. She took one street, then another. The sidewalk was
empty. Cars went by, spraying water on her feet and legs. The
gutters were flooded and sludge swirled around her sandals. Her
skirt was heavy with rain. She kept up a steady jog, no idea
where she was going. Bhagwandas Road was Jiggie Deeg's,
Jumna Road not hers to have. She remembered the windows,
though.

Kneeling and looking out.

Cully, full blown, filled the cavities of her mind, and she
started to run, as fast as she could, realizing that, all along, right
from the beginning, one turn after the other, she'd been headed

for him, straight through the maze of streets to him in Chandni Chowk.

She kept her pace. All she could see was his face now, aged ten or twelve or twenty-five. It glowed and beckoned, no age or imperfections, and she heard herself telling him, breathless, "There's no crash, Cully, no crash, don't you see? This is the truth. You had nothing to do with it."

Clear as clear, she imagined Cully sitting on his bed with her beside him, telling him, and he was silent and accepting, everything the same as it used to be.


But when she saw Cully's building, the doors on the balcony upstairs were closed, and she stopped running. Her spirits plummeted. Desperate that he wasn't there, she tried to catch her breath. Then she plodded ahead slowly, heavyhearted and forlorn. A little tea stall was open in the storm, but she decided to sit on the steps outside his door and wait for him up there where the iron railing stretched down to the ground.

He was closer to her there than anywhere else.

Cully was home after all. When she reached the third-floor landing, dripping wet, hair stringing down her neck, he opened the door and stood there, blocking it, big as the door itself.

"Cully," she exclaimed, "I need to talk to you."

Music was coming from inside his apartment. He didn't move, maybe he hadn't heard her over the noise; so she pushed ahead, thinking to turn off the music so they could talk. He let her pass, but when she turned to face him, she knew she'd made him angry by coming in. She started talking, about the storm, about how much she wanted to see him, and she remembers thinking her voice was too loud, competing with the radio.

"I've been trying to see Dr. Sharma ever since I got here," she said, not realizing she alone knew who Dr. Sharma was. "I just left him," she went on, "and I want to tell you what he said because it's going to make all the difference. I know it is to me, and . . ."

She looked around the room; it was different from before. Empty carton boxes were stacked against the wall, and the Mathuran horse was moved.

She was taken aback by its beauty. It lorded over the room with its majesty, and she found herself startled that an item of betrayal could be so stunning. "He was there," she said, distracted. "Dr. Sharma was at the house," as if Cully understood what she was talking about or knew the house in Golf Links.

She saw a hammer, too, and then that there was a great gaping hole in the back end of the horse. Chips of metal and terra-cotta were scattered about the floor.

Phoebe remembers noticing an energy in the room, something invisible yet electric, here with the doors closed, heat extreme, boxes, horse, a hammer, and a radio. She realized Cully hadn't moved since she came in.

A vein throbbed on the left side of his head. She could see it from across the room. It was like Louis' arm twenty years ago, the veins pounding as he lined up cigarette burns along the table.

Now there was only the sound of singing from the radio. "I'm sorry, Cully," she said soberly. "For running on so much. I'm not myself. Can I sit down?"

He didn't answer. Didn't move, either.

She sat on the edge of the bed, felt the clinginess of her wet clothes and hair. "They didn't die in an accident," she said. "That's what this is all about. That's what I'm trying to tell you."

He went over to the horse, frowning, as though he couldn't remember how the break in the flank got there.

"Can you turn the music down so we can talk?"

He bent down and began to pick up the pieces of the broken horse. There was no indication he even knew she was there. The shards were dark against the floor, and he deposited them carefully in his palm.

She was mesmerized by his preoccupation. He could have been a dancer, the routine was so precise. A minute or two passed. At first she thought he was cherishing the remnants of the horse, feeling their significance, but then she realized he was only cleaning up the mess. "Cully?"

His hands were rigid, like a mannequin's, fingers set in place.

"Did you just break it?"

He didn't speak.

"I think it's beautiful, even if it is false." The horse made her sad, yet another sign of how things had gone full circle, Guthrie, Suraj, and Deeg, everything twisted up and curling back in on itself, Louis burning cigarettes on the table, Cully breaking a

518

horse that wasn't real. "I have to talk to you. This is so important for both of us." Phoebe needed to tell him what had happened so badly that she was barely aware of him now. She was even oblivious of the fact tonight was Mirabai's wedding.

Cully kept on, picking up one shard, then another, wetting his fingertips with his tongue and wiping the floor of dust.

"I wish I didn't have to tell you, and I know it will be a shock, it was to me, but I don't know what else to do." She paused. "Haven't you always wondered about their death? How it all happened in Agra? He didn't even like Agra."

He continued to pick up the shards.

"On some level the accident never made sense to me. I couldn't see them driving to Agra." She wanted him to turn to her so she could tell him what had happened. "Do you think you could turn down the music?"

He put the pieces in the trash, crossed the room to where the radio stood, and bent over to turn the knob.

"Because they didn't die in Agra, Cully. They died right here."

He turned the music higher.

"Kady and Jiggie Deeg covered up what happened. They wanted . . ."

Higher.

". . . to protect us."

His hands were swollen. They looked like rolling pins attached to a palm. "I have to have a drink of water," she said, escaping.

In the kitchen, she drank from the faucet. When she came back she sat on the bed again. "Cully, I know this must be hard for you to hear. I wish we'd known it all along. It'd have been so much better. Kady should have told us the first chance he got."

Cully stared out the window into the grayness of the storm. She realized he was following the music.

"I love you and you love me," a girl was singing. "Tikkie tikkie tikkie tikkie tee."

He looked odd. Were his pants too small? Was that it? Had he gained weight? Everything about him seemed larger, swollen. Not just the fingers, but his buttocks, the line of his back. She pictured everything backed up inside him, clogged and engorged.

519

"The point is they didn't go to Agra. They went to the house in Golf Links. . . ."

"Do you know what day it is?" His voice when it came surprised her. It was hoarse.

"It's Monday."

"That's right."

"What'd you say to her? You must have said something." He sounded rigid. "You made her leave."

"She wanted to go back to Deeg. I had to help her."

"Do you know what time it is?"

"It's . . ." She brought her watch up to look, but before she could speak he said, "It's six o'clock. She's getting married right now. Do you realize that?" He banged his fist down on the flank of the horse.

Phoebe flinched.

"She's dressed," he said accusingly. "They all are." He was speaking more quickly. "The priests are there. The fire's lit. Do you know what that means? It means it can't be stopped. They're probably even on the elephants." His voice was angry now. "They're on the way to the palace. He's on the elephant. I mean, he's on it. The groom. Don't you hear the noise?" Suddenly he stopped talking, listening. "Hear it?"

"You mean the radio?"

"He's almost there." Cully was surrounded by guests, musicians, and a groom's entourage.

"It's what she wanted," Phoebe said.

"It's not what she wanted. She did not want to marry him." He took a step toward her, and she saw his eyes had gone small with anger. "Are you telling me you know her better than me?"

"I'm not saying I know her better. I'm just saying she wanted her life back."

"She wanted me."

"It was her decision to leave you."

"You made her do it. She'd never have left me if it weren't for you." He clenched his fists.

"Did you hear anything I said before?"

"You've interfered all over again."

"I don't like this about Louis and Thalia, either, but it's the truth and I'm trying to face it."

"You don't understand what you do to me. You're always

taking something away from me. Now it's Mirabai. You made me leave India, too."

"I did not." Phoebe pushed her hands against her hair, trying momentarily to block him out. "Didn't you hear anything, Cully? Kady and Jiggie covered it up to protect us. Louis killed her."

"I didn't want to leave India."

"Neither did I."

"But you made me."

"What were we supposed to do? Live here without any parents? Pay the bills?"

"You didn't want anything to do with India. You told me to forget India, forget Indian art, forget Louis, forget—"

"I was trying to help you get a job."

"I had a job."

"You were an assistant at Christie's. Is that what you wanted? I was trying to help you get a better job."

"What is it?" Cully yelled. "You don't want me to think anything good about myself? You want to ruin everything? Me and Louis?"

"I want you to face the truth. He killed her. Don't you think you should pay attention to that? There was no car crash, Cully. It wasn't your fault. You had nothing to do with their deaths. It wasn't you or your fight with him. It was everything else."

Suddenly Cully lunged at her and pounded his hands in the air a few feet in front of her face. "Stop it," he screamed.

"It was in the house in Golf Links," she persisted. "Think about it."

"You're trying to ruin my relationship with him."

"Well, there certainly wasn't any car crash and you weren't on his mind."

"Stop it! You're doing it again."

"What?"

"You're pushing me. You push me and push me and push me. And besides, what house in Golf Links? I've never been there, goddamn it. Don't you understand?"

"It's the house where he and Kady—"

"But I never went there," he yelled. "I never saw it. I never saw him. I never saw anything. You saw it, not me. Why're you always destroying everything I have?"

"I'm not," Phoebe said wearily. "Why do you keep saying the same things, over and over again?"

"I'm warning you," he said. "Stop it."

"Stop what?"

"What you're doing with your hair. The way you touch it. Do you have to play with it all the time? I mean all the goddamn time?"

"I'm just pushing it out of my face."

The vein on his head was throbbing so fast, she thought it'd burst.

"You're pushing me too far," he said. "You don't care about anyone. I've known it for years. You just toss your head and flick it." And with that he flicked his head, too, his face contorted in rage.

"I brush it out of my eyes, Cully. It bothers my eyes."

"What do you think it does to me?"

"It has nothing to do with you."

"I hate your hair. I hate it. If I could do one thing, I'd—"

"You have the same hair."

"I don't toss it around."

"What are you talking about? This is ridiculous."

"I bet there's hundreds, maybe thousands of people who hate you for the way you touch your hair."

"I don't mean it that way."

"You don't mean it that way? You want me to show you?" He grabbed a pair of scissors from the desk and pushed her down on the bed so fast she couldn't move. He had her pinned down with an elbow, his body on top of her so she could feel his stomach, legs, penis, it as engorged as the rest of him, and he had the scissors in one hand and was jabbing at her hair, then he grabbed the hair itself and cut great swipes of it.

She heard the scissors grind through her hair and pushed against him, but he was stronger, his bulk so great she could barely breathe, and she couldn't move, penis hard against her leg, like a log or weapon, and he kept cutting chunks of her hair. He brought it up in handfuls and waved it over her head like an Apache scalp then slapped it against her face, hard as he could. She screamed, more scared than she'd ever been.

She brought her knee up against his groin and kicked, and suddenly she was free, only he caught her by the arm and she was still screaming, but she couldn't even hear herself for the music. She was trying to break away and make for the door. He was still grabbing at her hair, trying to pull it out of her head. It was the only thing that gave her a chance to move at all.

She reached the door, turned the corner toward the stairs; he let go of her hair and reached for her with his hands.

"Don't. Please," she yelled, "Cully!"

He put his hands on her shoulders, pushed as hard as he could, and threw her backward down the stairs.

She fell hard. She hit the iron railing, then crashed against the stones. She could hear music from far away, but she couldn't see at all, blood in her eyes, filling them with darkness, her right leg up and hurt, even as her back and an arm were jabbed against the spokes of the railing. She came to a stop at the bottom, head below her feet, legs caught, she couldn't hear the radio anymore, only the sound of wind and rain, and she wiped away just enough blood so she could see Cully coming down the stairs.

He held his knapsack and a book of Indian art. She thought he was going to stop, but he didn't.

He stepped over her, didn't look or hesitate, and disappeared down the street, his left shoulder sloping slightly down, his arms swinging like he was mad. In the early evening darkness of the storm he blended into the yellow and brown of the empty street and was gone.

# ❧ 20 ❧

PHOEBE'S HAIR MINGLED WITH
water from the gutter. She smelled oranges and blood, and she
could feel grit and dirt in her mouth. The pain was so acute it
reached her inner mind. She imagined Louis and Thalia visiting
her, first one, then the other, bending down to cradle her, hands
addressing the places where she was hurt.

Her father stayed a long time, her mother barely lingered, but
she smelled of sweat and stress and her scent stayed on, mixing
with the pain. She wore a nightgown, he a suit. He wrapped her
in his jacket, little thing was all she was, she'd just been born,
and held her till she didn't bleed or ache, comforted her against
his body. But a longing had arisen in her, for a voice she knew,
for the woman who was halfway her, and hours later, or so it
seemed, Thalia finally came back.

First Phoebe heard footsteps in the yellow and brown of the
rainy night, then her mother bent down, skin moist, hands
trembling, smelling of sweat and fear, fear of a baby, that was
it, but to the baby, the woman was heaven, her breath upon her
face, her hands, like water, lapping at her body, her scent mixing
with the oranges and blood, this woman who'd been her home.

❧

Cully, she didn't see or imagine at all. She just felt the force of his blows reminding her over and over again exactly what he thought of her. There were no illusions left.


Down in Deeg, priests had started the wedding fire in the morning, laid the logs, sprinkled them with oil and scent. Now the bride was sitting on the ground beneath the gold canopy facing the fire. The painted elephants had come and gone. The ceremony had begun and the fire was a good five feet around and wild with flames. The groom was at Mirabai's side, crowds behind them.

Mirabai had jewels hanging from her ears, nose, forehead, neck, wrists, ankles, toes, and fingers, hundreds, even thousands, of diamonds, rubies, sapphires, and pearls. Her face showed through the gold brocade of a nine-yard sari. She looked serene, eyes cast down as in innocence, dark brows and little ears, cheeks and lips that had surely never felt a man's kiss or caress. Her sari, seventeen-karat gold, was so heavy Chumpi and another maid had had to help her carry it when she moved.

They were in the old palace on Lake Pichiti, the vast inner courtyard where all the women of Deeg had been married, for decades and centuries, since the Deegs rose up out of the desert and conquered the land. The sari was traditional, too, its abundant weight signifying wealth and consequence, all those things that never change.

Now, even as the storm to the northeast dwindled down in Delhi, the priest spoke about marriage and obedience, woman designed to produce and serve. Afterward the walk began. When it was done the two were joined, seven times around the fire they went, Chumpi and another following after the girl to carry the weight, she couldn't have done it alone.

Jiggie sat close behind her but before the ceremony was over, he stepped out of the crowd and got away, his plane waiting to take him back to Benares. He told Attar Singh that now one duty was done, he had to get back to the larger one, meditating on nothingness and forgiveness.

Maybe he was thinking about what he'd done to his children.

Five of them in all, three-fifths of them named Suraj.

In Delhi it was nearly ten when the landlady at Cully's building left her apartment on the second floor. She heard the music blaring up above, so she went to see the Am-ri-kan and note that he was home. But he was not there, so she shut the door and came on down.

In the darkness she only saw the body when she tripped on it.


The city ambulance came and Phoebe was put on a litter and taken through the streets to Safdarjang Hospital. She'd been there once before, the day she arrived in India and saw the male Caucasian body lying in the morgue.

This time she was alone.

The litter was laid on the floor of the hospital to wait. There was nothing to identify her, no one to bribe the staff to put her first in line or buy medicines, a sheet, a nurse, or privacy. For Phoebe the long, long darkness of the night, first lying in the street, then in a dim-lit hall at Safdarjang, was something as near to death, in metaphor if not in fact, as she had ever been.

# PART FIVE

###### ❧ I ❧

THEY SAY IN INDIA THERE ARE
only two seasons to the year, winter and summer.

They also say that life is creation, preservation, and dissolution. That the gods are not good and evil, but mixtures of both, and that rebirth is not a punishment, just a consequence, and what you haven't faced or learned in one life you face again, the next time around.

A monk from the northern mountains came to speak at the house of a friend of mine. He had tired eyes and a long beard, and he sat on the floor with us around, his orange clothes all he had to shield him from the air. He had retired to his cave above the Ganges but emerged from time to time to share his message.

"Man," he said, "must understand unity and connection and believe that he is one and the same as everything, the maharaja, the beggar, and the tree, the injured and the whole. There is no difference.

"We are now that which we were and that which we will be. Forest mulch, human being, and transcendent soul. We are all one and the same together."

Someone asked him, What about the rest of it? What about love?

He said it was too fleeting to count. "Something so effervescent and blinding, it dispels all else and conceals the truth."

The rains stopped and the land went back to the dry and dusty state it would maintain until the rains came again, cycles of life and death, just as the old man said.

It was hard, though, through September and October, to perceive of winter as the coming of death. The air was so fresh and exuberant, the sky so blue, that in Delhi, at least, it was the best season of the year. October is the month when Indians have their greatest celebration. Divali's like our Christmas, everything lit up, candles, presents, goodwill. It commemorates not just the end of summer and the beginning of winter, death, and rebirth, but the triumph of good over evil, too.

By October Phoebe could talk, and I told her about the old man from the mountains. But her recovery came slowly, and it came in stages, and in the beginning, strictly speaking, there was no capacity in her to find anything interesting at all. The vacuum left by Cully seemed so deep.


The last and longest phase of her recovery was spent at Kitty Chandradas' house. Phoebe had a suite downstairs and could move about easily, especially to and from the veranda, movement that the doctors said was crucial to her recovery. She specifically didn't want to be flown back to the United States. She was emphatic about staying here.

Before that we kept her at my house in the guest room on the second floor. Before that, of course, she was in the hospital.

She had a room to herself there, but her eyes were rarely open and she was unconscious most of the time; she'd had a bad concussion. She was covered with bandages, head, scalp, leg, and stomach, tied to tubes, monitors, and intravenous morphine and feeding equipment.

You may wonder who took care of her. We all did. Nurses and the doctors and, of course, myself. Harriet came as often as she could, and Kitty and Jyoti and Mr. Smith, who'd been Louis' CEO, and some others, Samiji and Tulsidas, for example, but, mostly who took care of her was Kady Suraj.

I got back from Deeg the day after her beating, and Harriet reached me right away. The landlady had called her first thing in the morning when the switchboard opened, and Harriet had

Phoebe moved immediately to one of the better hospitals. The landlady had ensconced herself upstairs at Cully's to be sure not to miss him when he returned, and Harriet had sent a clerk-chaprassi over to Kady's to wait to tell him too when he came home. But so far he hadn't showed up. Durr and the servants weren't there, either, and of Cully there was no sign at all.

Harriet said there was no information on who Phoebe's attacker was, and we accepted that. We couldn't figure out, however, why Cully's door was open and the radio playing.

Phoebe, of course, couldn't say until much later.

I finally reached Durr after two days. She was terribly upset by the news and told me I could find Kady at the Garden House. I drove out to get him, it was quite a ways, and brought him back to the hospital. He was grim and terrified, sat in the backseat with me, hand on the door the whole way so he could get out as fast as possible.

After that, he never left the hospital. Literally. He sat with Phoebe night and day. He washed her face, took her pulse, helped the nurses change the bottles and tubes, even the catheter and the bandages. He stroked her one good arm, held her hand. I don't know when he slept. At the most he dozed. I was the one who told Samiji several days later to bring him fresh clothes; Kady took to washing in the hospital bathroom. Toward the end of the fourth day, I made him drink some soup they sent up from the kitchen. He took a few swallows, then put it down, forgotten.

He looked both awful and wonderful. His eyes were haggard, chin covered with whiskers, hair unkempt. I told him she'd be all right. So did the doctors. They promised him she'd recover. But he couldn't believe it, not when she was living on machines and morphine.

The first change came after about ten days. It was obvious she was hovering on the edge of consciousness. She was squirming a lot and moaning. A fleet of things seemed to be trooping across her eyelids, they moved so much.

Kady had his chair pulled up to the bed, as always, but he was lying across her now, his arms holding him up so he wouldn't crush her. She started moaning louder, struggling with her attacker, I presumed. Kady had his hands on both sides of her face.

He was whispering to her. "Feeb," he said over and over again, "it's all right. It's all right. Everything will be all right."

She opened her eyes, amazingly blue against her white, bruised face. He was right there, inches away. She mumbled and tried to touch him, but she couldn't, of course, she was so weak the wind would blow her away, but her eyes were like flashlights, they were so bright. Kady kissed her face, nose, eyes, lips, and they clung to each other that way until suddenly she closed her eyes and was gone, asleep, and I had the good sense to hurry from the room, because Kady burst into tears. As I shut the door I saw him standing, his face in his hands, bent over sobbing, as relief and fear broke through his great reserve.


Afterward she wasn't sure if he'd been a dream or not. "Did he come and see me once?" she asked when she could finally talk. I told her he never left, he was there for days, round the clock, and when she first woke, yes, that was he.

After that he came to the hospital every day, but if she was awake, he left. That's what he did later at my house, too.

He and I became friends in that hospital room. I realized how much more to him there was than I had thought. He was on one side of the bed, I the other, Samiji usually seated on the floor somewhere, all of us inextricably bonded by this woman on the bed. I almost fell in love with Kady myself, because what paramountly came through to me about him, although I barely knew him then, was his overriding strength.

He seemed almost monolithic in his ability to wrench out his insides but nonetheless proceed. He never let up. He could be sensitive and thoroughly overwrought with feelings, but still transcendently sound and strong. Nothing seemed to threaten his basic system.

Now that he knew it was only a matter of time until Phoebe recovered, he told me that what happened in the future between them was up to her. He'd done what he could. He gave me very precise instructions. I was to tell her that he loved her and wanted to be with her, here or abroad, anywhere, he was ready, whatever she wanted. He would wait as long as she needed, months, years, but she had to initiate the first contact.

"I don't want to trivialize what I did to her," he said. "I know she won't want to see me right away, if at all. I want her to know I respect what she feels about me, this can't be easy, but I don't want her to have any doubts about me, either. For the first time in thirty years, my life makes sense, and if she won't have me, I still won't regret a thing. Everything will have been for the best."

He had already retired from public office, given up career, job, pensions, even a good bit of respect.


Of Cully, there was no word.

Phoebe eventually told me what had happened between them. "I may think I lost him," she said, "but I never had him. It was my imagination. I thought I was helping him. To him I was interference and a threat."

I told Suraj about Cully. He dealt with the police, used every bit of influence he had, which was still considerable, to make their search for Cully as aggressive as possible. The commander at Tees-he-zari with the burned-out face helped.

But Cully had disappeared all over again.

I have a friend here, an Indian who's a European-trained Freudian psychoanalyst. There are only three of them in Delhi, and my friend says that Indians' deepest fear is of being inundated by the masses of the Indian population, of disappearing into them. He doesn't fear being alone, as we do, but being swallowed up and rendered invisible. To them this personifies dissolution and destruction.

That was Cully's fate. He was just plain gone.


Phoebe's months of recuperation became one long moment of introspection.

To her friends it was unclear what she'd end up doing. Kitty thought she should go back to New York. Harriet didn't know. I thought she should stay. Kady had made clear what he wanted, but what Phoebe wanted remained a mystery.

During this time she did not want anything except to be left alone to think and, eventually, see as much as possible of me because talking to me became her chief mechanism for sorting things out. She explained her dilemma to me. Was she going to go home or stay here? Be with Kady or not be with Kady? And if she stayed here, what was she going to do professionally? She knew letting go of Cully was difficult, but basically the question was, how was she going to absorb everything that had happened and who was she going to be as a consequence? And about Kady, could she forgive his lies? She said she was determined not to go back to New York and be miserable without him, or vice versa, stay here with nothing but love and a married man to sustain her, no clear work or purpose.

"I let myself drift for years and didn't face things," she said. "I'm not going to let it happen again."

"You're making the stakes awfully high."

"The stakes are high."


She wrote a letter to Kady right before she moved from my house to Kitty's.

"Kady," it began. "My anger with you is not gone, but it is gradually dissipating. Increasingly I understand why you did what you did, and although I can't exactly forgive you, I may be able to forget it and just let it go.

"I have begun to miss you achingly. I feel you in the tightness in my chest and in the way I remember your toes and knees in a bed where I am, too.

"Didn't we have a good time together, Kady? We always did, right from the beginning, years ago. But you are a tortured human being, and I need that to stop if I am ever to be with you again. I can't take it anymore. I need you to be whole, too. That may be a tough thing to say to someone, but you have to put all this behind you, too, for your own sake as well as mine. I have to do the same.

"The days are very long now, but I'm getting much better. I can walk, although it still hurts a lot. I'll be moving to Kitty's soon where it's easier to get around. As I said, I'm still trying to sort things out. If I succeed at putting you out of my mind, that means I lose you again, and that doesn't seem the way to go. But living here with you, no husband, no legal relative, doesn't seem right, either. I wish I could do that, Kady. That would be the obvious answer. Unfortunately, I don't think I could sustain being unmarried and illicit in everyone's eyes, knowing you had a legal wife somewhere else. I don't think it's just because I'm 'conventional.' I think it's what my past has done to me. I need to belong.

"Thank you very much for taking care of me and coming to see me. Maybe someday soon I'll be able to tell you all this in person."

## ❧ 2 ❧

ONE DAY IN EARLY DECEMBER I went to Kitty's as usual, but for the first time Phoebe wasn't there.

The bearer said she was out.

"Out?" I exclaimed, because she'd never been out alone since the beating.

"She is calling Tulsidas at taxi stand and he is coming for her."

"How long has she been gone?"

"Long time, two, three, hours."

"When did she leave?"

"Nine o'clock."

"How was she dressed?"

"Werry fine."

I waited in the study. After a while I felt too much like a schoolmistress checking up on her and left, but two hours later I came back.

This time I couldn't find her, either, but Tulsidas was parked in the driveway. Inside, the bearer grinned at me conspiratorially and tiptoeing—it was siesta time—took me out back through the kitchens and the pantry, where servants were asleep on the floor. We came to a side door. There he turned the knob so it wouldn't squeak, and we looked out.

536

Phoebe was at the far side of the lawn at the dhobi's water faucet. She had a bucket, soap and water and was on her hands and knees on the ground, vigorously scrubbing a tie-dyed sari, the kind peasants wear, a big red block print with blue-and-green designs. For Indians it was so ordinary as to be inconspicuous.

The bearer shrugged. "She is going right out there without stopping to say any one thing to me."

"Did you ask Tulsidas?"

He looked shocked. "He is Chukker," he said.

I went in the study to wait.

After a while Phoebe came in. "Hi," she said cheerfully. "I didn't know you were here."

"What've you been up to?" I asked casually.

"Things."

"Oh. What have you got there?" She had the wet cloth in a bowl in her arms.

"Sari. I had to wash it, soften it up. Now I have to dry it."

"Sari? What for?"

"I'm going away. I want to be as inconspicuous as possible." She started to laugh. "Now I'll look like a hippie or a 'world traveler.' I'll wear beads, pull the sari over my head. No one will notice me. I can forget who I am and see what happens."

"Where are you going?"

"Benares."

City of the Dead, holiest spot in India, Jiggie Deeg's retreat.

"I have to let something in me die and I'm not coming back from there until it does. It's probably fear. I think that's what's blocking me. That after all that's happened, I'm afraid of changing even more, of letting go. But eventually that will go and something will come in its place. Then I'll have my decision. I'll know what to do."

## ❧ 3 ❧

SHE FOUND A TEMPLE NEAR THE
Ganges and persuaded the mahantji in charge to let her stay. He
led her to one of the rooms reserved for pilgrims. It was the size
of a closet with bars across the window to keep the monkeys out.
It had a light bulb in the ceiling and a charpoy cot for bed. He
asked if she had bedding. She said no, so he gave her some. It
smelled of human beings, but it had no bugs.

She felt comfortable. There was chanting at the altar day and
night, and she could hear the pilgrims on the river from her bed,
see the water itself from the temple grounds. To bathe or go to
the bathroom she had to go outside and cross the courtyard, so
she bought a bowl and peed in privacy in her room. For food
she went to a cook shop down the road, ate dal and rice with her
fingertips. She wasn't allowed to pollute the temple by eating
there, but the chef outside in the cooking stall fixed vegetables
if she brought them in.

During the day she walked the ghats along the riverbank. She
went from Asi Ghat in the south four miles north to the bridge
at Ramnagar, and in between she walked the streets and alleys
near the river, some so small a cart couldn't make it through or
two people abreast find a way to pass. She got up at four some
mornings and hired boys to row her upstream in a boat at dawn

538

when the sun cast a spectacular orange-and-purple glow. Often she sat on the ghats herself and waited for the sensation, whatever it would be, that would let her know the past had died, a snake shed its skin to reveal another, and that for her, finally, there were ashes to leave behind.

The steps of the ghats stretched from the water up the shore to the buildings, temples, schools, houses, and palaces, Jiggie's among them. They were covered with everything from sheets and laundry laid out to dry, to wild goats and sacred cows, people riding on bicycles, up and down the steps, nothing too hard for them, children playing hopscotch, naked sadhus and holy men, and such hordes of pilgrims and devotees, the banks were like subways at rush hour. There was no such thing as being alone here, if there was anywhere in India.

Phoebe had no interest in Jiggie, except that he was here trying to do the same thing as she, she thought. Often, though, she watched the widows and divorcées, thinking what could have happened to Mirabai and Durr. Most of them were old, but some were pretty and young. Phoebe wished she knew their stories.

Everyone bathed in the river. They submerged themselves fully dressed in the dirty, swirling waters, said their prayers, and turned seven times around to cleanse themselves before the gods.

Everything here was alive, throbbing like nowhere else she'd ever been; everything too was death.

The Manikarnika burning ghat was upstream, recognizable by the piles of logs and the bodies stacked up to burn. Its fires were always blazing, night and day. Smoke and the smell of flesh hovered over the city. Boats floated offshore, mourners dropping white-gray ashes in the river to be carried to Shiva's breast.

Even the river was dying. It was the only drainage system for the city, and what did not burn at the ghats came south in the water, too, the cycle of life at its most basic. The water was full of ashes and bits of bone. Phoebe even saw an arm, floating downstream, no more unusual than a flower or bowl for gods. And if the other side of the river so far away looked like a lovely beach, it was only white because of the human ash that washed ashore.

Phoebe was drawn to all this death. She remembered Harriet

saying she could only take Benares "so long," but with her it was the opposite. She even took to sitting in the water the way the pilgrims did and imagined that it was washing away her allegiance to the past.

She found herself drawn to the temples and began to sit in one daily, legs crossed and still. She felt encompassed by the stone and art. She didn't pray or worship, but she loved the iconography. All these multi-armed gods and animals were more familiar to her than Jesus or Mary, and although she didn't necessarily prefer them, they were more explicitly hers than anything else. People around her chanted, meditated, set down food so the gods could eat, but they left her alone. She could have felt the same in a cathedral or a library.

Her favorite temple was located on a street so narrow the first time she went a cow was sleeping and no one could get by. Old trees outside had pushed aside the roof and moved the stones. Inside, it was dark and full of beautiful statues that lined the walls. They'd been touched by so many hands through the centuries, though, you couldn't tell what they were anymore, Vishnu, Shiva, Ganesha, it was all the same.

One day Phoebe sat in back, wearing sari, beads, and a shawl, and wrote me a letter. "I'm trying to sort out what I feel when I come in here," she began. "It gives me a sense of what man has done in the name of his religious faith. These images around me aren't very good, much less beautiful than the Shiva or Cully's horse, but, no matter: They leapt freely out of the artist's faith and must have been difficult to sculpt because art, as a process, is difficult. As I sit here, though, I don't feel the difficulty. I only feel the calm of what they've done. I don't know if I appreciate God exactly, but he is here, summoned and acknowledged, all around me.

"The place makes me wonder if all art and all work, maybe even mine back in New York, is religious or at least intensely spiritual. Because it comes from a great and urgent drive to create and form and build. It represents an unwillingness on people's part to submit to, or be defined by, the mundane, or what was there, without them, before they came, to be willing to take great risks, emotional, financial, and even political, to do what they do. That they do it, that I do it, is important.

"It confirms something about yourself. It announces that you exist. What this place tells me is that all I've gone through ever since I came back here has been worth it. That it's my own great work, if you will, my own inner artist's struggle. That what I have been doing is defining myself, what I think and feel and want to do, what I believe and value. Isn't that what Kady was trying to tell me? That you try to rise above the everyday and see struggle for what it is? That it's something noble, really, not to be too corny about it. But by merely engaging in your struggle, you have, on some level, already succeeded, because it's the deepest form of living. Trying to define yourself. It's rebirth right here on earth."

The next day Phoebe went back to the temple.

"I sat in back," she said later. "I always sat in back. I didn't mind if I couldn't see the altar or someone came in front of me. I mean, it was theirs, not mine. I didn't want to get in their way. So I was just sitting that morning. I'd come from the Manikarnika burning ghat. I liked it there, actually, because it was so real. You can't get much more basic than that, and I guess you could say the ghats were still on my mind. I wasn't conscious of it too much, but I think the ghats left me raw and open. An Indian would say I was in an ethereal state because at that point my body didn't exist. I was in my mind, my soul, that's what the Indians would say.

"I began to think about what India used to mean to me when I was a child. I believed then that everything was one and that to believe in one thing was to believe in its part in everything else. The servants were always talking about that and saying that you were one and the same as God, and so that to love God, whatever God was, was to love yourself and believe in yourself.

"I took all that for granted then. They said life was a matter of reincarnation, and I believed that, too. And that cows were sacred and Shiva lived on Mount Kailash and Krishna was down in Goverdhan and ground-up flies cured headaches. It didn't occur to me not to believe any of it. Not until I came to America.

"Then sometime in New York, I forgot about belonging and everything being one, and that there is a system and a design, harmony and a rhythm, to things. Samiji used to point to the trees and say, 'This one growing, this one dying, all same, miss-sa'ab.' 'One thing coming, another going.' Kady said that, too. I remember one time we were in the house in Golf Links and he said that all is one and nothing's separate. I don't remember why he was saying it, but it was awfully important at the time. He said that on the one hand nothing matters, but on the other hand, the smallest thing in the world matters.

"And I remember asking him, wasn't that a contradiction? And he said no. It was one of life's great paradoxes. That you were a theme in the whole theme and that all our hearts were touched and linked on some level, and I thought it was all grand and that my life was wonderful because I understood such important things. But when I came back to India and saw him at the airport the first time, I knew right away that he'd forgotten that. Just like I had. I knew we'd both forgotten everything important.

"Anyway, sitting in the temple in Benares, all this came back to me. It touched me. I felt it very intensely. I felt I was reuniting with something I used to be. It felt very important. I felt Kady, too. He was as real to me as if he were sitting right there, and I knew I was opening up to him and to everything and that we were both going back to the way we had been before, because in order to go ahead, which was what we wanted to do, we had to go back and rediscover what we'd been before.

"I was sitting cross-legged and I even imagined that my vagina was opening up wide, yawning out into some huge awakening, taking in the stones beneath me. They were cold and I felt the hundreds of years beneath me like it was a river flowing in and out of me. I remember looking around to see if they'd opened a window because the temple seemed so much lighter. They hadn't, but I could see the carvings better, the gods and all their arms. In front of me a Brahmin was praying and people had left piles of food for him as offerings. I could smell the flowers. The altar was covered with jasmine flowers. The altar was a lingam, a large round oblong stone. It looked like an oversize penis, exactly what it was supposed to be. It was green, maybe black, almost a foot tall, five, six inches around, sticking straight up, and it was rough and grainy, but it had gotten smoother through the years from all the people touching it. They rub it each time they stop. Millions of people must have touched it and smoothed it down, put flowers on it, and food and oil. Indians think of it as the source of life, that it is life itself, and I thought that they were right. It is. I thought about the lingam and the yoni, the female part, that they were the source of everything. I never felt so strong.

"Afterwards I just felt different, and I came home."

## ❧ 4 ❧

IN DELHI PHOEBE DROVE OUT TO
the Garden House. She looked for one of Kady's cars, but the
street was empty. It was almost country here, a few houses,
widely separated, and in the distance smokestacks of a factory
rising above the field.

She told Tulsidas to wait, then clicked the gate open, walked
up the path. The house was low and squat and not too large, but
it had a nice veranda and looked like an English cottage set
among the green because it had vines growing up on it. The
garden was vast, about three or four acres in all, a meadow with
grass and flowers waving in the wind. It didn't look Indian. It
was too protected and removed, an island in a land where there
were no islands.

She still thought there was a chance he was inside, Samiji
could have taken the car and gone. She climbed the steps to the
door, but by the time she reached it, she knew he wasn't home.
She peeked in through a window. She saw the ceiling fans.
Turned off, they looked like huge dead bugs. She knocked and
jiggled at the door, but it was locked. She looked at herself
reflected in the glass. She had a long skirt and jacket and odd-
looking hair that came in different lengths. It was shorter on one
side than the other, but she'd fixed it so the asymmetry seemed
designed.

She went around the back of the house to find the sweeper. He must have recognized her because he looked frightened and backed away.

"It's all right," she said. "I'm his sister. He's gone away. He's disappeared. Can you let me in?"

A hut had been erected underneath the trees, just a tarpaulin, really, with stakes on the side, but it was spacious underneath and there was a water faucet, a cement basin. Most places didn't have any of that for sweepers. There were three of them, a woman and a child sitting in the back. "I just want to see the house and leave a message for sa'ab."

"He's not here."

"I know. Will you show me the yellow room?"

He was bent over and barely covered, a cloth about his thighs, although it was December. He was dark as a tire, skinny as a pipe, and not accustomed to being talked to very much, apparently, because he never did look at her, so it was like talking to a misshapen tree.

"Can I?"

He nodded. She handed him some money. He took it, then showed her the way in through the kitchen. She followed.

He was careful not to touch her or get too close, didn't, for example, use the doorknob to the kitchen, just pushed the door with his knee and left the knob for her.

The minute she stepped inside she could hear how empty the house was because her footsteps sounded hollow on the floor. There were no rugs, nothing to absorb the sounds. She ached for Kady and wished he were there.

The kitchen was modern and expensive, everything up on counters, not down on the floor. She looked for traces of Kady, but there were none. She asked if sa'ab had a cook. He said yes, but that when her brother and the girl were there, she had wanted to cook for herself.

He pointed ahead through an open archway. The dining room was on one side, the living room the other. Ahead was a hallway with rooms on the side. One door was closed.

"Is that it? The yellow room?"

"Yes."

"Why is it closed?"

"Sa'ab always has it closed."

"How long have you been here?"

He threw up his hands.

"So sa'ab hired you?"

"No, no," he said. "I came with the house. I even came with the land. I lived in a pipe before they built the house."

"Where is sa'ab? When is he coming back?"

The old man shrugged.

The living room was painted white. The sweeper started to turn on the fan. She said, No, don't. She didn't want anything blown away, the air in here still Kady's, even Cully's, and she wanted to breathe it in just as it was.

She looked at the books, pads of papers, little chits, letters. The whole thing seemed like an office.

He showed her the bedroom. It was small and nearly empty, just a closet, bed, a few clothes.

"Samiji's here," he said then, helpfully. "He comes sometimes."

"Has sa'ab been gone a long time?"

"One week. One month, must be."

He led her across the hall to the yellow room. She put her hand on the doorknob but didn't turn it. She waited, holding her breath, expectant. "I'll be alone in here," she said to the sweeper, and as she heard his bare feet disappear down the hall, she slowly turned the knob and opened the door.

The room was exactly what she'd imagined, nearly empty and bathed, now, in a fine pure yellow light that shone in from the the garden outside. The Shiva itself, across from her, seemed to have his arms out waiting for her to return. He had been here the whole time she lived in New York, when she went to school and got married, when Granny died, and she divorced, on and on, and all that time the Shiva was here, in Kady's keep. His arms were stretched out from his body, not in a position of embrace, but of balance and grace and power. She was drawn to go into the arms and be held. He was as big as she, nearly, standing amid his circle of flames, life eternal, and Phoebe smiled broadly and with amazement at the thought that he'd been here dancing against the wall for twenty years while she'd been dancing somewhere else.

But standing as his equal, her eyes into his, her shoulders near level with his own, became too much for Phoebe. The Shiva was too overwhelming, or she too tired, and without even thinking, she slid her back down along the far wall and sat on the floor.

546

The sunlight made the Shiva shine, and his surface looked a bit like water, it was so alive with light. He was so strikingly powerful an entity, she wondered how he could be false, and what was false, after all, if his comfort with life was so eternal?

From her position on the floor, Phoebe imagined the god's posture as even more noble and elegant than it'd been twenty years before. No dancer on a stage could look as grand as he. His eyes were shut; she waited for them to open. After a while they did, the one strong line the artist made now appearing as something open, now closed, then open again. That was the Shiva, she thought, its fascination in the way it changed, something endlessly in flow, and if you blinked, you imagined the legs had moved, the dancing was so real. It was ever changing, ever moving, never constant.

The room seemed deathly still, all the more because the Shiva was so breathtakingly alive. Phoebe pictured him in the hall at Jumna Road, now in the living room, now before the panel of windows, he, always, her rival in affection for her father and her brother, now sheltered here and put away because he was a secret. He was here, waiting all these years to appear again.

It took Phoebe a while to adjust to the fact that the god wasn't moving after all and that this was just one more afternoon in a lifetime of afternoons. He seemed full of blood and muscle, but he wasn't. This god was frozen in time, even as he personified the movement of time itself.

Phoebe smiled. She felt utterly peaceful and triumphant, a match at last for this god who'd been her overseer.


At the end she saw the sweeper again. "Tell sa'ab I was here, will you?" she said. "There's no hurry. Just tell him I came to see him and that I'm ready."

" 'Ready,' memsa'ab?"

"Yes. He'll know what I mean."

# ❧ 5 ❧

FOUR DAYS LATER SAMIJI CAME TO
Kitty's.

Phoebe flew out the door to meet him in the driveway. He handed her a letter. She tore it open. It was from Kady.

"I'm very happy to get your message," he wrote. "I want to see you as soon as possible, but I can't get away. I'm in the hills outside Jaipur, working. Can you meet me here? Samiji knows the way."

They flew to Jaipur. There Samiji rented a car and they drove in through the city, then out toward the north and west, where hills surrounded the city at a distance. The landscape reminded Phoebe of Deeg, which was not very far away: high desert plains with higher hills and forts that ran along the crest of the mountains. The colors of the earth were the same, too, a golden pink that turned to golden brown, then gray the farther out they got.

When they reached the hills, they climbed steadily. The twisting road was little more than a path, and the way was rocky. Giant boulders with their sheer sides and glossy surfaces were packed in everywhere. Goats were running all about, little scrawny things that danced and darted along the rocks as nimbly as if they were on a smooth paved surface. Near naked boys,

548

goatherds, ran after them, except when they stopped to stare at the car that was passing by.

After a while Phoebe took sharper notice of the stream that was falling headlong down among the boulders and remembered that Kady had his own private company now and was probably here to design a dam. She asked Samiji and he said yes, that was so. It was to be a dam.

He sounded proud.

The road kept going. There were shrines and villages along the way, handfuls of huts set down among the boulders, and, always now, the stream that poured down toward the plains, where it dissipated in the ground, unused.

Phoebe sat forward in her seat, up in front with Samiji for once, and peered directly out, determined to see Kady as soon as he appeared.

"Happy, memsa'ab?" Samiji asked her with a grin.

"Happy."

"Werry good."

"How much farther?"

"Not much."

They came around a bend and suddenly they were there, because up ahead, in the distance in a kind of indentation in the ground where the stream swirled out and looked more like a riverbed, she saw about thirty men, cars and equipment trucks, and dozens of village children.

Samiji stopped the car.

Phoebe peered out, looking for Suraj, found him way ahead, khaki trousers and a shirt, the sleeves rolled up, his back to her. Men were crowded around him. Some had maps. Others were surveyors. They were all too far away to notice her as yet.

"Let's wait here," she said. "Not interrupt."

"Better, yes, I think so." Samiji turned off the engine. "Sa'ab will come."

They got out and waited. Phoebe watched Suraj. He was the tallest. He was always the tallest. She could tell he was the one in charge from the way the people treated him. She could see where the dam would go, too, catch the water and establish a straighter flow down the hillside to the plains, where it would irrigate the fields for year-round crops and growth.

She thought to herself that there was a lot she had to learn.

Eventually the children noticed the car, and the boys did

handstands in case anyone there was looking. Phoebe saw Kady's head turn in her direction. She saw his face. It looked gorgeous, dark and strong and, right now, completely expressionless, just as she knew it would.

He found her with his eyes. Samiji waved.

Kady namasted her, two hands up, pressed to his forehead, then turned around and went back to work, just as if she wasn't there at all. Phoebe felt absolutely wonderful. She knew she'd been saluted, Indian style, and joined.

She went over to some rocks so she could sit and look back toward the plains. They stretched far into the distance, haze at the end where any line between land and sky was fully obscured. She felt she'd never been so content in all her life.

After a while Samiji spoke. "Missus Feeb."

She stood up and went around to the other side of the hillside. She knew Kady was coming.

There he was, striding up the indentation in the hills toward her. Children were following him, he was moving fast, and they were running along behind him trying to keep up, talking all the while. He came closer. He spoke to the children, clearly, so she could hear. "Woh meri patni hai," he said, winking at her. She's my wife.

Then he was in front of her, and in one long graceful motion he touched his forehead, chest, and heart, hand rolling as it went from one spot to the other, a movement that spelled devotion to a god or higher personage. Then he bowed his head and she bowed back.

The children watched, spellbound.

"Can you wait a while longer?" he said. "I'm sorry, but I'm not finished yet. I can't leave."

"That's all right," she said. "I don't mind. Can I walk up in the hills?" It was nearly three in the afternoon and the winter air was fresh.

"Take the children with you. Go take memsa'ab up into the hills," he said to them in Hindi. "Show her the lake and the shrine and how you can swim. Take good care of her," he said. "She's the most precious thing on earth."

The children stopped abruptly and stared at her, frankly disbelieving.

"No, it's true," Kady said, patting them on the head. "She's pure gold through and through, her eyes are sapphires, and . . . ."

The children took her back up into the hills, along little paths the goats had made, and up above they came to a lake, a small one that filled a gorge in the rocks where a shrine was built. The water was gray and green from the reflection of the rocks, the shrine covered with moss from the dampness. Some women were bathing in their saris; boys dived from the cliffs.

Phoebe sat at water's edge and everyone clustered around. The women fed her sweets and oranges and fingered her hair. The children said it was made of gold and everyone talked and eventually she borrowed a sari and, putting it on, dipped in the water, too.

It was colder than the Ganges, and she shivered.

The women said it was the god of her husband washing over her.

She said, Yes, that must be it, and when she was dressed again, back in among them, they asked what they hadn't dared to ask before. Was she Hindu or Am-ri-kan?

She said she was both.

But how could she be, they asked, and she said first she and Kady had been married in a Hindu ceremony, everyone breathless and listening now, then they got on an airplane and flew back to Am-ri-ka, where he met her friends and she was married again, Am-ri-kan style, by a judge.

That unleashed a torrent of questions because the women wanted to know what she wore at her weddings and what she said and what she put in the fire, and she answered everything they asked but said, only there was no fire, Am-ri-kans didn't have a fire, and the women said, But they must have bangles, and she said yes, they had bangles. Then they wanted to know if she wore them for both her wedding nights or just one, and she said both, and then they all shrieked in unison—obviously this was the question they'd been waiting for—How many of the bangles broke?

"All," Phoebe cried, grinning wickedly with delight, and the women screamed wildly in approbation at this proof of foreign passion.

It was nearly six when Kady came for her.

He drove her to a hunting lodge that was located in the hills near the dam site. It belonged to a local raja who'd rented it out for the duration of the project in return for cash.

Inside, it was warm. The servants had lighted the fires, and as the door opened Phoebe was greeted by heads of elephants and boars, antelopes and wild deer, that peered down from near the ceiling.

Samiji disappeared to see about dinner, and the two of them were left standing alone.

The hall was quiet. Neither spoke. Phoebe could hear the fire crackling in the big room that surrounded them and, in the kitchen, the sounds of Hindi voices and a dog barking.

Kady took her hands. They were standing face to face. She looked down at the floor, overcome with shyness. "Will you look at me?" he asked.

She shook her head.

"Then I'll look at you."

They were silent, and she realized he was waiting for her, going slow to give her time. She felt how much she loved him. "You've gotten thinner," she said, holding his long fingers, remembering how they seemed so important when she saw them at the airport.

"It's because I've been working hard. I'm very happy."

"Even without me?" she teased, feeling herself blush.

"Yes," he said, "but I never wanted anything in my life as much as I want you, Feeb."

She realized it was the American part of her that was shy and awkward, the other, the Indian, felt just right and even calm, because this was how an Indian woman would behave, modest in the face of such immense emotion. To be humbled was appropriate.

Kady took her face by the chin and lifted it up. "Are you hungry?"

She shook her head.

"You don't want to eat?"

"No."

"What do you want, then?"

"I want to go to bed," she whispered. "I want to be with you. I want . . ." Her voice so husky, it almost didn't . . .

"You don't have to say any more."

"No, I do. I want to say it all," eyes up. "I have to. I want to live with you, Kady. I want to have your children. I want everything there is between two people."

"Come," he said. "Let's go upstairs."

He turned, but she didn't move, just took a step forward and pressed herself in against his body so that all the warmth and strength of him was aligned next to her. Then she pushed her head into the slope of his neck and burrowed there while he wrapped his arms around her and held her. They clung together. His face was in her hair. His fingers moved along her scalp, finding the scars and tracing them. He bent down to kiss them and touched the length of her crooked hair and breathed into it. "I have something to tell you," he whispered.

"About Cully?"

"No. I'll tell you upstairs."

He took her down the hallway and up some stairs where there were more animals to look down on them. The hallway on top was lighted, too, everything pretty and faded, green paper on the walls, chairs outside the bedroom doors, pictures that spoke of eras when men had nothing to do but hunt and play at billiards, and women didn't exist at all, if the pictures spoke the truth.

He led her to a room with a great bed positioned to look out across an expanse of floor and a stretched-out tiger skin to a terrace outside. There was a fire and, across from it, the bath. He showed it to her, a room with a marble tub a good five feet square that looked out over the balcony and the hills, where winter clouds had rolled in and the sky was heavy and navy blue.

They intended to take a bath and talk in there, together, the lights off, look out the window from the tub, but instead she took off her sweater, then undid her blouse, and he came to help, and then he felt her shoulders and her breasts, her cheeks and hair, and said for her to come, now, to bed. So, with her clothes on the floor, his too, they moved the covers off the bed and he took her in his arms, just to kiss her, but then it became everything, so quickly they must have been ready for a long time.


Afterward Samiji scratched at the door and left a tray. Kady brought it in. The room was dark. He put more logs on the fire, pulled a cover off the bed and wrapped her up in it, gave himself another, and they sat on the floor in front of the fire. He poured tea and said they had to talk.

553

It was warm. The heat of the flames fanned out into the room. Outside, they could see the darkened sky and stars, a moon was coming up. "What did you want to tell me?" she said.

"It's about Durr. She's in Benares."

"Benares," Phoebe exclaimed. "What's she doing there?"

"She's going to stay there." Kady's voice was flat.

"Why?"

"She's not coming back. She's renounced."

Phoebe felt her heart stop. "How awful," she cried.

"I don't know," Kady said soberly. "I've thought and thought. It's what she wants."

"Why?"

"She says she wants to find peace. She wants me to divorce her and marry you."

Phoebe couldn't say anything. The glow of the fire seemed to be a million eyes, all of them Durr's. "But I didn't want her to go away. I never wanted her to suffer because of us. Why is she doing it? Does she want to be with Jiggie, is that it? What about her children and her grandchildren? She must want to be with her grandchildren."

"She wants me to be with you more."

Phoebe pressed her hand against her heart. She remembered Durr at the wedding twenty years ago and then later, telling her to take care of her husband. "Oh, Durr," she mumbled. "What do the children say?"

"They accept it. What can they do?"

"And she wants you to marry me?"

"Yes."

"But I feel like I want to protest. I love you, but I never . . ." Her voice petered out. She heard the voices of little boys. "What are they saying?" she asked.

"They're calling the goats."

She took his hand and gripped it hard. "Tell me exactly what happened."

"She decided. That's all. I gather it began with you the last time you went there. Remember?"

"Yes."

"She started thinking about it then. Except she must have been thinking about it for years. But you came back from Kashmir and you went there looking for Samiji and said you were going to Brinj. When you left, she said she shut the door and knew what she was going to do."

"Just like that? But what did I do?"

"I don't know, really. I think she just realized how much we . . ."

"Loved each other?"

"Yes. And she knew I'd never divorce her."

"You told her that?"

"No. She just knew it."

"And she decided that quickly?"

"That's what Jiggie did, too," Kady said. "He just decided one day he had to renounce and live in Benares, that that's what he had to do, to seek forgiveness, and he took Durr right up to Kashmir to tell her."

"Was she mad at him? Sad?"

"Both. At first she took it personally. I told her not to, but she did."

"When did she tell you she was going to renounce?"

"A month or so ago. I was at the house and she came to my bedroom. She hasn't been in there in years. I didn't know what to say to her. She asked if she could sit down. I said yes, of course. She said she had something to tell me."

"What'd she say?"

"That it was my turn. She kept saying that. That she'd had her chance for love and happiness for years and now it was my turn, yours and mine."

"Didn't you try to stop her?"

"I did. I could not bear to think I hadn't genuinely tried—for both our sakes. But she was adamant."

"But what's she going to do? I keep remembering all those widows and divorcées in Benares. Will she be like them?"

"She wants peace. She's not very different from you that way. She's deep and thoughtful."

"Will she live with Jiggie?"

"And Shyam. They'll live in the palace."

"Has she ever told her children about Jiggie?"

"That's the worst part," Kady said. "They don't know and they never will. But she told them about you. She said she was doing what she'd wanted to do all along."

"This could never happen anyplace else but India," Phoebe

555

declared. "All of it, from first to last. I feel blessed," she said. "By Durr. She has blessed us."

They were silent for a while, staring at the fire, hearing peacocks in the distance, and a dog.

"Can I meet the children sometime?" Phoebe asked.

"They're not 'children' anymore. I don't have much to do with them, you know."

"When you have a child of your own, you'll feel differently about them."

"I hope so."

"You will."

"There's one more thing," Kady said. "I've started divorce proceedings."

"Already? But you didn't know what I'd do."

"I knew what you'd do." He started smiling. "So did Durr. I never doubted it, really. I just didn't know when. You do want to get married, don't you?"

Phoebe pressed herself in against him. "I do. I just never thought it would happen. And I certainly never thought it would happen this way. I don't feel entirely happy about it."

"Neither do I. But I understand it better every day. She said it wasn't such a big price, and besides, I'd paid a worse price. We talked a lot. She made me understand it's not a sacrifice. It's just a change. An evolution. Three grown-up people doing what they have to do, you and me and Durr."

"Can we ever see her again?"

"If you want to. But not often because what she's doing is serious and you have to respect it. She and Jiggie will probably never even talk."

"Or touch?"

"They'll just be together."

"Could I see Durr to thank her? That would be important for me."

"Yes. You could tell her that," he said.

"Will you come with me?"

"I've already thanked her."

"Then I'll go myself. I'll go back to Benares sometime and tell her. I'll go when I'm pregnant. So she can bless us all, all three of us."

# ❧ 6 ❧

Time passed.

Phoebe and Kady weren't married yet, but they were living at the Garden House and the wedding date was set. A lot had happened. Phoebe had officially turned the foundation over to Alice, remained as a director, and was doing the legal work to start her export company. It was to be called "Guthrie and Suraj." A trip to America was scheduled, a second wedding planned there, and Kady'd worked it out with a punditji to have a fire at a wedding here. They were going to walk around it seven times, but the punditji wasn't going to say anything about men and women, chattel and so on, just about duty and devotion, one to the other, and therein to God himself. Phoebe said that was what she wanted.

It was planned that I'd be there, of course, and my husband, and a couple of friends of Kady's, Kitty and Jyoti, Harriet, some others, and Mirabai. They both insisted on Mirabai.

The big news was that they'd decided to have the wedding at the house on Viceroy Circle and to live there afterward.

I asked her was she sure, Viceroy Circle? Was he? They seemed very clear, something about continuity and respect, and that they'd need a lot of space for work and children.

What else? The Shiva was going to go in the entrance hall there and Cully's horse, smashed as it was, someplace else. They were going to keep the apartment on Fifth Avenue until she was ready to give it up. Then they'd get something smaller and cheaper, but they were both insistent they had to have a home in New York. There was a lot of talk too about godparents, even though there wasn't a baby or even a pregnancy. Stephen and Alice were to be the American ones, Mirabai and I the Indian ones.

For Phoebe, everything was family now. She'd found peace with Cully not being there. She'd even made plans to bring in the sweeper and his family from the Garden House and to hire Tulsidas full-time and give him a place there to live as well.

I said they'd have quite a houseful.

She looked thrilled. "It's very Indian," she said proudly.

There was Samiji, too. Not to forget him. He was going to be promoted to a room in the house proper, and she was trying to get him to bring his wife and children from Brinj. I swear she'd have found a way to bring all of us in, me and Kitty and Jyoti, probably even Harriet, if we'd agreed. She wanted to cement her ties with everything. She'd even started a hunt for Kamala and Moosselman, the old ayah and cook from Jumna Road.

Why not? she said. Why shouldn't they come back? Why shouldn't they all be together again?

So, by the time the first wedding approached, it seemed there was nothing more to happen but for the babies to appear and the fabric business to start, but there was one more thing.

It happened a few days after the divorce was final. She and Kady were supposed to fly to Puri the next day to lie on the beach and celebrate. Phoebe was out, scouting for an office. Kady was in the house alone, the Garden House.

A car pulled up outside and a clerk-chaprassi in a police uniform got out. He came up the walk to the door. Kady let him in. He said he had a letter for "Miss Phoebe Llewellyn Guthrie."

Kady took it. It was thick. He held it up to the window, but he couldn't make out the words inside. It was handwritten and had come from Tees-he-zari Station. He waited for her outside on the steps and when she came home, he gave it to her.

It was from the commandant with the burned-out face. "Why is he writing me?" she said anxiously, tearing open the letter. " 'My very dear Miss Guthrie,' " she began, reading aloud in a quick voice.

" 'I have not forgotten your visit to me last summer. Nor have

I forgotten your concern at the time that your brother, Mr. Cullen Guthrie, was of sufficiently attenuated mental capacity that you feared, should the police catch him, he would fail to notify you.

" 'He has not been caught, and this is not why I am writing you. But before I tell you why I should impress myself upon you at this time, let me express my relief that your injuries turned out to be no more serious than they were and that, as I understand it, you are completely recovered. . . .' "

Phoebe handed the sheet across to Kady, and they both went on reading to themselves in silence.

" 'To digress no further,' " she rushed on.

" 'I am writing because it is my personal and professional duty to inform you that your brother Cullen Guthrie was killed . . .' "

"Oh, my God," Phoebe cried, hands thrown up against her face. "He's dead."

Kady took the letter from her and read aloud. " '. . . January 6th in a bus accident on the outskirts of Deeg. But I believe it was not really an accident, but a suicide. I am informed that he walked straight into the path of an oncoming bus and could not have expected anything to happen except that precisely which did happen.' "

Kady stopped.

Phoebe had her head in her hands.

"Feeb," he said. "Look at this."

"What?"

"The date." He showed her the page.

She didn't look.

"The date of the accident. It's January sixth. He died—"

"Oh, my God," Phoebe exclaimed. "It's the same day they died. Keep reading."

" 'Due to the unusualness of your brother's personal appearance, namely his hair, the local police eventually made a connection between the body and the outstanding arrest warrant that was reactivated at the time of your injuries last summer—' "

"I can't bear it," Phoebe interrupted, her voice almost a moan. "Why did this have to happen? What a tragic waste. His whole life he never got himself together."

" 'My inquiries into this have had little result, but I will tell you everything and satisfy the personal obligations I feel toward you, based on the intense, even pleasant, nature of our meeting last summer.

" 'First, let me say that I am informed that your brother has not been seen anywhere in or around Deeg since his most recent disappearance September 9th, or anywhere else, for that matter.

" 'Therefore,' " Kady read on, squeezing Phoebe's hands with his own as she leaned against him, " 'I am unable to tell you what your brother was doing up until approximately four-fifteen January 6th when he was first spied by the bus driver.

" 'The bus was following an ancient route that runs from the distant site of Pushtu Fort straight into town. Pushtu Fort is a sprawling empty place that centuries ago was the first bastion of the Deegs. There's even a legend the gods used Mount Pushtu to descend to earth. This fort lies some twenty miles outside the city of Deeg up on the crest of a hill and commands a broad view of the surrounding plains. From the extensive information I received about your brother from your friend Mr. Suraj at the time of your injuries, I am of the opinion he was drawn to the site and probably stayed there. Hippies do live there from time to time. They eat goats and vegetation and drink from the mountain streams.

" 'I propose all this on the chance that it may provide you some understanding of his frame of mind.

" 'At any rate, the highway in question extends from Pushtu Fort across the plains, then runs along the edge of the city until it reaches the palace grounds. There, it makes an abrupt right turn, in order to skirt these grounds, and heads into the center of town. It appeared to the bus driver that your brother had been following this road on a parallel course from inside the fields, and at the precise moment when he first saw him, he was headed straight in for the palace itself. That seemed to be his destination. But then, as the driver watched, your brother changed course dramatically and proceeded toward the bus itself.

" 'This vehicle, lest you think he might not have seen it, was big and yellow and had baggage and chickens piled on top.

" 'The driver saw your brother approaching,' " Kady continued, " 'but thought nothing of him except to note that his hair was a striking color and that he was, of course, Caucasian—' "

Kady stopped.

"Go on," Phoebe said, her voice shaking.

" 'Beyond that he did not notice anything, except that the man was walking fast and his left shoulder was sloping distinctly toward the—' "

"Left."

" '—and that his arms were swinging in a fashion that was vigorous. The driver thought no more of him, however, except to assume that he would slow down in order to accommodate the priorities of a fast-moving bus.

" 'Seconds later, however, he saw him again, and this time he was at the side of the road, proceeding with the same strength and vigor, and the driver realized he wasn't going to stop at all. Indeed his eyes were open, his arms were swinging, and so, even as the driver slammed on his brakes, your brother headed straight into the wheels of the bus and died.' "

"Uh-h-h-h," Phoebe moaned.

" 'That, Miss Guthrie, is all I have learned, except that the body is not much damaged. To everyone's surprise. This leads me to wonder if, at the last, your brother was blessed, though why the gods might bless him, I am not in a position to know. Perhaps you do. Perhaps he was in some inner way innocent of the awful things he did?

" 'The authorities kept his body in the morgue in Deeg for quite some time, but since there was no identification in his pockets and they are not very efficient in these rural cities—they didn't even notify the embassies in Delhi—eventually they burned the body. They did have the wherewithal to keep the ashes, however. Had someone not eventually noticed the arrest warrant and the yellow hair, we might never have known of this at all.' "

"I want to bring him here," Phoebe interrupted. "I want him to go in the Jumna River, the same as Louis and Thalia."

" 'Finally, as a matter of official identification,' " Kady went on, " 'let me say that the body in question was that of a male Caucasian somewhere between the ages of 30 and 40, roughly 6 feet 2 inches long, weighing approximately 190 pounds. He had a scar on his upper left hand shoulder that appears to be old and yellow-white hair not unlike your own except that it was apparently falling out.

" 'The body is described as "very very white." This may simply be a phrase Indians use for Caucasians, but from my inquiries it is my impression that it is not. That it is intended to

561

suggest some state of being that had settled upon your brother that was not entirely healthy.

"'He did, to summarize, appear out of nowhere, stride across a field until which point he strode directly into the path of a moving bus.

"'That is it.

"'Miss Guthrie—' This is more personal now," Kady said, looking up. "Do you want me to read it or . . . ?"

"No, go on."

"'That which brought us together has now ceased. That is the manner of life. Things come and things go. It has required some effort on my part to locate you at this place where you now reside with Mr. Suraj, and so I am taking it upon myself to assume that whatever sadness my information may bring you today, you are nonetheless well and thriving. It is my consideration that this is what you deserve, in this and every life to come.

"'Perhaps, if I may say it, your brother did not. For all that you were both born here in India, born to the same parents and lived in the same house, there the similarities would seem to end. Your paths were different. I have found this to be the case with life. People are different, just as I am different, rather than they are the same. No one path is the same as any other, no matter how much we may think they are.

"'Myself, I believe the gods do this on purpose. They delight in presenting us with obstacles.'"

Kady let the last page flutter to the ground and settle.

"Oh, my," Phoebe said mournfully. "I have loved him and loved him for some thirty years. I couldn't have loved him more."

Kady held her tight.

"What's it like there?"

"Pushtu Fort? It's desolate, windy. A lot of the walls've crumbled."

"Is it pretty?"

"You'd think so, and maybe Cully would, but I don't. You just see India, you know, fields and haze and a lot of scrub. The view is spectacular, I guess. You want to go there?"

"Not yet. Maybe he died in a state of grace," she said. "Maybe he felt remorse."

"Maybe the gods are forgiving."

"Do you really believe all that? About the gods and all?"

"I don't know," Kady said. "Probably not."

"What do you believe?"

"In you."

"No, seriously."

"I guess in a kind of justice and balance. That we create our own future, to the extent that we practice humility and recognize our faults. And desires." He fingered her hair.

"What else?"

"I don't know."

"But what about the gods?"

"I don't know. I guess, to me, they're an extension of our own consciousness, a metaphor for internal forces."

"So they don't exist?"

"I don't think so."

"So you don't believe in Shiva and Vishnu and—"

"No," he said. "Not particularly. I feel affectionate toward them and what they represent in us."

"What do you mean?"

"Well, take Cully. He was too intent on dissolution and destruction, that side of Shiva, but he had no interest in rebirth and creativity. He had no sense of the cycle of things, the endless coming and going, that one thing becomes another."

"He was sick."

"Yes, of course he was sick, but I'm trying to put it in an Indian context. That's what you want, isn't it?"

She nodded.

"In Indian terms, he didn't know about God. He didn't know about the comings and goings."

"Like how you're going to come alive again in a baby inside of me one day."

"That's right," Kady said, smiling. "That things transform." He took her hands again and held them.

"If it's a girl, I want to name her Durr, Kady. Is that all right?"

"We'll have to talk about that. You really want a baby, don't you?" He was smiling at her, kissing her fingertips.

"I do," she said, "I really do."

"Diapers and crying and not sleeping at night?"

"Yes, but you see, I really just want you, every which way I can have you, and a baby's you. I want a family. I want our

563

families to be transforming themselves so that a thousand years from now"—Phoebe was grinning—"the gods will look back and say that here, right here, at the end of the twentieth century, on Viceroy Circle, the lives of Guthrie, Suraj, and Deeg changed, and—"

"Deeg, too?"

"Oh, yes, absolutely," Phoebe said with conviction. "And they headed out on a different course. That with us, the era of deterioration and sadness ended and the families became wonderful again. Don't you like that idea?"

"Yes," he said.

"I do," she said. "I really do."

## ABOUT THE AUTHOR

Lacey Fosburgh, who was born and raised in New York City, was a longtime reporter for the *New York Times* in New York and San Francisco. The author of a number of magazine articles, her two books are *Closing Time: The True Story of the Goodbar Murder*, and *Old Money*, a novel of disinheritance.

She first went to India on a Fulbright grant in 1964 and has spent a total of about four years there.

She lives in Mill Valley, California, with her husband, David Harris, the writer, daughter, Sophie, and stepson, Gabe.